A TEXTBOOK OF
HOUSEHOLD ARTS

Stella SoundaraRaj has long and wide-ranging experience in the field of home science and nutrition. She has worked in various capacities in this area and was also Director of Collegiate Education, Madras - the first woman to be appointed to this post. She has conducted seminars, orientation programmes and workshops for teachers. The Krupskaya UNESCO award was given to the Directorate of Non-formal and Adult Education, Tamil Nadu in 1982, when she was the director. Dr SoundaraRaj has several papers on home science, education and allied subjects in leading journals and magazines, apart from three books including this one.

A TEXTBOOK OF
HOUSEHOLD ARTS

FOURTH EDITION

STELLA SOUNDARARAJ
M.Sc. (Lond.), B.T., Ph.D.
(Formerly Director of Collegiate Education, Madras)

With a Foreword by
Mrs GRACE TUCKER, M.A.
Formerly Deputy Minister of Education
Government of Mysore

Illustrated by
G. SOUNDARARAJ

Orient BlackSwan

A TEXTBOOK OF HOUSEHOLD ARTS

ORIENT BLACKSWAN PRIVATE LIMITED

Registered Office
3-6-752 Himayatnagar, Hyderabad 500 029 (A.P.), INDIA
e-mail: centraloffice@orientblackswan.com

Other Offices
Bangalore, Bhopal, Bhubaneshwar, Chennai, Ernakulam, Guwahati, Hyderabad, Jaipur, Kolkata, Lucknow, Mumbai, New Delhi, Patna

First published by Orient Longman Pvt. Ltd., 1963
Reprinted 1965, 1966, 1968, 1971
Second Edition 1972
Third Edition 1974
Reprinted 1979, 1981, 1982, 1983, 1984, 1985, 1987, 1989, 1990, 1991, 1992
Fourth Edition 1996
Reprinted 1997, 1999, 2001, 2003, 2004, 2005, 2006, 2008
First Orient Blackswan impression 2009

Reprinted 2011

ISBN 13: 978 81 250 0951 1
ISBN 10: 81 250 0951 5

Typeset by
Graphic Letters (Pvt) Ltd.
New Delhi

Printed in India at
Vardhman Printers
Delhi.

Published by
Orient Blackswan Private Limited
1/24 Asaf Ali Road
New Delhi 110 002
e-mail: delhi@orientblackswan.com

TO MY CHILDREN

Foreword to the First Edition

This textbook on household arts by Smt. Stella Soundararaj comes at a time when the demand for such a study is on the increase. In other fields of knowledge such as industry, agriculture, science, economics, history, art and archaeology, India has made rapid strides since Independence; but in the art of keeping house, old methods hold us in bondage. No doubt conventions of the past were wise and valuable for those times; but the hourglass pours out hours, days, years and centuries, bringing in their wake radical changes and demanding a like change in all spheres of life. In this busy world of industry, the human being looks more and more for a happy and peaceful home, a quiet corner to which to retire and feel at peace. And what this book sets out to do is to show the housewife how to create such a lovely spot.

Home-making sounds simple enough, but its underlying principles are so forceful that a successful home-maker is bound to send out into the world people who are healthy and happy and prepared for all the vicissitudes of life. The author of this book has woven the ingredients of Home Science—plan of the house, beauty of the home, food and cookery, child care, etc —into the art of home-making in such a fascinating way that it makes interesting reading not only to the student of home science or the housewife but also to the other partners of the home, the father and the children.

In conclusion, I commend to all this lucidly written book which brings into focus methods of making a success of the home, the institution whose individual success implies the progress of a nation and whose failure would mean the deterioration of a nation. May its reading and study help to create an atmosphere of love and joy in each home of this our beautiful land.

Grace Tucker

Preface to the Fourth Edition

An important aspect of education is helping young people to form a scale of values. The Government of India and the state governments have recognised the value of the study of Home Science as a major subject for students of Higher Secondary schools and also colleges.

This book covers comprehensively and very effectively various aspects and diverse fields of Home Science. It has been updated and made suitable by incorporating new sections. Adequate illustrations, figures and informational tables have been supplied to make understanding easier and clearer. The test papers given at the end provide a tool for informative feedback and evaluation as well.

While the purpose of the book is to serve as a text for the Higher Secondary schools (both vocational and academic), it can also be used as reference in libraries, colleges and schools. Thus the book is both a text and a reference book and a valuable guide for anyone interested in household arts.

Stella SoundaraRaj

Contents

1. The Home

It is an indisputable fact that every human being spends a good portion of his time at home. The importance of the home cannot be sufficiently emphasized. The home can make or mar one's well-being. The test of a civilized nation is the quality of the homes its people live in. It is imperative therefore to develop a science and art that contribute to this end. Home-making and housekeeping take on a new urgency in an age when civilization is speeding up in an unprecedented fashion. People have a tremendous responsibility and it is only proper that men and women should take to this science of home-making with enthusiasm and commitment.

In a world of fear, suspicion and hate, the common person has a cozy haven of love, affection and trust in his home. It is his private paradise, his place of contentment and concord in a world of discord and discontent. When wars and rumours of war get on our nerves and fill us with worry, the home remains the place of peace, quiet and tranquillity. All that goes in to making the ideal home can best be realised only in an improved form of residence.

Homes have undergone change from the days of the primitive savage to those of civilized man. The cave which shielded primitive man from the ravages of the weather was superseded by the hut when shelter and safety from wild beasts became the chief concern. The modern home has far greater physiological and psychological implications. Comfort, health, economy, beauty, living space, convenience, hygiene and all that contributes to the development of the personality and material well-being of the members of the family have to be taken into account. For this we need a good house.

The house and its surroundings

One should not build a house in a hurry. Great care should be spent on the planning and many factors should be taken into consideration however small they may be. Factors such as careful selection of the site and surroundings, the pattern of structure, size, number of rooms, and the materials to be used all deserve careful consideration. There is no need to accept a partially satisfactory, stereotyped layout when a little extra thought could help you to get a house you and your family would enjoy living in.

Site

Care should be exercised in the choice of the site for a house. This should be such as to command fresh air, proper ventilation, good water supply and sufficient space. The locality also should be healthy.

The house should not be located near a factory or an industrial concern. It should not be situated in a crowded area or be surrounded by obnoxious public drainage or stinking open gutters, or be too near public conveniences. However, it is not advisable to go to the other extreme and buy a site in a remote place simply because it is cheap or because you hope the neighbourhood will become important after some years. It is safer to build in a neighbourhood that is already developed. Other factors to be taken into consideration in your choice of a site are physical features, the quality of the soil, sanitary requirements and practical conveniences.

Physical features

The house should be erected on elevated ground. This will give it a wider and brighter view and will also afford better facility for drainage, since the rain-water will flow away from the house instead of collecting around it in puddles. A house near the sea is good for health on account of sea breeze, but this also carries with it the disadvantage that the salt-water spray corrodes the iron work and causes it to rust. Furthermore, plants do not thrive too near the sea.

Soil conditions

Rocky surfaces afford a good foundation, but are hard for excavation and levelling. They create difficulty in laying drainage pipes, carrying water, etc. Moreover, they are unsuitable for maintaining a garden round the house.

A top layer of soft soil with hard soil at a depth of 3 to 4 feet is best suited for construction. The next best is gravel and sand. Soil containing much clay is not satisfactory because it easily gets water-logged.

Sanitary conditions

From the sanitation point of view, stagnant pools of water, tanks, lakes and unused wells in the neighbourhood of the site are not desirable.

Reclaimed land filled with debris and refuse is unhealthy for building purposes, as it will give out obnoxious gases and will be a breeding place for flies and mosquitoes. Moreover, it is hard to make a firm foundation in it. Corporation or municipal sites with modern sanitary facilities are the most suitable.

Practical conveniences

A site in a busy locality, though desirable from a business point of view, may not be suitable because of the dust and the constant din of vehicular traffic.

The site should be as near as possible to a railway station, a hospital, a post office, a bank, a school and a market. However, it is not always possible to obtain a site near such places. One has to weigh the pros and cons before finally deciding. For instance a family with many school-going children will find it advantageous to have a house near a school.

As far as possible the house should not be located in an area given to quarrels and unruly behaviour.

Plan of the house

In planning a house, one should remember the following points:

Aspect

The arrangement of the doors and windows in the outside walls of the house should be such as to allow the inmates to enjoy the sunshine, breeze and view of the landscape. Preferably the kitchen should have an eastern aspect, while the bedroom should face the south.

Privacy

It is important to have privacy in the bedroom, study and the toilet. The kitchen should be away from the living room.

Prospect

It is important that the house should have a proper prospect to create a good impression on a person who views it from outside.

Grouping

The rooms must be arranged in relation to one another; for example the dining-room must be close to the kitchen.

Roominess

It is necessary to fix the cupboards and shelves in such a way as to make the best use of the space available.

Sanitation

Provision should be made for proper lighting, ventilation, cleanliness and other sanitary conveniences in the house.

Flexibility

It is ideal to arrange for flexibility in the use of the rooms so that they can be utilised for more than one purpose; for example, a living room can be converted into a bedroom at night. Flexibility is especially important for those who live in flats.

Apart from the locale of a house, the immediate surroundings also should be carefully considered. These are the garden and courtyard or backyard. They are important because they can be aids to beautifying the house and serve some useful purposes in the family's social and economic life and in promoting good health.

The garden is the cultivated ground around the house. It adds beauty to the house and gives it a sylvan setting. Flower-beds with phlox, zinnias, chrysanthemums, sunflowers; flowering shrubs such as roses, ixora or cannas; crotons; creepers like bougainvillaea or jasmine; flowering trees such as gulmohur or champak can be used to provide a distinctive charm to one's abode.

In a plot at the back of the house a kitchen garden can be planned. Brinjals, lady's-fingers, chillies, coriander, greens, etc. can be grown there. Useful trees like drumstick, plantain, guava, papaya, mango, coconut, etc. can be planted in the ground adjoining the house.

A garden, either with a lawn or without, will be ideal for social purposes such as tea or dinner parties, conversation and the like; for outdoor games, especially for children's play and for the family to sit out in the open and enjoy the fresh air. The garden can also supply fresh flowers for putting in vases, wearing in the hair or for other such purposes. It can also yield home-grown vegetables and fruits which will be fresher and thus healthier than what you buy in the market.

The courtyard is the paved and enclosed ground in front of the house. Potted plants, statuettes, a small tank with water-lilies or lotus plants and a fountain may be provided to make it attractive.

The backyard is the enclosed space at the back of the house. It can be used for household activities such as laundering, carpentry, etc. It often contains structures such as a poultry-run or a cattle shed. These should be kept clean to safeguard the health of the inmates of the house.

The cleanliness of the area around the house is of very great importance. The dead leaves should be swept up and removed from the garden. Regular weeding should be carried out for the healthy growth of the plants one grows and to give the garden a neat appearance. Shrubs should be carefully pruned, otherwise they will have a ragged growth. Poultry-runs and cattle sheds should be kept spick and span lest they become breeding grounds for disease-producing germs. The dead leaves, cow-dung and sweepings from the poultry-run may be dumped in a pit and covered with earth to serve as manure for the garden. Dirt and refuse should be properly disposed of either by burning, burying or by dumping in dustbins provided by the municipality or corporation. The health of the persons living in a house depends as much on the cleanliness and sanitary conditions prevailing inside as well as outside the house.

Allocation of space in the house

To play its manifold role, a house has to be suitably and

adequately planned. Its efficiency, convenience, comfort, neatness and charm depend largely upon the way in which the various rooms are designed and constructed. While palatial buildings may have scores of rooms affording great scope for living and moving space, great skill is needed in the case of small cottages and flats so as to utilise all available space to the best possible advantage.

In planning a house, the needs of those who will occupy it must be taken into consideration. It should be so built as to foster a harmonious family life and at the same time minister to the privacy of the individual members. For gracious living the essential purposes for which allocation of space is necessary are cooking, dining, sleeping, study, nursery, storage, toilet and reception of guests.

Living and reception rooms

Living-room

Whatever be the size of the house, it must have a living-room. This is where the family sits and relaxes. The living-room also serves as a reception room to entertain visitors or guests. It may be used for listening to the radio, playing cards, carrom or chess. It should be well lit and well ventilated and should provide maximum comfort for the perfect relaxation of all members of the family. It should be situated on one side of the house, with an entrance from the front verandah. None of the activities of the house should be interrupted by its location.

The room should be equipped with suitable furniture and drapery and should be at least 15 feet by 12 feet. Its size should be determined by the kind of furniture needed. Equipment and furniture may be provided for activities such as conversation, reading, writing or study, entertaining, music, games and so on.

The chairs or sofas should be comfortable. There should be a table for books and magazines and a reading lamp. For writing or study, a desk, chair, book cases, waste paper basket, etc., should be provided. A music system, cassettes and records, a musical instrument, a TV, etc. can all be placed in the living-room.

The arrangement of the living-room should be such as to

allow enough room to move about.

The living-room should be simple in design and well proportioned. Its ceiling should be neither too high nor too low. There should be enough wall space for hanging pictures and decorative articles. Small potted plants in brass bowls and flowers in vases can be used with advantage to decorate the room. If it is large enough, a wall shelf for exhibiting curios can be provided.

The flooring also should be as attractive as possible.

Reception room

A reception room is of more value to a hotel, an office or an institution rather than a private house. In large homes a room in the front portion of the house can be used for this purpose. In smaller houses a verandah adjoining the living-room serves as a reception room. Such a room often comes in handy for receiving visitors. It is enough to furnish it in a meagre way.

Bedrooms

Privacy should be the keynote for the bedroom. Comfort and protection from noise should also be taken into consideration since bedrooms are intended for rest. The bedroom should be well away from the living-room.

It should be properly ventilated. It is essential to have the windows so placed as to give a through breeze, especially during warm weather. The room should have enough sunshine, preferably the morning sun.

A good size for a bedroom is 15 feet by 12. Children of different sexes above ten years of age should have separate rooms, one for the boys and another for the girls. The ideal bedroom is divided into three areas: one for sleeping, one for dressing and one for storage of clothes.

The bedroom is meant for rest and sleep, and therefore the bed forms the centre of interest in the room. It should be placed with the head against the wall and with sufficient space to move around for making the bed. Also it should not be visible from outside when the bedroom door is open.

The bed should be resilient enough to yield to the body and yet support it in a comfortable position. It should neither sag nor be too hard. Mattresses are filled with just about everything from feather to air. Foam rubber ones are good as they are easy to keep clean, harbour no insects, do not produce any allergy, are resilient and last a lifetime; but they are very expensive. Cotton mattresses can also be bought and used with advantage. Even if funds are low, a good mattress should be purchased.

Bedspreads should be heavy enough to stay in place and of a material that can be laundered or cleaned easily. The sheets should be of clean, white material and should be about 2 feet longer than the mattress on all four sides, so that they can be properly tucked in. Each bed should have one or two soft pillows.

In South India, cots made of wood and woven with coconut fibre ropes or palm fibres are commonly used. They are airy and are ideal for summer. Palm fibre cots can even be used without a mattress. Some varieties can be folded up and put away during the daytime to save space. Cots which are woven with broad, cotton or nylon tape are also used in India. Apart from these, mats made of reeds are also used for spreading on the floor and sleeping.

The dressing space in the bedroom should be away from the beds. It can be just a screened off portion of the room with a dressing table and a mirror inside.

A closet built in the wall can be used for keeping clothes. A chest of drawers can be used but a wall cupboard is better as it does not take up space.

Dining-room

The dining-room should be adjacent to the kitchen so that it is easy to carry the cooked food in and serve it. However, it should be so situated as not to reveal all the paraphernalia in the kitchen. If the kitchen is well planned, even a covered verandah adjoining it can serve as the dining-room. The dining-room should be properly protected against flies and other insects.

A rectangular room is most suited for use as a dining-room. The dining table should be oval or rectangular in shape. The dining chairs should be straight-backed and without arms.

A wash-basin for washing one's hands after meals can be provided in one corner or preferably in the passage or verandah just outside the room and near the door. Provision of one or two wall cupboards inside the dining-room will be useful for storing dinner sets, tea sets, cutlery, etc. A sideboard on which to put the food to be served is also useful in a dining-room.

The equipment necessary for dining Western style is:

Soup plates, full plates, half plates, quarter plates, different sized bowls or dishes with lids for different courses, jugs, tumblers, cups and saucers, spoons, forks and knives of various sizes and shapes depending upon the use to be made of them, and serviettes. The dining table may be glass-topped, laminated or provided with a table cloth or lace cloth, with table mats.

For dining Indian style, such elaborate requirements are not necessary. People sit on wooden planks or mats and eat with their hands, often from plantain leaves instead of plates. The vessels needed are suitable degchis for rice and other vessels for sambar, side dishes like pugaths, chutneys, pickles, pappads, spoons for serving and tumblers for water. The vessels used may be of brass, stainless steel or even aluminium.

Kitchen

The kitchen should be well planned, clean and comfortable. It should be airy, well lighted and ventilated, and with a lot of space to work in. As far as possible, it must be proof against flies, mosquitoes and other sources of infection. Therefore, it should have barred windows and ventilators with wire gauze. The door should be a gauzed spring door which can open inwards or outwards according to convenience. For safety, the swing door may be protected by ordinary wooden doors on the outside. Absolute cleanliness should be maintained in a kitchen, because the germs and bacteria grow fast in food, and thus food may become a source of contamination.

The location, size and orientation of the kitchen, the position of the cooking area, sink, cupboard, etc., have a direct bearing on the comfort and convenience of the person who works in it.

The kitchen should be at the back of the house, adjoining the dining room. In some houses it forms a separate unit behind the house, connected to the main building by a covered passage.

It should normally have 100 to 150 square feet of floor area. Its optimum size is to be determined by the amount of cooking to be done, which depends upon the number of people in the family and the size of parties the family gives. Further, the amount of storage space desired and the number of activities to be carried on in a kitchen also have a bearing on its size.

The location of doors and windows greatly influences the arrangement of kitchen equipment. They should be so placed as to leave undisturbed floor and wall space for cupboards, shelves, etc. They should be wide enough to afford a view of the surroundings in order to break the monotony of kitchen work.

The kitchen floor should be paved with durable, smooth, grease-proof material. This will facilitate easy cleaning. The corners formed by the walls should be rounded. The floor should slope towards the drainage to facilitate cleaning.

Adequate provision must be made for storage. The storage space should be so located and designed as to enable easy access to the objects required. In arranging cooking vessels, care should be taken to keep the heavier ones on the lower shelves and the lighter ones on upper shelves.

It is convenient to have shelves not more than a foot deep. Vessels which are used often should be within easy reach.

Those who can afford it may buy a refrigerator and install it inside or near the kitchen.

All containers should be clearly labelled and neatly arranged on the shelves. They should be so arranged as to ensure clear visibility of all articles.

The grinding stone should be kept on a raised platform. Proper facilities for washing it and for the drainage of water should be provided.

A sink is an absolute necessity in a kitchen. It is necessary for washing hands, fruit and vegetables, for cleaning crockery, cutlery and glassware and for drawing water for mixing, cooking and drinking. There should be drain-boards on both sides of the sink on which to put washed utensils. Provision should be made for a towel rack, soap-holder, a shelf for scrubbing material, etc.

A low tap close to the floor level is also useful for cleaning the bigger vessels.

The kitchen should have a table for mixing flour and cutting vegetables. It should also be provided with a garbage bin for collection and disposal of peelings, waste products, etc.

A kitchen must have a stove, and if one can afford it, an oven. The stove should be placed at least two feet above floor level to facilitate working without having to stoop.

The kitchen table, stove and sink should be conveniently placed so that the housewife can do her cooking conveniently with a minimum of movement.

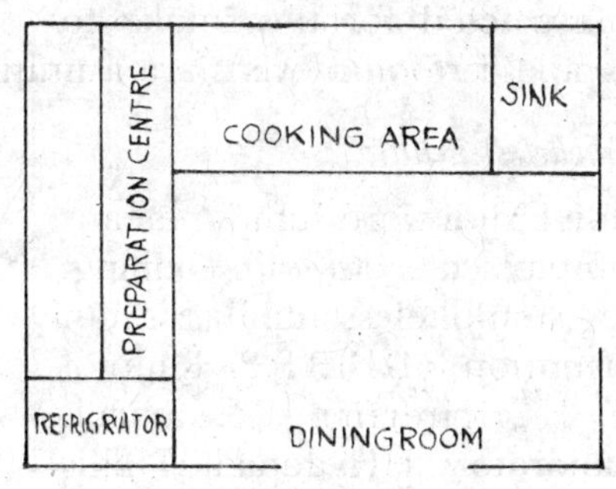

L-Shaped kitchen
Fig. 1

Adequate storage space should be provided near the table, stove and sink, for keeping groceries and cooking utensils, pots and pans and cleaning materials.

Types of stoves and ovens

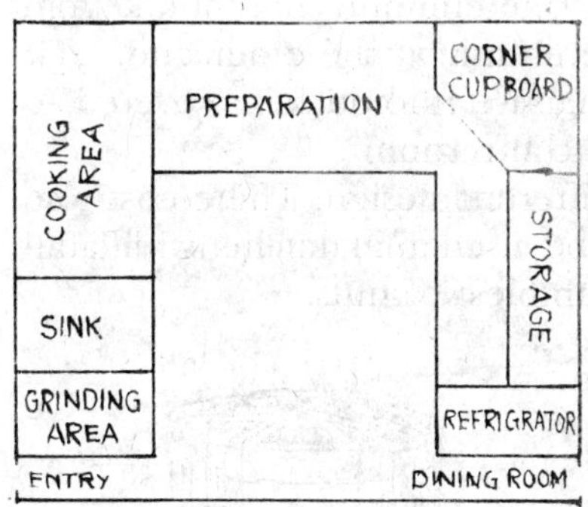

U-Shaped kitchen
Fig. 2.

The type of stove and oven used depends upon the fuel available and its price. One should buy as modern a type as one can afford. To be economical, a stove should give maximum heat with minimum fuel. It should be convenient and easy to use.

The different types of stoves and ovens are firewood ovens, electric ovens, gas stoves, coal stoves, charcoal stoves, oil stoves, etc.

Firewood oven

This is the commonest type of oven in most parts of India, though rather old-fashioned. If proper chimneys are not constructed for the smoke to escape, firewood ovens are a nuisance.

Firewood oven
Fig. 3.

Smokeless "chula"

The Hindi word "chula" means a fire-place or stove for cooking. The smokeless chula is an invention of Dr. S.P. Raju of the Engineering Research Laboratories, Hyderabad. This chula can be fed with firewood or coal. The consumption of fuel is very small compared with the firewood oven since every calorie of heat available is used in cooking. It is shaped like the letter L and has three holes, each 8 inches in diameter on which the cooking vessels are placed. The fire is lighted at one end and the smoke and heat are drawn through to the chimney at the other end. If any of the three holes is not in use it should be covered to prevent the smoke escaping into the room.

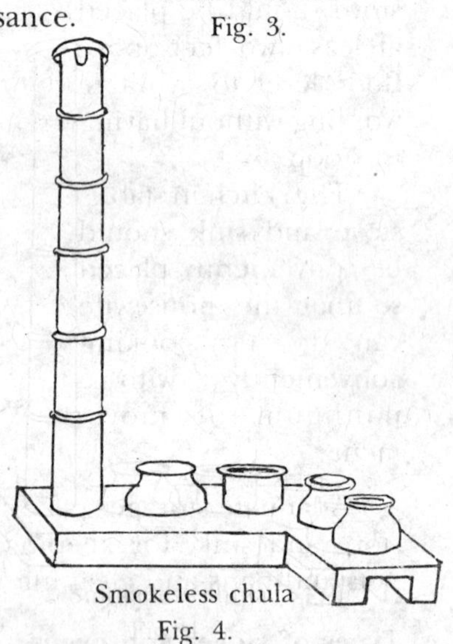

Smokeless chula
Fig. 4.

Smokeless chulas are of different designs. The cost also varies considerably. They can be used in kitchens with all modern amenities or in the humblest of huts.

Charcoal sigri

A charcoal sigri, made of iron, is not very expensive. It is advantageous because it produces no smoke, but the consumption of charcoal may not suit our pockets. Further if the room is not well ventilated

Charcoal sigri
Fig. 5.

there is the danger of carbon monoxide poisoning through the fumes of the unconsumed gas given out by the charcoal.

Oil stoves

Oil stoves have the advantage that they can be used in places where there is scarcity of electricity and gas. They are economical and portable and can be easily lit and managed. They are available in various sizes. Clean kerosene oil should be used in them. Their efficiency depends upon how regularly wicks are trimmed and how clean the stove is kept. Unless they are kept clean the smell of kerosene oil that emanates from them will be nauseating. They should be kept away from draughts while in use.

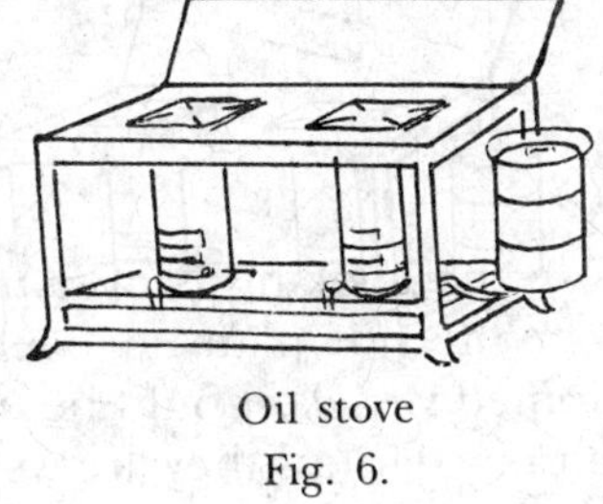

Oil stove

Fig. 6.

Gas stoves

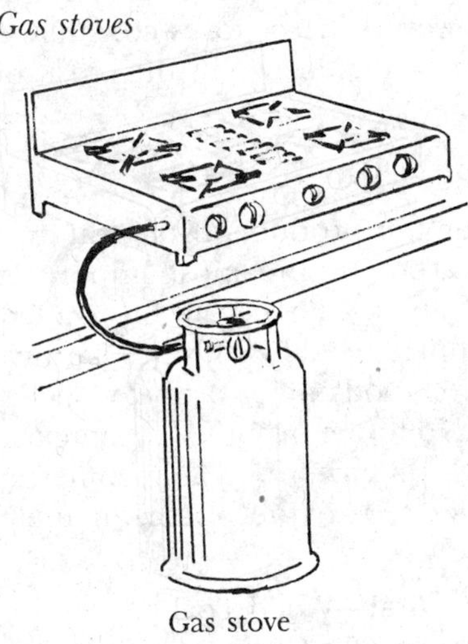

Gas stove

Fig. 7.

Gas stoves are commonly used in India mainly in big cities. A gas oven is relatively cheap and inexpensive if the gas is cheap. Gas stoves are also easy to clean and very simple to use. However, one should be careful to switch off the gas when the stove is not in use because it is poisonous and inflammable.

Electric stoves

Electric stoves are not common in India and are used only by a small minority of people. They are labour saving, convenient and efficient and produce no smoke or soot to dirty the cooking vessels. The current should be switched off a little

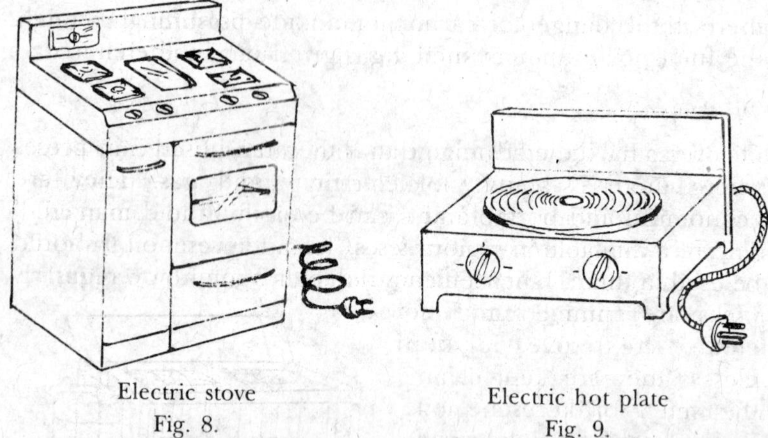

Electric stove
Fig. 8.

Electric hot plate
Fig. 9.

before the cooking is over because there is always some heat left in the hot plate to complete the cooking. Special flat-bottomed vessels should be used on them to prevent waste of electricity. Unless they are well constructed there is the danger of getting an electric shock. However, these stoves consume a lot of electricity and prove very expensive if the cost of electricity is high.

Types of fuel

Combustible substances used for the production of heat and energy are known as fuels. Carbon is the most important constituent of the majority of them. They can be graded according to the amount of heat produced by a given quantity. They have a variety of uses: to cook food and to propel vehicles on land and sea and in the air. No home or industry can exist without them. Our concern with them here is their domestic use. The different kinds of fuel used in the home, in their natural or prepared state, are:

Solid Fuels	:	Natural—Wood, coal. Prepared—Charcoal, coke.
Liquid Fuels	:	Natural—Petroleum. Prepared—Kerosene.
Gaseous Fuels	:	Natural—Natural gas. Prepared—Coal gas, water gas and acetylene.

Electricity
Solar Cooker

Solid fuels

The solid fuels are wood, coal, charcoal and coke.

Wood

This is a well-known and widely used fuel. Any twig, stick or log of wood used for cooking food becomes fuel. It is a cheap type of fuel. There are many varieties of firewood. Some burn quickly without giving out much heat, while others burn steadily for a long time. The wood of portia, casuarina, tamarind, margosa and acacia trees is commonly used for fuel in India. Expensive wood is seldom used as fuel unless it is considerably decayed or ravaged by white ants. Wood is dried and cut into the desired shape before being used as fuel. When it is used as fuel some heat is wasted owing to the evaporation of the water contained in the wood. When one end of a piece of wood is burnt, an oily liquid can be seen to ooze out at the other end. The more oil there is in the wood the better it burns. The wood of the eucalyptus tree is rich in oil and burns very well. People living in the Nilgiris use it for fuel.

The disadvantages of using wood as fuel are many. It does not help to cook food quickly. During the rainy season and when it is wet it is difficult to kindle. It is difficult to store because it occupies too much space. Some kinds of firewood give out too much smoke and make a person cough, shed tears and feel suffocated. Such fuel dirties the kitchen and makes it dark and sooty with smoke. Using wood for fuel also means depleting forests.

Cowdung

In Indian homes cowdung cakes are used as a supplemental fuel along with firewood. However, they are good fertilisers and it would be more appropriate to use them as manure. They are unhygienic since a lot of insects multiply where they are stored. They should not be stored when wet as they will become breeding places for flies which are carriers of infectious diseases.

Coal

A period during the formative stages of the earth is known by scientists as the "Carboniferous Age". Owing to some phenomena the trees and other objects of that period were burnt and buried. Those forests of a bygone age are the suppliers of coal to modern man. Coal is the product of heat and pressure on vegetable and animal matter through many generations. Coal is dug out from underground mines in many parts of the world. The coalmines of England have contributed greatly to the wealth of that country. In India coalmines exist in Singareni in Andhra Pradesh and Raniganj in West Bengal. Lignite is found in Neyveli in Tamil Nadu. Coal is black or brownish black in colour. It is hard, heavy and shiny. It contains mostly carbon. It gives intense heat but produces smoke and thus darkens the wall. There are different forms of coal such as lignite, bituminous, anthracite and so on. Coal is mostly used for industrial purposes.

Charcoal

Charcoal is a black, amorphous and brittle substance. It is the charred remains of wood heated out of contact with air and is widely used for domestic purposes all over India. It is easy to light. When lit it glows red and burns till completely consumed.

Coke

Coke is prepared from coal in the same manner as charcoal from wood. It is the residue obtained by heating coal out of contact with air and is cheaper than coal. It is difficult to ignite coke, but when once lighted it gives out much heat and burns slowly and steadily without much smoke.

Liquid fuels

The liquid fuels are petroleum, petrol, spirit, kerosene, alcohol, etc. Kerosene is commonly used in Indian homes for lighting a fire and for oil lamps. Since it is a cheap fuel, it can also be conveniently used for stoves.

Gaseous fuels

Though gas is used mostly in laboratories in India, in today, gas is also used for cooking purposes in metros like Bombay, Delhi, Calcutta, Madras and other big cities where LPG (Liquefied Petroleum Gas) is available.

Liquefied Petroleum Gas

Liquefied Petroleum Gas (LPG) is defined as a hydrocarbon which is gaseous at normal atmospheric pressure and temperature but may be converted to the liquid state even at normal temperature by the application of moderate pressure. Although they are normally used as gases they are stored and transported as liquid in steel or aluminium cylinders with a valve outlet. When the valve is opened, the liquid changes back to gas and can be piped to an appliance for use. LPG is either propane (C_3H_8), butane (C_4H_{10}) or a mixture of the two.

Advantages

1) It is economical.
2) Heat can be regulated by means of automatic regulators.
3) It is a first class cooking medium as its calorific value is considerably more, and
4) It is convenient to use and does not blacken the wall.

Disadvantage

LPG is one and a half to two times heavier than air and if LPG escapes, it tends to settle near the floor, creating a safety hazard. If it burns without an adequate air supply, some of carbon will not be converted to carbon dioxide(CO_2) and it will be deposited as carbon (soot). A dangerous situation thus will arise by producing a dangerous gas, carbon monoxide, which can he lethal if breathed in.even small quantities. Hence care should be taken to turn off the gas tap securely when not in use as gas can cause carbon monoxide poisoning if it is not lighted.

Cowdung gas

The Indian Agricultural Research Institute, after many years of investigation, has worked out a cheap and simply operated plant by which cowdung can be fermented so as to yield a sufficient quantity of combustible gas which can be used for cooking. The residue that remains can be used as manure for crops. These plants have been installed in some villages and have been found to work very successfully.

Consumption of the dung of four animals regularly will give 100 cubic feet of gas daily, which can be used for both cooking and lighting purposes. The blue flame of the gas is hot and smokeless, which makes cooking much cleaner and quicker.

The gas plant operates on the simple principle that when dung or any organic matter ferments in the absence of air, a combustible gas called methane is produced. The fermentation tank is a brick-lined well 12 feet deep and 6 feet in diameter, which is filled with cowdung made into a liquid paste with water. This is then covered with an iron drum 5 feet in diameter and 4 feet in height, introduced upside down into the well. This serves to cut off air and provide the necessary conditions for fermentation. The gas produce bubbles into the inverted drum which begins to float and rise. Through an opening on the top of the drum the gas can be led to the kitchen by pipes and used.

In this process, no loss of manurial constituents takes place. In fact, the removal of only the heat constituents in the form of gas makes the residue actually a richer manure than the original cowdung. No fly breeding takes place in the dung slurry.

The adoption of this gas plant is one of the solutions for the difficult problem of fuel in villages.

Electricity

Though electricity is the commonest fuel in many advanced countries, its use for cooking is a luxury known only to a few Indian families. It gives intense heat very quickly. The heat can be regulated according to need. It is convenient and labour-saving. Electricity minimises the work of the housewife, while making for maximum efficiency. There is no smoke or dust, and the kitchen can be kept spick and span. But electric cookers are very costly and far beyond the means of most Indians.

Solar Cooker

An important domestic, solar thermal application is that of cooking. Over the past 30 years, a number of designs of solar cookers have been developed. Box Type Cookers with no reflector or with one reflector are simple to use and require little attention.

Parts : The Solar Cooker consists of :

a) **Enclosure**—It is rectangular in shape and is made up of inner silver and outer metal or wooden box.

b) **Insulation**—The enclosure is insulated at the bottom and sides.

c) **Top Cover**—The top cover contains two plain glasses fixed in the wooden frame.

d) **Absorber Tray**—The tray is painted black (dull in colour) so that it can withstand the maximum temperature attained inside the cooker.

e) **Reflector mirrors**—The addition of the mirror helps in achieving enclosure temperatures which are higher by about 15° to 20°C. It is hinged on one side of the glass frame and its inclination can be varied so as to be adjusted to reflect the sun's Rays into the box. Cookers with reflectors on all four edges have also been built.

Working mechanism

Solar radiation enters through the top and heats up the enclosure in which the food to be cooked is placed in shallow vessels.

Dimensions

60 × 60 × 20 cms.

Temperature

100°C.

Serving

For a family of 5 to 7 people.

Use

To prepare pulses, rice, vegetables which are readily cooked.

Advantages

(1) No attention is needed during cooking.
(2) No charring of food or overflowing.
(3) No pollution of utensils and atmosphere.

Disadvantages

i) Cannot be used to cook chapatis and puris as it requires high temperature and also needs manipulation.

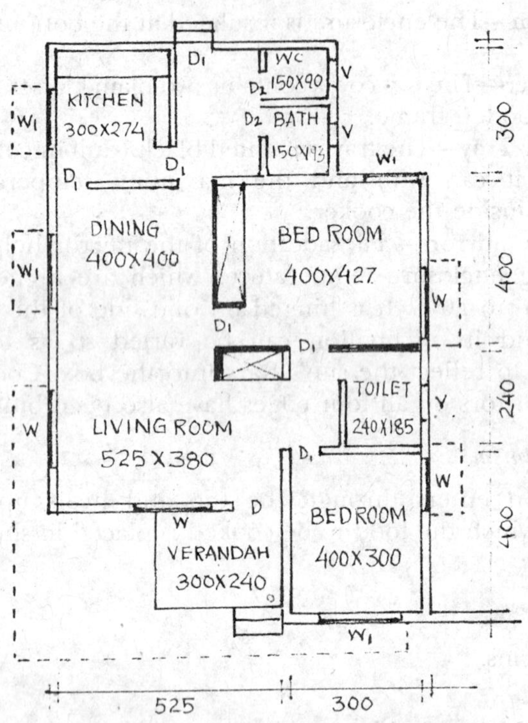

REFERENCE

PLINTH AREA 1183 sqm

D DOOR	105X213
D1 DOOR	90X213
D2 DOOR	75X213
W WINDOW	182X137
W1 WINDOW	122X137
V VENTILATOR	90X60

(ALL MEASUREMENT IN CENTIMETRES)

PLAN OF A HOUSE FOR A HIGH INCOME GROUP FAMILY

Fig. 10. Plan of a house for a high income group family

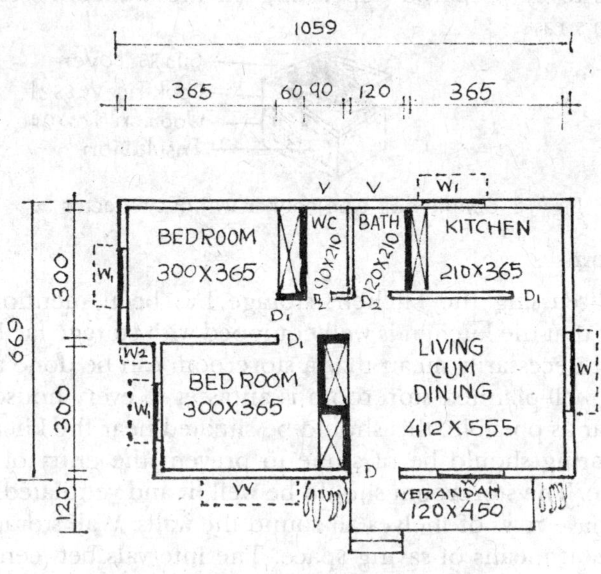

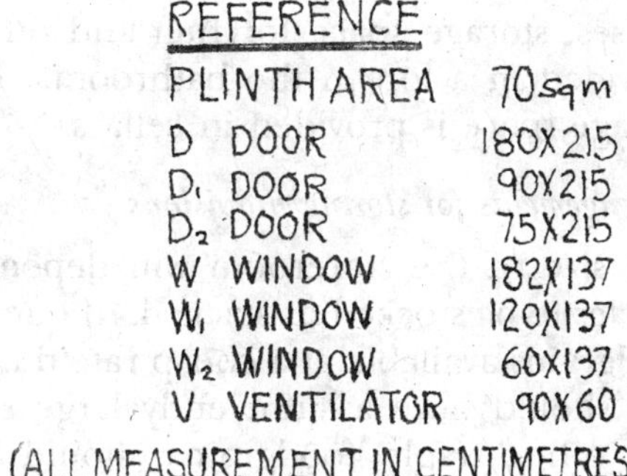

REFERENCE

PLINTH AREA	70 sqm
D DOOR	180X215
D_1 DOOR	90X215
D_2 DOOR	75X215
W WINDOW	182X137
W_1 WINDOW	120X137
W_2 WINDOW	60X137
V VENTILATOR	90X60

(ALL MEASUREMENT IN CENTIMETRES)

PLAN OF A HOUSE FOR A
MIDDLE INCOME GROUP FAMILY

Fig. 11. Plan of a house for a middle income group family

ii) One has to cook according to the sunshine and the menu has to be prepared depending on the availability of the sun's rays.

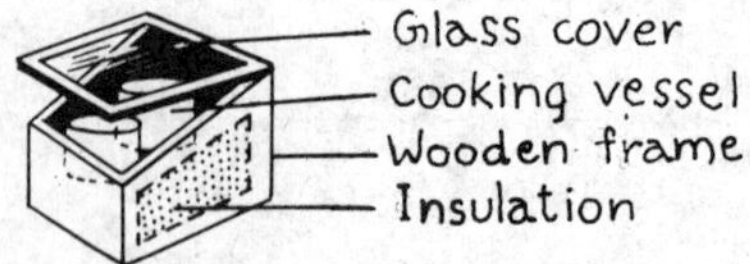

Fig. 12. Simple box type cooker without reflector

Storeroom

While discussing the kitchen, storage has been mentioned. The fact that the kitchen is well equipped with storage facilities does not necessarily mean that a storeroom can be done away with. A well-planned storeroom is an asset to every house.

As far as possible, this should be situated near the kitchen. The flooring should be of stone to prevent the entry of rats and mice. The storeroom should be well lit and ventilated and should have rows of shelves all round the walls. Wall storage is an efficient means of saving space. The intervals between the lower shelves should be larger and between the top ones smaller to facilitate the storing of different-sized articles.

In some houses the space below a stairway is covered and used as a storeroom, while in others, places such as back verandahs are covered and utilised for the purpose. In some houses, storage space for fuel and other forms of lumber is provided in a loft in the bathroom. In some, underground storage space is provided in cellars.

Arrangements for storing provisions

The size of the storeroom will depend upon the nature of articles to be stocked or stacked. If one desires to store in bulk foodgrains available at a cheap rate during the harvest season, one should have a sufficiently large storeroom. Wheat, rice and other staple foodgrains should be stored in air-tight wooden boxes with tin lining or boxes made of tin, galvanised boxes or drums to prevent the entry of grain weevils and other household pests. Neem leaves put with grain safeguard it from attack by insects. The containers should be cleaned and aired from time to time.

Spices and condiments can be stored in air-tight tins,

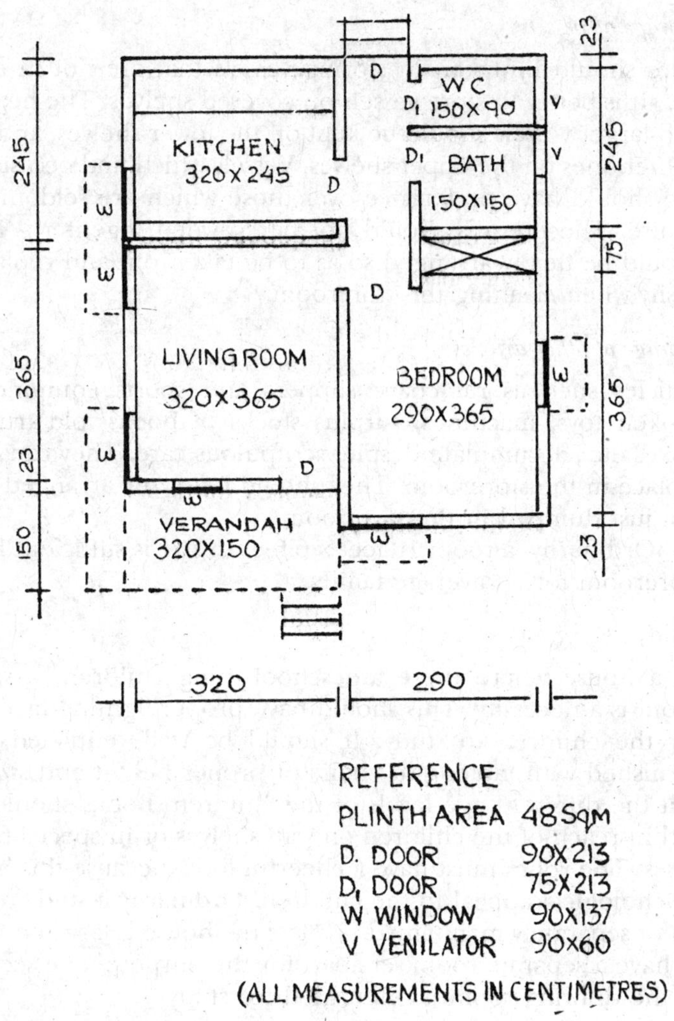

Fig. 13. Plan of a house for a low-income group family

bottles, boxes, plastic cases, etc. They should be properly labelled.

Storage of vessels

Care should be taken in storing vessels that are not in daily use. It is better to store vessels on covered shelves. The heavier and larger vessels should be kept on the lower shelves, and the lighter ones on the upper shelves. Vessels which find occasional use should have preference over those which are seldom put to use. The utensils should not be crowded together. They should be neatly arranged so as to be taken out and replaced easily when cleaning the storeroom.

Storage of other articles

Articles such as raincoats, slippers and sports equipments, broken toys, machines, surplus stocks of books, old trunks, boxes etc., accumulate despite scrupulous care. They can find a place in the storeroom. They should be neatly arranged and not just dumped in the storeroom.

Ordinarily, a room 10 feet × 6 feet in size is sufficient for a storeroom for an average family.

Study

In a house where there are school-going children, a study room is a necessity. This should have proper lighting facilities for the children to study. It should be well ventilated and furnished with tables and chairs of proper height and size to suit the different age levels of the children. Books should be within reach of the children on wall shelves or in special book cases. The room must have a cheerful look, because this has a psychological appeal to the children. Ordinarily a study room is not separately maintained. Unless the house is large enough to have a separate room set apart for the purpose, one section of the drawing room is often used for study.

Nursery

The nursery should be situated close to the parents' room. The floor and wall surfaces should be easy to clean. The floor should be devoid of cracks. Care should be taken in fixing the electric lights so that no wall plug is within reach of the child.

Overhead fixtures are advisable. A night light with a bulb of low wattage, preferably tinted, should be installed.

Enough storage space within the child's reach should be provided for keeping its clothes, playthings etc. The room should contain a blackboard or some writing-board with writing materials such as chalk. This will prevent the child from scribbling on the wall.

Children enjoy physical experiments such as crawling, standing up, walking, climbing and jumping. The furniture should have rounded ends, and be strong and sturdy.

Bathroom

Practical aspects should be considered first in planning a bathroom. Convenience and privacy should be its keynote.

The purpose of a bathroom is to provide facilities for washing, bathing and shaving. Hence the size should be such as to facilitate all these functions. The minimum should be 6 feet × 10 feet.

The flooring should be glazed for easy cleaning. Mosaic flooring is suitable. The wall also should have a glazed or polished surface, at least to a height of 3 feet from the floor level.

The present-day tendency is to have a bathroom attached to every bedroom. The bathroom should have closed storage space for keeping soap, shaving kit, toothpaste, toothbrush, towels, etc. A towel rack, a clothes stand, and a mirror are also necessary. A wash-basin, a bath-tub, a shower and a tap should be provided in a bathroom. In the Indian style of bathing, water is stored in a large tub or vessel and the bather uses a mug for pouring water.

In some houses the lavatory also is inside the bathroom. This is a convenient arrangement. The flush type of lavatory is the best. In constructing a lavatory, one should remember the following points.

It should be properly designed so that the excreta is washed away automatically into a receptacle or container without soiling the sides.

The materials used for construction should be non-absorbent thus preventing soil pollution.

The lavatory should be properly ventilated to prevent its giving out any foul odour.

Even a flush lavatory has to be kept clean. The lavatory basin should be cleaned daily with detergent and the room also washed with phenol or some other disinfectant daily.

How to make the best use of a one-room apartment

An ideal home should have excellent facilities for cooking, dining, sleeping, entertainment, bathing, toilet, children's activities, study and storage. In these days of economic stress, in countries like India, not all can afford a house with all these amenities. Most people live in one-room apartments. They have to make the best use of their single room. This demands careful planning. Activities should be located efficiently, and those that do not conflict should be clubbed together. Furniture should be kept to a minimum and be only what is absolutely necessary. Light furniture which may be folded easily when necessary, should be provided to enable easy transition from one activity to another. Versatile built-ins help to save space. Some modern pieces of furniture come in parts and sections which can be built into storage units and room dividers according to one's own design. There are some pieces of furniture which can serve dual purposes, as for example a convertible sofa which becomes a bed. Such multi-purpose furniture is now available in the market. The living room can be partitioned off from the dining-room by a large wooden partition with shelves on either side. Curios, books, etc., could be placed on the shelf facing the living-room, whereas crockery, cutlery and other dining-room equipment could be stored on the shelves on the dining-room side.

The living-room can be converted into the bedroom at night. The dining-room can serve as a 'study'. The dining-room section should be large enough to play the part of a kitchen as well as an eating place.

If wooden partitions take too much space, cloth screens can be used as room dividers.

By carefully planning the one-room apartment and fitting it with minimum furniture and equipment, a family can enjoy a comfortable life.

2. Interior Decoration

A simple house can be made to look attractive by decorating its interior tastefully. Interior decoration is a creative art which can transform an ordinary house. It is the art of adjusting the space and equipment to suit the fundamental and cultural needs of the dwellers and thus creating a pleasant atmosphere.

The value of an article depends upon its suitability to the home and its inmates. It should be **useful**. This is the central concept in planning and furnishing the home. Furniture should be comfortable. Storage space should be provided with due regard to convenience.

The articles and furnishings should be **economical** in the sense that they are worth the time, energy and money required to keep them clean and in good condition.

The articles used in a house should be **beautiful**. Beauty is the element or quality which pleases the senses and uplifts the spirit. The principles of beauty and those of design are the same. The elements of design are line, direction, shape, size, colour, texture and value. These are plastic elements which can be adapted to suit the individual taste. The originality evinced in their selection and organisation is the art of interior decoration. The combinations should be expressive, unified by a basic conception, rich and varied, and should have harmony, balance, proportion, rhythm and emphasis.

Every home should have an **individuality** of its own. This is the quality which differentiates one home from another. It reflects markedly the very personality of the occupants.

Thus by combining use, economy, beauty and individuality, one is able to create a unique charm in the house one lives in, reflecting the refined and cultured tastes of the inmates.

Importance of good taste

In some people good taste is inborn. They have an eye for beauty and are capable of setting up a neatly arranged and beautifully planned home. A tastefully set up home is pleasant, agreeable, exciting, interesting and satisfying. In choosing furnishings for the home, decorating it with flowers, or selecting clothing, good taste is important.

A house should be artistic in all respects. We must know how to use art in simple ways, appreciate beauty in common things, and develop good taste.

Art and good taste should go together. Since art is involved in most of the objects in a house, one should have a knowledge of the principles fundamental to good taste. These are flexible guides which can be modulated according to one's tastes. Good taste has been described as "doing the right thing, at the right time, in the right way".

One can improve the appearance of one's surroundings if one has proper judgment of design and colour in furnishing the home. There are certain principles which help one to cultivate good taste. One should have a knowledge of the guiding principles of good design, of the harmony of colour, and of structural and decorative principles. Design involves **line**, straight, slightly curved and deeply curved; **direction**, vertical, oblique or horizontal; **shape,** formed by lines and direction such as square, diamond, circle, etc; **size**, depending on the degree, small, smaller, smallest or big, bigger, biggest; **texture**, as fine, medium, coarse; and **colour**, as yellow, blue, red, etc.

Design is classified into two groups, as **structural** or **decorative.** Structural design is that which is suitable to the purpose for which the article is made, befitting the materials used and suitable to the processes by which it is made. Design added to enhance the beauty of an article is called decorative design. If the specific designs of birds, flowers and other natural objects are used, the design is naturalistic.

Fundamentals of design

Design is the backbone of graphic arts like metre and rhyme to poetry. It aids one's aesthetic appreciation of objects. Design, which is a part of art actually becomes a part of our lives and personality and influences the enjoyment of everything we do, and of everything we select.

Design is defined as any arrangement of line, form, colour,

space, value and texture. It involves the proper choice of forms and colours and arranging them aesthetically and tastefully. A good design shows an orderly arrangement of the material used and in addition enhances the beauty and charm of the finished product.

Designs are classified into two kinds: structural and decorative. Structural design is that which is suitable to the purpose for which the article is made, befitting the material used and the processes by which it is made. It is the design made by the size, form, colour and texture of the object, whether it is the object itself in space or a drawing of it on paper. All objects have structural design. The requirement of a good structural design are four-fold.

1. The design must be suited to its purpose.
2. It must have correct proportions.
3. It must be simple.
4. It must be in consonance with the material from which it is made.

If these four requirements are fulfilled, the object will have lasting satisfaction.

Figure 16 (a) shows a good structural design of a porcelain cup—simple and functional. In Fig. 16 (b), the flower vase has a poor structural design. Its proportions are faulty and the object looks unbalanced and unstable. It appears top heavy, as the base is small and there is every chance that the vase will tilt in the slightest wind.

(a) A good structural design
(b) A poor structural design
Fig. 14.

A good structural design could be made more beautiful by decoration. A good design added to enhance the beauty of an article is called "decorative design". The decorative design should fulfil several requirements.

1. The decoration should be used in moderation.
2. It should be placed in structural points to strengthen the shape of the object.
3. The decoration should be restrained enough so that the background space is simple and adds dignity to the design.
4. The decoration should be suitable for the purpose for which the object is made.

Hence, a decorative design provides the surface enrichment of a structural design. Any lines, colours or materials that have been applied to the structural design for the purpose of adding a richer quality to it constitutes its decorative design. Thus the structural design is essential to every object while decoration is the "luxury" of design. If the specific designs of birds, flowers, and other natural objects are used, the design is called a naturalistic one. Lack of moderation in design will make the object look bizarre.

If a design is to give maximum amount of satisfaction, it should not only be beautiful, but should have individuality, character or style, and utility. The importance of combining utility with beauty should be emphasized in any structural or decorative design. For instance, a chair may be very attractive with pleasing decorations and graceful curves. But it may be uncomfortable to sit on. The chair may not provide good support for the back. The curved piece of decoration which may be at shoulder-level, or the arm rest, may cause much discomfort. Despite the chair being beautiful, its design is poor since it is not functional. In Fig. 17, though the structural design of the vase is very appealing, the decorative design is too emphatic and makes the vase look unnecessarily ornamental for a flower arrangement.

Fig. 15. Decorative design

It will definitely take the eye off the flower arrangement and destroy the very purpose for which it is intended. On the other hand if it is displayed as an ornament for show and not as a flower vase the design is certainly acceptable.

In our everyday life we meet with a number of designs. The three essential aims of a good design are: order, beauty and utility. A man with good taste may use an ordinary piece of canvas and some paints and create a masterpiece of art while another person using the same material may produce something worthless. It is just the variation in the qualities of order and beauty—order that denotes organization or structure, and beauty that shows character through the interpretation of an idea by an individual. The organizational ability of an individual could be developed by applying the principles of art in one's everyday life.

The principles of art can be thought of as the yardsticks with which we are able to measure a design or an object. The following art principles are the bases for judging good design:

1. Harmony
2. Proportion
3. Balance
4. Rhythm
5. Emphasis.

Harmony

Harmony means unity or a single idea or impression. That is, it produces an impression of unity through the selection and arrangement of consistent objects and ideas. When all the objects in a group seem to have a strong family resemblance, that group illustrates the principles of harmonious selection. It makes no difference whether we are dealing with interior decoration, garden layout or dress design. There must be harmony if one is to create an integrated and beautiful effect. Harmony is the fundamental requirement in any piece of design or work. It is therefore the most important of all the principles in design. There are six aspects of harmony. They are harmony of line, shape, size, texture, colour and idea.

Proportion

Proportion means the relationship of sizes or areas to one

another or to a whole. Therefore, it is sometimes called the law of relationship. Every time two or more things are put together, good or bad proportions are established. Some individuals have a natural or inborn instinct for correct proportion and whatever combinations they plan are sure to please the eye. However, a person could easily acquire this unique trait by experience. Proportion is the principle of design which is achieved when the different sizes are successfully grouped in any arrangement, so that they are "in scale"— that is, the elements making up the structure have a pleasing relationship to the whole and to one another. Generally speaking, large furniture belongs in large rooms; likewise, a small room requires small-sized furniture, patterns and accessories. A very small chair next to a very massive one would be "out of scale". Furniture that seems too small for a room should be arranged in groups. Then the size of the group and not the size of each piece becomes the unit for comparison.

Appearance can be changed by the use of strong vertical or horizontal lines. Horizontal lines tend to increase the width of an object or a room while vertical lines make a room appear higher.

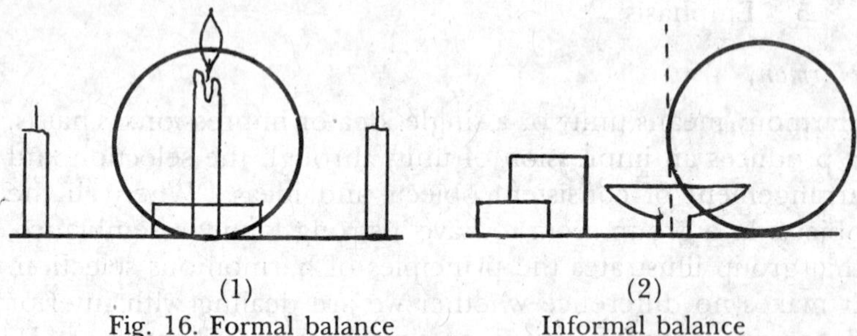

Fig. 16. Formal balance Informal balance

Balance

The next principle in design is "balance". Balance is composure or equilibrium of forces. It is rest or repose. This restful effect is obtained by grouping shapes and colours around a centre in such a way that there is equal attraction on each side of the centre. Balance is necessary for a sense of equilibrium, stability, and permanence.

Balance in design can be explained simply as balance in weight. The only difference is that it is not so much a question of how much an object weighs as how much the object attracts.

Balance is of two types: formal and informal. If objects are similar in appearance, they will attract the same amount of attention and therefore should be equidistant from the centre. This kind of balance is known as formal or bi-symmetrical balance. A design which has a formal balance gives a feeling of dignity and stateliness. If however the objects do not attract the same amount of attention, they must be placed at different distances from the centre. Large objects placed close to a visual centre may be balanced by smaller objects placed at a greater distance from the visual centre. This second type is called informal balance or asymmetrical balance. Informal balance gives the impression of spontaneity, freedom of movement and casualness. Balance in design is so natural that an individual is not even aware of it when it is present, but when it is violated there is a sense of disparity, distraction and discomfort.

Rhythm

In design, "rhythm" means an easy connected path along which the eye may travel in any arrangement of line, form or colour. Rhythm relates to movement. But in a perfectly plain space there is no movement. The moment a pattern is placed

Fig. 17. The design radiates from the centre and creates a feeling of rhythm

upon the plain surface, the eye will begin to travel along the lines suggested by the object or pattern. Rhythmic movement can be obtained through repetition of shapes, progression of sizes or through an easily connected continuous line movement.

Emphasis

Emphasis means having a particular point of interest with every other detail subordinate to it. Though a design or an arrangement may be well balanced, its proportions good, and its contents in perfect harmony, it may still be dull and uninteresting. In spite of its merits, the eye will pass over it because there is no particular point to arrest the attention—the arrangement lacks emphasis. Therefore emphasis is the art principle by which the eye is carried first to the most important thing in any arrangement and from that point to every other detail in order of importance. Emphasis should be put on a few things; non-essentials should be eliminated. The problems to face are: what to emphasize, how to emphasize, how much to emphasize and where to place the emphasis. The test for judging emphasis are simplicity and beauty. Certain areas or objects can be emphasized or attention could be attracted by grouping objects, by using contrasts of colour or values, by using decorations, by providing sufficient plain background space around objects, or by using unusual lines, shapes or sizes.

With the development of our appreciation of these principles, our conception of the term 'principles of design' broadens and deepens. Good design never goes out of style. These principles are never static. They are flexible guides to be used in producing desired results and developing a capacity for good taste in an individual.

Study of the colour chart

Colour removes the drabness from life and enhances the beauty of objects. Its appeal is universal. The charm of a painting depends upon the colours used by the artist apart from the technique employed in the presentation of the subject matter. To understand why some colours are to be preferred to others it is necessary to know something about the nature and language of colour. Colours mean different things to people of different professions, such as the physiologist, the chemist, the physicist, the psychologist and the artist.

One can assess the value of colour in three ways: in light, in vision and in pigment. The important question in the study of colours is what colours complement each other in the three media of light, sight and pigment.

There are several theories regarding colours in pigment. One of the simplest is the Prang Colour System.

Prang Colour System

Just as objects have three dimensions, length, breadth and thickness, colours have three features. They are:

Warmth or **coolness**, referred to as the **hue** or the **name** of the colour;

Lightness or **darkness**, otherwise known as the **value** of the colour; and

Brightness or **dullness**, also called the **intensity** or **chroma** of the colour.

Hue is the name of the colour such as red, green, etc.

Value is the lightness or darkness of the colour. It ranges between high-light, light, wan-light, middle, high-dark, dark and low-dark. White is the highest value as no hue is as light as white. Black is the lowest value as no colour is so dark as black.

Intensity or chroma is the brightness or dullness of a colour. Intensity of a colour is usually achieved by mixing it with its complement, and sometimes by mixing it with gray.

According to Prang, all colours may be obtained from the three primary or basic or fundamental colours, yellow, blue and red. These three colours cannot be obtained by mixing other hues.

When two primary colours are mixed in equal proportions, a binary or a secondary colour results, as follows :

Yellow plus blue	... Green
Blue plus red	... Violet or purple
Red plus yellow	... Orange

Yellow, blue, red, green, violet and orange are commonly called the **standard colours**.

When a primary and a neighbouring binary colour are mixed, the following six intermediate hues are obtained:

Yellow plus green ... Yellow-green
Blue plus green ... Blue-green
Blue plus violet ... Blue-violet
Red plus violet ... Red-violet
Red plus orange ... Red-orange
Yellow plus orange ... Yellow-orange

The three primary hues, the three secondary hues, and the six intermediate hues constitute the outer circle in the Prang Colour Chart. However, there are possibilities of indefinite gradations between each of the intermediate colours such as blue, blue-green, green, yellow-green and so on.

When two binary colours are mixed, a tertiary colour results; for instance green plus orange—tertiary yellow.

A mixture of two tertiary colours gives a quarternary hue such as tertiary yellow plus tertiary blue—quarternary green.

In the Prang Colour Chart, the colours are arranged in a circle with yellow at the top centre. Violet falls directly opposite on the same vertical line.

Blue lies on the right side and red on the left side of the vertical line.

The inside circle of the colour chart consists of the six standard colours one half neutralized; and in the centre of the circle occurs gray.

The colours at the right side of the circle are the cool hues and those on the left are the warm hues. Red and orange are the warmest and blue the coolest. Green is between warm and cool.

Warm hues make objects appear larger and nearer; cool hues make them seem reduced in size and far off. While warm colours are cheerful, cool colours are calm and restful. White complements black; heat complements cold; and cool and warm colours complement one another.

Light values increase the size of objects; dark values decrease it.

The colours in the outer circle of the colour chart are of high intensity; those inside it are of low intensity. Objects with colour of full intensity are striking and brilliant. Objects with colour of low intensity are sober. In using colours of full intensity one should be cautious lest a daring and flashy effect is created.

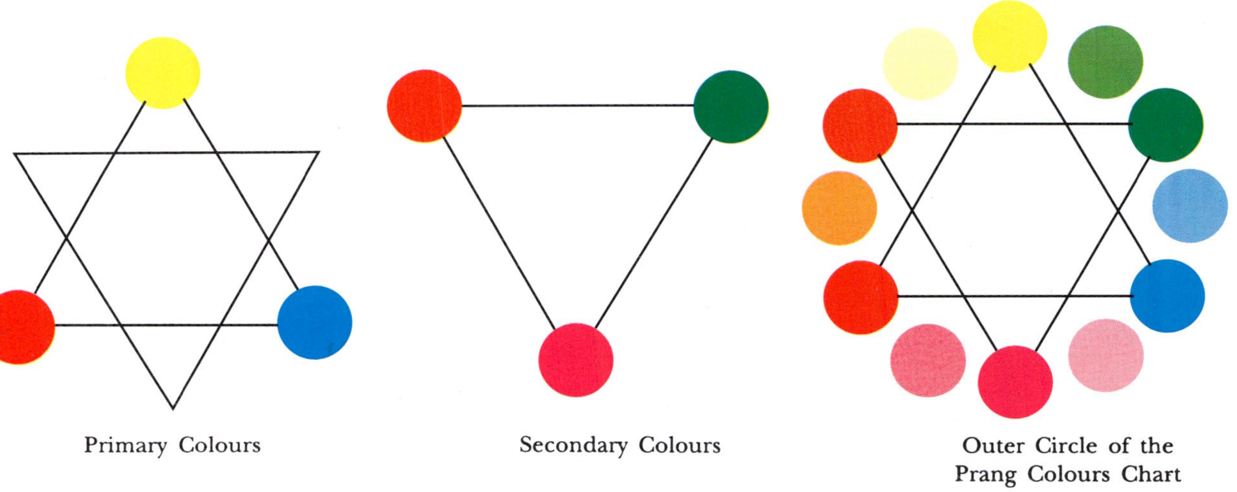

Fig. 18. COLOURS

Colour combinations

As discussed by the Goldstein sisters in their "Art in Everyday Life", successful use of colour combinations cannot be easily achieved. Careful study and patient experimentation are necessary. The principles involved are the same as in the case of design. They are:

Harmony or Unity,
Contrast or Variety,
Balance or Rest,
Rhythm or Easy Movement,
Emphasis or Centres of Interest, and
Proportion or Beautiful Sizes.

All these contribute to beautiful colour effects.

Certain colour combinations are pleasing to the eye, while others are loud and jarring. The standard colour harmonies are :

harmony of Related Colours, and
harmony of Contrasting Hues.

Harmony of related colours

Related colour harmonies are obtained by using colours which are similar. There are two ways of doing this: Monochromatic Harmony and Analogous Harmony.

Monochromatic harmony

This is also known as **one hue** or **one mode harmony**. In this only one colour is used. There may be difference in values or intensities. The neutrals, black, white and gray may be used in any harmony. In monochromatic harmony, charming effects can be obtained through a contrast in the textures of the materials used.

Analogous harmonies

In analogous harmony, colours which are next of kin or neighbouring in the Prang Colour Chart are used. They provide a greater and more interesting variety than monochromatic harmonies. The colours used should be of different intensities and values, such as an analogous harmony of yellow-green, green and blue-green. Analogous harmonies are quiet and useful.

Harmonies of contrasting colours

There are four ways of obtaining contrasting harmonies. They are:

Complementary Harmony,
Double Complementary Harmony,
Split Complementary Harmony, and
Triads.

Complementary harmony

When colours which are directly opposite to each other in the Prang Colour Chart are used, they produce complementary harmony. They are excellent for room and window displays. Complementary harmonies can be obtained by using Yellow and Violet, Blue and Orange, Red and Green.

Double complementary harmony

When two adjacent colours and their complements are used together, they form double complementary harmony. One hue should be outstanding and it should be used in a large amount. For instance, Yellow and Yellow-Orange to Violet and Blue-Violet can be used for double complementary harmony.

Split complementary harmony

When a primary or an intermediate colour is used with the colours on either side of its complement, the combination produces split complementary harmony. For example, Yellow when used with Red-Violet and Blue-Violet, or Yellow-Orange with Blue and Purple will form split complementary harmony.

Triads

Four equilateral triangles can be formed within the Prang Colour Chart. The colours forming the points of the equilateral triangle constitute the triads. Thus the four triads formed are:

The Primary Triad created by the three primary colours, Yellow, Blue and Red.

The Secondary Triad, formed by the secondary colours, Green, Violet and Orange, and

The two Intermediate Triads consisting of the intermediate colours, Yellow-Green, Red-Orange and Blue-Violet, and

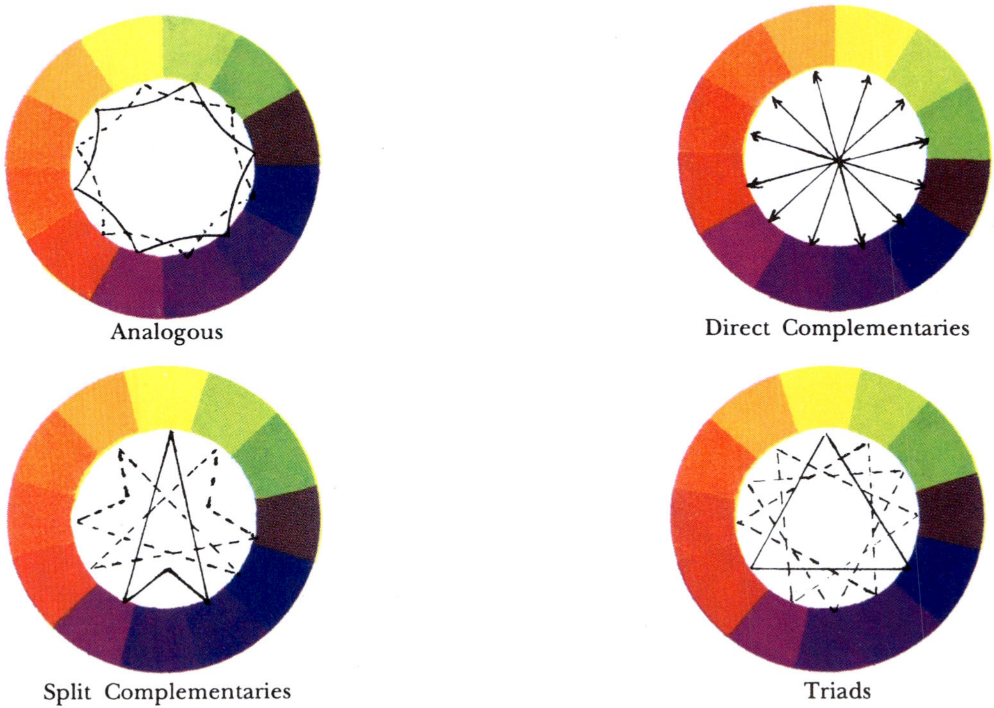

Analogous

Direct Complementaries

Split Complementaries

Triads

Fig. 19. COLOUR HARMONY

Red-Violet, Blue-Green and Yellow-Orange.

Triads form the richest of all harmonies, and afford a pleasant variety of combinations.

Colour harmonies are "recipes" for combinations.

Though there are varieties of colour harmonies, one should use caution and discretion in the selection of colours and their harmonization. The texture of the cloth also has a bearing upon the harmony, since some materials produce better effects than others, bringing out forcefully the natural charm of the colours used in the combination. If dark colour harmonies are used indiscriminately, they will produce a bizarre effect, either too bright or flashy.

Balance in colours

Apart from harmony there should be balance in the use of colours. Larger areas of a colour should be quiet and subdued in effect; smaller areas should show strong contrast. This constitutes what is known as the 'Law of Areas'. The contrasts may be in hue, value or intensity.

If tan and brown is used with bright red-orange, the colouring will be monotonous. If an opposite hue such as blue, green or blue-green is added, the effect will be satisfactory through the introduction of a Balancing Colour.

Apart from the selection of bright and dull hues, balance in colour can also be achieved by repeating some colours or values in various parts of the arrangement. This "repetition" is also known as "crossing".

Rhythm

Rhythm and balance are closely related. Rhythm is well-known in connection with poetry, music and dance. The skilful flow of colour in lines or slopes produces a rhythmic effect on the eye. Rhythm can also be achieved through the use of gradations in hue, value and intensity.

Emphasis

In the use of colour, there should be a point of emphasis or an outstanding or predominant colour effect. A main colour should be used distinctly or in various values and intensities. Some idea, colour, value or direction must be the dominant

factor. The background must be less emphatic than the objects portrayed on or placed against it.

Proportion

A subtle variation in proportion of the colour used can produce interesting effects. Colour combinations will be monotonous if equal proportions are used. The Greek proportion of 2 : 3 or 3 : 5 : 7 will produce a pleasing effect. According to the Law of Areas, if the colours differ in forcefulness, subdued colours should be used in larger areas and striking hues in smaller spaces.

Use of colour in the home

However commonplace one's life may be, it can be made bright and cheerful by the use of colour in the home. A magical effect can be produced by colours since they can transform darkness into light, dullness into brightness, gloominess into cheerfulness and drabness into beauty. The home is a colourful place with its different coloured furniture and accessories such as draperies, rugs, pictures. Colour plays a vital psychological role in home life. It is of primary importance in the emotional life of the occupants. Further, the selection and use of different colours, and coloured materials in the home expresses the character and individuality of the people who live in it.

Some colours produce certain characteristic effects. Orange, red and peach are stimulating, green-blue is soothing. Blue is serene and cool, but in excess causes depression. Green is easy on the eyes and is symbolic of freshness and youth. Violet is cold and austere. It is the colour of royalty. Yellow is vibrant and strong, cheerful and gay.

In using colours, the quantities used should be kept in mind. While a small area of brilliant red may be attractive, all the four walls of a room painted red may be a strain on the nerves and eyes, and cause emotional unrest. Some colours are more appropriate than others for certain rooms in a house. A bedroom, for instance, is a place of rest and quiet. Hence a colour which produces a peaceful atmosphere such as blue or blue-green should be chosen.

The dining-room should have a cool restful colour so that

one may be in a pleasant mood when one eats. Since a kitchen will be spoilt by smoke, buff, blue-grey or smoke-green should be used.

Bathrooms should have fresh, clear and stimulating colours, such as ivory or cream, so that the bather may have a clean and refreshed feeling.

It is a good idea to repeat one colour from a room in the colour scheme of the adjoining room. This produces a feeling of continuity as one moves about a house.

The type of colour and pattern used in a room should express the purpose for which the room is intended. Rooms that are lived in for long hours at a time should appear peaceful and the colour used should be restrained. Rooms that are used only for a few hours a day or in which there is a bustle of activity can stand bright colours and lively patterns. If a room gets too much sunshine a dark colour may be used to subdue the light. On the contrary, a room which does not get natural sunlight should be brightened up by a vibrant colour such as yellow. In general, in hot climates, light, cool colours of dull intensities should be used.

If the rooms are crowded, dark colours should not be used since they will add to the cramped appearance. If a room is small, it should be painted with light colours or cool ones to create an illusion of space. A low ceiling will appear higher when it has a lighter hue than the colour of the wall. A large room will appear smaller and cosier when warm colours such as peach, soft tan or rust are used. Wood work and draperies that differ in colour from the walls also make the room look smaller. A square room appears different in shape when one wall is contrasted in colour with the others. If a room is too long and narrow, the short walls should have a contrasting colour to the long ones, to make it look wider and shorter. Skilful use of colour is the best way of giving individuality to a room.

Choice of suitable pictures

The selection of pictures in the home, like the choice of colours, depends in the taste of the inmates. Strictly speaking, the picture used in a particular room should be in conformity with the activity carried out in that room, or with the purpose for which the room is used. The fundamental idea of the picture should coincide with that of the room. There should be a harmony of feeling between the picture and the room. Pictures and paintings should, as far as possible, adhere to the principles of colour combination. They will be effective if the colours bear some relationship to the surroundings. The paintings should neither clash with the surroundings nor be made to look dull and weak by the colour of the walls, etc.

Colour is perhaps the quality most universally enjoyed in pictures. Quiet and bright colours are both stimulating, and have their own bright special appeal. Dull, monotonous pictures are depressing. Moreover, pictures should be in natural colours.

Good pictures should be selected for use in the home. Such pictures should have the following characteristics:

a well organised theme,
a good pattern, and
a good colour scheme.

Only three things should guide one in the choice of a picture. They are: (1) the person who chooses the picture and his or her whole family should like it; (2) it fits in with the general decor of the house, and (3), it has some semblance of principles of good design.

The verandah, hall or **living-room** often serves as a place for receiving visitors. Since the room is used for entertaining a variety of persons, the pictures adorning the walls should depict themes of general interest. Portraits, photographs of personalities, and abstract paintings are suitable for the living-room. Landscapes, seascapes and murals go well with almost any type of living-room.

The **bedroom** is a place of rest. The pictures used in a bedroom should suit the personality and the emotional balance of the inmates. They should necessarily symbolize love. A portrait of someone you love could also be used in a bedroom and hung on the wall facing you when in bed, so that you can look at the loved one while lying down in bed. Landscapes do not enrich the bedroom, but if they have a romantic, colourful or emotion-rousing scene they may be used. Even an old piece of lovely brocade can be used to adorn the bedroom.

The pictures used in a **dining-room** should be cheerful.

The theme should be such as to enhance the appetite. Still life paintings of fruit, fish, etc., can also be used.

The pictures used in the **nursery** are either of lasting interest or of more or less temporary appeal. Children may be allowed to choose pictures that please them for their own room. The themes may be of educative value or of such a nature as a growing child would come to appreciate more and more. The pictures used in a nursery should arouse the enthusiasm and curiosity of the children and channel them towards increasing their knowledge.

The pictures used in a **study** should not distract the powers of concentration of the child. They should create an atmosphere favourable for study and clear and original thinking. Pictures of educative value and maps fit into the spirit of the room.

Religious pictures create an austere spirit and feeling in a room. Pictures of sacred themes which imply worship require a special setting. They are out of place in a room of gaiety and noise. They are more in tune in personal rooms, and rooms specially allotted for prayer, meditation and worship.

At present, the new School of Modern Art is becoming popular and there is a great opportunity to buy a colourful picture by a young artist who may eventually become famous. It is better to have one good painting than several nondescript prints.

Framing of pictures

The frame should suit the picture. The type of frame chosen should be in harmony with the picture. A delicate painting should obviously have a delicate frame. Normally, plain frames are better than decorative ones, since frames with elaborate carving and design will attract more attention than the picture itself. The frame should be just a space for the picture to rest against the wall and not be prominent.

Location of pictures

Where a picture is located or hung depends upon the available wall space, the furniture arrangement, the need for enrichment and illumination. They are used over pieces of furniture like davenports, sofas, chairs, tables, chests of drawers, grand pianos and the like, to enrich the setting. Keeping them low enables one to view them comfortably, relates them to the furniture so as to form a unit, and gives an emphasis to the room. When pictures find a central place on the wall directly above the furniture, they give a static, stable symmetry. Pictures should get sufficient light for their beauty to be appreciated. Light pictures should find a place on fairly light walls, and dark pictures on dark walls. Dark pictures may also find a place over a dark piece of furniture.

Hanging pictures

Small pictures should be hung on walls with small free areas and larger pictures in large wall spaces. For the sake of "Shape Harmony", tall pictures should be hung in vertical wall spaces and broad ones in horizontal spaces. A room in subdued colours can be made vibrant by hanging a colourful picture in it. A more spacious feeling can be created in a room by hanging landscapes or seascapes.

Pictures should be hung neither too high nor too low, but in such a manner that the centre of interest is at about eye level.

In successful picture arrangement, emphasis plays an important role. There must be sufficient plain space around the picture. Pictures should not be hung in isolated spots.

Pictures should be hung in spaces which need enrichment. Small pictures should be grouped together. Pictures should be hung with their bottom edges on a level. If that is not possible the next best is to have their top edges on a level. They should be hung flat against the wall and not tilted. The wire or string used for hanging a picture should not be visible.

Much of what has been said in general about pictures relating to their selection, suitability for various rooms, location and hanging, applies equally to calendars, paintings and photographs.

Choice of curtains, cushions, etc.

Curtains

Curtains and draperies are used for controlling light, heat and noise. They provide privacy. They are also aids for beautifying the home. Curtains of various materials such as cotton, plastic, nylon, are available in the market. Curtains and draperies are used mostly on windows and doorways; however, in some homes they are also used as space separators for partitioning rooms. Apart from the material selected, the manner in which they are hung can also add charm and dignity to the room.

Small rooms put on an appearance of size if the colour of the curtains and draperies blends with that of the walls. Appropriateness to the room or the window should be the major criterion in the selection of curtains. Rooms with low ceilings look higher if draperies extend from the floor to the ceiling. Dark and gloomy rooms can be brightened by the use of light coloured draperies. Rosy pink or yellow curtains add warmth to a cold room. On the other hand, pale blue or green draperies provide a cool atmosphere.

A pleasing colour scheme for a room may be secured by selecting for draperies a material in which the background is of the same colour as the wall. Curtains with large designs suit only large rooms, while those with small designs are fit for use in small rooms. If the material used for curtains, draperies, cushion covers, bedspreads, and chair upholstery contains patterns with large designs, it will produce a confusing effect.

Narrow windows may be made to appear broad by the use of suitable curtains. The curtain material should be bulky with horizontal lines predominating. The use of pelmets, and half curtains will also add to the width of the windows.

On the other hand, windows can be made to look longer by using full length curtains with vertical lines and narrow trimming.

Cushions

Cushions are used for comfort and relaxation. These accessories lend charm and colour to the room. They may be round or square in shape to harmonize with the shape and size of the furniture on which they are placed. It is better to have the cushions strongly contrasting in colour with the draperies, upholstery and walls, to prevent dullness.

Rugs and carpets

Rugs and carpets add charm to the flooring and provide colour and pattern to the home. Their design and colour should be in harmony with the general colour scheme. They should be of durable material. They help to alter the apparent size and shape of a room. Wall to wall carpeting will help to make the room appear larger. It will promote a feeling of luxury and formality as well as serenity and quiet.

Other articles used for decorating the home

Apart from pictures, draperies, upholstery, cushions and carpets, there are other accessories that serve for decoration. There is no limit to such items. They range from ashtrays to mugs and from statuettes to lampstands. Wall clocks of different sizes and shapes also play the role of decorative accessories. Even colourful and shapely pebbles and seashells serve this purpose.

Nowadays a variety of attractive articles for decorating the home can be bought in the market. Beautifully painted birds and beasts made of wood, clay or glass, which can be fixed to walls, paintings done on gramophone records, wood inlaid with ivory, depicting charming scenes of folk art, etc., carved centre tables and the like all beautify a home.

Accessories to beautify a home can be made at school or at home or picked up from gift or curio shops. A variety of beautiful shells can be picked up on the beach or bought from vendors. Various attractive articles made of seashells can be bought quite cheap. One often acquires charming souvenirs during one's trips to various places in India and abroad.

Small articles should not stand alone. It is better to have a setting with several miniature articles than a single 'eye catcher'. In the selection of decorative articles, one should avoid things which tend to accumulate dust and thus lose their original charm. It is always better to select articles that have a personal appeal to the owner.

Some people collect curios as a hobby. It is unnecessary to be a copyist in accumulating attractive articles. However attractive a thing may be, it will lose half its worth if it is not displayed properly. Normally decorative articles find a place on tables; however, special niches, corner shelves or stands, specially designed glass stands on walls, glass-fronted shelves, bookcases, etc., may be used for displaying them. Colour is an important factor to consider in selecting accessories. They should be chosen with a view to introduce a contrasting colour or to echo a major theme. A decorative article should not strike a colour note all by itself. When a number of such articles are grouped together they must have something in common, such as size, shape, texture or colour to present a harmonious appearance. Ashtrays, cigarette containers and lighters are charming table-top accessories. Even a non-smoker should provide an ashtray in the living-room or reception room for the use of his guests. Ashtrays used on dinner tables should be in harmony with the dinner or tea sets used.

Mirrors and book-ends also serve as articles of decoration. Further, mirrors give an illusion of space and are effective in a small room. The bookcase in the home need not necessarily be stacked with books. Attractive effects can be achieved by leaving spaces in the book shelves and filling them with china or pottery figures.

Pictures and ceramics in the living-room accentuate colour effects. By the use of accessories, one has an opportunity to incorporate the complementary colours in their pure state. Pure colour spots can also be introduced here and there in the form of attractive lampshades.

Original pieces of creative sculpture can achieve striking and stimulating effects in the living-room. If too many accessories are used in a bedroom with deep-tone walls, the room will look congested and the restful atmosphere may be lost. It is better to have the barest minimum of accessories in a bedroom. If the smaller accessories have the same colour as the walls, draperies and upholstery, they will merge and be lost in the colour scheme. Therefore, these smaller accessories should preferably be of strong contrasting colours to prevent dullness. A work desk should have no accessories on it as they hinder the efficiency of work. It should be uncluttered and put in a quiet corner.

Attractive accessories can be introduced in the dining-room in the form of brightly painted pottery and water pitchers.

Even ordinary things of everyday use can become decorative accessories by the manner in which they are placed in the house. The principles of design such as balance, rhythm, emphasis, harmony and proportion are also applicable to the arrangement of decorative accessories.

Use of plants and flowers as decoration

Plants as decorative articles

However much a person may try to beautify the home through artificial means such as coloured draperies or curios, one is seldom satisfied without turning to nature. Few decorative objects give the natural charm and dignity that plants, flowers and fruits can give to a home. Plants are inexpensive assets, are always refreshing and provide the necessary variety of form and colour which are of main importance in interior decoration. Plants which are normally kept out-of-doors have claimed a place inside man's dwellings and have come to be regarded and accepted as a part of the furnishing scheme. Apart from the intrinsic beauty of shape and colour, rhythm and balance, provided by the leaves and flowers of plants they are also good for the health, as they help to purify the air during the daytime. Further, the psychological and moral effect of plants on one's mind is also of primary importance. The fresh, pleasant and cheerful atmosphere created by plants and flowers stimulates pleasurable emotions and alleviates feelings of depression and dejection.

Plants as decorative articles can find a place in any part of the house. Potted plants can be used in the corners of a room, on special stands, on table tops, on window-sills, shelves, and special niches. Potted plants can be fitted into brackets fixed on walls as decorative pieces.

Different varieties of palms, cactus and other succulents, conifers like the Christmas tree, begonias, coleus, ferns of various kinds and pothos (money plant) are some of the plants commonly used in the home for interior decoration.

The attractiveness of plants in the home depends also to a large extent on the type of container in which they are grown. These may be of concrete, ceramic, brass, copper, aluminium or wood either natural grain or painted. Ceramic containers can be bought in any colour; but those in neutral, unobtrusive colours are preferable. Sometimes a green container is nice because it seems to blend with the foliage of the plant.

In selecting and using plants for interior decoration, care should be taken to exhibit big, bold plants for major effects, and tiny ones on a coffee table, in shelves, niches, and small windowsills. On large tables and cabinets, plants 30cm or 60 cm in height will be appropriate. Several plants of the same kind can be grouped or distributed in a pleasant pattern; or, as a significant source of embellishment, different types of plants may be used for interior decoration.

Use of flowers for interior decoration

In all God's creation there is nothing so beautiful, attractive, elegant and colourful as flowers. They are universally admired, loved and adored. No interior decoration can be complete without the presence of a few flowers in a room. Flowers suit any room in the house and give tremendous variety and interest. They add glamour and charm to one's home life, apart from enlivening the appearance of a well-kept room.

In former times flowers were stuffed into a vase and left on the living-room tables as an adornment. Today, arranging flowers has become a fascinating hobby, and a specialized art. The Japanese are considered to have developed it to perfection and it is said rightly or wrongly, that it will take a person 20 years to master the Japanese art of flower arrangement.

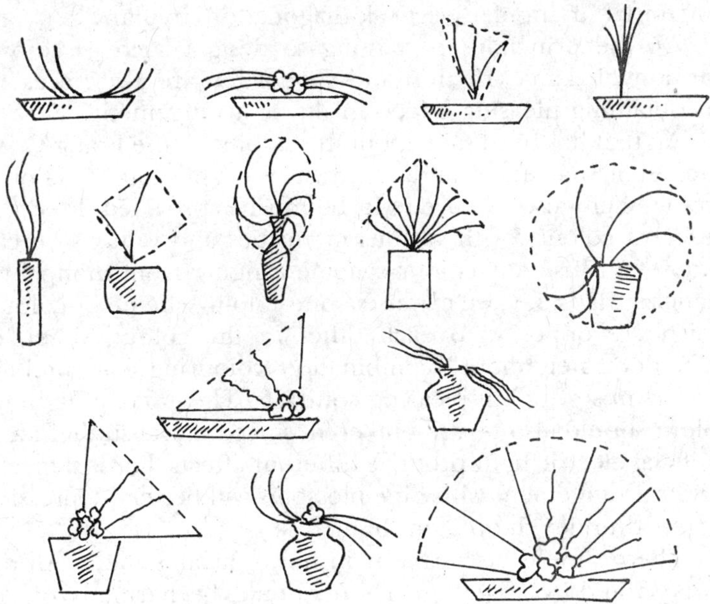

Fig. 20. Patterns in flower arrangement

Flower arrangement can be studied best by observing flowers in their natural setting on the parent plant. The big flowers grow at the bottom, smaller blossoms appear above them, and buds sprout at the top. Flowers appear above one another in a step-ladder fashion. At times even an isolated or solitary flower captures one's attention and exhilarates. A person can draw inspiration by observing the natural flower composition and copy it for artistic arrangement inside the home.

The function of flower arrangement is to present a centre of interest, to decorate the home by accentuating the colour scheme of the interior and creating an atmosphere of loveliness. If fragrant flowers are used in flower arrangement, their sweet smell is an added attraction.

There are manifold ways of arranging flowers. However, the arrangements should be in conformity with nature as far as possible. Though one need not follow hard and fast rules, one must work within the broad limits of good design to achieve pleasing effects. The designs may be in the shape of a diamond, oval, fan, the letter 'L' or 'S', crescent, or be horizontal, triangular, vertical, diagonal or circular.

All the principles pertaining to design, such as colour, harmony, balance, rhythm and proportion are also necessary for obtaining pleasing effects in flower arrangement.

All that has been said about the colours in the Prang Chart and their harmony and contrast is applicable to flower arrangement also. Nature in its bounty has provided flowers in different colours, with various intensities and values. We can choose and use any colour scheme ranging from monochromatic to triads, i.e., we can use a one-colour scheme or colours which are opposite to each other in the colour wheel, or "next-door neighbour" combination colouring, or combine colours in strong but pleasing contrasts. The effect of light on colour should also be remembered, since natural sunlight and artificial electric light produce different effects. For instance, a flower arrangement with blue blossoms will be very depressing if viewed under fluorescent light.

There should be harmony in flower arrangement. All the parts should go together. There should be harmony of the flowers, the container and the setting in which the arrangement is exhibited. Harmony can be achieved in the colour, shape and number of leaves or flowers used.

Balance also should be considered in flower arrangement. This may be semi-formal or informal. It may even be formal at times.

However, it is better not to have arrangements with two sides exactly alike. One side should not look heavier than the other; nor should the bunch of flowers be jammed together in the container. The arrangement should have distinctive parts. For instance the central part should clearly dominate the whole arrangement, and the other parts should support it. The centre of interest must always be placed near the bottom of the arrangement. The heavier, larger, and more brightly coloured flowers should be placed near the lower centre. Short flowers do not look well in high vases, but tall flowers can be used successfully in low bowls if the diameter of the bowl is large enough to give the impression of balance.

Any flower arrangement should be delightfully rhythmic, whether in line, size or colour. Rhythm plays an important role and enables the eye to travel easily from one part of the bouquet to the other parts.

Flower arrangements should conform to some proportion. The size of the entire arrangement should be in scale with the space it fills in the room. The flower with the longest stem should be so placed that its head comes above the centre of the container. Though the stem may curve one way or the other, the blossom should be on or near the central axis. The stems of the others should be cut to suitably proportioned heights. There are no exact measurements or proportions for successful flower arrangements. Generally, if tall vases are used, the tallest stem should be one and a half times the height of the vase. In broad containers it should be as much again as the width of the bowl.

Flower arrangements should have **movement.** The basic movements are: vertical or slightly spreading; outward spreading; horizontal; and downward. The character of the movement should be in harmony with the home.

There should be continuity between the container and the flowers. In fact, the container could be related to the flowers by allowing some of them or their leaves to conceal its rim.

Containers

The function of the container is to support the flowers and foliage. In principle, flower arrangements should be in containers appropriate to their setting in the home. The container should normally be subordinate to the flower arrangement. It should be of the right size, shape, colour or material. Almost anything that will hold water can be used as a flower container if special containers are not available. Household pots, vessels, tumblers, milk jugs, goblets, pitchers, bottles, shallow dishes, bamboos and baskets can be used. A person who enjoys exhibiting versatility in flower arrangement can show ingenuity in making any article act as a vase.

Plain coloured containers display the blooms to good advantage. Suitable colours for vases are soft earth colour, brown, tan-gray, gray-green, soft dull blue and white. One should choose containers with a neutral or soft colour and a milder appearance than the flowers in them. As far as possible, containers, important as they are, should not detract one's attention from the flowers or foliage they hold. On no condition should the background mar the beauty of the flower arrangement. It is always advisable to have the arranged flowers exhibited on a plain background. The containers may be put in any available place, such as table tops, or fixed on the wall.

If the flower vase is to be placed on a large table or piano, a large container and fair-sized blooms will be necessary. A low container is usually preferred for the dining-room table.

The texture of the flowers is also important when selecting a container for them. Delicate flowers should have delicate containers, and coarser blooms need a heavy pottery container.

Selection and storing of flowers

Successful flower arrangement presupposes a proper selection of flowers. The flowers selected can have curved or straight stems. The stems should be as long as possible. Flowers should be gathered either early in the morning or soon after sundown, that is, at dawn or dusk, but never when the sun is burning hot. It is better to select buds or flowers just blossoming than flowers in full bloom as the latter are liable to shed their petals or droop and wither fast.

The stems of flowers should be cut clean, on a slant, with a sharp knife and never be broken with the hand. Even the use of scissors is not satisfactory because it compresses the stem cells. Soon after cutting, the stems should be immersed in water, exposing only the petals or the corolla of the flowers. If the cut end of the stem exudes latex (milky juice or sap) it should be singed for a few minutes over a lighted candle and then quickly immersed in water. The leaves close to the base of the stem should be removed.

The flowers should be wrapped either in a piece of paper or a broad leaf, such as the banana leaf, above the stem ends and stored in the dark corner of a room in a bucket of water to protect them from sunlight if they are not arranged and used soon.

Flower holders

The stems must be held firmly in place in flower arrangement. It is not possible to arrange them well without some type of flower holder inside the container, which enables you to keep them where you want them. The most satisfactory flower holder is the pin type which has sharp spikes upon which the stems can be firmly anchored. A number of flower holders can also be improvised with crumpled wire, split twigs, etc.

Styles in flower arrangement

There are three main styles in arranging flowers, known as the traditional, the oriental and the modern.

The **traditional style** is a formal arrangement. A mass of flowers of all kinds, colours and sizes are used together in a decorative container. The arranged flowers present a multi-coloured, mass effect.

The **oriental style** is in fact the Japanese mode of flower arrangement. The most striking characteristic of this is that it gives the impression of a natural growing plant. The arrangement is simple, symbolic, meaningful and informal. The stems are so arranged that their lines form an attractive pattern. The flowers are placed in such a fashion that their shape and colour produce the best balance. The flowers, while maintaining their individuality, fit and merge into the strikingly planned design.

The flowers or clusters chosen are always in odd numbers, three, five, seven or eleven. The arrangement has three main branches whatever be the number of flowers used. The three branches are symbolic of Heaven, Man and Earth. The main branch, which is the longest, soars upward and signifies Heaven. This stem should be half as long again as the vase or even twice as long. The smallest branch points downwards, representing the Earth and is a third the height of the vase, while that of medium height, spreading sideways, symbolises Man, and is the same height as the container. If more than three stems are used, they are cleverly arranged so as to give the impression of three. Any number of flowers can be used as auxiliaries to provide the proper balance to the arrangement.

The **modern style** of flower arrangement is a combination of the traditional and oriental styles, with a leaning towards the latter.

Floating arrangement

Flowers can also be attractively arranged in a different fashion. Drawing one's inspiration from such flowers as the lotus, waterlily and hyacinth, one can arrange them in such a way that they seem to be floating in a pond or tank. The floating arrangement can be made in shallow bowls and trays with flowers whose stems are short. The largest, highest and most attractive flower can be allowed to float in the centre, with the others grouped around. The flowers should not completely cover up the water. Flowers of different colours may be used in this type of arrangement.

Other varieties of arrangement

Dry arrangements with fruit, vegetables, seed pods, bare branches, driftwood and other such materials are also in vogue. This lasts for a long time. Varieties of grasses, flower plumes of tall grasses and the sugarcane, the clustering flowers of palms, all these lend themselves to pleasing decorative arrangements. Even feathers in containers, especially peacock feathers, if well arranged, present an exotic, novel appearance and are suitable for interior decoration.

Selection of furniture

Our home, our clothes, our pictures, books and furniture all proclaim to the world the kind of person we really are. We should therefore make a definite effort through the knowledge and appreciation we have gained, to express in our choices and arrangements our best personal qualities.

Furniture in its limited definition means movable objects of utility.

The correct choice of furniture is a very important aspect of home furnishing. A bad choice will not only mean a loss of money but it also prevents the family from enjoying the right and correct type of furniture. The following factors should be considered while selecting furniture.

Family characteristics

The type of family: This is very important specially in selecting furniture for a living room. The personality and interests of the members, traditions in the family or their social and economic status should be taken into account. The outdoor type of family might choose wrought iron or cane furniture with brightly coloured cushions. The formal type of family might select rosewood or fine teak wood furniture and heavy draperies. They might add some antique pieces in their decoration. The informal type of family may also select rosewood but may upholster them in simple fabrics.

Family's pattern of living: Families who are fond of entertaining should select a different type of furniture from that selected by a family whose members prefer more studious and quiet activities. The entertaining type of family needs nests of tables, tea trolleys, game tables, etc.

Families that spend more time working and reading, need large desks, bookcases, lounge chairs and good lamps. The furniture should be suitable for any of these interests.

Needs of individual members: The habits and needs of individuals in the family should also be considered—work needs (desks, etc.), leisure-time activities (shelves for records or cassettes, bookcases), personal habits (people who are in the habit of reading in bed need a good bed-side lamp).

Physical needs of individual members: The stature of the person who is to use the furniture must be considered in the selection. Furniture should fit people just as clothes do. Tall people need extra-long beds and mattresses, short people need shallow-seated chairs. A work table should suit the height of the worker. Health demands must also be considered. People with weak backs need firm mattresses on their beds. People who are allergic to feathers can use foam rubber for cushions.

Use and economy

This means that the "form of the furniture should follow its functions".

Flexibility or multi-usefulness: Furniture that can be used in more than one room or for more than one purpose saves money. The kind of furniture that makes this adjustment possible is known as "multi-use furniture".

Furniture that is well selected should be such that it can be used in any house and situation. Many families are apt to live in more than one house in their life time. Examples of such multi-purpose furniture are individualized storage pieces like chests, interchangeable dining-room chairs, bedroom chairs, adaptable tables, extendable dining table, card tables, etc. In contrast to these are single-use furniture such as dressing tables and big dining tables for a buffet which can only be used for one purpose.

Convenience and comfort: Convenience applies especially to storage facilities and to the ease with which frequently-moved furniture can be handled, (e.g. pull-up dining chairs). All furniture however should be lightweight so that they can be easily shifted. Heavier pieces could be on casters (wheels). Comfort applies mainly to furniture on which we sit or sleep but the height of tables, desks and work surfaces should have sufficient leg-room under them.

Quality of furniture

There are four important factors to be considered for the quality of furniture: (1) furniture construction (2) quality of wood (3) quality of upholstery and (4) reputation of the firm where the furniture is bought.

Looking for bargains may be wise in shopping for other things but not for furniture, since cheap furniture goes to pieces quickly and hence is a waste of money.

Construction: Construction of furniture such as chests and desks and light chairs can be easily checked for quality. The back and undersides of drawers and the bottom of light chair-seats can be checked for their finish and smoothness. A good piece of furniture is never rough anywhere. The quality of cabinets or chests can be checked by seeing to it that on the inside there are dust-proof partitions between the drawers. There should also be a proper centre guide or grooving on the underside of the bottom of each drawer so that it will pull out evenly and smoothly, and the front of the drawer should be dovetailed into the sides.

Fig. 21. Dovetail joining

The corner blocks of case furniture as well as chairs and tables should be glued and screwed in and not nailed.

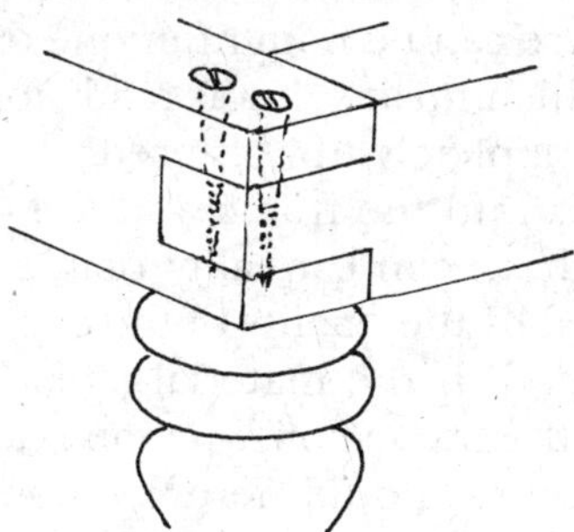

Fig. 22. Screwed-in corner

These points of construction can be seen easily by examining the furniture. What cannot be seen should be accepted on faith, based on the reputation of the firm. The points that cannot be seen are the dowelling together of the frame, the joining where great strain is anticipated, and the general quality of wood and workmanship.

If a piece of furniture is highly decorated with a great deal of carving it may be either beautiful hand-carving or unattractive moulded wood-fibres. The first is a mark of excellent quality throughout. The second is a manufacturer's effort to cover up poor workmanship. Good proportion, good line, and good quality need no decoration to attract attention.

Quality of wood: A hard wood is desirable for furniture because it does not dent easily with long wear. Walnut, mahogany, gum wood, oak, teak and rosewood are some of the woods suitable for furniture.

Gum wood is sometimes used in under-construction or for legs of inexpensive mahogany tables or chairs. This cuts the cost of furniture tremendously but does not weaken the furniture or spoil its appearance since gum wood takes up stains of any wood easily.

Use of veneer is not necessarily a mark of inferior quality. A good, well-applied veneer may be stronger than solid wood of the same thickness. Veneers cannot be used for carved furniture.

Seasoned wood always marks superior quality. Defects and faults in the wood should be detected before buying furniture.

Quality of upholstery: This is another mark of value. A good piece of furniture can be bought in one of the two ways: (1) in muslin cover which means that is ready for upholstery or a slip cover, or (2) completely upholstered. In the first, every paisa spent on it goes into the frame and the construction work of the piece. In the second, quality of the piece as a whole is usually indicated by the quality of the covering as well as by the finish of the wood. If the material looks 'flashy' it may be an indication that the frame construction is also of a poor quality. A piece of furniture should never be bought with the idea of re-upholstering it with a better covering later. In all probability the frame will not be worth re-upholstering and the cost will be out of proportion to the total value.

The reputation of the firm: This is one of the most important considerations especially when buying upholstered furniture. It is necessary to rely on the integrity of the firm in such invisible matters as construction of the frame, the number and quality of the springs, the number of times they are tied, the quality of stuffing and quality of the webbing. If any of these things are misrepresented, there is no way to prove it until the furniture goes to pieces. Hence it is necessary to deal with a reputable firm in buying specially-upholstered pieces. A guarantee of any kind means nothing if the firm that gives it goes out of business.

Economy in selection

In setting up a budget for furniture the wise buyer economizes on the pieces that do not take a great deal of wear. For example, the quality of wood in a bookcase can be sacrificed since the books are more important. End tables need not be of top quality as well, since people notice the articles like ashtrays, lamps etc., placed on them, rather than the table. Hence such things need not be of top quality if the budget does not permit.

The large bulk of the budget for the living-room furniture should be spent on such furnishings as desks, chests, sofas and lounge chairs, since these receive constant wear, and comfort is necessary in their selection. In bedroom furniture, quality of mattress and beds are important. The greater part of the budget for furniture and equipment should be spent on articles that will be subjected to constant wear and that must provide physical comfort. Savings can be made on pieces where comfort is not a primary consideration and where wear is negligible.

Arrangement of furniture

Furniture is intended for comfort, rest and relaxation. It should be of good structural rather than decorative design, to serve its purpose. It suggests stability rather than movement. Therefore, it is better to select furniture which has straight lines and restrained curves.

In arranging the furniture in a room one should be guided by the considerations of utility, scale, rhythm and harmony. The arrangement should contribute to livableness more than anything else. The furniture in the hall should be so arranged as to convey an air of hospitality, but not too much intimacy. Articles of furniture must be so arranged that it does not become necessary to shift them too often.

The general arrangement should be based on utility. The sofa-sets in the hall which are used by the members of the family to sit and chat should be comfortable. They should be so placed as to form a unit. Similarly the furniture used for a music group should be different from that intended for conversation.

The person who selects and arranges furniture should have taste and an understanding of **scale**. Bulky articles should not be put in a small room so as to overcrowd it. If large pieces of furniture have to be used in a small room, their number should be kept to a minimum. If small articles of furniture are used in a large room, they should be arranged in a group, to form a sizable unit.

If furniture is arranged without much thought, it will present a scattered effect. Any point in the room that needs particular emphasis may be accented by the pattern in which the furniture is arranged. There should be line-movement in the arrangement of furniture to produce harmony.

There should be a proper order in the arrangement of furniture so as to create an impression of spaciousness. The larger articles should be put in place first, and then the smaller ones introduced as space fillers. For instance, the sofas should be arranged first, then the teapoy and other smaller articles should be placed in the spaces between them. One should not leave too large gaps between pieces of furniture, or the arrangement will lack unity.

The various articles of furniture should harmonize among themselves and with the room, in size, shape or colour. It may not be possible for the furniture to fit snugly into the pattern in which the room has been constructed or to agree with the room in all respects, size, shape and colour. It is sufficient if it agrees with the room in one or two of these respects. Failing that, a person should try to arrange the furniture in such a fashion as to obtain as much harmony with the design of the room as possible. Size-harmony, shape-harmony and colour-harmony of the pieces of furniture among themselves and between furniture and room should be aimed at. Moreover, the furniture and decorative objects should be so arranged as to carry the eye towards the centres of interest, where it should rest for a while.

In the disposition of furniture, one should exercise three policies: elimination, rearrangement and concealment. If pieces of furniture do not suit a particular room, they should be replaced by fresh ones that do, if one can afford them. Sometimes, with a little imagination, thought and planning, the furniture in one's possession may be rearranged to harmonize tolerably well with the pattern of the room. Agreeable changes in the appearance of the room can be effected by suitable alterations in the arrangement of the furniture. It is desirable to keep out of view, such articles of furniture that do not combine favourably with the style of the room. Concealing furniture sometimes helps to prevent unsightly and jarring objects from infringing on the pleasant setting of a room. By the use of slip covers, one can conceal defective and unattractive furniture and also harmonize it with unrelated furniture. Further, unshapely furniture may be relegated to some inconspicuous space against a background with which it can merge without any violent contrast.

In furniture arrangement, what should be kept, where it should be kept and how it should be kept must all be borne in mind. One need not dilate on incongruities and oddities in furniture arrangement, as for instance, bedroom furniture straying into the dining-room. Such absurdities are evident and must be avoided. We frequently see that, for the sake of convenience, people sacrifice principles, and pieces of furniture get discordant and sadly misplaced, presenting a deplorable sight.

Line, colour, size and shape of the furniture should be exploited to the maximum advantage to fit the furniture to the room. This creates a feeling of pleasant satisfaction arising from aesthetic appeal and effective usefulness.

SUGGESTED COLOUR SCHEMES FOR A HOME

Scheme II

Room	*Walls*	*Upholstery*	*Draperies*	*Accessories*	*Floor Coverings*	*Furniture*	*Remarks*
Living Room	White	Turquoise	White background with turquoise and green print	Potted plants, porcelain or ivory figureines, table lamps.	Forest green	White cane	The colour scheme has been selected from the draperies; turquoise, the basic colour, has been used for the upholstery, green has been repeated in the carpet, white serves to unify these two colours.
Bedroom	Pale green	Green and yellow bed spread	Yellow draperies.	Accents of orange, e.g., a vase, picture, table lamp.	Yellow bed rug.	Mahogany	A cool, serene colour scheme, accents of orange add warmth.
Dining Room	Cream	—	Deep yellow and green striped	Pictures, vase etc.	Yellow linoleum.	Light with green seats	This colour scheme creates a cool effect and there is an illusion of space.
Guest Room	Cream	Apricot and green bedspread upholstered chair in red	Apricot	Pictures, etc.	Red bed rug.	Light wood	A cool scheme; warmth is introduced through the addition of red.
Kitchen	Pale green	—	Pale yellow	—	Deep green linoleum.	Cream	A cool colour scheme, pleasing and not harsh on the eyes.

SUGGESTED COLOUR SCHEMES FOR A HOME

Scheme I

Room	*Walls*	*Upholstery*	*Draperies*	*Accessories*	*Floor Coverings*	*Furniture*	*Remarks*
Living Room	Dove Gray	Blue Gray (checked) small red cushion on the upholstery	Blue Gray (self)	Table lamps vases and ornaments	Red carpet	Light wood.	Blue and Gray are cool, restful colours; their attraction is heightened by the red carpet. This colour scheme is an example of the primary triad, the yellow being accented in the light wood furniture and red accents in the form of small cushions.
Bedroom	Pale pink	White top with pink and white gingham frill	Pink and white check	Table lamps and pictures.	White bed rug	White wood.	An ideal colour scheme for a girl's room, the cool soft colours give a restful effect.
Dining Room	Pale turquoise	—	Hand-woven cotton striped in blue, green and yellow and a small amount of black	Brighter yellow accessories.	Dark green linoleum	Mahogany or rosewood orange upholestered seats	Pale colour gives a feeling of serenity; warmth and cheer is introduced through the vivid orange.
Guest Room	Pale blue	Turquoise bedspread, Tan upholstered chair with yellow cushions.	Yellow	Pictures, table lamps, etc.	Tan.	Mahogany	This colour scheme gives the room a sunny appearance, serenity is introduced through the pale blue walls.
Kitchen	Pale blue	—	Cream and orange patterned	—	Orange.	Cream	A colour scheme which is ideal for a kitchen with dreary outlook.

SUGGESTED COLOUR SCHEMES FOR A HOME

Scheme III

Room	*Walls*	*Upholstery*	*Draperies*	*Accessories*	*Floor Coverings*	*Furniture*	*Remarks*
Living Room	Pale green	Yellow, small brown and red cushions on the upholstery	Green and Yellow patterned	Table lamps, pictures, vases	Deep green	Mahogany	Yellow and green are cool colours; warm accents are introduced in the form of small brown and red cushions.
Bedroom	Pale yellow	Mauve bedspread	Mauve nylon or transparent material.	White table lamp pictures	Yellow bed rug	White wood	These pastel shades harmonize and are easy on the eye, creating a cool effect in the room.
Dining Room	Dove gray	—	Lilac and green printed	Pictures, vase, etc.	Green linoleum	Chromium with purple seats.	This colour scheme will give the room a cool appearance and also create an illusion of space.
Guest Room	Pale pink	Green bedspread Deep pink upholstered chair	Green	Pictures, vase, table lamp, etc.	Deep pink bed rug	Mahogany.	This colour scheme will be suitable for either a male or female guest; the pink is warm and inviting and the green adds a cool touch.
Kitchen	Pale pink	—	Deep pink and cream	—	Deep pink linoleum	Cream with chromium fittings	A colour scheme which would take the drudgery out of any kitchen.

It is not necessary to have a great variety of colours in the home. At times people prefer the closely knit colour schemes, that give a feeling of serenity and quietude. A colour thread is often used, i.e., any one colour which acts as a unifying factor is repeated in most of the rooms of the house. This has practical value in that any article that is in the colour selected as the colour thread will look well anywhere in the house. Suppose, for instance, that yellow is the colour selected for the colour thread; then, if the dining room chairs,upholstered in yellow, they can be used, if necessary, in any room of the house and will at once fit in with the rest of the furnishings.

Fig. 23. HARMONY OF COLOURS

1. Monochromatic	2. Direct Complementary	3. Analogous	4. Split Complementary	5. Double Complementary	6. Triad
(a) Dark orange with	(a) Red with	(a) Green with	(a) Yellow with	(a) Orange & Yellow	(a) Red
(b) Blue orange	(b) Green	(b) Blue Green	(b) Red Purple	(b) with Purple	(b) Yellow
		(c) Yellow Green	(c) Blue Purple	(c) Blue Purple	(c) Blue

should be shown in selecting dress materials of various colours.

One can avoid monotony in dress by using different values or intensities of the same colour or by combining different colours.

Any colour scheme in dress may be made more interesting by means of an accent on contrasting colours. However, the colours used must give the impression of belonging to each other. White, black and gray can be used with any intense colour.

Colour and texture

The texture of a fabric may affect a particular colour either adversely or favourably. Lighter shades suit thinner fabrics better than darker shades. Darker shades and colours are becoming in thicker material. Pale lilac, for instance, may be unbecoming in a heavy khadi cotton sari; but it will look charming in nylon or georgette. Garments that are meant to last for some years should not be too conspicuous in colour or too flimsy in material. Some dark colours fade fast or look dull in material of certain textures.

Colour and age

Generally speaking, anyone can wear whatever colours he or she likes, provided the choice is of the right hue and blend and the texture of the material does not spoil the effect of the colour. Young, active and vigorous people can pick and choose and can use to advantage clothing of either related or contrasting colour harmonies. However, only clothing of related colour harmonies is suitable for use by quieter or older persons. Further, consistent with the dignity of age, persons past middle age will do well to wear clothing of duller intensities, rather than flashy and gaudy colours.

Colour and occasions

The time, place and occasion also influence the choice of colour in dress. Bright and cheerful colours befit festive occasions, parties or marriages. White, silver, yellow and gold are most suitable for weddings, and generally adorn the bridal array. Men use clothing of dark coloured material such as navy blue and black for formal dinners and dances. People

3. Colour Schemes in Dress

Colour schemes in dressing play an important role in the lives of men and women since they help to bring out their personalities. A man may be muscular and well proportioned and a woman shapely and attractive, but if the colour of their attire does not suit them, their personalities will suffer. The colours of the clothes worn should suit the wearer and help to enhance his or her appearance. The colour values should set off the wearer's better features and subdue the less attractive ones. At all events clothing should be in good taste and never gaudy or flashy.

The choice of colour in clothes is usually influenced by a person's complexion, age, size, personality, status and income, as well as by the occasion and the season. The colour of the clothes should match the hair, skin and eyes of the wearer. Appropriate colour in clothes gives the wearer individuality and self-confidence. It enhances his or her personality and makes a favourable impression upon those with whom the person comes into contact.

People have colour preferences in dress as in many other things in life. What one woman likes another woman may dislike. People may use suitable colours in dress through sheer instinct or from experience and experimentation, or because they have learnt and planned methods of harmonizing their clothes. However charming and colourful the clothes may be in themselves, they will not look attractive if they do not go well together.

Colour combination

As in the case of interior decoration, colour harmony in dress can be achieved through various colour schemes such as monochromatic, analogous, direct complementary, paired or double complementary, split complementary, triadic and tetradic. Some colour combinations in dress have harmony and some others produce a note of discord. The utmost caution are also affected by sentiment in the use of colours. White for purity, saffron for austerity and piety and green for felicity are general colour associations. While some people shun black, associating it with sorrow and sadness, others have a positive preference for it. Some married women are prejudiced against plain white because it is associated with widowhood.

Some colours are more flattering than others. Magenta, purple, flaming-orange, royal-blue and emerald-green, which are very flashy, do not lend themselves to everyday wear.

Seasons also have a bearing on the choice of a particular coloured garment. Cool colours such as white, blue, lavender and green are refreshing in summer, while warm colours such as red, orange, pink and yellow are suitable in winter. Warm colours are those containing red and orange. Cool colours have a predominance of blue. Green, for instance, is a cool colour suitable for summer; but yellow-green is considered to have enough warmth to warrant its use in winter, especially when used in combination with a warm contrasting colour.

Colour and light

Garments to be worn in the daytime should be selected in daylight. Apparel for evening wear or for use at night should be viewed under artificial light. Electric light can play the most extraordinary tricks on colour. Red can turn to brown, orange to dirty khaki and yellow to acid yellow-green. So one should be on guard against optical illusions while selecting fabrics by electric light.

Colour and emotion

Since most people are susceptible to emotional appeals, the impact of colour on the emotions must be taken into consideration when choosing clothes. Dull colours are depressing, while bright colours contribute to sprightliness and gaiety. If one wears dowdy colours, one will feel dowdy and look it. People must feel happy with their clothes if they are to look their best. Sober colours give sobriety, flashy colours make one coquettish.

Colour and character

Shakespeare said, "The apparel oft proclaims the man".

Equally may it be said that colours are an index of character. Some people do not like to dress in gaudy colours. Others prefer bright colours. It is said that if you prefer

Purple: You are magnetic; Red: You are passionate;
Pink: You are truly feminine; Blue: You are coolly competent;
Green: You are neighbourly; Orange: You are sociable;
Yellow: You are idealistic.

Colour and personality

One should select garments whose colours will suit and set off one's personality and not clash with one's complexion. A dark-skinned person should avoid wearing clothes of deep dark shades and hues. A person with a rosy skin should give a wide berth to garments of pink; similarly, a person with a yellowish complexion will not look well in yellow.

Light colours unlike dark ones make a person look larger. Warm colours should not be used indiscriminately. They are quite suitable for thin and fair persons. A timid, shy, quiet, reserved and retiring person can take shelter under rich, dark and dignified colours to express her personality traits. A vigorous person with healthy complexion can wear the most striking contrasting colour combinations.

Colour apparently increases or decreases the size of a person. Bright colours make one look larger, while brown, gray, green, dark, blue and black make one look smaller. A tall lady will look shorter in a sari and blouse of different colours. Monochromatic colour schemes with vertical stripes or small figured patterns and soft colours make a short person look taller. Bright colours with bold designs and horizontal stripes greatly accent the stoutness of a bulky person. Thin persons look slightly heavier if they wear bright colours.

Dainty fabrics suit slim people. Thin, gauzy materials in striking colours do not suit heavy-hipped, broad-backed ladies. A person with a small waistline should wear a choli and sari of different colours. A woman with large waistline should resort to monochromatic colour combinations to make her waist look smaller.

Nature has endowed the human figure with a good body structure. Therefore, clothes and their colour should rhythmically accentuate the shapely proportions of the wearer by their flowing lines.

SUGGESTED COLOUR SCHEMES IN DRESS

Colour scheme	*Colour of sari*	*Colour of choli*	*Colour of accessories*	*Colour of jewels*	*Remarks*
Monochromatic	Mauve	Violet	White and silver chappals White handbag	Silver jewellery.	Mauve and violet are in monochromatic harmony. Variation is introduced in the form of white accessories and silver jewellery. Suitable for both day and night wear. This type of harmony is ideal for stout persons who wish to appear slimmer.
Analogous	Yellow	Green	Green chappals Green handbag	Green bead neck lace. Green glass bangles. Green and Yellow bead earrings (Jimikies).	The ensemble is in analogous harmoney suitable for college or day wear.
Complementary	Red orange sari, with blue-green border and embroidered motifs	Blue green	Blue-green chappals and handbag.	Long gold chain with a large pendant with green stones. Gold earrings and gold bangles.	Red-orange and blue green are in complementary harmony, more suitable for a tall person and for evening wear. This combination is ideal for persons with a small waist.
Split Complementary	Shell pink sari with Lilac border	Pale green	Lilac slippers and handbag	Pale green and Lilac plastic bead necklace. Pale green and Lilac glass bangles. Pale green bead earrings.	This combination is in Split complementary harmony, more suitable for morning wear. In hot climates, these pale colours are suitable.
Triad	Deep blue sari with yellow border, red and yellow embroidered motifs and red and yellow tassel.	Yellow	Red chappals and handbag	Plain gold jewellery.	This combination is an example of the Primary Triad and is suitable only for evening wear.

4. Cleanliness and Care of the Home

A home should be clean and tidy. It should be free from foul smells, cobwebs and dirt. The health of the inmates depends on the care they take to keep the house spotlessly clean and sparkingly bright. Though a house is designed in the modern fashion and built on the most up-to-date lines, and fitted with the latest equipment for comfort and convenience, if it is not kept clean, it will become unfit for living. Therefore, cleanliness in a house is of utmost importance.

Fig. 24. Sweeping

The task of keeping the house and its surroundings clean, hould be executed systematically and the proper methods mployed. The methods adopted will depend upon the kind f unclean matter to be removed. Cleaning should be carried ut from the ceiling to the floor. All the necessary equipment, uch as a good step-ladder, ong-handled brushes, brooms, dusters, dust pans, mops, carpet beater, polishing cloth, buckets, or pails for water, soap, disinfectants, polishes for metal, ilver, wooden furniture, floor, tc. should be kept handy and hould be ready before the leaning process is begun. The oom also should be kept tidy and everything in it should be n the right place.

Fig. 25. Step-ladder

Fig. 26. Brushes, brooms and duster

Cleaning is the removal of all dust, dirt and foreign matter. Daily, weekly, monthly and periodical cleaning has to be carried out in every house.

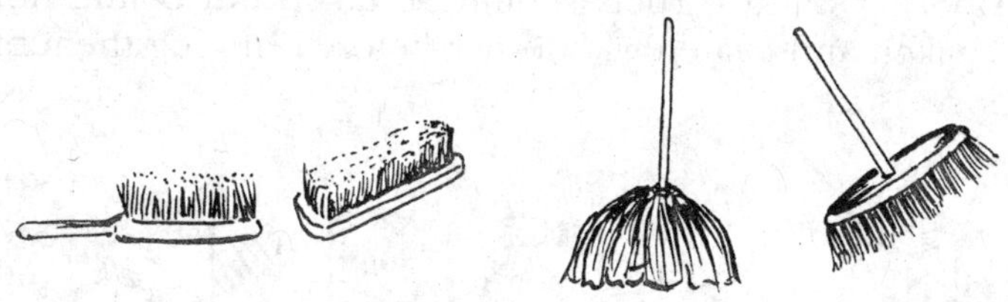

Fig. 27. Brushes, mop and carpet beaters

Vacuum cleaners

Vacuum cleaners and their tools or attachments are the most labour saving devices available for removing dust and other soil from many of the large and small surfaces in the home. One reason for using vacuum cleaners and floor polishes is to decrease the amount of human energy expended in cleaning. An additional means of decreasing the work of cleaning is to keep as much dirt as possible out of the home. The size of the house as well as the type of cleaning done are important factors to be considered for selection of vacuum cleaners.

Daily cleaning

Sweeping the floor and window-sills, dusting furniture, brushing doormats and carpets are daily tasks.

Dust and dirt accumulate in rooms which are used often. The dust should be swept, collected, removed and disposed of.

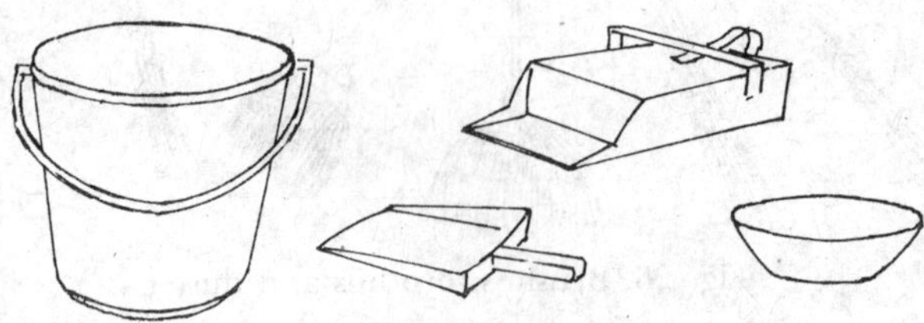

Fig. 28. Bucket, dustpans, etc.

Dust should be removed not only from the floor, but from walls, window-sills, pictures and furniture as well.

Doormats and carpets should be taken out of the house and shaken and beaten with a stick before bringing them back in.

Fig. 29. Polishes, disinfectants, etc.

The doors of a room should be closed while sweeping to prevent dust from being scattered about by a sudden gust of wind. A damp cloth should be used to wipe the room after sweeping. After sweeping the floor, the carpet should be put down again. Then the furniture should be dusted with a duster which should be shaken frequently to get rid of the dust it has gathered.

The main entrance to the house often gets dirty because it is open to frequent use. It is a good practice to remove one's chappals or shoes before entering the house, as is done in most Indian homes. Doormats and scrapers are an asset at the front door. This will enable people to wipe the dirt off their shoes before entering the house. The room commanding the main entrance should be cleaned first; the staircase needs attention next.

All the living rooms should be swept daily. The bedroom needs special care. It should get the benefit of sunshine daily. All the windows should be opened wide to let in the morning rays of the sun. The bedding should be aired daily and shaken out every now and then. Curtains should be taken down and shaken out periodically.

Ashtrays should be emptied and washed daily. Waste-paper baskets and dustbins should be emptied. Cleaning slop-basins, cisterns, and bath fittings should also be a part of the daily routine. Open drains should be checked and cleared of obstructions.

Doors and windows should be wiped clean. Lamp shades, flower pots and decorative articles such as vases should be wiped and cleaned or polished as the case may be.

Urinals and latrines should be washed and sprayed with a disinfectant daily.

Weekly cleaning

Since a person will have a number of daily chores to accomplish, it may not be possible to clean the house thoroughly every day. So the house and its belongings should be given a more complete cleaning at stated intervals, for instance, weekly. Preferably a holiday in the week, a Saturday or Sunday, is allotted for this purpose.

At least once a week the furniture and other household articles should be taken out and put in the sun. The bedding and covers should be sunned. The wall surfaces, corners and ceilings should be carefully swept. Cobwebs should be swept away. The floors should be thoroughly washed with soap and water. Shelves and cupboards should be scrubbed and washed. Sinks should be cleansed with a cleaning powder like Vim.

Polishing mirrors, metalware and a few pieces of wooden furniture, wiping and dusting pictures and washing glassware should form part of the weekly cleaning. Since it may take too much time and energy to polish all the furniture and large metalware even once a week, the larger articles can be polished in rotation.

Pillow cases and other bed linen should be changed at

least once a week. Table cloths and towels also should be laundered every week.

Cleaning of floors

Floors should be cleaned of dirt, dust and any other foreign matter. It is advisable to sweep the floor as many times as possible, especially when there are young children in the house. The floor should be washed with water regularly using a disinfectant such as phenyl in addition. Some kinds of flooring require mopping and waxing. Care should be taken to wipe the floors with water if milk or coffee is split or crumbs are scattered, to prevent ants and flies from congregating at the spot. Ink or any other stains should be removed or washed off.

Cleaning of walls

Walls should be swept carefully and dusted. There should be no cobwebs clinging to the corners of the walls or ceilings. The walls should be white or colour-washed at least once a year, if not once in six months.

Cleaning of windows

The windows should be cleaned and dusted. If there are glass windowpanes they should be cleaned with a moist cloth. A little ammonia can be added to the water to clean greasy windowpanes. Methylated spirits can be used for removing stains. Window frames should be carefully guarded against the attack of household pests. Wasps should not be allowed to build nests on them. They should be painted once a year, or oftener if necessary.

Window glass cleaning liquids

Window cleaners consist of a water miscible solvent, often isopropyl alcohol, to which a small quantity of synthetic detergent and possibly an alkali, are added to improve the polishing effect of the cleaner. Some also contain a fine abrasive. The cleaner is applied with a cleaning rag and rubbed off with a clean, soft cloth. Water or water to which some methylated spirit has been added, does the job quite well and much more cheaply but entails more rubbing.

Cleaning of mirrors

Both glass and frame should be dusted. The glass should be smeared with a paste of whiting, such as white chalk, and then wiped, starting from the centre and working outwards. The paste should not be allowed to stick to the frame.

Finally, the glass should be polished with a piece of smooth linen or tissue paper.

Cleaning of pictures

Pictures should be dusted and cleaned daily. Once a week they should be removed from the walls for a thorough cleaning. The glass should be wiped with chamois leather dipped in methylated spirits and water and then dried with a clean soft linen cloth. Care should be taken to clean the back of the pictures also, to remove dust, dirt or foreign matter.

Cleaning of beds and bedding

Bed linen should be aired and sunned daily, if possible, and changed at least once a week. The bed should be made every day.

After returning from a bus or train journey, the bedding should not be straightaway brought into the house and spread on a cot. It is possible that it may contain bed bugs and germs gathered in the course of the journey. Therefore, it should be put in the sun, and the sheets, etc., washed.

The bedsteads should be sunned regularly and properly searched for bugs. Steps should be taken to eradicate the pest, if there is evidence of their presence.

Cleaning of furniture

Furniture should be dusted and cleaned with a slightly moist cloth and then dried with a clean cloth. It should be put in the sun at intervals. Varnished, polished or painted furniture give a neat appearance to the room. New wood should be rubbed with a soft duster. For old wood, furniture polish should be used. Cracks and dents should be carefully sealed with hard wax lest they become the haunt of bugs.

Making of furniture polish at home

The following are the methods of preparing furniture polish at home.

Method I

Turpentine	...	2 parts
Methylated spirits	...	1 part
Linseed oil	...	2 parts
Vinegar	...	1 part

The above ingredients should be put in a beaker and shaken well to form an emulsion. This home-made polish is useful for dark wood. The turpentine and vinegar in it help to remove the grease, while the oil is useful for keeping the wood in good condition.

Method II

Beeswax	...	14 g
Turpentine	...	250 ml

The beeswax should be heated over a moderate fire until it melts. After removal from the fire, turpentine should be added and stirred till the mixture has cooled.

Method III

White wax	...	14 g
Petrol	...	500 ml

The wax should be broken into small bits and these bits should be put in a bottle and petrol added. The bottle should be corked properly and left for nearly a week for the wax to dissolve and the mixture to become creamy.

Cleanliness of the surroundings

Not only the inside of the house but also its surroundings should be kept scrupulously clean. The compound should be systematically swept and cleaned.

The garden should be weeded properly. Dead leaves and dry twigs should be removed. There should be no thick undergrowth. Piles of stones, and heaps of manure should not be left in the surroundings lest they become breeding places for flies, scorpions, snakes, deadly spiders and centipedes.

Water should not be allowed to stagnate in the vicinity of the house, since weeds in standing water will become ideal places for breeding mosquitoes. Water in tanks and wells should be kept covered.

Cowsheds, stables, kennels and poultry runs should not be

located too near the house. The flooring of these sheds should be of such material as will facilitate its washing and cleaning with water everyday. Cowdung should be removed immediately and disposed of properly.

The drains around the house should be kept covered. They should be inspected to ensure free flow of drainage. Disinfectants should be poured into the drains.

Waste products should not be indiscriminately thrown away in the compound. Peelings of vegetables and fruit, waste paper and dust should be deposited in a dustbin in the compound. This should be kept covered with a tight lid. The refuse in it should be burnt once a week.

5. Textile Fibres and Clothes

The word "textile" comes from a Latin word meaning "a woven fabric or raw material for weaving, such as cotton or wool". The fibres used in the manufacture of textile fabrics are many and varied. Fibres form the fundamental units in fabrics. The fibre is a very fine, hair like material that is very small in diameter in relation to its length. It is the beginning of all clothes. Fibres are the basic units from which textile yarns and fabrics are made. Yarns are the strands obtained by twisting the collected single fibres together more closely to increase the strength of the cloth or fabric manufactured.

Cellulose fibres

Natural cellulose fibres—cotton, linen, jute, hemp, etc. are those that are obtained from the stem, seed or leaf of certain plants. These fibres develop naturally during the growth of plants. Rayon is the man-made cellulose fibre which is obtained by dissolving and re-dissolving natural cellulose from pine trees.

Cellulose fibres are good absorbents and good conductors of heat and electricity. It is comfortable to wear clothes made of cellulose fibres, especially during summer because of their greater absorbency. The fabrics made of cellulose fibres can be boiled to sterilize them and there is no special precaution to be taken while ironing. They burn freely and quickly. Moth and mildew harm cellulose fabrics.

Cotton

Cotton is a cellulose or vegetable fibre and is the most widely used textile fibre. It is the seed hair of the cotton plant. Cotton fibre is short, its length ranging from 1 cm to 5 cm. Immature cotton fibre is cylindrical in shape but when it ripens the fibre flattens and twists.

Textile fibres can be classified as follows:

Cotton fibre is quite strong but has less elasticity than that

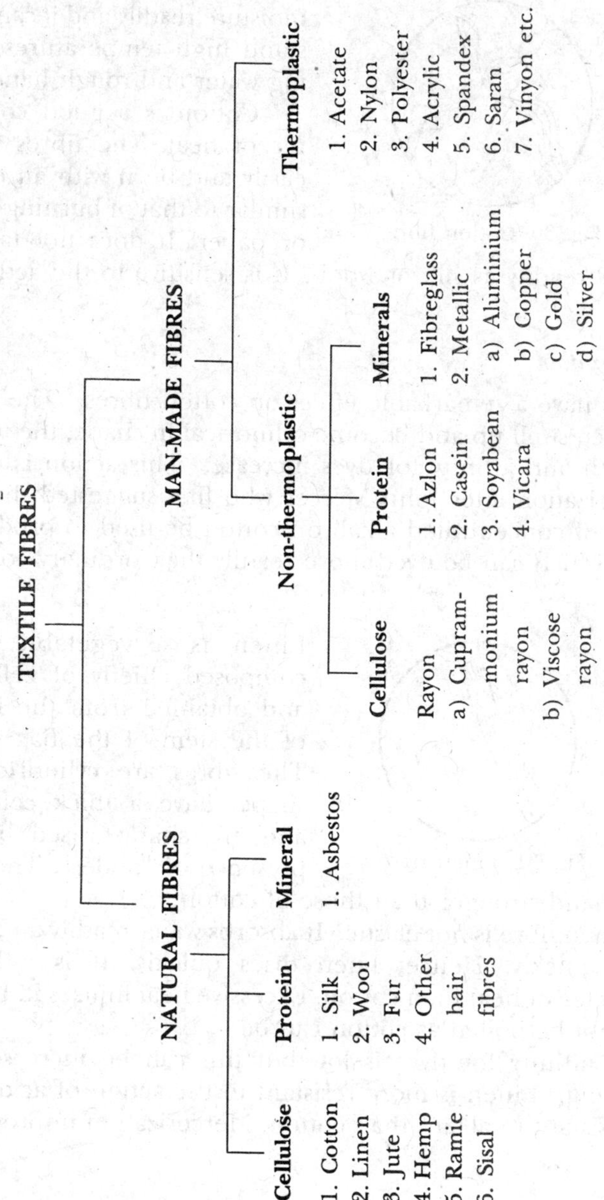

TEXTILE FIBRES
NATURAL FIBRES
Cellulose
1. Cotton
2. Linen
3. Jute
4. Hemp
5. Ramie
6. Sisal
Protein
1. Silk
2. Wool
3. Fur
4. Other hair fibres
Mineral
1. Asbestos
MAN-MADE FIBRES
Non-thermoplastic
Cellulose
Rayon
a) Cuprammonium rayon
b) Viscose rayon
Protein
1. Azlon
2. Casein
3. Soyabean
4. Vicara
Minerals
1. Fibreglass
2. Metallic
a) Aluminium
b) Copper
c) Gold
d) Silver
Thermoplastic
1. Acetate
2. Nylon
3. Polyester
4. Acrylic
5. Spandex
6. Saran
7. Vinyon etc.

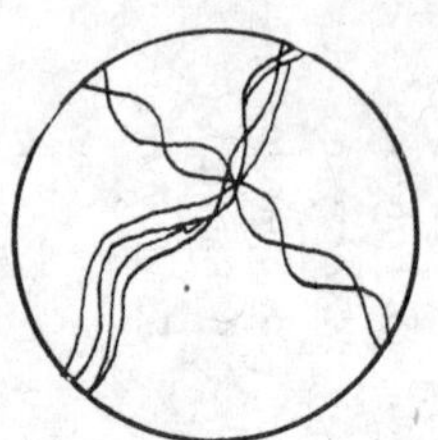

Fig. 30. Cotton fibre

of silk or wool. Cotton absorbs moisture readily and it can withstand high temperatures, boiling water and rough handling.

Cotton is a good conductor of heat. The fibres ignite easily and burn with an odour similar to that of burning wood or paper. It does not take in dyes as readily as silk or wool. It is sensitive to the action of acids.

Mercerization

Alkalis have a remarkable effect on cotton fibres. The fibres contract, swell up and become cylindrical in shape; the tensile strength and affinity for dyes increase. This action is called mercerization after John Mercer who first suggested that the action of concentrated alkali on cotton be used to produce a fabric which can be dyed more readily than ordinary cotton.

Linen

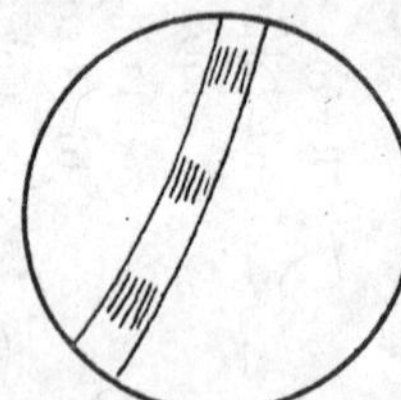

Fig. 31. Linen fibre

Linen is a vegetable fibre composed chiefly of cellulose and obtained from the inside of the stem of the flax plant. The fibres are cylindrical in shape, have a thick cell wall and are characterised by the presence of "nodes". They are longer and stronger than those of cotton.

Linen fibre is not elastic. It absorbs water readily and gives it up quickly. Hence, linen dries quickly. It is a better conductor of heat than cotton. Excessive heat injures it. Hence it cannot be boiled as cotton can be.

Its affinity for dyes is low but this can be increased by bleaching. Linen is more resistant to the action of acids and less resistant to alkalis than cotton. Mercerization improves its lustre.

Rayon

Rayons are of vegetable origin. They are a regenerated

cellulose, the chief source of which is wood pulp and cotton linters. Two kinds of rayons, namely viscose and cuprammonium, are obtained from regenerated cellulose, the differences being due to the different chemicals used in making the cellulose into a solution.

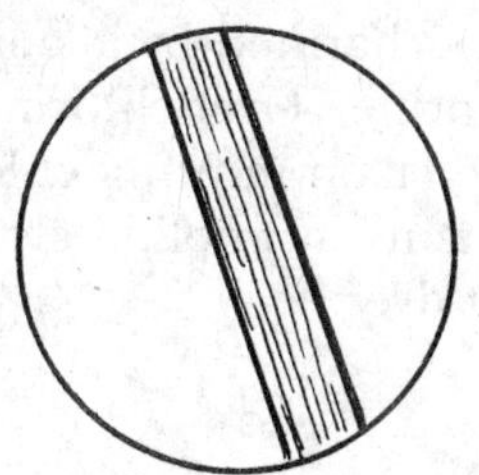

Fig. 32. Rayon viscose fibre

Under the microscope, the viscose fibres appear to have many lengthwise striations, whereas the cuprammonium fibres appear to be round filaments.

Rayon fibres are quite strong but lose their strength when wet. Hence when washing rayon fabrics, care should be taken to avoid soaking and friction for fear of tearing and stretching the fabric.

Rayons are good conductors of heat. They have great affinity to dyes. Acids weaken rayon fibres. Alkalis have a harmful effect but under controlled conditions mercerization is possible. Rayons absorb more moisture than cotton but do not give out moisture as readily as cotton and linen. They burn faster than cotton with a smell of burning paper.

Protein fibres

Natural protein fibres are products of animal growth. Man-made protein fibres are made by dissolving and re-dissolving protein from animal sources and from grains.

Protein fibres do not burn readily and are self-extinguishing. In a cool, damp climate it is comfortable to wear fabrics made of protein fibres.

Wool

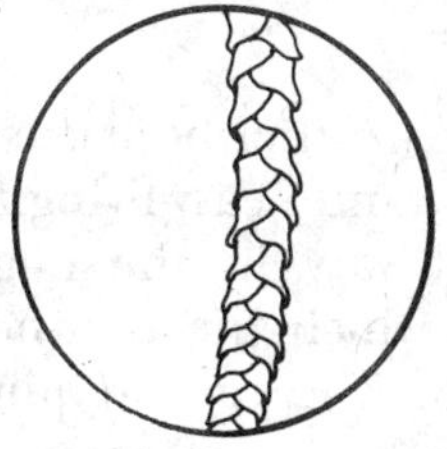

Fig. 33. Woollen fibre

Wool is the hair fibre of sheep. Its fundamental substance is a protein. Hence it burns with a characteristic odour of burning hair, but not readily. Under the microscope, it is seen to be a rounded fibre with a characteristic epidermis of horny scales or serrations. When woollen garments are washed in hot water and with friction, the scales melt and therefore the garments shrink. Hence heat and friction are avoided in washing woollen garments. Woollen fibre is elastic. It is also a bad conductor of heat. Hence woollen garments keep the body warm.

Wool is fairly stable to acids and is harmed by alkalis. It absorbs a considerable quantity of chlorine. Over-chlorination weakens it. Therefore, care should be taken in using chlorine as a bleaching agent for removal of stains in woollen clothes.

Wool has a great affinity for most dyes.

Silk

Silk is an animal fibre obtained from the cocoons of a species of caterpillar which feeds upon mulberry leaves. Silk fibres are characterized by their extreme fineness and great length. They have great tensile strength and elasticity.

Silk fabrics are smooth, lustrous and not fluffy. Therefore, they can be cleansed easily. Silk burns quickly with a characteristic odour of burning hair (burning protein).

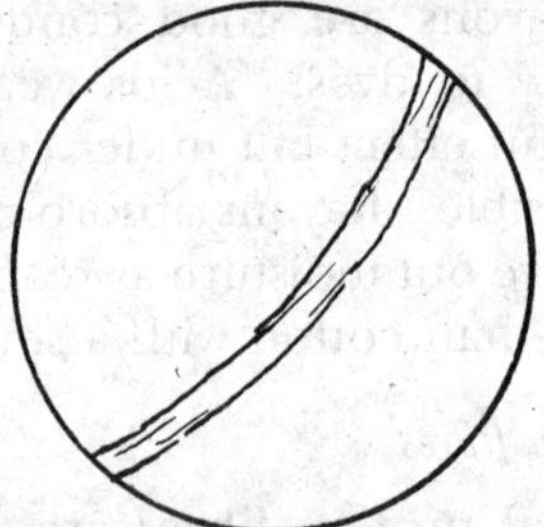
Fig. 34. Silk fibre

Strong acids dissolve silk. It is less sensitive to alkalis than wool. It is a poor conductor of heat. However, it is comfortable, both in winter and summer, because it absorbs moisture very readily. Dyestuffs are also absorbed by silk readily.

Raw silk, as seen under the microscope, consists of a double filament, coated irregularly with sericin (a fixing fluid secreted by the glands of the silkworm).

Thermoplastic fibres

Fibres that are softened on heating are thermoplastic fibres. They have been called "magic fibres" and "easy-living fibres". They are all sensitive to heat, but vary in the degree of sensitivity. There are many ways by which the thermoplastic fibre fabrics have made living easier. The time required for washing, drying and ironing clothes has been reduced to a minimum, and ironing is sometimes unnecessary. The thermoplastic fibres have good strength and resistance to rubbing. They resist wrinkles. They absorb very little moisture. They have good resistance to moth, mildew, insects, etc.

Nylon

Nylon fibre is the first man-made fibre to be built up from chemicals in a laboratory. It is a smooth, round fibre, resembling cuprammonium rayon and is almost translucent.

It was the first synthetic fibre manufactured. It is the strongest per unit of weight of all the fibres except dacron (polyester). Nylon fibre is strong, tough, elastic, lustrous and smooth. It retains its strength when wet. It does not absorb moisture but dries quickly. This property of not absorbing moisture is a disadvantage because it means it cannot absorb sweat either.

Nylon fabrics do not shrink because of their low absorbing power. The low absorbing power of nylon makes it uncomfortable to wear. Nylon is a poor conductor of heat. It is affected by high temperature. A hot iron will melt nylon fabrics.

Care should be taken while ironing nylon. Low temperatures of the iron (132°-148° C) do not affect nylon. Nylon fibres do not burn but melt from flame with the smell of burning rubber which stick on to the surface and form a hard bead.

It is resistant to moth, mildew, insects and other organisms. It is affected by strong mineral acids but not by dilute acids. Alkalis have no harmful effect on it. Nylon fibre is not resistant to bleaching. Hence bleaching should not be resorted to in the removal of stains from it.

The fibre is transparent when seen under the microscope, without any striations.

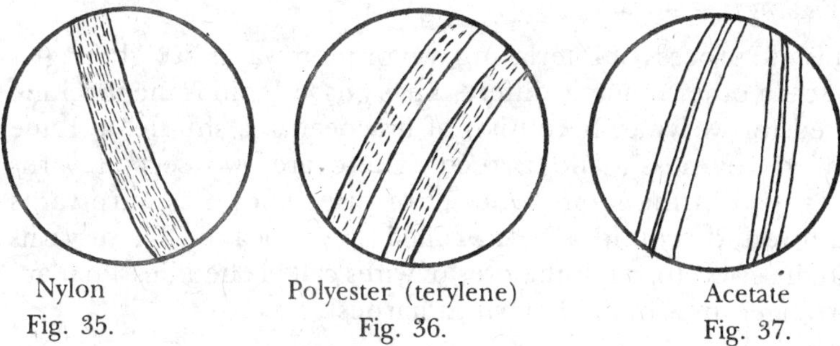

Nylon
Fig. 35.

Polyester (terylene)
Fig. 36.

Acetate
Fig. 37.

Polyester (Dacron or terylene)

Polyester is made by reacting an acid with an alcohol. Like nylon, polyester melts from the flame forming a tan-coloured bead. It has the ability to resist heat damage. Polyester has the ability to impart strength, and is wrinkle-resistant. Therefore, it is easy to take care of fabrics while washing. Absorbency is very low and hence it resists the absorption of stains carried by water. Polyester is generally resistant to acids and alkalis and can be bleached with mild bleaches. It is resistant to bacterial attack and to damage by sunlight.

Acetate

It is a fibre derived from cellulose in which the cellulose has been chemically changed by a reaction with acetic acid during the manufacturing process. It appears to be a smooth cylinder with a canal-like structure when seen under the microscope. Acetate burns freely, melts and decomposes into a black ash. It gives off an acetic vinegar-like colour while burning. Strong acids and alkalis damage acetate fabrics. Bleaches like chlorine bleaches are not harmful. Acetate is not affected by moth and mildew.

Fabric construction

A fabric is a structure made from yarns and fibres, and from non-fibrous substances such as plastics, rubber or metal. Of these, fabrics manufactured from yarns are the most expensive and complex ones. Weaving, knitting, braiding and lace making are some of the processes by which fabrics are made from yarns. Weaving and knitting are the most commonly used methods of fabric construction.

Weaving

It is the process of interlacing two or more yarns at right angles to each other in many different designs. A loom is the machine used for weaving. It consists of two beams, a shuttle, a frame called "harness", and a reed. There are two sets of yarns arranged in the loom. One set of yarns known as warp yarns are wound around a beam called "warp beam". These yarns are inserted through the eyes of wires called "heddles" that are arranged in a frame known as harness.

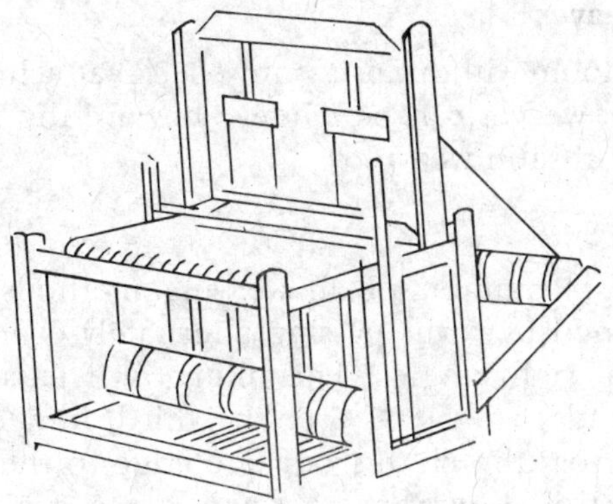

Fig. 38. A simple loom

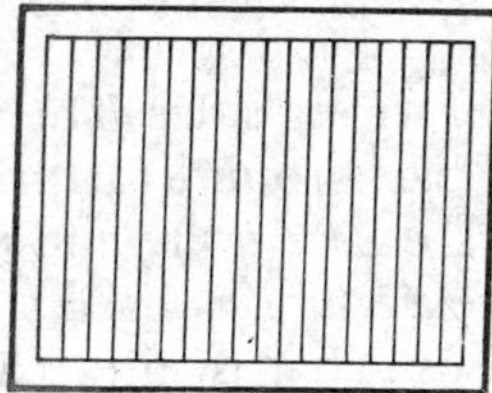

Harness with heddles
Fig. 39.

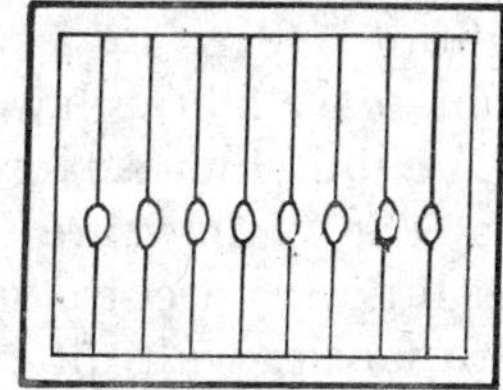

Reed
Fig. 40.

In a simple loom there are two harnesses which are raised alternately. During this process of raising and lowering of harnesses a gap — 'shed'— is formed. This process of forming the shed is known as "shedding" which is the first step in weaving. When a shed is formed, a boat-like shuttle moves fast through it with the second set of yarn called "filling yarn". This step is known as "picking". The next step consists of the reed pushing the filling yarn back to the cloth which is wound on a cloth beam. This step is known as "beating up". Thus the three steps involved in the process of weaving are:

a. Shedding: the raising and lowering of harnesses to form a shed.

b. Picking: passing the shuttle through the shed to insert the filling yarn.

c. Beating: the reed pushing the filling yarn back into place in the cloth.

The basic weaves

On a simple loom without using any special attachments, three types of basic weaves can be made. They are the plain weave, twill weave and satin weave.

Plain weave

It is the most common of all weaving methods. The plain weave is formed by yarns passing alternately over and under each other at right angles. The filling yarn passes over one warp yarn, under the next, over the third, under the fourth and so on across the cloth from one edge to the other. The second time, the filling yarn goes across after taking a turn at the edge by passing under each yarn over which the previous filling yarn passed and over each yarn under which the filling yarn has passed on the previous line. This is repeated throughout.

Plain-weave fabrics have no right or wrong sides. The plain surface of the cloth serves as a good background for printed designs. The plain-weave fabrics get creased easily and yarns unravel little from cut edges. Plain-weave fabrics have a wide range of fabrics with different end-uses. That is, they can be made in any weight, from very thin to very heavy fabrics.

Fig. 41. Plain weave

Twill weave

The characteristic of the twill weave is a woven diagonal line called "wale" pattern. It is formed by each warp or filling yarn passing over two or more filling or warp yarns with the interlacings being shifted by one step either to the right or left. For twill weave there should be a minimum of three harnesses in the simple loom.

Fig. 42. Twill weave

The surface of the twill-weave fabric has an interesting texture and beautiful geometrical designs. The fabrics are soft, pliable and have more crease recovery than other fabrics. Some twill-weave fabrics are serge, gabardine, denim, etc.

Satin weave

In satin-weave fabrics, the surface pattern is absent. The surface is smooth and shining, similar to that of silk. The satin-weave fabric has long floats passing over several yarns before interlacing with a single yarn, followed by another long float.

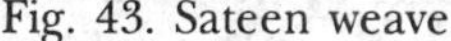

Fig. 43. Sateen weave

Fig. 44. Satin weave

If the long floats of the yarn on the right side of the material are along the warp direction (along the length) the fabric is known as satin. Such fabrics are slippery when rubbed in the lengthwise direction. If filling yarn has long floats on the right side along the width it is known as sateen. The slipperiness of the fabric is in the widthwise direction.

The satin fabrics have a definite right and wrong side. The satin-weave fabric is quite strong, durable, pliable and resistant to wrinkles.

Textile finishes

As yarn and fabric come from the spinner, weaver or knitter they are in crude form. They are harsh to touch and always contain impurities. Very often they are soiled and may have oil stains. Fabrics in this condition are normally referred to as "grey goods", which have been woven on a loom and have received no treatment to improve the appearance. These grey goods undergo the next process called "finishing".

A finish is defined as anything that is done to fibre, yarn or fabric either before or after weaving or knitting, to change the appearance (what you see), the feel (what you feel with the hand), and the performance (what the fabric does). A finish may be either permanent or temporary. A permanent finish lasts the life of the garment, whereas a temporary finish lasts until the garment is washed or dry-cleaned.

Functions of finishes

Finishes are applied to cloth for various reasons. They are :

a. to improve the appearance or the usefulness of the fabric
b. to impart or improve service qualities, such as resistance to abrasion or rubbing, resistance to moth or insects
c. to improve suitability and utility
d. to produce variety by dyeing and printing
e. to increase the weight or stiffness
f. to produce imitations.

Dyeing and printing

Dyeing and printing are the two colouring methods used in textiles to produce variety. In dyeing, the colouring substance penetrates the fibre and becomes a part of their structure. In printing, the colouring matter is applied on the surface of the cloth with the help of a substance to bind the colouring matter and the cloth. The colouring substances used for dyeing and printing are dyes and pigments. The differences between the two kinds of colouring substances are given below:

Dyes	Pigments
Soluble substance.	Insoluble substance.
Penetrate into the fibre and are fixed by chemical action, heat or other treatment.	Do not penetrate fully. Held mechanically on the surface by a binding agent.

Methods of dyeing

Colour is applied at various stages of production of fabrics: before spinning, after spinning but before weaving or knitting, and after weaving and knitting.

Before spinning

There are two methods of applying colour before the fabric is spun.

Stock or fibre dyeing is the process by which dye is applied to loose fibres before spinning the yarn. This process is expensive but there is good penetration of dye.

The other method is **solution or dope dyeing**. This consists of adding coloured pigments to the spinning solution. It is an inexpensive method but there is high resistance to fading of colour.

Yarn dyeing

This is done after spinning but before weaving or knitting. Yarns are dyed in skeins or packages. Packages of yarns are wound on a perforated cylinder. By the movement of the dye and the packages on the cylinder, the dye is absorbed by the packages of yarns (skeins). Yarn dyeing is less costly than raw stock dyeing.

Piece dyeing after weaving or knitting

The woven or knitted fabrics are dyed by means of immersing the fabrics in a dye solution. Piece dyeing usually produces solid colour fabrics. Piece dyeing is done a great deal, because it is economical for the manufacturer as the colours in fabric can be obtained according to the rapid changes in style.

Classification of dyes

Dyes are classified as natural or synthetic. Natural dyestuffs have been used from ancient times. The relatively recent discovery of the synthetic dyes have however diminished the importance of natural dyes. The latter were obtained from plants, insects, wood and minerals. Indigo, a blue dyestuff is a vegetable dye that is extracted from a plant. Tyrian purple is the royal purple colour obtained from one kind of insect and hence it is an animal dye. This dye is not in common use.

Synthetic dyes are man-made dyes obtained by mixing certain chemicals whose bases are either salts or acids. At present, synthetic dyes have practically replaced natural dyes. The first synthetic dye was discovered by William Henry Perkin in 1856. This was an accidental discovery which led to the further discovery of coal-tar dyes.

Dyestuffs may be classified according to their method of application to a cloth. The principal synthetic dyestuffs are :

1. acid dyes
2. mordant dyes
3. basic dyes
4. direct dyes
5. developed direct dyes
6. disperse dyes
7. naphthol or azoic dyes
8. pigments
9. vat dyes
10. fibre reactive dyes

Acid dyes

They are organic acids which are obtained in the form of salts. They are applied directly to fibres, from solutions containing acid, such as sulphuric acid, acetic acid or formic acid. Wool, silk, nylon and polyester (terylene) can be dyed with acid dyes. Bright colours are obtained with acid dyes. Colours are fairly durable when washed but not quite durable when drycleaned or exposed to light.

Mordant dyes

These dyes have no affinity to fibres. Hence a substance known as "mordant" is used with the dye. The mordant has an affinity for both the fibre and dye. Chromium salts are commonly used as the mordant; hence mordant dyes are also known as "chrome dyes". Mordant dyes are applied on wool, cotton and silk. The metallic compound of the mordant combines with the fibre and the organic dye, and forms an insoluble colour compound in the fibre.

Basic dyes

These were the first synthetic dyes discovered. They are salts of various organic bases. They are applied to wool, silk, nylon. The colours are brilliant and are not durable when washed, exposed to light or rubbed.

Direct dyes

They are salts of colour acids. Cotton, rayon and linen are dyed directly with the direct dyes without the use of a mordant. Direct dyes may be applied on silk. A wide range of colours which are not brilliant can be obtained. The colours are generally not durable.

Developed direct dyes

These dyes can be applied directly to the cloth and may change to a new colour on the fabric if treated with nitrous acid and certain other chemicals called developers. They are applied to cotton, rayon, silk and linen. Cloth dyed with developed direct dyes may be washed satisfactorily at home, but they are not durable when exposed to sunlight.

Disperse dyes

These dyes were originally known as acetate dyes because these were used to dye acetate fibres. Now the disperse dyes are used on acetate, polyester and nylon. Disperse dyes are slightly soluble in water, but they are kept in colloidal suspension by sulphonated oils. The colours are durable and resistant to light, washing and perspiration.

Naphthol or azoic dyes

These dyes are used on cotton and are commonly used for printing on cotton. The cotton cloth is immersed in beta-naphthol that has been dissolved in caustic soda and then immersed in basic dyes. The colours are very durable even when frequently washed.

Pigments

They are insoluble colouring matter without any affinity to fibres. Therefore pigments are dispersed with a binder which helps to fix the pigment on the cloth. They are padded or printed on cloth. Almost all types of fibres can be coloured by pigment dyeing or printing.

Vat dyes

They are insoluble but are reduced to leuco compounds which are soluble in alkali. Finally these dyes are re-oxidized by air or oxidizing agents. Cotton, rayon, nylon and some other synthetic fibres can be dyed with vat dyes. The colours are generally durable and are the most satisfactory of all dyestuffs.

Fibre reactive dyes

They are applied by means of physical absorption or mechanical retention of an insoluble particle by the fibre. The colour then becomes a part of the fibre. Cotton, silk and wool can be dyed with this type of dye. First, the dye is padded on the fabric and dried. The second padding is done with an alkali which completes the process of colouring the fabric. Then the fabric is exposed to extreme heat, steam or air. The colours are very durable and can be washed and drycleaned.

Printing

Printing is the application of colour in the form of a design, on a fabric. It is the controlled application of colour to selected areas on the cloth. For printing, the dye is in the form of a paste. There are a number of printing techniques. The chief ones are as follows:

Block printing

It is the most popular technique of handicraft. It is the earliest form of decorating fabrics. Block printing consists of carving a design on a block of wood or linoleum block and dipping the block in a pan of dye paste and then stamping it on the surface of the fabric to be printed. If two colours are in the design two different blocks are prepared with the necessary different outlines carved.

Stencil printing

This is similar to block printing. The only difference is, instead of cutting the design on wood or linoleum, waxed paper or thin copper sheets are used. Through the cut-out portions of the stencil the dye paste is brushed. Depending upon the number of colours needed the required number of stencils are cut.

Direct roller printing

It is a machine-printing technique, and is most commonly used in printing cloth today. It is similar to the way a newspaper is printed. The design is etched on copper rollers which are covered with the dye that is needed. When the dye-covered roller comes in contact with the fabric, the design is transferred to the fabric.

Discharge printing

It is done on a dark background. The fabric is immersed in a suitable dye solution and dried. A discharge paste containing chemicals to remove the colour is printed on the dyed fabric. The chemical in the paste bleaches the fabric where it is applied. Therefore the design area is lighter in colour than the background colour.

Resist printing

As the name implies, a resisting material like wax is applied on a plain white or light-coloured fabric. Then the fabric is dyed in suitable dye solution. Care should be taken to avoid heating while dyeing because the wax may melt and there will not be any resistance. After dyeing the waxed cloth, the wax is melted and removed from the cloth. This type of resist printing is known as batik.

Another form of resist printing is called tie and dye (bhandhaner or chungudi). It is a hand process where fabric or yarn is tied in certain places with waxed thread or string. After tying, the cloth is dyed in a cold, dye solution. After drying the waxed thread can be removed.

Care of linen

A well-kept house should not only be clean, but also stocked with proper household linen. This term denotes articles for household use made of wool, silk, cotton, linen and various other materials. Linen will not last long or look fresh or pleasing unless well cared for. The greater the care we take of it, the longer it will last, and the better it will serve. The amount of linen needed depends on the number of inmates, and the status of the family. It is better to have a little more rather than too little, so as to be prepared for emergencies. Normally, a household should have three sets of household linen, one in use, one with the dhoby and one spare set on the shelf.

Under the heading of household linen, the following articles are necessary:

Table linen, such as table-cloths, table-napkins, sideboard cloths, tray cloths, tea-cloths, table mats, etc.

Bed linen, such as sheets, pillow cases, blankets, bed-spreads, mosquito nets.

Bathroom linen, such as bath towels, face towels and roller towels.

Other household cloths such as dusters, floor cloths, curtains, cushion covers, etc.

Storage of linen

A well-planned linen closet is a great help in keeping linen in good condition. The cupboard should be clean, cool, airy and dry and contain plenty of racks for storage. The shelves should not be too deep. Shelves are preferable to drawers. It is best to arrange the various linen on different shelves and label the shelves according to their contents. Linen should be arranged according to size, the top shelves being used for storing larger articles which are used only occasionally and the bottom shelves for smaller articles which are used often. Only clean linen should be stored here and dirty articles put in a separate box known as the soiled-linen box. Normally, the soiled-linen box is made of wood with perforated sides. In some houses soiled-linen is kept in covered baskets.

Before being put away, the linen should be properly mended. It should not be allowed to get very dirty or remain dirty for long. It should be changed frequently and washed by the best methods before putting it away again. The storage space should be free from household pests, such as moths which damage the linen. The shelves should be properly cleaned at intervals, the contents removed, aired and sunned. The shelves should be sprayed with suitable insecticides.

All stains should be removed from the linen before it is stored. Household linen is liable to be stained by animal or vegetable, grease, dye or mineral stains. It may also be stained by being scorched by a very hot iron.

Stains may be removed by applying an absorbent dissolved in a common solvent like water, petrol or turpentine; or by bleaching with lemon juice, sour milk, hydrogen peroxide, etc., depending upon the type of stain. Removal of stains is a process requiring the utmost care; otherwise the original appearance and texture of the linen may be marred.

Some general rules for stain removal

Linen or any other material should be washed the moment it is stained. The stains are easy to remove when they are fresh; otherwise they may become permanent and difficult to remove. All stains should be removed before laundering.

Some reagents used for stain removal might have injurious effects on the colour, texture and finish of a particular fabric.

	Type of Stain	*Nature of Stain*	*Reagents Used*
1.	**Animal Stain** **Examples:** blood, egg, milk, meat, juices, ice cream, etc.	Animal stains contain proteins; hence heat should be avoided while removing them.	Cold water, salt, soap, borax solution, a few drops of ammonia.
2.	**Vegetable Stain,** **Examples:** tea, cocoa, coffee, fruit juices and wine, grass.	Vegetable stains are acidic; therefore, alkaline reagents should be used to remove them.	Warm water, borax, glycerine, hydrogen peroxide, benzene, starch paste.
3.	**Dye Stain.**	May be acidic or alkaline; hence the reagent used, for removal of stain, should depend on the nature of the stain.	Water, soap, dilute alkali, dillute acid, alcohol, cold bleaching powder solution.
4.	**Mineral Stain,** **Examples:** iron, mould, ink.	Mineral stains are compounds of a metal and dye. Therefore acidic reagents should be used first to act on the metal, followed by dilute alkaline solutions to neutralize the acid reagent and to remove the dye.	Water, soap, cut tomato, lime, sour milk, starch, paste, oxalic acid, borax solution, methyl alcohol.
5.	**Grease Stain,** **Examples:** oil, paint, varnish butter, tar.	Grease stains are caused by the grease and specific colouring matter in it; hence grease solvents and grease absorbents should be used.	Water-solvent soap, french chalk fuller's earth, kerosene, turpentine, alcohol.

Hence before attempting to remove the stain, this effect should first be tested on the fabric, inside a seam or hem, and should be used only when the fabric is found to retain its original appearance after the application of the reagent.

It is easy to remove a stain when one can identify it. Specific reagents should be used for known stains, while unknown ones should be first treated with dilute solutions, followed later by concentrated solutions if necessary.

Bleaching should be resorted to only when all other treatments fail.

Once the stain is removed, the reagent should be rinsed out thoroughly. If acid reagents have been used for stain removal they should be neutralised with an alkaline rinse, and vice versa, before rinsing out with water.

For silks and synthetics, mild dilute reagents only should be used and alcohol should be avoided altogether.

It is best to use only small quantities of the reagent. This can be done successfully by applying the reagent drop by drop with a medicine dropper.

When hot water has to be used for removing the stain, it is convenient to hold the stained portion over a basin and pour the boiling water from the spout of a kettle.

Sponging a stain helps to remove the stain without the reagent penetrating the fabric. The stained portion should be placed over an absorbing pad like a blotter and the reagent should be applied lightly with a circular movement, starting from the outer edge of the stain and going towards the centre. This prevents the spreading of the stain.

Perspiration and scorch stains form a class by themselves. Bleaching in sunlight is usually effective in removing them. Mild bleaching reagents like ammonia can also be used.

Grass stains require special treatment. Kerosene, turpentine and solvent soaps are generally used.

Laundering

Laundering is the process by which dirty clothes are made clean by washing and ironing.

Washing is done in different ways according to the material to be washed. The method of laundering cotton garments differs from that for silk. Laundering is doubly imperative because, apart from removing the dust and dirt of the soiled clothes, it cleans them of the germs that they may harbour. Washing and ironing are heavy chores and can be lightened by the use of suitable equipment and materials.

Laundry equipment

The essential household equipment for laundry consists of sinks or tubs and buckets, or bowls and basins; spoons and containers for preparing starch, and stirring blue; washing soap or soap flakes; materials for stain removal, scrubbing brushes, scrubbing boards, clothes rack, line and clothes pins, an iron and ironing board.

Washing of cotton and silk

The process of laundering includes sorting, pre-treatment, soaking, washing, rinsing, starching, blueing, drying, ironing, and airing.

Sorting

Before washing, clothes should be sorted on the basis of their

(a) Fibre of texture: Cotton together, silks separately;

(b) Size: Bigger articles such as bed linen and table linen together and smaller clothes such as kitchen cloths and dusters separately;

(c) Use: Personal clothes together, household linen separately;

(d) Colour: Dark ones should be separated from white and light-coloured ones;

(e) Degree of dirt: Heavily soiled garments in a group and slightly dirty ones separately.

Pre-treatment

Garments that are torn or ripped or need mending in any way should be mended before washing.

Stained garments should not be mixed with unstained ones and washed. Stains should be removed first before the stained clothes are put into the wash tub.

Pockets and cuffs should be turned before washing.

Soiled spots, like neck, pockets, etc., which may be very

dirty, should be washed with soap, before soaking.

Soaking or steeping

Clothes should be soaked in water before washing. The length of time required for soaking depends on how dirty they are. Lightly soiled clothes should be soaked for 10 minutes and heavily soiled ones for about 30 minutes. The time may be curtailed if warm water is used, as it quickly dissolves the dirt. If the clothes are soaked for an unduly long period, the fibres will become soft and the dirt will get lodged more firmly. As hot water will harden the protein matter and help fix dirt, soaking of linen in it should be avoided. Non-fast colours, silks and synthetics should not be soaked.

Washing

Washing should be done in soft water. If water is hard, washing soda must be added to soften it. (Temporary hardness can be removed by ordinary boiling, while permanent hardness can be removed by water softeners such as washing soda or borax.)

Detergents must be used for washing. The quantity needed depends on the quality of the water and on how dirty the articles are. If the water is soft, a smaller quantity of detergent is enough.

The detergents may be cakes of soap, such as Sunlight soap, soap powder, or flakes such as Lux or 501, or it may be a soapless by-product of petroleum like 'Det' or 'Surf'. Soiled parts of clothes should be soaped well and washed.

The temperature of water used should vary according to the fabric to be washed; for instance, 95°F (lukewarm) for wool, 100°F (warm) for silk and 140°F (hot) for cotton. The time taken for washing should be 2-3 minutes for wool; 10 minutes for silk and 15 minutes or so for cotton.

For coarse material and strong cotton, friction can be applied by the use of scrubbing board or scrubbing brush. On the other hand, in washing delicate cottons and silks, the clothes should be kneaded and squeezed or agitated in the soapy water with hands or a stick or a plunger. Too much friction weakens the silk fabrics.

Using soda with soap for washing instead only for softening the water results in weakening the cloth. Chloride of lime (bleaching powder) should not be used to whiten clothes as its effects are detrimental, resulting in the rotting of the cloth. Beating clothes too hard on stones while washing is not advisable as it may tear them.

Rinsing

Clothes should be rinsed once or twice in warm water for removing the soapy water. The final rinse should be done in cold soft water. This helps to retain the whiteness of the fabric.

In the case of silk, the final rinse should be done in cold water to which a little methylated spirit or lime juice may be added. This will help clear the colour, renew the sheen and stiffen the silk.

Starching and blueing

To save time, to avoid wasting starch and blue and to obtain good results, starching and blueing may be combined in a single process. The necessary amount of blue should be added to the prepared starch. The 'blue' is tied up in a piece of muslin cloth and squeezed into the starch solution till the required depth of colour is obtained. Coloured articles are not blued. Only blue articles or white cotton clothes are blued. Blue is used for giving a good colour to the washed clothes.

Articles of household linen, such as tray clothes, table mats, etc., are heavily starched, while clothes are given only a light stiffening. Handkerchiefs, towels, underwear, dusters, babies clothes, etc., should not be starched. Starching helps to keep clothes clean and fresh for a longer time.

The water containing starch and blue should be stirred well before the clothes are put in, to prevent the blue from settling to the bottom. The garments should be squeezed well in the water for the starch to penetrate into them. Garments with fringed lace or crochet edges should not be completely immersed in the water containing starch and blue. They should be carefully put in with the edges gathered together. The edges may be treated with a dilute solution of starch afterwards.

Preparation of starch

The following is the recipe for the preparation of starch:

Starch	...	1 Table spoon.
Cold water	...	2 Table spoons.
Borax	...	1 Table spoon.
Candle wax	...	½ Table spoon.
Boiling water	...	1½ Pint.

The starch should be mixed with cold water to form a paste. Borax and wax should be added to the paste. Borax gives a shine to the garment, and wax makes the ironing easy by helping the iron to slip over the surface of the garment and not stick. The boiling water should be poured in, while stirring quickly all the time till the solution becomes clear. Finally, this full strength starch should be diluted immediately with an equal volume of cold water.

In some homes the strained water from cooked rice is used for starching clothes. Starch may be prepared from rice, tapioca, maize or potato.

Gelatin may be used as a stiffening agent for cotton fabrics. It contributes greatly to the ease of work and the smart appearance of the garment. A small packet of gelatin should be dissolved in 8 cups of cold water. Boiling water should be added till the mixture is clear. The quantity of gelatin should be varied to suit the thickness of the fabric and the desired degree of stiffness. The garment should be dipped in the solution and hung on the line to dry completely. The stiffening usually lasts through 2 or 3 launderings. If any of the solution is left over, it can be kept for future use. Gelatin stiffening is especially desirable for dark cottons as it does not leave a gray or white deposit. Garments stiffened with gelatin look just like new and unused fabrics.

Gum arabic is often used for stiffening silk clothes.

Drying

Washed, white cotton garments should be hung in the sun to dry, as sunlight bleaches clothes, quickens drying, disinfects and freshens them. Coloured cotton fabrics and silks should be dried in a shady place. It is better to hang fabrics up to dry without wringing them. Instead, the moisture should be squeezed out with the hands and the clothes should be smoothed carefully on the line. This will lessen the amount of ironing needed.

Ironing

The equipment necessary for ironing is an iron, ironing table and iron stand or asbestos mat on which the hot iron may be placed. Different types of irons such as the flat, charcoal, electric and thermostatic, in which the heat can be regulated to suit the fabric, are available in the market.

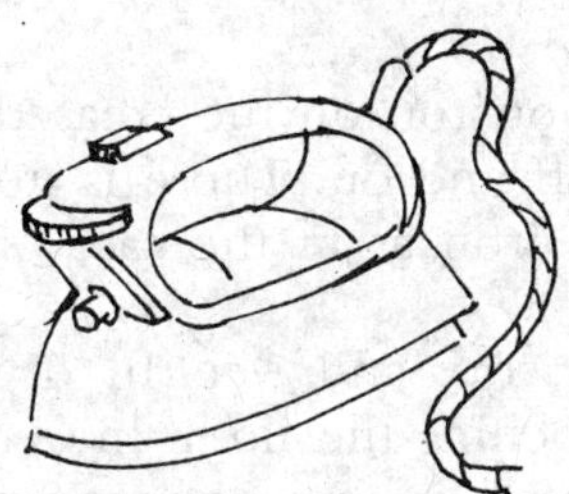

Fig. 45. Electric iron

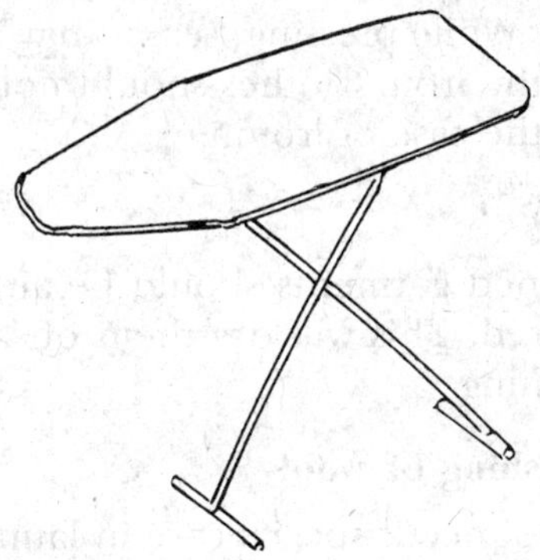

Fig. 46. Ironing board

Garments hung up to dry should be removed from the line while still damp, for ironing. If dry, they should be sprinkled with cold water to soften the texture before ironing. When sprinkling fabrics with water as a preparation for ironing, it makes the work easier if you fold the garments smoothly and carefully instead of bundling them up or crumpling them tightly. Silk should be ironed when evenly damp. Water should not be sprinkled on it as it leaves marks. Therefore, if the silk clothing is dry, it should be wrapped in a wet turkish towel to make it damp and then ironed with a moderately hot iron.

An ironing board is convenient. If a table is used, it should be covered with a blanket overlaid with a cotton sheet.

Before ironing, care should be taken to see that the iron is clean, and has the proper temperature. If too hot it may scorch the garment or even burn a hole in it. Cottons should be ironed with a hot iron and silks with a warm one.

Garments should be ironed on the right side for a glossy effect. Embroidery and lace should be ironed on the wrong side, placed on a soft pad, so that the pattern is not flattened out. Double or thick parts and seams should be ironed first on the wrong side and then on the right.

When ironing clothing like blouses, the sleeves should be ironed first, then the neck, front, and finally the back.

Pressing

Pressing is the process of placing a hot iron on the creased portion of a garment and lifting it off and on. There is no backward and forward motion of the iron as in the case of ironing.

There are two kinds of pressing: dry and wet. In dry pressing the iron is used without dampening the cloth. In wet pressing a damp piece of muslin is spread on the garment for pressing.

While pressing, seams may be opened with the pointed tip of the iron. Clothes should not be stretched while pressing as in the case of ironing.

Airing

Ironed garments should be aired thoroughly before they are stored. This will dry them off and remove the heat left from ironing.

Washing of wool

Wool needs special care in laundering because of its tendency to shrink or stretch. Woollen fibres have rough scales which are softened by moisture, heat and alkalis. These softened scales interlock when friction is applied and this results in shrinking. The texture of the fibre is affected by the use of alkalis. Hence in washing woollen garments, friction should not be used and excessive heat and alkalis should be avoided. If the water is hard, it could be softened by using a few drops of ammonia.

Preparation

The surface dust should be taken out. The outline of the garment should then be marked on a newspaper before commencing the washing.

Steeping

Wool loses its strength when wet. Hence woollen garments should not be steeped. Very dirty ones may be steeped for a few minutes in warm, soft water.

Washing

In laundering woollen articles, both the washing and the rinsing water should be prepared before the garments are made wet. The washing water should be lukewarm (95-100 degrees F), and the articles should be washed by kneading and squeezing only. Soiled parts can be attended to by patting extra soap solution over them until the dirt is removed.

Rinsing

The temperature of the rinsing water should be the same as that of the washing water. Sufficient quantities of rinsing water should be kept ready, as thorough rinsing is essential. If soap is left in the fabric, it will damage it and give out a bad smell.

A little citric acid may be added to the last rinsing water.

The water should be squeezed out by pressing the garment between the palms. A wringer may be used for heavy woollen articles.

Drying

After removing the moisture, the garment should be placed on the newspaper on which its outline had been marked, and pulled back to its original shape, using the outline as a guide. Woollen articles should not be dried in the sun since the texture of the fabric is affected by heat. Hence washed woollen clothes should be dried in a shady place where there is a good draught. Heavy and large articles could be hung for drying, but small and delicate articles should be dried on a flat surface.

Finishing

Woollens in general are finished by pressing while slightly damp. If dry, a damped muslin can be placed over them and pressed. A hot iron should not be used. Woven fabrics may be ironed lightly.

Airing

The articles should be thoroughly aired before storing.

Mending of clothes

"A stitch in time saves nine" is a very common proverb. The

ability to mend neatly is a means of saving, as the articles in use are made to last much longer than they otherwise would. Mending is the art of repairing any article, either clothes that are worn or house or bed linen, by means of patching or darning.

Patching

The two common types of patch are plain or print patch and flannel patch. To patch a hole in a garment, the following steps are carried:

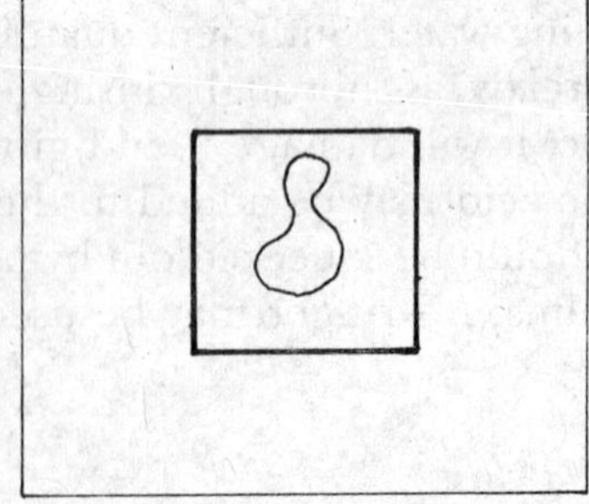

Fig. 47. Step 1—Mark a square around the hole

Step 1: Make the hole in the garment even by cutting a square form around the hole. (Fig. 47)

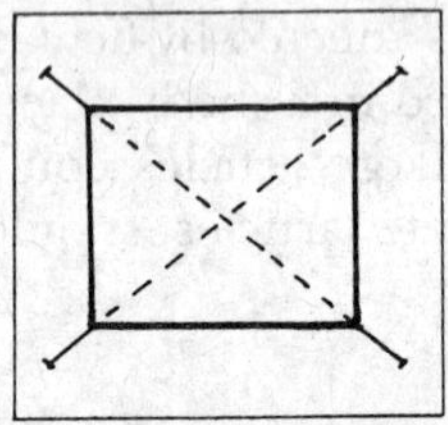

Fig. 48. Step 2—Cut along the diagonal creases ¼" (0.5 cm)

Step 2: Cut the corners of the squared hole diagonally upto one half of a centimeter. (Fig. 48)

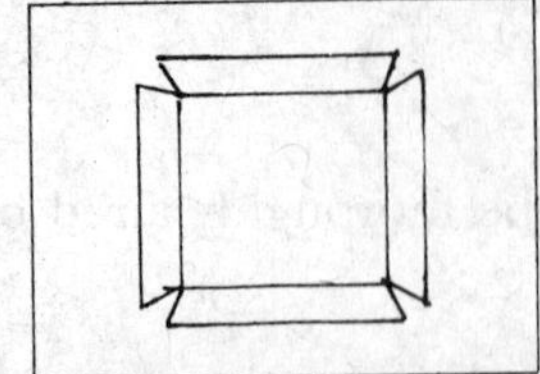

Fig. 49. Step—3 Fold back the flaps of the square

Step 3. Fold back the edges of the squared hole towards the wrong side along half a centimeter margin from the edges. (Fig. 49)

Step 4: Prepare a patch by cutting another square piece of cloth of the same material, of the same colour, the square patch being 2.5 cms more on all four sides. This is the patch to be placed on the garment with the hole to be mended with a patch.

Step 5: Fold half a centimeter along the edge of the patch.

Step 6: Place the prepared square patch over the evened square hole to be patched by matching the wrong side of the area to be patched in the garment with the right side of the patch.

Step 7: Fold the outer edges of the patch piece under and pin the patch carefully over the garment.

Step8: On the right side, hem the square hole of the patch neatly (Fig. 50).

Step 9: Complete the patching by hemming the patch to the garment by hemming the outer edge as pinned earlier in step 7 (Fig. 51).

Step 10: Press the patched area to make the folds and corners neat.

The same procedure is followed for plain patch and print patch. Special care should be taken for print patch in matching the printed design on the garment with the design on the patch. Use matching thread.

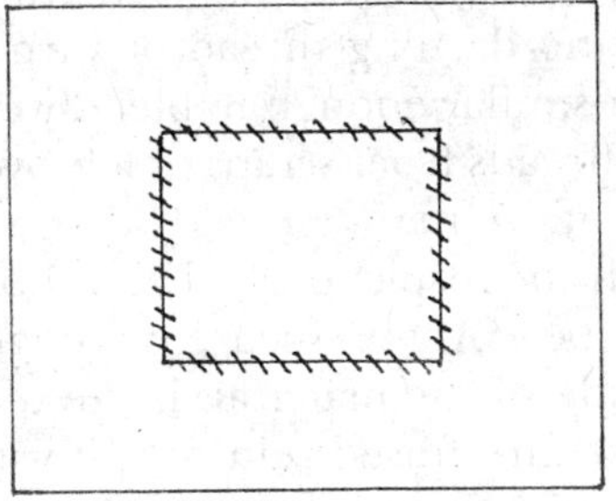

Top sew the square of the hole to the patch underneath

Fig. 50.

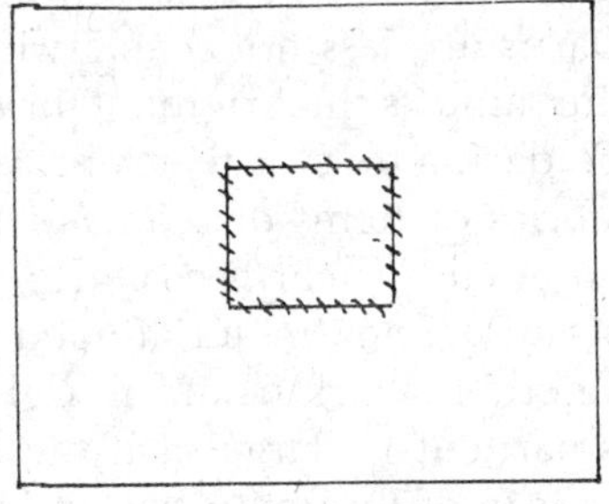

Complete the outer folder edge patch to the garment on the wrong side

Fig. 51.

Flannel patch

The shape of flannel patch may be either square, oblong or triangular. The patch should be 2.5 cm more all round than the area to be repaired. The edges of the patch are not folded.

The right side of the patch is placed on the wrong side of the garment. The centre of the patch should be placed over the centre of the hole. Carefully pin the garment and the patch together in position. Tack as close to the edge as possible. First use herring-bone stitch to attach the patch to the garment. Then the hole should be completed by stitching the same stitch (herring-bone). To make even herring-bone stitch do one row of tacking, after first tacking close to the edge of the patch about one centimetre. When working the corners of the patch and hole, care must be taken to work squares at the corners.

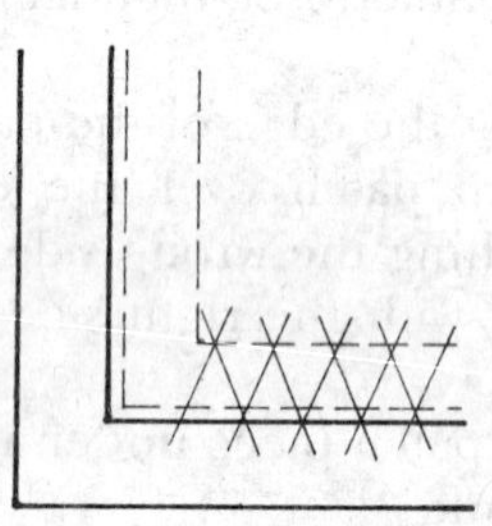

Fig. 52. Right side of patch on wrong side of garment fixed with herring bone stitch

Darning

It is a method by which new threads are supplied in the place of thin or worn-out woven ones. It is a form of hand weaving. Darns are less noticeable when the darning thread or yarn is the same as the original fabric or similar enough to blend well. To darn a hole or tear, unravel threads from scraps of left over fabrics or hems or seams of the garment.

A cut or tear is easier to darn inconspicuously than a hole because a new material need not be woven to secure two edges together. Work from the right side of the material. If the tear is particularly large or if the edges are frayed reinforce it with a piece of thin material underneath. There are three kinds of tears or cuts requiring slightly different darning procedures.

Straight tear

A straight tear is one form of cut in which either warp or filling threads are broken. Thread the needle with a matching thread or a strand of thread unravelled from hem or seam. Work from the right side by bringing the two cut ends closer. Do not knot the thread. Leave about 5 to 10 cms of thread-end free on the underside. Begin darning about 0.5 cm or 1 cm above and to the right side of the tear. Use small running stitches. After completing one row of running stitch take a turn for the next row of running stitches after leaving a small loop at the corner. Stitch back and forth at right angles to the tear and parallel to the threads of the fabric. When crossing a tear, make a stitch in one row of the tear and stitch in the next row going under it. Such alteration makes a firmer, harder darn. Stitches should extend about one centimetre beyond the tear, but the length of rows should be varied a bit to avoid a continuous clean cut edge of darning.

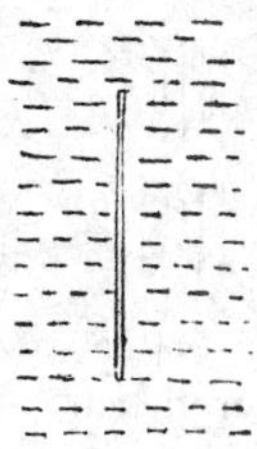

Darning a straight tear
Fig. 53.

Diagonal tear

In this the warp and filling threads are broken. Because the cut is on the bias of the fabric, it is likely to stretch or fray badly. For this reason it is advisable to stitch rows of running stitches along the length as well as width of the cloth. In this way the rows of stitches cross at the tear and strengthen the tear.

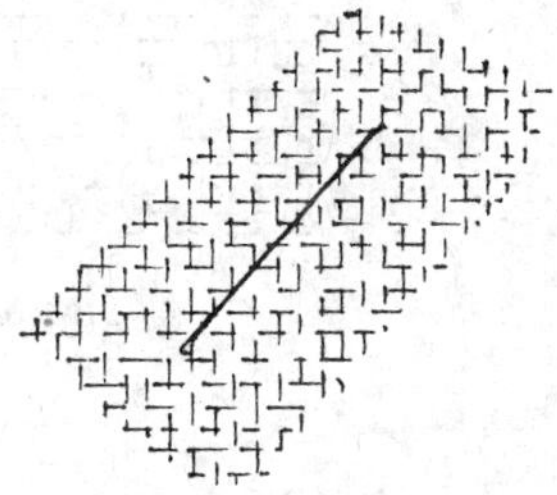

Darning a diagonal tear
Fig. 54.

Three-cornered tear

The three-cornered tear is the common right-angled tear. Darn each side as for straight tear allowing the darn to overlap at corners. Such crossing of threads adds strength to the corner.

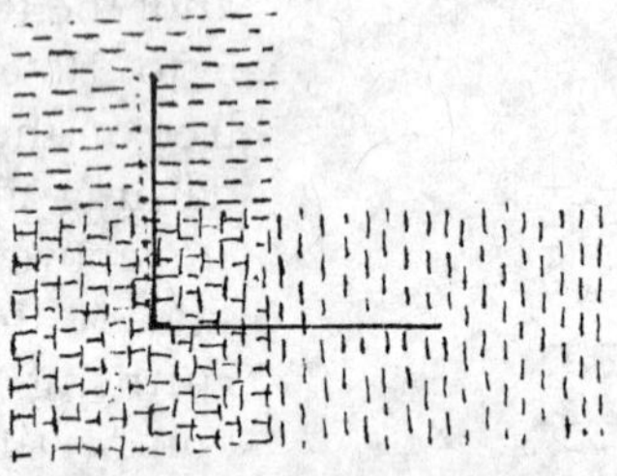

Fig. 55. Darning a three-cornered tear

Darning a hole

Before darning a hole, trim the uneven edges. Make the hole a neat shape. Keep the fabric flat. Without knotting the thread, stitch rows of small running stitches along both ways (that is along the length and width of the hole). By stitching in both directions the open area of the hole gets darned by the interlacing of the thread used for darning.

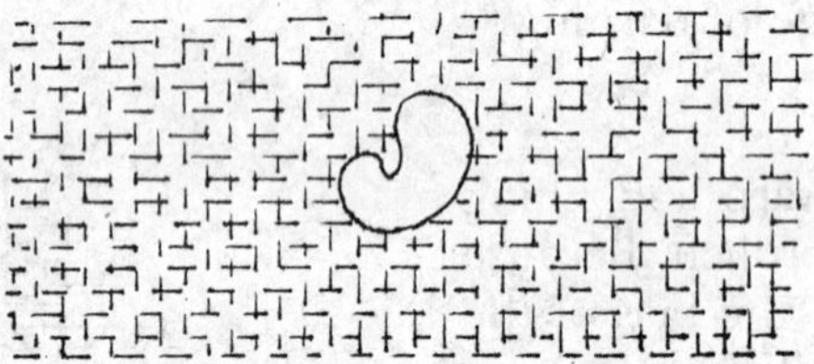

Fig. 56. Darning a hole

6. Common Household Pests

Man does not live alone. His habitation becomes the haunt of insects, birds and beasts. Some of these do him good, others, harm. The latter are the dreadful pests against which man has to guard, to live a healthy life. The common household pests are ants, bugs, mosquitoes, cockroaches, crickets, flies, silverfish, termites, fleas, ticks, lice, clothes moths, grain and furniture weevils, wasps, spiders, lizards, scorpions, mice, rats, bandicoots, reptiles such as toads and snakes, etc. These bring disease and sometimes death to human beings; hence they should be eradicated. Some of these pests are the direct cause of diseases; some others are the indirect agents that transport and deposit disease producing germs in man's habitations and food. Man wages a constant war against these foes.

The enemies of mankind can be divided into three categories, based on their harmful tendencies, as **blood suckers, polluters of food and destroyers of property.** The blood suckers are mosquitoes or gnats, sandflies, bed bugs, ratfleas, ticks and lice. Those that pollute and taint our food are flies, ants and cockroaches. Destroyers of property are those that destroy woollen goods like the clothes moths; those that devour artificial silk, starched clothes, paper and paste, like the silverfish; those that destroy wood, like the white ants and furniture weevil; and those that destroy foodgrains like the grain weevil.

General rules for preventing the breeding of pests

There are certain general rules to prevent insects from breeding in the house. One should keep the house and its surroundings clean and dry. Water should not be allowed to accumulate and stagnate in the vicinity of the house. If tanks and fountains are kept in the garden area of the courtyard, they should contain fish that will destroy the larvae of the insects; or the water should be sprayed with crude oil or kerosene. Broken vessels, unused tins, etc., should not be indiscriminately stacked in and around the house. Poultry runs, cowsheds, stables and out-houses should be kept clean and dry. All the cracks and holes in the walls, floors and ceilings should be plastered. The house should be systematically and frequently white-washed. Doors and windows should be well painted. Bedsteads and furniture should be inspected regularly. Dustbins should be kept closed with tight-fitting lids. Food should be kept properly covered. Strong-scented plants like tobacco, tulsi and neem should be grown around the house. Hygienic living is absolutely necessary. Children should not be allowed to ease themselves wherever they please, in and around the house. Insecticides like kerosene and sulphur gas, repellants such as incense, camphor, naphthalene balls, smoke of neem or tobacco leaves; etc., may be used to keep away or destroy household pests.

Mosquitoes

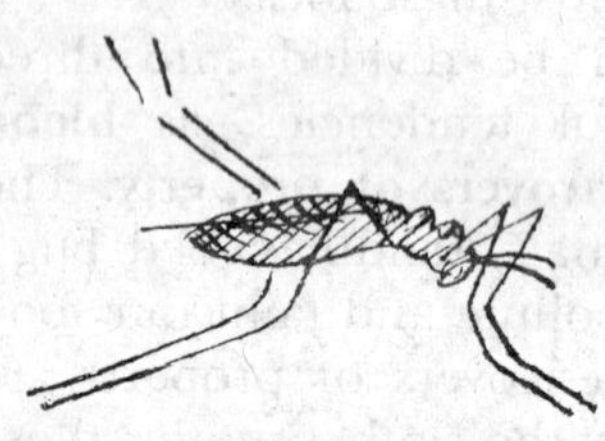
Fig. 57. Anopheles

Mosquitoes are household pests that harm us by sucking our blood and injecting disease germs. There are three different types which are harmful to man: the **anopheles** which spread **malaria**; the **culex** which is the carrier of **filaria**; and the **aedes** or **stegomyia** which are the vectors of **dengue** and **yellow fever.**

Life History

The female mosquitoes lay 100 to 400 eggs at a time on water. Within a period of 1 to 3 days the larvae emerge from the eggs. They swim about in the water and feed voraciously. After 7 or 14 days they attain the **pupa** or **nymph** stage. The head gets enlarged. The pupa resembles a "comma". Within 24 to 48 hours the pupa

Fig. 58. Culex

becomes straightened out and lies flat on the surface of the water. The pupa case bursts and the **imago** or adult mosquito emerges.

Only female mosquitoes are blood suckers. The male lives on vegetable juices, etc. The anopheles attack people at night, while the aedes bite even during day.

Control of mosquitoes

Mosquitoes can be controlled from spreading diseases by personal protection against adult mosquitoes, eliminating their breeding places, destroying larvae and killing the adults.

Personal protection

One should sleep under mosquito curtains. Rooms should be well-ventilated since the mosquito cannot propel itself against strong currents of air. Incense and other repellants like neem leaves, tobacco leaves, camphor, etc., may be burnt in the house at night to keep them away. The exposed parts of the body should be rubbed with repellants like eucalyptus oil, oil of citronella or turpentine mixed with olive oil. The repellants should be non-toxic and they may also be applied to the clothing. Insecticides, kerosene emulsion, petrol or patent mixtures available in the market may be sprayed in cupboards, book shelves and dark places regularly. Rooms may be sprayed with insecticides at night.

Elimination of breeding places

Water should not be allowed to accumulate and stagnate near the house. Wells and tanks in the vicinity of the house should be kept properly covered. Broken pots, old tins, etc., should not be kept inside the house or allowed to lie around it. Drains should be properly covered and free flow of water should be ensured. Kerosene should be sprayed on the surface of stagnant water around the house.

Destruction of larvae

Mosquito larvae can be destroyed by spraying kerosene on the water where they have been hatched; by dusting Paris Green (a poison) or by the application of emulsified larvaecide. In wells and tanks, fishes which feed on the larvae should be reared.

Destruction of adult mosquitoes

To destroy adult mosquitoes, the best method is to trap them inside rooms by closing all windows and outlets and fumigate the room. In recent years it has been found by scientists that some species of mosquitoes have developed immunity to many of the insecticides sold in the market. However, the use of insecticides in the form of residual sprays, surface sprays or direct sprays are helpful in their elimination in most cases.

Bed bugs

Bed bugs belong to the category of household pests which are blood suckers. They are man's constant companions. They migrate from house to house or are imported from trains and buses and public places where people congregate, like hotels and cinemas and ill-kept offices. These are flat, oval creatures that exist wholly on human blood. They can live in a quiescent stage for several months together if they do not get a blood donor. They live in cracks and crevices of walls, floors, bedsteads and other furniture, and in boxes and books. They are said to transmit several diseases including kala-azar, but it is a theoretical conjecture and not a proven scientific fact as in the case of mosquitoes.

Fig. 59. Bed bug

Control measures

It is difficult to keep bugs away because they manage to sneak into the house by hook or by crook. All cracks and crevices on ceilings, walls and floors should be plastered and covered. All possible lurking spaces like bedsteads, furniture and boxes should be wiped with kerosene, kerosene emulsion and creosote. Cracks, crevices and holes in which they live should be sprayed or squirted with gasoline, benzine or kerosene containing pyrethrum. Cots and other furniture, quilts, rugs, pillows, mattresses, mats, etc., should be sunned and aired properly. Fumigation with hydrocyanic acid, sulphur dioxide, or ethylene oxide mixed with carbon dioxide is useful. In the destruction of both the eggs and the adults, boiling water is very effective.

Fleas

There are many varieties of fleas, such as dog flea, rat flea, cat flea, etc. They live on different kinds of animals before they come to live on human bodies. Fleas are parasites. They attack man in the absence of their normal hosts. The deadly bubonic plague is passed from rat to man by the rat-flea when its host, the rat, dies. Disease germs are not only carried by fleas but also multiply in them.

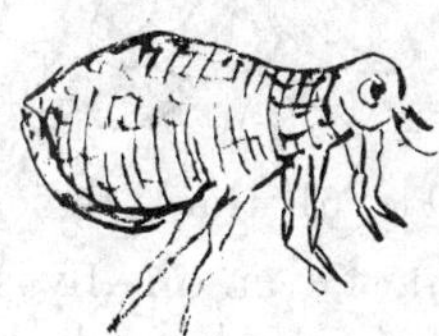

Fig. 60. Rat flea

When an infected flea jumps on to a person, bites him and drinks his blood, the disease is transmitted to him. Fleas can jump to a height of 9 inches. Unlike mosquitoes, where only the female lives on blood, both the male and the female flea suck blood.

The female flea lays eggs on the fur coat of animals. These eggs fall to the ground and hatch into larvae. The larvae feed on refuse and live in cracks and crevices on the floor. They pass through the pupa stage before they become adult fleas.

Control measures

Cleanliness of a house and its surroundings is an absolute necessity. The cracks and crevices on the floor must be filled up. If a room is infested with fleas, it should be sprayed with insecticides. To get rid of living fleas from our pets such as dogs, the animal should be washed with a solution of kerosene emulsion or some patent medicine. Since direct sunlight kills fleas, infected pets, linen and bedding should be exposed to the hot sun. Measures taken for the extermination of rats will prevent the spread of bubonic plague.

Flies

Of the household pests which pollute our food, the most dangerous are house flies. They are carriers of diseases. They transmit disease germs through their vomit or faeces. Germs cling to their legs and are deposited wherever they sit.

The female fly lays eggs on decaying refuse of all sorts and excreta of human beings and animals, especially horse dung.

A female house fly lays about 100 to 500 eggs at a time.

Fig. 61. House fly

The eggs hatch into larvae called maggots within 8 to 24 hours. They attain the pupa or chrysalis stage in 2 to 5 days. The adult fly emerges from the pupa within seven days.

Since during the hot season and the monsoon a single fly can give rise to millions of flies, the extermination of even one fly is of utmost importance for the personal health of the householder.

Control measures

The house and its surroundings should be kept clean and tidy. Garbage bins should be kept tightly covered. Children should not be allowed to defecate around the house. Stables and cowsheds should be kept clean. Manure should be kept covered with a layer of sand. All food-stuffs should be kept completely covered.

For destroying adult flies, fly papers, fly traps, and D.D.T. may be used. Fly papers are available in two forms — ribbons and flat sheets. Fly papers can also be made easily at home, by heating together two pounds of resin and one pint of castor oil, until the mixture resembles molasses and then smearing this on the paper while hot with an ordinary paint brush. Flies can also be killed when present in small numbers, by a fly swat.

During the season, when the flies swarm in number, the room should be sprayed with a disinfectant.

The eggs can be destroyed with kerosene, borax or chloride of lime (bleaching powder).

If flies abound despite all precautions, wire netting over windows and doors, especially of the storeroom, kitchen and dining-room, is absolutely necessary.

Cockroaches

While flies pollute food-stuffs by day, cockroaches are the nocturnal pests which sally out of their haunts at night to taint our food-stuffs.

Cockroaches are of several sizes and varieties. Their favourite haunts are the kitchen, the pantry and the dining-room.

Fig. 62. Cockroach

They eat and damage the leather bindings of books, scraps of particles of food of all kinds and the leather of shoes and boxes.

The female carries the eggs in a sac which can be seen protruding from the anal region. The sac containing the eggs is deposited in murky places. The young are hatched within a few weeks.

Control measures

The places where cockroaches congregate give out a foetid odour. Thorough cleaning should be carried out to remove the unpleasant smell. The house must be fumigated to destroy cockroaches. Food particles must not be left scattered around. Dining tables should be wiped spotlessly clean. Scattering some repellent like borax, pyrethrum or sulphur in bookshelves will prevent their attacking the books. Spraying their haunts with patent insecticide helps to eliminate them.

Clothes moths

The clothes moth belongs to the category of household pests which cause damage to our property. It particularly destroys woollen clothes, furs, rugs, blankets and upholstery. The moth itself is harmless. It is the larva of the moth that causes destruction.

The moth lays its eggs on woollen clothes or other garments. They hatch within a week. Soon after they are hatched the larvae or caterpillars start feeding on the material on which the eggs are laid. They drill holes in clothes and thus destroy them.

Fig. 63. Clothes moth

Control measures

To keep clothes free from the attacks of the clothes moth, they should be brushed well and shaken before storing. Dirty clothing should be laundered and not allowed to remain unwashed for long. Before storing furs and woollen garments, they should be carefully wrapped in newspapers, because the smell of the printing ink is repulsive to the clothes moth. It is better to keep them in airtight tin-lined boxes. Cupboards, chests of drawers and almirahs should be sprayed with some patent insecticide like D.D.T. The use of moth balls is a great aid in preventing the moths from attacking clothes.

Silverfish

Fig. 64. Silverfish

These little pests derive their name "silverfish" from their silvery appearance and smooth gliding motion. They cause serious damage to books, papers, photographs and paintings. They are fond of glue and starch. Starched clothes and artificial silk are also attacked by them. They are a menace to our libraries.

Control measures

Books should be taken out fairly frequently and dusted clean. Garments which are to be stored should not be starched. Book racks, cupboards and chests should be frequently dusted and fresh pyrethrum powder or D.D.T. applied. The best method of preserving pictures and photographs is to have them constantly cleaned. Photographs framed with glass in front should be tin-lined at the back. This will prevent the entry of silverfish.

Weevils

In a household, one may find both grain and furniture weevils. They resemble beetles.

Grain weevils

This household pest can breed only in grain. There are many varieties that attack cereals like rice, pulses like red gram, dal, and flour. The rice weevil has a rostrum or snout about 2/3 the length of the thorax. It breeds in any cereal.

The female bores a hole in the grain, lays its eggs and then seals the hole with a gelatinous substance. On an average, it lays 5 eggs a day. A single female may lay 200 or more eggs. The larvae are hatched within the grain and pupate inside it.

They tunnel through the endosperm and destroy the grain. They develop fast when the grain is moist. From egg to adult stage, the grain weevil takes about a month.

Control measures

Grain should be kept as dry as possible. Cleanliness also is of utmost importance. The containers should not have any holes. Old and new stocks should not be mixed together. Before refilling a container, it should be thoroughly cleaned and sunned. It is also advisable to spread the grain out in the hot sun at intervals. Grain should be kept in a cool dry place in airtight tins or jars. It should not be kept unused for too long in containers that are not properly sealed. However, the measures taken to destroy these pests might affect the foodstuff also; hence, great care must be taken about the mode of destruction so as to prevent the foodstuff from getting poisoned. The remedy should not prove worse than the disease.

Furniture weevil

As the name indicates, these weevils live on wood. They destroy wooden furniture, by boring holes into them and nesting inside.

Control measures

Furniture should be inspected regularly. Holes or cracks should be properly examined for weevils. The weevils should be killed with a thin long sharp article, like a knitting needle. If possible an insecticide should be sprayed or squirted into the holes. The holes should then be sealed with melted paraffin.

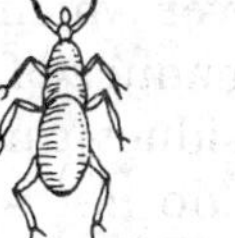

Fig. 65. Grain Weevil, Wood weevil

White ants

Of all household pests, the most destructive are **white ants** or **termites.**

There is no end to the damage done by them to wood and wooden articles. Wholesale destruction of pandals, wooden shacks, wooden beams of houses, door frames, doors and windows are wrought by these pests. At times, they tunnel their way right from the ground through the wooden supports, making their way right up to the ceiling and destroying it. White ants prefer dark, secluded, damp places where their nefarious activities are least likely to be discovered or interrupted. Termites build mounds of earth or galleries and live in colonies like ants and bees.

Fig. 66. White ant

Control measures

Wooden posts erected on the earth should have a cement foundation. If they are planted directly in the ground, the sunk end should have a thick coating of tar. As soon as termite colonies are detected, the mounds or galleries should be knocked down and the white ants destroyed. Boiling water or kerosene emulsion may be used for exterminating them. Patent white ant destroyers are available in the market for liquidating them.

General

Practising good house keeping and spraying insecticides on surfaces over which the insects are likely to crawl will be an effective manner of getting rid of insects. However, unless the poison residues can and will be removed by washing and or stripping, do not use any spray or dust solution or bait that contains such poisonous materials as DDT. DDT is poisonous to higher animals and man. Therefore its usage as an insecticide is very limited and is not recommended.

The major household insecticides used are propoxur and allethrin.

Propoxur (Baygon)

It is a carbonate insecticide having contact and stomach poison with quick down effect and long residual action. It is effective against flies, mosquitoes, cockroaches and other household pests. It is available as 1% oil based spray for household purposes.

Allethrin is a pyrethroid insecticide used in mosquito coils and mats. It is available at 0.04% concentration in mosquito mats.

Insecticide sprays, aerosol

Aerosol containers deliver a fine spray which does not moisten surfaces as coarse sprays do; aerosol sprays do not give lasting protection.

Always read and follow the directions on the container. You may buy these insecticides in ready to use pressurised containers that deliver a coarse spray or you may buy a liquid sprayer that delivers a continuous coarse spray. When the spray dries, it leaves a deposit (thin layer of insecticide) which kills insects that crawl over it.

Napthalene balls are used in closets in which the articles (clothes) are stored. When this chemical evaporates, it produces a vapour that is in sufficient concentration, kills the moths in the closet.

An area frequented by cockroaches can be painted with a mixture of lime, water and a small quantity of salt, and the insects will be gone in a short time. Chrysanthenaum flowers are rich in pyrethrum that is deadly poison to roaches. Save the blooms, and let them dry. Shred them slightly and scatter them in storage places and in other favourite haunts of roaches. This will help in getting rid of cockroaches.

A little cinnamon spice in the corners of drawers, cupboards or other areas will discourage silverfish. Pyrethrum powder, obtainable where insecticides are sold, are an effective remedy for most household pests.

Pesticides and insecticides used improperly can be injurious to man, animals and plants. Always follow the directions and heed all precautions on the labels.

Store pesticides/insecticides in original containers out of the reach of children and pets and away from foodstuff. Apply pesticides selectively and carefully. Avoid prolonged inhalation of a pesticide spray or dust. After handling a pesticide, do not eat or drink until you have washed, keep children and pets away from sprayed surface that have not dried. Apply all chemicals as sparingly as is consistent with efffective control.

Dispose of empty pesticide containers by wrapping them in several layers of newspaper and then place them in your trash can.

Part II
Income and Expenditure

7. The Meaning of Income and Expenditure

Income

In every household income and expenditure play an integral part in the life of the family.

The more the income the better the standard of living and amenities. The income may be what is earned by way of salary or wages by one or more members of the family. It may also be supplemented by inherited landed property, rent from houses, interest from invested money or profits from business.

Further there may be additions to the real income in a family, not in the form of cash, but of free amenities, resulting in saving of expenditure. For instance, the family may live in free quarters, enjoy free medical care or get free education for their children. The size of the family is also a factor to be taken into consideration in determining the real income. A person drawing Rs. 100 per month who has one child is better off than a person drawing Rs. 200 but with three or more children.

Whatever the income, the efficient management of money is a requisite for a happy, successful and peaceful family life.

Expenditure

The normal items of expenditure for a family are food, clothing, lighting, schooling of children, and the like. Happy is the family that can live within its means. No family will have enough money and savings unless it follows frugal ways of spending. One must cut one's coat according to one's cloth. If one does not manage personal finances properly, one cannot be free of financial troubles. Though expenses will be high if the family is large, cutting out unnecessary expenditure will enable the householder to manage within his income. A point to reckon with in balancing income and expenditure at any time is the cost of living. In pre-war years, the cost of foodstuffs and other articles was much lower than in these days. A family with an income of Rs. 100 per month twenty years ago was probably better off than one drawing Rs. 500 per month today. Times have changed and the prices of articles have increased considerably owing to scarcity and inflation. Families, therefore, have to incur expenses beyond their means because of circumstances over which they have no control.

Though there are variations in expenditure in different families, the following factors affect one's spending.

Actual money income of the family derived from all sources; size of the family, including not only the father, mother and children, but other dependents, such as grandparents, in-laws, etc.

Age and sex of the children. The fewer the children the less the expenses. As children grow up, more money has to be spent on their education, clothing, food, etc., till they can earn for themselves.

The profession of the father is another determinant of expenditure. A doctor, for instance, may have to spend quite a lot for setting up a clinic, equipping it properly and maintaining it.

The skill of the person who runs the home is another factor controlling expenditure.

The normal standard of living of the family affects it too. The town or village in which the family lives has also to be considered. A family living in a city like Madras will have to spend more than one living in a rural area.

The locale of the house also affects expenditure. A house situated in a busy part of the town will normally entail more expense than one situated on the outskirts.

Social and religious customs of the family also contribute to the spending.

Personal choice, preferring one expenditure to another is to be taken into consideration also. One person may have a liking for expensive perfumes and jewellery while another may have simpler tastes.

Spending may also be affected by the measures taken in the family to make provision for the future.

Since so many considerations influence one's spending, a householder, especially one belonging to the middle or low income group has to be continually on his guard to make both ends meet.

Household budget

The household is a miniature business centre catering to the various needs of the inmates. It may be a business enterprise under a sole proprietor or run under joint partnership of two persons; or it may be managed by a number of partners. In some houses the father alone manages the business of running it; in others the father and mother have joint responsibility and in some others the father, mother and other earning members of the family all have a finger in the pie. However, it is not correct to call housekeeping "a business" in the strict sense of the word, since it is not a profit-making body like a commercial enterprise.

Importance of a planned budget

The human body receives food, expends it on warmth, energy and movement, and stores the excess in the form of fat. Similarly in a household, salaries and other income are spent on the three main necessities of food, shelter and clothing; and a portion is put by for a rainy day.

Budgeting helps a household to spend money carefully, since "a paisa wisely spent is a paisa saved". It is an intelligent guide to spending. It balances the future and the present wants, making suitable allocations for spending and saving. It helps a person to save with ease, prevents frivolous or extravagant spending and falling into unnecessary debts and keeps one free from financial worries and anxieties. A household budget is a carefully prepared spending plan and guide based on the actual family income. Budgeting helps in the better distribution of funds for more satisfactory living. It enables a family, "to live within its income" or "to make life what the family would like it to be"; hence its importance.

Steps in household budgeting

The household budget varies according to the size and needs of the family, as well as its social and economic standing. Therefore, no two budgets can be similar. However, there are three stages in household budgeting which are common in all cases. These are:

1. the proposed expenditure based on the anticipated income;

2. an accurate record of all expenses incurred and incomes derived; and

3. checking or reviewing the expenses from time to time to see how favourably they compare with the original budget drawn up.

While preparing a budget, one should have a clear idea and full knowledge of one's present needs and their relative importance. This will enable the householder to eliminate such of the expenses as can be safely omitted without present or future loss.

The household budget should normally be drawn up to cover a whole year. This will, as far as possible, eliminate the effect of unforeseen expenses which do not occur every month. A budget should always be a balanced one, namely the income and expenditure should tally.

Chief budget items

The components of a budget are determined wholly by the needs of the family. It is customary to classify expenditure under a variety of budget headings. This helps to divide a lengthy list of different kinds of apparently unrelated items into workable units. It can then be further split into smaller items so that no important item is overlooked. The following are some of the essential heads to be borne in mind while formulating a budget.

Housing or shelter
Food
Clothing
Operational or housekeeping expenses
Education
Sundries and other personal expenses
Savings

These major items are further divisible into many more minor items. This will enable the householder to consider the relative merits of the various items, and make it easier for him to determine the correct proportion of expenditure to be devoted to each head and to each item within each head. Thus the family will be prepared for all probable demands on its income.

Housing or shelter

This budget head includes charges on a rented house, such as the actual rent paid, and the repair charges paid by the tenant, if any. In the case of houses, obtained on "hire purchase system", from co-operative housing societies, it will include payments on principal, interest charges, taxes, special assessments and repairs.

This does not include sums paid towards the purchase of the house or site, lighting, fans, telephone, cleaning charges, etc.

Food

The expenses incurred in the actual purchase of groceries, meat, fruit and vegetables, eggs, milk and other articles of food are included under this head.

The cost of cooking equipment, fuel, wages for the cook, if any, and the like are not included.

Clothing

As in the case of food, in clothing only such of the items as are bought from a shop or dealer are included. These may be garments, shoes, hats and other accessories, for the husband, wife and the children, and also furnishing fabrics and tailoring expenses.

This does not include cleaning and washing expenses.

Housekeeping expenses

All the miscellaneous expenses for running the house such as electricity, telephone, water, fuel, washing, servants' wages, as well as other expenses incurred in connection with housekeeping activities are included under this head.

Education

In former years, in India, education was given a minor place in budgeting and included under sundries. Education since Independence plays an important role in resurgent India. The Government is taking bold steps to make the country literate. Therefore, it is right on our part to allot a prominent place to education in budgeting and treat it as a major item of expense.

Under this head are included all expenses incurred in connection with schooling, such as tuition and other fees, as well as cost of books, note-books and other school equipment.

Sundries or personal expenses

All other items of expenditure in a household which are not included under shelter, food, clothing and education, find a place under this miscellaneous head of accounts.

Family expenses of a cultural nature for the recreation of the members of the family, in dances, dramas, films, *kalakshepams,* music recitals and the like, doctor's fees, cost of medicines, club fees, church subscriptions or donations to temples, transportation charges, personal expenses of the individual like cigarettes, sweets, toilet articles, etc., are included here.

Savings

Savings are a means of providing for future wants. They consist of money put aside for future spending. Saving is an essential item in budgeting.

Engel's Law

A German statistician named Ernest Engel made a statistical analysis of budget facts by research. The principles enunciated by him through his study of family budget are known as Engel's Laws of Consumption. They are: "As income increases, the proportion of income spent on food decreases, though the actual amount of money spent on food increases.

The proportion spent on sundries, cultural wants, recreation, education, health, etc., increases, as income increases.

The proportion spent on shelter, clothing, lighting and fuel remains practically unchanged whatever the income may be".

Formulation of family budgets for different income groups

A satisfactory budget assures at least a minimum standard of living in terms of adequate food, shelter, clothing and other necessities. The adequacy of food is tested by meeting calories and proteins and other nutrients recommended by the Indian Council of Medical Research and of housing in terms of the space specified by the National Building Organisation (NBO) and of clothing by the family practices that is the model value of the amounts of clothing bought at various income levels and of other items included in the budget by the model value of the items concerned.

Specimen budget

Engel's Laws can be seen to operate by studying the following table of budgets of various income groups. This budget relates to a family of four consisting of father, mother and two children aged 12 and 17 and living in the city of Madras. For the sake of comparison, the income levels have been fixed at Rs. 1500, Rs. 3000 and Rs. 9000 per mensem.

Specimen Budget

Items of expenditure	*Low Income Group Rs 1500*		*Middle Income Group Rs 3000*		*High Income Group Rs 9000*	
	Percentage spent	*Actual amount spent* Rs	*% spent*	*Actual amount spent* Rs.	*% spent*	*Actual amount spent* Rs.
1. Food	50%	750	40%	1200	30%	2700
2. Shelter	15%	225	15%	450	15%	1350
3. Clothing	10%	150	10%	300	10%	900
4. House-keeping	5%	75	5%	150	5%	450
5. Education	5%	75	10%	300	15%	1350
6. Sundries	8%	120	10%	300	12%	1080
7. Savings	7%	105	10%	300	13%	1170

Remarks: As income increases, the proportion (%) spent on food decreases; whereas the proportion spent on shelter, clothing and housekeeping remains the same. As income increases, the proportion (%) spent on education, sundries and savings increases.

Thrift and savings

Saving is made possible in a household by taking a long term view of things. Even in the insect and animal world, saving is effected. Foodstuffs are stored for future wants. Similarly, human beings ought to put some money by as a provision against future needs.

Today's income may be sufficient for today's needs. But the future may bring increased need or decreased income or both. Savings enable one to face the future bravely, because one is armed to keep the wolf from the door.

The financial emergencies for which the householder should make adequate provisions by saving are:

Fall in income through accident, sickness, old age, death, unemployment, reduced wages, etc.

Increased expenditure caused by illness, loss by fire, robbery, inflation.

The need to invest money at an opportune moment, in the acquisition of a house or land.

Investment in some business that pays dividend or interest which adds to one's income.

Acquisition of consumer durables, such as a music system, refrigerator, or car.

Pleasure trips or sight-seeing tours embarked upon during a vacation.

Gain of power and prestige for oneself and one's family.

Provision for one's family to guarantee security of life and property.

Furthermore, the individual savings of a family have a bearing on the working capital of the society at large and increase the nation's productive power.

Every individual and family of average efficiency should save something regularly from their income. A householder should be economical and thrifty. She should realize that her prudence and forethought are in themselves assets amounting to additional income. She should try to get the best value for all the money she spends. Her aim ought to be to secure the greatest amount of goods with the minimum of labour and expenditure. Above all she should not be pennywise and pound foolish.

Being stingy or niggardly is not the same as being thrifty or economical. It is not necessary for a householder to be in affluent circumstances in order to save. Though the rich are better able to save than the poor, it does not logically follow that the poor cannot save at all. Even the poor can save according to the measure of their income, provided they are frugal.

A householder should cultivate the habit of saving. Indeed, she should be imbued with a passion to save. In most cases, the desire to save is motivated by a desire to safeguard oneself against the future. It also depends largely upon the ties of affection that bind the family. Often in Indian families this is a major factor. Though one may have the means to save, no saving can be effected if there is no will to do so.

Methods of saving

Savings can be in many forms, simple and complex. They can be effected by putting money in banks, or post office savings bank, by joining co-operative societies, investing in chit funds, nidhis, insurance, shares in joint stock companies, etc. With a view to helping the common man formulate the habit of saving, the Government of India has been introducing, from time to time, schemes such as National Savings Certificates, prize bonds and the like. Annuities, cumulative deposits, contributory pension, provident funds, stocks and bonds, hire purchase to buy houses, cars, etc., on a monthly instalment basis, are further incentives to saving.

One can save haphazardly by putting aside any surplus money that is left over after incurring all the essential expenditure or one can save systematically by drawing up a short or long term scheme or plan of saving. Systematic and consistent saving is better than haphazard efforts.

Institutions of saving banks perform many financial functions. A bank gives commercial, personal, mortgage and other types of loans. It receives deposits for savings, current and fixed deposit accounts. It also performs other duties such as renting safe-deposit boxes, issuing letters of credit and travellers cheques and the like.

A householder interested in a systematic savings plan can have recourse to savings, current or fixed deposit schemes in a bank.

Savings account

Banks promote thrift by receiving small deposits. The minimum balance to be maintained can be as low as Rs. 2 in some banks. Banks also have ceilings for the maximum amount that can be received by way of deposits in a savings account. A pass book is given to the saving depositor. All transactions such as deposits, withdrawals, credits of interest declared on the deposits, are promptly recorded in the pass book. Deposits may be made at any time, but interest is calculated for a minimum period of three to six months. Withdrawals are limited to one or two a week, and often, restrictions are placed on the maximum amount that can be withdrawn at a time.

Withdrawals can be made by presenting the pass book and the necessary requisition slips for the amount to be withdrawn. Withdrawals by cheques are allowed by most banks.

Current account

In a current account, the minimum balance to be maintained is higher. Withdrawals are by cheque and any number of withdrawals can be made. The rate of interest on deposits is lower than that in the savings account.

Fixed deposit account

In the case of a fixed deposit account the bank receives the money on deposit from the client for a fixed period. In return, it pays interest on condition that the money is not withdrawn before the expiry of the period. The rate of interest is higher than that on current accounts or savings accounts.

Post office savings bank

The post office savings bank has greatly helped working class people to save money. An account can be opened with as small an amount as Rs. 2. The maximum amount that depositor can have in the savings bank account at any time is Rs.15,000.

Withdrawals are allowed only once a week and the amounts to be withdrawn are also limited, but deposits can be made any number of times. The reason for this restriction is that the post office savings bank system wants to encourage saving but discourage spending.

Co-operative societies

Co-operative societies are organizations owned by the members who invest their money by buying shares in the societies. The investors are known as shareholders. The societies help to eliminate "middlemen" who exploit the consumers by coming between the producer and them, buying from the former and selling to the latter at a profit that is often out of proportion to the cost of the goods.

In co-operative societies, as the consumers are also the owners and are selling to themselves, they buy at the proper price and sell at the proper price. Whatever profit is made is divided among the shareholders.

Chit funds

Chit funds are very old methods of saving and raising money. They encourage people to save according to their capacity. They provide a ready means of getting a lump sum which can be utilized for some special purpose, while payments are in instalments. Chit funds have to be registered with the government when they call for public participation. There are different varieties known as the "lottery chit", the "auction chit" and so on.

Lottery chit

Some individual or other gets together a number of acquaintances or friends, who undertake to make periodic payments of specific sums for a specific period, say Rs. 10 per month for a period of 12 or 24 months. The promoter or the organizer usually gets the first month's total collection. During each succeeding month the names of persons contributing are written on pieces of paper and one is picked out. Thus the person to whom the chit fund is to be paid is decided by lottery every month.

Auction chit

In an auction chit fund the monthly collection is put up for auction among the members. The one who bids the lowest amount, in other words, offers the highest discount, is paid the fund after getting from him the necessary security to ensure his future monthly payments. Next month the successful bidder of the previous month drops out of the auction, although he continues to contribute. Thus each member gets the amount once and at each auction the discount or the amount saved is divided up among all the subscribing members. The last member gets the full amount. The discount on each bid depends on the urgency of each member's needs and the degree of competition.

Nidhis

Nidhis were originally temporary societies of members who contributed monthly a certain amount which was then available as loans to members. The origin of the Nidhi scheme dates back to about 1850 when a fund for officials in Madras was created to save them from the money-lenders who charged very high rates of interest. The Madras officials decided to start a fund of their own which would offer needy persons with fixed incomes an opportunity to borrow at reasonable rates.

Nidhis now have to be registered under the Indian Companies Act. The objectives of Nidhis are:

to afford facilities for saving;
to give relief to members from the burden of old debts;
to grant loans for special purposes.

Loans are given to outsiders also on sufficient security, but preference is given to members, and loans are given at reasonable rates.

Small Savings Schemes

The small savings scheme in operation are of significant relevance, especially for salaried class and other fixed income group investors.

The small savings schemes of the Government of India are broadly classified into the following groups.

1) Indira Vikas Patra

Investments made in this doubles in 5½ years. Simple interest works out to 19.18% per annum. There is no limit on investments. They are available in denominations of Rs 200, Rs 500, Rs 1000, Rs 5000 and Rs 10,000 and can be purchased at half the face value.

2) Kisan Vikas Patra

Investments made under this scheme double in 5½ years for the Kisan Vikas Patra purchased on or after 24th April '92. The interest works out to 18.18%. It is available in denominations of Rs 100, Rs 500, Rs 1000, Rs 5000 and Rs 10,000.

3) National Savings Scheme

This is a tax benefit scheme. The interest payable is 11% per annum on the lowest balance at credit between the close of the 10th day and at the end of each financial year. A minimum amount of Rs 100 and multiples of hundred can be contributed.

4) National Savings Certificate (VIII Issues)

The scheme provides double benefit. It provides interest and also saves tax on income. It carries interest at the rate of 12%, compounded half yearly. It is issued in denominations of Rs 100, Rs 500, Rs 1000, Rs 5000 and Rs 10,000.

5) Public Provident Fund

The current rate of interest is 12% per annum and the minimum subscription in a financial year is Rs 100 and maximum is Rs 60,000. It saves tax and hence is a tax benefit scheme.

Insurance is saving collectively instead of individually. It involves the setting aside of sums of money in order to provide compensation against loss resulting from particular contingencies. The contingency is expected to affect only a certain proportion of the number of the insured and the participants of the scheme are able, therefore, by paying a comparatively small sum into the fund, to guarantee themselves against heavy financial loss, e.g., from fire, loss of cargo at sea, death of the bread-winner, etc. Insurance organizations furnish protection against sickness, fire, etc. Business enterprises would be very limited in scope if they were not safeguarded against loss by insurance. Insurance can be classified as life insurance, casualty insurance, life annuities and so on.

Life insurance

Life insurance is a contract between an individual called the insured and the insurance company, whereby the former makes a money payment each year or at stated intervals to the latter in return for which the latter agrees to pay a certain amount after a specific period or at the death of the former, if it occurs earlier, to a third party named in the contract and known as the beneficiary. Life insurance is a provision so designed that a man shall in his life time make as adequate a financial provision as he can for his family in case of his death. The contract is called the policy, the periodical payment is called the premium and is payable monthly, quarterly, half-yearly or annually.

Most life insurance companies carry various types of policies such as limited payment life policy, endowment policy, etc. As we all know, the life insurance business has been nationalized in India and the Life Insurance Corporation now deals with all life insurance.

In limited payment life policy, the payments are for 10, 15, 20, or 30 years as may be agreed upon. The rates of premium in this type of policy vary with the age of the person insured, the sum insured, and the number of years the policy is to run. In life policy, the proceeds are payable on the death of the insured.

Endowment policies provide for definite contingencies like marriage, education, building a house, etc. For example, the educational policy is an endowment policy which matures when the child is ready to enter college. The money is available then from the insurance company to defray the student's college expenses.

Casualty insurance

The most common types of casualty insurance carried by families are fire, health and accident insurance, automobile insurance, and so on. Very wealthy families may even go in for burglary insurance.

The fire insurance policy covers losses resulting from fire. Health insurance provides protection against disability. An automobile insurance policy provides for the protection of the car against damage. Burglary insurance provides protection against loss by burglary.

Life annuities

The annuity can be bought either for oneself or for someone else. Premiums are paid for a given number of years and when the policy matures, the company commences paying the person or his assignee a stipulated amount per month or year for a stipulated period or for life. It works exactly like a pension. Thus it guarantees the continuance of an adequate income even after the retirement of the annuitant from employment.

Investment is the placing of money, more or less permanently, in some form of property in order to secure an income. It assumes that the principal will be safe and later recoverable when desired and that in the meantime, interest, dividends or rentals will be received more or less regularly.

In investing money, certain factors are to be remembered.

1. Safety of the principal.

2. The income yield—whether it will be regular and certain.

3. Ease of sale.

4. Management and care required.

Money can be invested in bonds, stocks or shares or in buying land.

Bonds are purchased from corporate bodies or the government. The individual is the creditor and in return the institution pays a specified amount of interest on specified dates. Gilt-edged bonds are those of the highest grade. The organizations issuing these bonds have long records of payment of interest and principal and therefore the bonds are easily marketable. Low grade bonds are those issued by companies having poor financial records.

When an individual buys stocks or shares in a company he becomes part owner of the concern and thus gets dividends. An investor looking primarily to the safety of the principal will be attracted to bonds. On the other hand, a man looking for a high return on his investment will be interested in stocks and shares. The purchase of any security is a good investment if the price is low enough in relation to the expected returns and fits into the investment plan of the individual.

Part III
Personal Hygiene

8. Importance of Personal Cleanliness

What is personal hygiene? Personal hygiene is concerned with the maintenance of a person's own health, for which he alone is responsible. Cleanliness is the prerequisite for the healthy growth and normal development of any individual. For good health, cleanliness with regard to the food we eat, the air we breathe, the water we drink, and the clothes we wear, and cleanliness of the body, both internal and external, are all essential.

Care of the skin

Keeping the skin clean is absolutely essential in hot countries like India, where people sweat a lot, for the regulation of the body temperature. During perspiration the sweat glands give out sweat, which contains some inorganic salts and a little urea, besides the fatty acids which give it its characteristic odour. It is absolutely necessary that the waste matter of perspiration be eliminated, as has been proved by many experiments on animals, and by the classic case of the little boy who lost his life at the Coronation of Pope Leo X. The boy was gilded all over with gilt paint to represent an angel at one of the coronation ceremonies. The gilt paint blocked up all the sweat pores and the boy died within a few hours.

If the sweat glands are blocked up by dirt not only is their action interfered with but the dirty skin also becomes a perfect breeding place for skin diseases like eczema, itches and the like. If parts of the body are moist with perspiration, a tropical fungus will readily grow there. For personal cleanliness and healthy living, one should take proper care, especially of certain parts of the body, such as those behind the pinnae of the ears, the axillae, groin, etc.; if not, a nauseating odour will emanate.

Workmen in lime quarries, coal mines, cement factories

and flour mills are affected a great deal, if they do not take proper care of their skin.

Further, the skin should not be exposed to extremes of climate. Dry, hot weather tends to singe and burn it and produces ulcers and heat boils. One should also guard against prickly heat in hot climates by taking proper care of the skin. Unnecessary exposure to cold will result in frost bite, which can be avoided by suitable clothing and conserving of the skin.

Bathing is the simplest, easiest and most common method of keeping clean. It is not only the easiest way to personal cleanliness but also a beneficent tonic for the skin and internal organs. Sweat and dirt and the secretions of sebaceous glands are removed while bathing. Frequent washing of the parts of the body which sweat most and produce unpleasant odours is absolutely necessary.

The best cleansing agent is a warm bath, with the use of soap. Further, warm baths are stimulating and energizing on cold days. A warm bath after a vigorous game will have the effect of an efficient massage. At night one should invariably take a bath with warm water to avoid chills and catching cold.

However, fairly strong and healthy people may take cold water baths. This gives a feeling of pleasure. Cold water baths help to tone up the system, and even those accustomed to hot water baths should practise taking cold baths now and then.

The best time for taking a bath is the morning. One should not take a bath after a full meal, or when one is thoroughly exhausted. Personal towels should not be used by others. Sticking to this rule safeguards one from contagious skin diseases.

Steam-baths are resorted to in cold countries. Oil-baths are a speciality in India and soap, soapnut powder and turmeric are used for them. A daily bath, whether it is in a tub or under a shower, cold or warm, steam or oil, river or sea, ensures a life of cleanliness.

Care of mouth and teeth

In personal hygiene, care of the mouth and teeth is important. The mouth should be washed immediately after every meal. It is also advisable to gargle with warm water or salt water or a solution of potassium permanganate. The mouth should be specially cleaned carefully after eating strong-smelling food such as garlic, onion or fish. Breathing through the mouth is unhygienic. It should be avoided especially while sleeping. If it is unavoidable owing to some deformity or a cold tie a piece of gauze around the mouth while sleeping. If the mouth is not kept clean, sores and ulcers will result. Also one should not take extremely hot food, as it will hurt and harm the delicate membranes of the mouth and lips. Since the tongue will invariably be coated with residues of the food taken, it should be scraped and cleaned well while washing the mouth.

The teeth should be cleaned carefully and thoroughly at least twice a day, on getting up in the morning and before going to bed at night. "Cleaning with the twigs of a banyan or a neem tree will strengthen the teeth" is a common Tamil saying. Villagers clean their teeth in this way. In urban areas toothbrushes have replaced neem-twigs, though toothpastes containing neem are much in vogue. However, whether in rural parts or in urban areas, cleanliness of the teeth is of utmost importance to every one. Scrupulous cleanliness is the best of all preservatives for them. Lacking toothpaste or toothpowder, even common salt is excellent for cleaning them.

If the teeth are not cleaned well, food accumulates between the crevices and causes them to decay. The gums also are affected. Decaying teeth cause many maladies, including digestive disorders. Some people have the bad habits of constantly chewing pan, rubbing the teeth and gums with snuff, and chain-smoking. Their teeth get stained, dark, and nicotine-coated. Clean teeth are pearly white and ivory bright.

Children often suffer from caries owing to deficiency of vitamin D, or calcium, or phosphorus, or due to acid-forming bacteria. They should not be allowed to eat too many sweets. Toffees, chocolates, biscuits and other sweets should not be given to them especially just before they go to bed. They should also be trained early in life to clean their teeth properly and regularly. Thumb-sucking should be discouraged and prevented as it can lead to deformed or protruding teeth. Children should never be allowed to taste and swallow sweets or to eat things taken out of someone else's mouth and offered to them. A piece of fruit after a meal will help to clean the teeth.

Nearly 90% of the infections we suffer from are carried into the body and the blood stream through the mouth. Water, food and air are the main vehicles through which microbes enter the various systems of the human body. The utmost care should therefore be taken about what we eat and drink. Food which is exposed to flies and insects, should not be eaten, nor should sweets and other things carried by hawkers openly through the streets. Water should be boiled and filtered before drinking. If eaten raw, fruits and vegetables should first be washed clean. Over-ripe and rotten fruit should not be eaten just because it is cheap. It is better not to drink from the tumblers of others or eat from a plate used by someone else. Cleaning tumblers and plates with soap and hot water is a wise precaution for health.

Care of the nails

Nails should be cleaned properly and cut short, otherwise dirt will lodge under them, and may carry infection. Washing hands properly, especially the fingers and nails, before taking food is essential. Biting nails is not only a bad habit but a very unhygienic practice since in the process infectious microbes lodged under the nails are directly transferred to the mouth. Little children enjoy playing on the ground with earth and sand, soiling their hands. Parents should wash the children's hands with soap, paying particular attention to their nails, when they come home after play.

Care of the hair

The hair should be oiled, brushed and combed daily. Massaging it when taking a bath will strengthen its roots. Different kinds of oil should not be used as such indiscriminate use may cause the hair to decay and fall out. One should not use the brush, comb or hair clips of another person. If the hair is not oiled and combed carefully it may get tangled, matted and become a happy home for lice. Neglected hair causes dandruff. Washing the hair with soap or soapnut powder and shampooing it at least once a week is a healthy practice.

Clothing in relation to personal appearance

Primitive men and women dressed themselves in leaves, grass, barks of trees, feathers and skins of animals. Some aboriginal tribes in India and elsewhere still follow this practice. Today, through mechanical devices, we produce enormous quantities of cotton, satin, silk, velvet and woollen materials of attractive designs. Synthetic products such as plastic, nylon, rayon and the like are also available as dress materials. Well-tailored clothes add greatly to the personal appearance of men and women today. Clothes make the man.

Purposes of clothing

The principal purposes of clothing in this civilized world of ours are: protection against heat, cold and external injuries, maintenance of normal body temperature, decency, and personal decoration. Clothing is, to borrow Bacon's phrase, "for delight, for ornament and for ability." A well-dressed person has poise, looks smart and neatly groomed, and, psychologically speaking, can move in any society without a feeling of inferiority. Being well-dressed gives one a feeling of security, and at the same time enhances one's looks and personal charm. One should always be neatly and immaculately clad. That does not, however, mean that one should be foppish.

Selection of clothes

Three factors are important in the choice of clothes: beauty, usefulness and cost. Apart from the intrinsic beauty of the material one should also consider whether it goes well with the other garments worn. If the clothes worn go well together they will look more beautiful. Harmony enhances the beauty of the garments worn and makes the wearer more attractive. Harmony not only of material but also of colour is necessary for sartorial grace.

It is not right to wear a soft, expensive silk saree with a coarse cotton blouse. Large patterns and horizontal stripes and bands do not suit short figures. Soft, clinging material helps to give the impression of height and slenderness. Unless one is tall, well-proportioned and has a commanding personality, one should avoid all flashy and startling designs. Workaday clothes should be simple, neat and easily washable. Further, things worn should fit the occasion. For instance dress or lounge suits are stipulated for dances. Imagine a person dancing to the hot music of Rock-'n-Roll clad in a dhoti! Similarly, it would be incongruous for a lady to be wearing an expensive silk saree and doing her cooking in the kitchen! The time, place and occasion should be the guiding factors in the choice of what to wear.

Health and comfort are as important as aesthetic requirements in the choice of clothes. Self-consciousness should be shed if one is to be truly well-dressed. However, if one is improperly or inappropriately clad, one cannot easily ignore the feeling of discomfort. Clothing should not be disgracefully short nor so unusually long as to hang loose on the body or sweep the floor. A perfect fit gracefully accentuating the contours of the body, should be aimed at.

Tight-fitting clothes are not advisable, since they curtail circulation and respiration, affect the digestion and the action of the muscles, and are injurious to health. Clothes should allow freedom of movement for limbs and muscles to ensure that the internal organs carry out their work normally. The weight of the clothes should rest on the shoulders or be equally distributed over the body. Sarees should not be tied too tight around the waist. Actually loose clothes are warmer than tight ones. Clothes should not be heavier than is actually necessary for warmth.

Choice of clothing is guided by climatic conditions also. While cotton dresses suit the Indian summer, heavy woollen dresses are necessary to withstand the European winter. In obtaining material for clothing great attention should be paid to its wearing qualities, such as strength and durability, fastness of colour and washing properties. The dyes used should not have any irritating or poisonous effect on the body.

Care of clothing

Take care of your clothes and they will take care of your looks. Clothes give better service when well kept than when neglected. In order to keep up a good standard of personal appearance one should keep one's clothes in good condition. They should not be allowed to get too dirty. Dirty and soiled clothes are a veritable asylum for disease-producing germs. One should never let clothes get too dirty or let them remain unwashed for too long. As perspiration has a nasty odour and a deteriorating effect on fabrics, clothes should be carefully washed and put away. For reasons of health, clothing should be worn clean, changed as often as possible and washed frequently and systematically. The proverbial "stitch in time" is very necessary in the care of clothing, especially in the case of socks and vests or banians. A tear in a saree or a pair of trousers should be darned or patched before it has a tragic effect on the garment and a comic effect on the appearance. Frayed collars and sleeves should be mended soon. Torn clothes, worn sleeves and frayed collars are a blot on one's appearance. Missing buttons should be replaced quickly. Clothes should not be allowed to get stained. Ink-blots, coffee stains and betel-juice marks on clothing do not speak well of the wearer; hence they should be removed quickly. For the sake of personal appearance, clothing should be worn neatly pressed or ironed and not wrinkled, crushed and crumpled. Articles of clothing should be folded and put in the closet, or hung up on a clothes-hanger on the clothes-rack, to retain their shape. If garments are hung directly on a nail or hook, they not only lose shape but also run the risk of getting torn. One should wear clothes properly brushed so that their sheen is not dulled. In fact the more you care for them the better they will serve you.

Wearing wet clothes too long is dangerous for health. If you get drenched in the rain, you should change into dry clothes quickly to avoid catching a cold or getting pneumonia. If laundering is not done properly by the dhoby, one is liable to get the skin-disease known as dhoby's itch. If the dhoby does not steam dirty clothes properly, the germs from other people's garments may be transferred to one's own and produce infectious disease like ring worm. So if clothing is given to a dhoby or laundry for washing, instructions should be given that it must be properly boiled. Even perfectly clean clothes can pick up germs and harbour them, especially if one is in contact with a person suffering from some infectious or contagious disease. It is better to have a bath and change your clothes after visiting a person suffering from a contagious disease.

Day and night wear

For personal health and cleanliness it is a good practice to take off the clothes you have worn during the day and put something else for the night. Though to all appearances what has been worn during the day may look neat and clean, it cannot have escaped the effects of sweat and dust. So it is more hygienic to take it off and put something else on for the night. It is better to have special clothes for night wear. These should be of thin material and sufficiently loose. If tight, they will affect respiration and will be uncomfortable. For proper sleep and rest, loose and clean clothes should be worn at night.

Proper footwear

In the past, in China, a girl's feet were tied tightly to arrest their growth, since small feet were considered beautiful. Such beauty treatments are injurious to health. In India, chappals or slippers are generally worn. These give freedom of movement to the toes and the foot is well aired. Usually slippers do not distort the feet so much as shoes. Since shoes completely envelope the feet, less air gets to them and the soles and sides sweat, at times, profusely.

Shoes and sandals should conform to the normal outline of the feet and not squeeze or distort them. Shoes with pointed toes constrict and compress the toes and thereby deform the feet. Further, tight shoes produce corns on the toes and produce blisters round the heels.

Made-to-order shoes are better than ready-made ones. The proper measurement of the feet resting on the ground with all the toes in a normal, relaxed position should be taken for making shoes. Shoes should be neither too large nor too small. The sole should be flexible since, if it is tight, it will impede the muscular action of the foot while walking. The leather should be soft and pliable. Shoes with broad toes are better than those with narrow, pointed toes. Walking shoes should be comfortable, or they will cause an unseemly gait. They should also match the colour and material of the costume worn.

It is customary in India to remove one's shoes or chappals at the threshold of a house. Hygienically it is a good practice not to wear shoes or slippers inside the house. It is common among some Indians to spit in the streets for no reason. Urinating at the road-side and defecating on foot-paths have not ceased despite efforts by social workers, health propagandists, municipalities, corporations and the government to instill a civic sense into the citizens. Such being the case, shoes and slippers worn on the streets are bound to gather dirt and disease producing germs. So, it is better not to use shoes worn outside the house inside the home.

Care of shoes

Proper care of shoes is necessary. If the soles get worn out they should be resoled. The heels usually get worn down soon and should be repaired lest they deform the foot. Crooked heels do not speak well of the wearer. Shoes should be kept on shoe-trees to prevent their losing shape and developing unwanted creases when not in use. As an alternative, tissue paper can be stuffed in tightly. The shoes should be cleaned and left to air when taken off. Shoes should be cleaned and polished regularly and frequently. It is good for the leather and makes the shoes last longer as well as look better. White canvas shoes can be cleaned with paste or liquid cleaner. Suede shoes should be brushed with a stiff brush and dusted. It is bad for leather shoes to get wet, as water destroys the pliability of the leather and weakens the stitching of the shoes. When shoes have been exposed to rain, they should be taken off, wiped and put to dry as soon as one gets home. Rice or other cereals may be put in wet shoes as they will absorb all the moisture in them. It is a good idea to wear socks along with shoes as they lessen the likelihood of perspiration. Shoes should not be too tight or short, cramping the toes. On the other hand, they should not be too loose, leaving unfilled space at the toe. Socks should be washed and dried in the sun or they will give out a fetid smell and cause ulcers on the feet. Torn socks should be mended before they are worn again. Some people put talcum powder inside the socks and shoes before wearing them, to prevent bad odour, absorb perspiration and avoid fatigue of the feet.

Part IV
First Aid and Home Nursing

9. First Aid

What is first aid? Living as we do in an age of science, with space-ships circling the earth, rockets landing on the moon and the growth and development of industries at a remarkable speed, we are today, as never before, prone to accidents. Everywhere people are digging deeper, building higher and moving faster. Fainting inside a smoke-filled, ill-ventilated factory, getting a few fingers crushed out of shape by the toothed wheel of a machine, or being knocked out of one's senses with multiple injuries and broken bones, by a rashly driven car, are everyday occurrences of city life. The immediate help rendered to a person in case of injuries or sudden illness, before the arrival of the doctor, is known by the self-explanatory term "First Aid". First aid serves as a temporary measure to alleviate pain, prevent aggravation of injury, promote recovery, or save the life of an injured person.

Qualities of the first aider

The essential qualities to be developed in a first aider are fellow-feeling or sympathy, gentleness, tact, observation, perseverance, dexterity, resourcefulness, discrimination, explicitness and physical and mental alertness.

General emergency action

(a) Keep calm, reassure the casualty and keep away onlookers.
(b) Send for medical aid.
(c) Remove casualty from sources of further danger or injury.
(d) Try to stem any copious bleeding.
(e) If casualty is unconscious, loosen tight clothing and lay him down with head on one side to prevent him choking in his own saliva or vomit.
(f) Give other specific first aid treatment as appropriate.

(g) Make casualty as comfortable as possible and do not move him more than necessary.
(h) Keep him warm by means of blankets or other covering placed under as well as over him.
(i) Do not give liquids if internal injuries are likely, otherwise give sips of water or hot, sweet tea or coffee if asked for.
(j) Do not give alcoholic drinks.

Bites from animals

(a) Thoroughly wash affected part and apply a clean, dry dressing.
(b) Take casualty to doctor or hospital for anti-tetanus or anti-rabies injection.

Bites or stings from insects

(a) If sting is embedded in flesh, remove with tweezers or point of sterilized needle.
(b) Wash area of bite or sting with cold water or, if in mouth, give mouthwash of bicarbonate of soda and call for medical aid.
(c) Do not scratch or rub the spot as it may aggravate the infection.
(d) If swelling and redness begin to spread, seek skilled medical attention.

Bleeding from cuts and wounds

(a) If bleeding is serious lay casualty flat and, if a limb is affected, raise it as high as possible to reduce blood flow. (This is not desirable if the limb is also fractured).
(b) Gently expose the wound, causing as little movement as possible.
(c) Compress the bleeding point with a clean pad and a tight bandage and if necessary, press the dressing on the wound with thumbs. Do not apply more pressure than is necessary to stop the bleeding.
(d) If serious bleeding in a limb persists, apply tourniquet above the point of injury, by use of a pad under the tightened bandage. Loosen tourniquet every 15-20 minutes, otherwise gangrene may set in.

(e) In some cases it may be advisable to stop the blood flow by pressing an artery with the thumbs against an underlying bone.
(f) Keep casualty warm.

Internal bleeding

(a) May be concealed within the body, coughed or vomited through mouth, or passed with urine or excreta.
(b) Summon urgent medical aid.
(c) Keep casualty warm and as comfortable as possible.
(d) Do not give any food or drink.

Convulsions and fits

(a) Place casualty in area where he is not likely to injure himself when thrashing about.
(b) Put pencil, spoon handle or similar article between teeth to prevent biting of the tongue.
(c) Gently restrain any violent movements which might cause injury.
(d) Loosen any tight clothing and raise chin to stretch the neck and help breathing.
(e) After recovery keep him quiet and calm until a doctor arrives and do not leave him alone until it is apparent that any mental confusion has cleared.

Dislocation

(a) Support the injured part in the most comfortable position and prevent all unnecessary movement until medical aid is obtained.
(b) Do not attempt to replace the dislocated part.
(c) Otherwise treat as you would, fractures.

Fainting attacks

(a) Lay person flat on back with head on one side to prevent choking in own saliva or vomit.
(b) Loosen any tight clothing.
(c) Splashing cold water on face sometimes helps recovery.
(d) Keep rested until fainting has disappeared.
(e) If fainting persists, obtain medical aid.

Heart attack

(a) Loosen collar and tight clothing and give plenty of fresh air.
(b) Keep him calm and resting until medical aid arrives.
(c) Do not give alcoholic drinks or other stimulants.
(d) If breathing stops give artificial respiration by mouth-to-mouth breathing method.

Types of wounds

A man shaving his face with a razor blade, a person cutting vegetables with a knife, a person walking barefoot on the street and treading on a bit of broken glass, or one handling a sharp instrument carelessly are all liable to get wounded. A wound is cut in the skin which becomes an outlet for blood and a gateway to disease-producing microbes.

An injury caused by a sharp instrument, like a razor blade, wherein the blood vessels are cleanly cut and bleed freely is known as an "Incised Wound".

"Lacerated Wounds" are such as have torn and irregular margins. These may be caused by the toothed wheel of a machine or the clawing of an animal. The bleeding is either delayed or less but the wound is liable to get septic quickly.

A person stabbed by a knife or pierced by a sharp-pointed instrument sustains a deep-seated wound of which the mouth is small, although the injury is deep and may affect the internal organs. This is called a "Punctured Wound."

"Contused Wounds" are caused by a heavy weight crushing a limb, or a direct blow by some blunt instrument. The tissue ligaments, muscle fibres and cartilages get torn and bones may also be broken.

Treatment of wounds

In the treatment of wounds much depends on the physical condition of the patient and the nature of the injury; nevertheless there are some general rules.

It is advisable to get the patient to lie down, as he bleeds less in this position.

It is advisable to raise the bleeding part above the level of the heart to arrest the free flow of blood, unless there is a fracture.

The wound should be properly exposed, after removal of soiled or dirty clothing and cleaned of dirt or any other foreign matter.

As a blood clot acts as a natural agent for preventing further loss of blood, if one has formed, it should not be tampered with.

Application of direct pressure over the wound with the thumb, or over a pad, if available, may stop the bleeding. Pressure should be applied to the sides if a foreign body is embedded in the wound, or if there is a piece of broken bone inside the injured part.

An open wound is liable to get infected; hence application of an antiseptic is a wise precaution to take.

The wound should be dressed and padded and tightly bandaged, if there is no projecting bone or foreign body in it.

When there is a foreign body or protruding bone, pads should be fastened around the wound but not so as to press on the protrusion, and the wound then dressed and bandaged.

Bleeding nose

In the case of a bleeding nose, the patient should be seated in a draught of air, in front of a door or open window, with the head tilted back and the arms raised above the head.

He should be asked to breathe through the mouth.

Any tight clothing around the neck and chest should be loosened.

An ice-pack or cold compress should be applied over the nose and on the spine at the level of the collar. The feet should be placed in hot water.

The injured person should be warned not to blow his nose.

Bleeding from the ear

In most cases, bleeding from the ear indicates a fracture of the base of the skull.

In such cases though the natural temptation will be to plug the ear with cotton-wool or dressing, it should not be done. Instead, the patient's head should be inclined towards the injured side, and a dry dressing applied over the ear lobe and bandaged lightly.

Shock

A man, who is run over by a lorry, with a limb severed and suffering great pain, one who has an artery cut by a stab-wound and has excessive bleeding, a person who is informed of the sudden death of one very dear, a person walking on a forest path and confronted by a tiger, a person suffering from a griping belly ache due to acute appendicitis, or a careless workman treading on a live electric wire, may suffer shock. From the examples cited, it will be observed that factors such as excruciating pain, profuse bleeding, emotional upset, fear, medical emergencies, and electricity produce shock. Shock is a condition of prostration of the body and cessation of normal faculties resulting from sudden exhaustion of vital energy. It is a state of circulatory collapse, nervous tension, and at times unconsciousness.

Depending on the cause, shocks are classified as nervous, haemorrhagic, toxic and electric. They may come on singly or one form may lead to another and thus produce a combination of forms. Further the degree of shock may be aggravated by the age, constitution, mental make-up and emotional maturity of the patient: Shocks also vary in appreciable degree according to the circumstances, or the type and severity of the factors which induce or cause them. Shock can be a killer. It is a common cause of death when the patient is not killed outright in an accident.

Nervous shock

This sets in fast and produces just giddiness or complete unconsciousness. A sudden fall in blood pressure leading to draining of blood from the brain is a characteristic feature of nervous shock. Pallor, cold and clammy skin, feeble pulse, irregular breathing, dilation of pupils, general debility owing to loss of muscle tone are signs and symptoms of nervous shock. Properly treated, the patient will recover quickly.

Haemorrhagic shock

This is usually preceded or accompanied by nervous shock

and most of the symptoms are similar. The patient will have a desire to consume large quantities of water but suffers from nausea if fluids are administered to quench the intense thirst.

Toxic shock

Serious injuries such as crushing, compound fracture of large bones or of the spine and severe burns produce toxic shock especially when infection supervenes in the injuries. "This type of shock is due to the production of toxins which is a poisonous substance formed due to infection or putrefaction of body tissues because of serious injuries and which gains entrance to the blood stream, or to the loss of fluid from the blood into the tissues.

Generally, profuse sweating, especially on the forehead, air hunger, feeble pulse at first but rapid later, dilated pupils, pale, cold, clammy skin and a faint feeling are common symptoms in nervous, haemorrhagic and toxic shocks.

Electric shock

Prompt and intelligent action is called for in cases of electric shock, as delay may prove fatal. If the patient is still in contact with the live conductor, before attempting to free him the current must be switched off. In case this is not possible, the rescue worker must stand on a dry, thick wooden board, or rubber mat and pull the patient away. Better still, use a dry wooden pole to push the patient away. In cases of electric shock the patient usually becomes unconscious and struggles for breath as respiration is partially or even wholly suspended. If breathing has stopped, artificial respiration should be resorted to. After restoration of normal breathing, treatment for any burns sustained by the patient may be given.

Treatment of shock

Shock is dangerous as it takes a large toll of lives. It is a wrong notion that its treatment should commence only after the local injury has been attended to fully. Immediate steps should be taken to counteract it.

The patient should be removed from crowds or from a stuffy atmosphere. Excepting in the case of severe injury to the spine, he should be made to lie on his back. The head and shoulders should be kept low. The legs should be kept raised unless they are injured. Tight clothing should be loosened and wet clothing, if any, removed. The patient must be allowed fresh air. The patient's face should be sprinkled with cold and hot water alternately. Any visible bleeding should be arrested and injuries treated. If the pulse is weak, the palms and soles of the patient should be rubbed vigorously. Artificial respiration should be given if breathing is faint or has stopped. The patient should be kept warm, wrapped in thick blankets. Hot-water bottles should be applied over the covering. Excepting in cases of severe bleeding or injury to an internal organ, hot strong coffee or tea with plenty of sugar or a little dose of brandy if available, should be given, to stimulate the patient.

Apart from this attention to the physical condition of the patient, a psychological approach should also be made. Soothing and reassuring words should be spoken to the patient, encouraging him to think lightly of his injuries, and no undue fuss should be made over his physical malady. No one should be allowed to discuss his condition within his hearing. The patient should be shielded from any emotional excitement or worry.

Artificial respiration

In cases of drowning, suffocation, strangling, gas-poisoning, or shock, there is a deficiency of oxygen supply to the body. Want of oxygen prevents the lungs from performing their work of oxygenating the blood, and thus leads to a dangerous condition called asphyxia. It is characterized by partial or entire cessation of breathing which may lead to loss of consciousness and often, death. Asphyxiation calls for prompt attention if the life is to be saved. It should not be presumed that the patient is dead if there are no apparent signs of breathing. Immediate steps should be taken to ensure proper breathing. When natural breathing is failing or is not discernible artificial means of making the lungs work properly are attempted. This artificial respiration is absolutely necessary in most cases of asphyxiation.

There are three kinds of artificial respiration, named after their inventors, Schafer, Silvester and Holger Neilson.

Schafer's method

In Schafer's method, the first aider lays the patient in a prone position with arms extended above the head, and the head turned to one side to keep his nose and mouth away from the ground. He faces the patient's head and, kneeling on both knees near the hip joint of the patient, sits back on his heels. He places his hands on the loins of the patient, on each side of the backbone, with wrists almost touching, thumbs forward and fingers close together. Keeping his elbows straight, he swings slowly forward allowing the weight of his body to be communicated to the patient's loins. The pressure makes the abdominal organs push the diaphragm which forces out the air from the lungs causing expiration. Then the first aider slowly swings back on his heels relaxing the pressure. This causes the abdominal organs to fall back, and the diaphragm to come down, causing inspiration. The first aider alternates these movements by a rhythmic swaying forward and backward twelve times a minute at the ratio of two seconds pressure and three seconds relaxation. He continues to give artificial respiration till the patient regains breathing or a doctor examines him and pronounces life extinct. In cases where natural breathing commences, the first aider synchronizes his movements with the patient's natural breathing. Then he applies friction to the limbs to promote circulation. He revives the patient if he is unconscious and gives him stimulants if he is able to swallow.

Silvester's method

The patient is laid on his back with shoulders supported on a cushion so that the head hangs backwards. The first aider kneels at the head of the patient and grasps the patient's forearms firmly below the elbow. He then draws the patient's arms upwards, outwards and towards himself with a sweeping movement, pressing his elbows towards the ground. This causes the chest cavity to expand and air is drawn into the lungs, i.e., inspiration takes place. Then the first aider seizes the patient's flexed arms slowly along the same route and presses them firmly against the front and ribs of his chest. This drives the air out of the lungs and causes expiration. These movements must be carried out rhythmically at the rate of 12 per minute. It is advisable to have an assistant hold the tongue of the patient firmly with a handkerchief during the rescue operation.

Holger Neilson's method

In Holger Neilson's method the first aider places the patient on his stomach. The forehead of the patient is made to rest on his hands. The first aider sits at the head end, and presses his hands on the back of the patient. To effect inspiration the first aider grasps the patient's upper arms near the elbows and pulls them towards the head to expand the chest cavity.

'Rescue breathing'

Though the methods mentioned above are recognized ones which have been systematized, there is the age-old method of artificial respiration in which the first aider puts his mouth to the mouth of the patient. He blows air into the patient's lungs as though he were blowing a balloon, and makes the patient's lungs work.

Time should not be unnecessarily wasted by feeling the patient's pulse, going for help, moving him or looking for equipment as every second is vital.

The patient should be placed on his back. His head should be tilted backwards from the neck as far as possible so that, from above, the first aider looks straight into the patient's nostrils. With the head in this position, the air-passage to the lungs is wide open.

The first aider should open his mouth wide and seal it round the patient's mouth. At the same time, the patient's nostrils should be blocked by the first aider's cheek.

The first aider should then blow a strong breath of air into the patient, remove his mouth and let the patient to breath out. This procedure should be followed at the rate of 10 per minute. Between breaths, fluids if any, should be drained from the patient's mouth. The blowing of air into the patient's mouth should be continued till the patient starts breathing by himself.

If the first aider breathes about twice as deeply as usual, the exhaled air will contain more than enough oxygen for an adult victim.

In Switzerland "rescue-breathing" has replaced other methods of artificial respiration in all the major life-saving organizations.

Sunstroke

Long exposure to the hot sun without proper protection causes sunstroke. The patient becomes unconscious. His face becomes livid and his skin hot and dry. His pulse becomes full and pounding and the temperature of his body is raised. Sunstroke can be fatal. It is common in many hot countries, including India.

Treatment

The patient should at once be removed to a cool, shady place where there is free circulation of air. Tight clothing should be loosened and he should be stripped to the waist. He must be fanned vigorously. An ice bag should be applied to his head and spine till the body temperature comes to normal (98.4°F). His body should be sponged with cold water. The patient may be given Epsom salts in a tumbler of cold water when he regains consciousness. Then he should be placed under medical care.

Poisons

Any substance, whether solid, liquid or gas which, when taken into the body in sufficient quantity is capable of destroying life, is known as a poison. Poisoning may be accidental or intentional. Poisoning may be through the skin by injection, through the lungs by inhalation, or through the mouth by swallowing.

Injected poisons

Poison can be injected into the body by a hypodermic syringe; by the bites of venomous snakes like the cobra or by rabid animals; or by the stings of insects like the centipede and the scorpion. Life is endangered by coma and asphyxia.

Treatment for bite of a poisonous snake

If the bite is on a limb, a tight constriction between the bitten part and the heart as near to the trunk as possible should be applied to delay the poison entering into the circulation of the blood. The constriction should be relaxed for a period of one minute once in twenty minutes and re-tightened. After washing the wound well, the bitten part should be kept below the level of the heart and bled by a few incisions with a clean knife. The wound should be washed with potassium permanganate. The patient should be kept calm and warm and given stimulants. Artificial respiration should be given if the patient's breathing fails. Medical aid should immediately be arranged for.

Gas poisoning

Inhaling smoke or poisonous fumes of fires or stoves causes gas poisoning. Life is endangered by asphyxia. Unless severely poisoned, the patient may appear deceptively well. Unconsciousness with difficult breathing can be noticed in the cases of severe gas poisoning.

Swallowed poisons

Swallowed poisons include carbolic acid, lysol, iodine, corrosives (strong acids and alkalis); excessive amounts of alcohol such as beer and wine; pain-relieving or sleep-inducing tablets taken in large quantities; decomposing food and seeds or fruits of plants such as those of datura or nerium. Particularly severe symptoms are caused by corrosives which burn the lips, mouth, gullet, and stomach and cause intense pain. Potassium cyanide and strychnine produce convulsions. The patient is in a state of profound collapse. Irritants such as food poisons cause severe pain in the stomach, nausea and vomiting. Opium and bromide poisoning induce a tendency to fall asleep, developing further into stupor and coma. The pupils of the eye become minutely contracted to a pinpoint.

General rules for treatment

If the patient is unconscious and breathing has stopped, artificial respiration should be given. A doctor should be sent for with particulars of the suspected poison and obvious symptoms such as burnt lips and mouth. If the patient is not unconscious and his lips and mouth are not burnt, he should be induced to vomit by putting a finger inside the patient's mouth, or by giving emetics such as two teaspoonfuls of common salt in a tumbler of water. If the lips and mouth are burnt, thereby revealing that the poison is a strong acid or alkali, an antidote should be given to soothe the instant effects of the poison.

Antidotes

Half a litre milk is the simplest antidote generally used. Raw white of egg beaten up with sugar is also a good antidote. If this is not available, even warm water can be used as an antidote.

If the nature of the poison taken is known, special antidotes may be administered, if available.

Special antidotes

Given below is a table of antidotes that can be used to neutralise the poisons mentioned against them.

Poisons		Antidotes
Corrosive acids such as sulphuric acid, hydrochloric acid or nitric acid.	...	Two tablespoonsful of magnesia powder in a pint of water. If magnesia powder is not available, powdered chalk may be substituted or a pint of soapy water used.
Corrosive alkalis	...	Two tablespoonsful of vinegar or lemon juice in half a litre of water.
Carbolic acid (Phenol)	...	Two tablespoonsful of epsom salts in half a litre of water.
Tincture of iodine	...	Half a litre of thin starch paste.

In the case of corrosive poisons, after the antidote has been given, olive oil, butter, barley water or gruel should be given to relieve the pain.

In cases of irritant poisons, after the emetic, or the

substance given to induce vomiting, has acted, give a dose of castor oil.

In the case of hypnotic poisons, such as opium or bromide, after the emetic has been given, keep the patient awake by making him walk about, and sprinkling cold water on his face, neck and chest. Strong black coffee may also be given.

Metallic poisons

The metals which are liable to cause poisoning are lead, brass, arsenic and copper.

Lead

The symptoms of acute lead poisoning are usually those of acute gastroenteritis. Chronic poisoning is manifested chiefly by anaemia, constipation, abdominal pain, paralysis, especially of the extensor muscles of the forearm, arterio-sclerosis, convulsions or delirium. Usually lead poisoning is contracted through dyes used in colouring foodstuff. The action of salt and tamarind on lead also produces poisonous matter.

Brass

Brass poisoning is contracted through the inhalation of the fumes of this metal in brass foundries.

Arsenic

Arsenic poisoning may be due to over-drugging with arsenic. It may be acute or chronic. The symptoms are violent purging and vomiting. The treatment is to administer freshly prepared dialysed iron or peroxide of iron or magnesia and then give an emetic followed by soothing drinks like milk, gruel, etc.

Copper

Copper poisoning is rare. Copper itself is harmless but sulphite of copper (blue vitriol) and acetate of copper (verdigris) are poisons. Vessels made of copper and brass are generally given a coating of tin on the inside (tinning) in order to prevent the production of that green poisonous substance (verdigris). Copper vessels should never be used for cooking purposes unless they are properly tinned.

Treatment

Milk or white of an egg can be given as an antidote, followed by washing out the stomach.

Prevention of poisoning

"Prevention is better than cure" is a well-known maxim. The truth of it may be borne in mind particularly with reference to poisoning. The following preventive measures are valuable to protect children. Bottles containing medicines should be properly labelled. Those containing poisonous substances must be clearly marked, preferably with the word "Poison" written boldly in red on the labels. It is better still to keep poisons isolated and locked up, far out of reach of children. Medicines should not be taken in the dark as one cannot see the label on the bottle.

Fractures

Fracture is the term used to indicate that a bone is broken or cracked. Fractures may be caused by **direct force**, as for instance from a severe blow; **indirect force**, as for example when a bone breaks at some distance from the spot where the force is applied, or by **muscular contraction**, as in the case of fractures to the knee-cap caused by a sudden violent contraction of the muscles attached to it.

Types of fracture

There are three main types of fracture. They are the simple or closed, the compound or open, and the complicated.
Simple or closed fracture is one in which the bone is broken and there is no wound leading to it.
Compound or open fracture, in contrast to the simple or closed fracture, is one where a wound bleeds down to the broken bone. In some cases the broken bones or the fractured ends protrude through the skin.
In the **complicated fracture**, as the very term indicates, in addition to the broken bone, there is either an injury to some important internal organ or dislocation of a joint.These main types apart, there are some other varieties of fractures.
In the **comminuted fracture** the bone is broken into several bits. In the **impacted fracture** the broken ends of the bone

are driven into one another. Children's bones are pliable and cartilageous and not hard and calcified like the bones of adults. Therefore, they bend and crack, or get partially broken without breaking right across. Such fractures are known as **greenstick fractures**. **Depressed fractures** occur in the upper part of sides of the skull. The broken part of the bone is driven inwards.

Falls, blows and accidents are the chief causes of fractures. Most falls can be prevented by better lighting of door-steps and staircases. One should walk with care on slippery and wet floors, especially in bathrooms, and rooms which have waxed and polished floors; similarly on moss-covered ground. It can be disastrous to leave fruit-peels, especially banana skins, on the floor or ground. Even wet cowdung or damp clay soil may cause a fall if carelessly trodden on.

General signs and symptoms of a fracture

The following signs and symptoms indicate fracture:

The injured person complains of pain at or near the place of fracture.

There will be swelling around the seat of fracture.

The affected part will be tender and the patient will have discomfort when gentle pressure is applied there.

There will be loss of power of the fractured limb.

The fractured limb will be deformed.

The injured person will feel uncomfortable on moving the limb, and there will be unnatural mobility at the seat of fracture.

One can at times see a pronounced irregularity of the fractured bone.

In moving the affected limb one may even hear the crepitus grating or rough crackling of the fractured bone.

By enquiring how the accident happened one can get some helpful clues for the diagnosis of a fracture.

Fracture of a bone is usually followed by shock.

Treatment of fractures

Of the elementary rules to be observed in the treatment of fractures, the first and foremost is that the fractured limb should be steadied and supported.

It should be kept in as natural a position as possible.

With the use of splints, or using the patient's body for support, the fractured bone should be bandaged and immobilized. If splints are used they should be padded.

Bandages should be firm and neither too tight nor too loose.

When body splinting is adopted adequate padding should be used to secure comfort and maintain immobilization.

Splints should be fixed above and then below the seat of fracture.

The injured part should be well supported.

The patient should be treated for shock, and medical aid arranged for.

In case of doubt the first aider should treat the injury for fracture.

Bleeding should be stopped and wounds treated before attending to immobilization of the fractured part.

As far as possible the fracture should be fixed before the patient is removed for proper medical care. Improper handling of a simple fracture may at times lead to compound fractures. Compound fractures are much more serious because of the danger of infection entering from the surface wounds.

Sprains, burns and scalds

Sprains

Sprains occur at joints such as the ankle and wrist. If the ligaments and parts around a joint are stretched or torn by a sudden wrench or twist, the joint is said to be sprained.

The characteristic signs and symptoms of a sprain are: pain at the joint; inability to use the joint without experiencing increased pain; swelling and later discolouration.

Treatment of sprain

The limb should be placed in the most comfortable position, preferably elevated, and movement should be prevented.

The joint should be exposed and a firm bandage applied.

The bandage should be kept wet with cold water.

If the patient has no relief, the bandage should be removed and retied.

The sprained part should be given complete rest.

In doubtful cases treatment should be as for fractures.

Burns and scalds

An injury caused by **dry heat** such as fire or a piece of hot metal, contact with high-tension electric current, friction or corrosive chemicals, such as concentrated acids or alkalis, is known as a "burn".

In direct contrast, an injury caused by **moist heat** such as boiling water, steam, hot oil, tar or improperly applied poultices is termed a "scald".

Burns and scalds produce identical effects such as reddening of the skin, formation of blisters, and charring of the epidermis or total destruction of the deeper tissues.

The great danger of burns and scalds is from shock and septic infection of the wound.

Treatment of burns and scalds

If there are blisters they should not be broken. Clothing should not be removed as the area of burns or scalds including the clothing over it is sterile for a short period and all efforts should be made to keep it so. The burnt or scalded part, as also the clothing, should be covered with dry, sterile dressing. The affected parts should be bandaged firmly with cotton pads if there are no blisters, and lightly, if there are blisters. The patient should be kept warmly wrapped up in blankets. The burnt or scalded part should be kept at rest. Plenty of warm drinks, especially warm weak tea with a lot of sugar, should be given to the patient.

If medical help is not available, further treatment may be given as follows:

The first aider should wet the area of the burn, including the clothing, with warm alkaline solution, such as two teaspoonsful of baking soda or one teaspoonful of common salt to a tumbler of water at body temperature. This will relieve pain and minimize shock.

If burns are caused by corrosive acids they should be thoroughly washed with baking soda solution. Burns caused by alkali should be washed with vinegar or lemon juice in water.

If the first aider does not know whether the cause of the burns is acid or alkali, or if any neutralizing agent is not available, he should wash the affected part with plenty of warm water and remove the clothing gently. Then he should give treatment in the same way as for burns and scalds.

When a person's clothing catches fire

People working carelessly at the stove, run the risk of their clothing catching the fire. In case a person's clothing catches fire, he or she should not panic and run about, nor run out into the open air, as that will aggravate the situation A breeze might fan the fire to such an extent that it could prove fatal. The patient should not be allowed to become panic-stricken. The first aider should quickly wrap a blanket around the patient, lay him or her on the ground and put out the flame by smothering it.

If one's own clothing catches fire and no other help is available, one should cover oneself with a thick blanket, and put out the flames by rolling on the ground.

10. Home Nursing

What is home nursing? Home nursing is the care of the sick at home. The doctor decides the course of treatment and the nurse carries out his orders. She does all that is necessary to make the patient comfortable and to ensure conditions essential for his recovery.

Choice and preparation of the sick room

The sick room should be large and airy and have a cheerful, sunny atmosphere.

It should be conveniently situated, away from the noisy part of the house, preferably adjacent to a shady verandah, and have an attached bathroom.

It should not be encumbered with unnecessary furniture. A bed, two tables, two chairs and an easy chair will suffice.

Care should be taken as to the position of the bed. It should not be in a draught or in direct sunlight. It should be so placed as to enable the patient to look out of the window.

Flowers may be used to decorate the room, their choice determined by the likes and dislikes of the patient.

All the furniture should be well protected. Tables should be covered with oil-cloth. The sick room should be scrupulously clean and tidy.

The daily cleaning of the room should be carried out systematically, but should be done quietly and quickly after the patient's bed has been made and he has been comfortably settled down.

A cloth damped with a weak disinfectant should be used first for dusting, and then a dry duster to wipe up the moisture.

Bed pans and urinals should not be kept inside the sick room.

They should be brought in when needed by the patient and removed soon after use.

The bedsteads should preferably be of iron and fitted with a good mattress. It should be about 2 metres long and 1.08 metres wide. It is better to protect the mattress with an oil-cloth.

How to make a bed

In making a bed the criterion should be the comfort of the patient. Though the neat appearance of the finished bed adds to the well-being of the patient and the tidiness of the sick room, under no circumstances should the comfort of the patient be sacrificed to this end. The bed clothes under the patient should be tight and smooth and those over him light and loose.

Scientific bed-making saves time and effort and provides comfort. It is easier when someone assists the nurse from the opposite side of the bed. The following procedure may be adopted for bed-making using the undermentioned articles.

The first requisite is a **firm mattress with cover.**

An **underblanket** should be smoothened of all crinkles and creases and firmly tucked under the mattress.

An **undersheet** should be tightly drawn and tucked under the mattress first at the head, then at the foot, and lastly at both sides making mitred or square or envelope corners. The envelope corner effect is achieved thus: One should stand facing the head of the bed and tuck the sheet well under the mattress. With the left hand one should lift the edge of the sheet, holding it at right angles to the mattress. Then the sheet should be tucked under the mattress with the right hand. After smoothing the sheet with the palm of the right hand, the part of the sheet held in the left hand should be dropped over the right. The sheet should be pulled tight before being tucked in, first at the centre and then under the corners. This should be repeated for all the four corners of the bed.

A **mackintosh cloth or oil cloth**, extending from the waist to the patient's knee, should be spread across the bed and tucked well under the mattress on both sides.

A **draw-sheet**, serves to protect the undersheet and mattress and keep the patient dry and clean. The draw-sheet

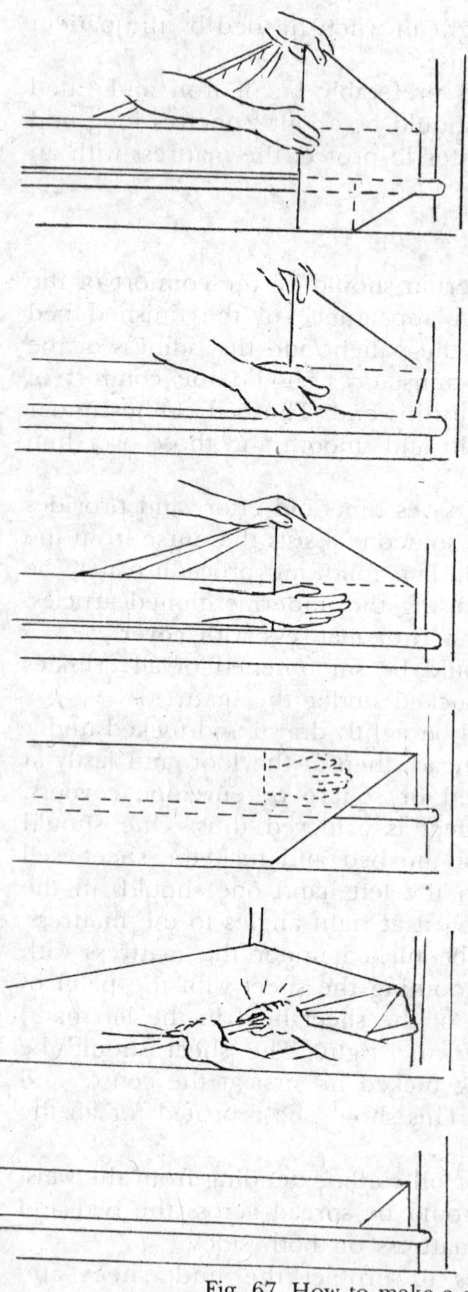

Stand facing the head of the bed.

Tuck the sheet well under the head of the mattress.

With your left hand lift the edge of the sheet, holding it at right angle to the mattress.

Tuck the sheet under the mattress with your right hand.

With the palm of the right hand, smooth the sheet against the mattress, holding the sheet in place against the mattress.

Drop the part of the sheet held in the left hand over the right hand.

Grasp the sheet with your hands.

Pull the sheet tightly before tucking under the mattress, in the centre first, and then at the corners.

The square corner is completed.

Fig. 67. How to make a square corner

can be more easily changed than the undersheet, when soiled, and can be more easily kept free from creases. It can be made by folding an ordinary sheet lengthwise so that it is wide enough to cover the oil-cloth completely. One end of the sheet should be tucked under the mattress on one side of the bed. The sheet should be spread smoothly across the bed. The remainder should be folded and placed under the mattress on the other side. One or two pillows in pillowslips should be placed at the head of the bed, with the closed end of the pillowslip facing down. The pillows should fill the case firmly at the bottom.

The **top-sheet** should reach right up to the head of the bed so as to leave plenty to turn down. It should be well tucked under the mattress at the foot of the bed, and half way along the sides.

A **light, warm blanket** should be spread over the top-sheet but not so tight as to restrict the free movement of the patient.

A **soft and light counterpane** may be used if the patient desires it. On well-made beds the sheets are smooth, without wrinkles or bulges.

Changing sheets for a patient in bed

A good deal of patience and quick efficiency are needed for changing the sheets of a patient in bed. It is convenient to have two persons working, one on either side of the bed, and keeping the fresh sheets in readiness. All the bed-clothes should be first untucked. After covering the patient with the top-sheet, the pillows should be removed, shaken and aired.

The patient should be turned gently on one side. He should be supported in this position and kept covered all the time.

The soiled under-sheet, oil-cloth and draw-sheet should be rolled along the length to lie in a long light roll close against the patient's back.

The clean sheets, rolled lengthwise to half the extent, should be placed against the soiled roll. The unrolled portion should be smoothened and the under-sheet, oil-cloth and draw-sheet, tucked in.

The patient should then be gently lowered on his back over the two rolls and then rolled over on his other side. He should be supported in this position and kept well covered.

The dirty roll should now be removed and the clean roll unrolled, smoothened and tucked in. The under-sheet should be first tucked in; then the oil-cloth and the draw-sheet.

The patient should then be lowered on his back gently.

The pillow or pillows should be put under the patient's head.

The bed-clothes should be replaced and neatly tucked in, allowing enough room for him to move his legs.

Sponge bath

A patient should be given a daily wash. It is essential for keeping his skin clean and adding to his comfort. A washing bowl or a large basin, a jug of hot water, a bucket to pour the dirty water into, soap, two flannels, bath and face towels, bath powder, a clean set of clothes, and any other article or substance required, should be kept ready beside the bed.

The windows should be closed.

The patient should be covered and his clothing removed without disturbing or inconveniencing him.

The washing should be carried out with speed and utmost efficiency, avoiding exposure of the patient. Washing should start from the face and then proceed to the neck, arms, chest, abdomen, legs, feet and then the back. The washed parts should be carefully dried and immediately covered up.

Soap should be applied to one of the flannels and the face soaped. The face should then be wiped with the other flannel wetted with hot water. Water should be squeezed out and not allowed to drip from the flannel. A towel should be placed beneath the part washed in order to prevent the bedsheets from getting wet.

Only the parts to be washed should be exposed and, the rest of the patient's body should be kept carefully covered. Water should be changed if dirty, and as often as necessary, after bathing the trunk and again after bathing the legs and feet, and so on.

Attention should be paid particularly to clean and dry the back of the ear, the axillae of the armpits, groin, and the area under the breasts in the case of a woman patient.

The bony prominences, back and folds of the skin

should be gently massaged with a soapy hand, washed, dried and dusted lightly with bath powder.

The patient should be dressed in a clean set of clothes.

The bath clothes should be removed from the room and left to dry elsewhere. No wet cloth should be left inside the sick room.

After combing the patient's hair, the bed should be smoothened of all wrinkles. Particles of dirt, fallen hair, etc., should be removed. The bedsheets should then be neatly tucked in under the mattress and the patient left to rest in comfort.

The clinical thermometer

The clinical thermometer is the instrument used for measuring the temperature of the human body. It differs from other thermometers in the following ways:

The scale is graduated only from 95° to 110°F.

The normal body temperature of 98.4°F is indicated by an arrow or marked clearly with a red line.

There is a constriction in the mercury thread to prevent the mercury column coming down of its own accord, as soon as it is removed from the patient's mouth. The thermometer

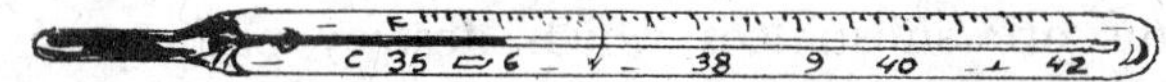

Fig. 68. The Clinical Thermometer

has to be shaken down after the temperature is taken, to get the mercury back into the end, well below the arrow mark of 98.4°F.

To take the temperature of the body, the clinical thermometer may be placed either in the mouth or axilla in adults, axilla or groin in children, and rectum in infants of up to one year when specially instructed by the doctor.

Clinical thermometers have also the Celsius scale marked on them and the graduation is from 36°C to 42°C, and the normal body temperature being marked with an arrow at 37°C.

How to take the temperature

The first thing is to check whether the mercury level is below the arrow mark. If not the thermometer should be held at the top end and given a few sharp jerks to bring the mercury level below 95°F.

The thermometer should be rinsed in cold water and dried and then its end placed under the patient's tongue.

The patient should be asked to breathe through the nose and cautioned against talking, opening his lips or biting the thermometer.

The thermometer should be left in the patient's mouth for at least 2 minutes to assure an accurate registering of temperature.

The thermometer should be removed from the patient's mouth and wiped dry. The temperature should then be noted and the reading recorded in the daily chart.

The mercury column should be shaken down and the thermometer left in an antiseptic lotion.

If a patient has had a hot drink, fifteen minutes should be allowed to lapse before taking his temperature in the mouth. The temperature should not be taken under the armpit or in the groin just after the patient has been bathed or washed.

Disinfectants

Disinfectants are substances which destroy pathogenic microbes and so prevent infectious disease from spreading. Disinfection means destruction of the specific organisms of infectious or contagious diseases.

In the use of disinfectants one should not only know the qualities of the product used, but the quantity to be used and the degree of concentration. It is also absolutely necessary for the disinfectant to come in direct contact with the micro-organisms. Since most disinfectants are poisonous they should be kept carefully locked up, far out of the reach of children, and used with caution.

Different kinds of disinfectants are available; but the simplest and most easily procurable ones should always be used.

Classification of disinfectants

Disinfectants can be classified as natural, physical and chemical.

Natural disinfectants

Nature's own fresh air and sunlight are disinfectants that destroy most germs.

Physical disinfectants

These include heat in its various forms, and may be applied as dry heat and moist heat.

Dry heat

Burning

Burning is the best means of disinfection. It should always be employed for articles of meagre value such as rags, pillows, old mattresses and the like.

Hot dry air

Leather articles, books, etc., are liable to be spoilt by the action of water and steam. Hot dry air is the best disinfectant for them. To ensure the destruction of bacteria and spores, the temperature must be high and the heating prolonged.

Moist heat

Boiling

Boiling in hot water is one of the most efficient methods of disinfection. Infected articles can be disinfected within about 20 minutes by boiling. Bed linen and other such articles are best disinfected by boiling. However, boiling is a slow process and is not suitable for woollen articles which will shrink if boiled.

Steaming

Steaming is the most efficient and practical way of applying moist heat for purposes of disinfection, since steam has a penetrating power infinitely more rapid than dry heat.

Chemical disinfectants

A variety of chemical disinfectants are available. The choice of a chemical disinfectant depends on the nature of the infection to be combated and the resistance of the organism. Chemical disinfectants can be solids, liquids or gases.

Solids

Lime or **chunam** is one of the common solid chemical disinfectants used for disinfecting latrines and bathrooms. **Bleaching powder** is also a well-known solid disinfectant. **Boric acid** or **boracic acid** consists of white crystals. It is colourless, odourless and has a slightly acid taste. It is a mild antiseptic used for cleaning eyes and mouth. **Iodine** is extracted from seaweed and chili saltpetre. In its pure state it exists as a solid, in the form of heavy, strong-smelling, steel-coloured flakes. It is used at the time of surgical operations. **Potassium permanganate** consists of purple crystals. It is used for mouth washes, gargles and douches. **Perchloride of mercury, hydrarg, perchlor, mercuric chloride, corrosive sublimate** are names for a heavy, white, poisonous crystal which has an acrid, metallic taste. It is a powerful disinfectant.

Biniodide of mercury is used as a disinfectant for hands in surgical work. **Sulphonamide** is taken in tablet form as an internal antiseptic.

Liquids

The common liquid disinfectants are **carbolic acid** or **phenol**, **lysol, Dettol, Condy's fluid** and **hydrogen peroxide.**

Gases

When a gas is used as a disinfectant, the process is known as **fumigation. Formaldehyde, chlorine gas**, and **sulphur dioxide** are some of the gaseous disinfectants. Formalin is a solution of the gas formaldehyde and is used as a spray for disinfecting the walls and floors of a room. Paraform tablets used as disinfectants give off the gas formaldehyde, when heated. Chlorine is a poisonous gas with a greenish-yellow colour and a disagreeable smell. Chlorine in minute quantities is a suitable and powerful agent for the purification of water supplies.

Stock solutions of disinfectants

It is better to have a home equipped with the following stock solutions of disinfectants for ready use.

The stock solution of carbolic acid or phenol has a strength of 1 in 20, namely, 1 part of carbolic acid and 19 parts of water. Lotions of carbolic acid may be used in the following strengths:

1 in 20 for disinfecting bedsteads, furniture, mackintoshes, leather articles, combs, etc.

1 in 100 for gargles and for disinfecting hands.

Potassium permanganate is used in the ratio of 1:5000 for mouth-washes and throat gargles.

If perchloride of mercury is stocked in addition to the above, the solution should be 1 in 1000 for use; if formalin, 2% solutions in water and iodine 2% solutions in spirit.

Since most of the disinfectants are virulent poisons, utmost care should be taken in storing them. Bottles and containers should be properly labelled and kept securely locked up out of reach of children.

How to disinfect a room

The method employed for disinfecting a room depends on the nature of the infection. The different methods of disinfection are spraying, fumigating and washing. The following procedure may be adopted for disinfecting a room.

Articles of small value should be burnt.

Contaminated linen should be immersed in a pail containing a disinfectant.

Articles such as crockery should be boiled in a container for a minimum period of half an hour.

Mattresses, blankets, rugs, bedspreads and the like should be disinfected by fumigation.

Cupboards and shelves, should be opened out, drawers of tables and almirahs should be emptied and left fully open and exposed, so that the disinfecting gas may permeate the nooks and corners properly.

Windows should be securely closed and paper pasted over any crevices in the window frame and over key holes. The room should be completely gas-tight before fumigation.

After getting the room ready in the above fashion, the

formalin lamp which liberates formaldehyde gas should be lighted. After it is lit, the person who lights it and anyone else who may be in the room should quickly leave the room, close and seal the door securely. The room should be kept locked up for twelve hours.

If the room cannot be made gas-tight, its walls should be sprayed and its floors washed with a suitable chemical disinfectant. Each article in the room should be separately dealt with.

While disinfecting a room great attention should be paid to the floor, as infected vomit, urine and stools generally fall on the floor and contaminate it, and germs, fleas and flies thrive therein. The walls should be sprayed and washed with formalin or a similar disinfectant, and the floor with an acid solution of perchloride of mercury, bleaching powder or phenol or any other suitable disinfectant.

Domestic cleanliness scrupulously maintained is the safest and surest way to combat the spread of infection. Washing the hands with soap and water, rinsing the mouth with a solution of potassium permanganate or Condy's fluid, washing of bathrooms and latrines with phenol, systematic exposure to sun and air of clothing, mattresses, bedspreads and blankets contribute greatly to healthy living.

Part V

Child Care and Family Relationships

11. Child Care

Prenatal care

Parenthood is one of the most important undertakings in life. A perfectly healthy woman usually goes through pregnancy without much trouble. Evil results can be prevented by adequate prenatal care.

Benefits of prenatal care

1. One of the commonest disorders of the expectant mother is "toxoemia". If allowed to progress, it sometimes ends in a serious condition known as "eclampsia" accompanied by convulsions or fits and unconsciousness. By regular examination during pregnancy, much can be done to prevent the development of toxoemia and eclampsia.
2. In some women, the birth canal is very small, so difficult and obstructed labour follows, greatly endangering the life of both mother and child. By adequate prenatal care, such a difficulty can be foreseen and prevented.
3. A baby is normally born 'head first', but if buttocks or feet come first, it is dangerous for the child and there is very little chance for the baby to be born alive and uninjured. By proper prenatal care, this wrong position of the baby can be discovered and corrected in the last weeks of pregnancy.
4. By following the advice given by the doctor regarding health and diet, much can be done to ensure that the child after its birth will be healthy and will be able to resist illness and disease.
5. During prenatal care, the blood of pregnant women is examined in order to discover conditions which might affect the mother and the baby, and special treatment will be given if necessary.

Minor troubles of pregnancy

Watering of the mouth

Some women notice an excess of saliva in their mouths. The remedy is to eat small meals rather than three large meals. Women with unhealthy teeth and gums are much more likely to suffer from excessive salivation than those with clean and healthy mouths.

Morning sickness

This is more common in the first than in subsequent pregnancies. Morning sickness is due to the adjustments made by the body to the changes of pregnancy. Whatever the cause, a woman should avoid the unpleasantness of morning sickness by paying attention to her diet, by having a quiet mind, by thinking of the joys of having a child and expecting a normal delivery.

Constipation

This is common during the later months of pregnancy when the enlarged uterus presses on the rectum. Constipation can be avoided by taking plenty of green vegetables and fruits. Vitamin 'B' complex is also helpful.

White discharge

During pregnancy, there is normally some increase in vaginal secretion. This prepares the passage for the baby by making it soft and smooth. If the discharge is excessive, it is due to infection and needs treatment.

Backache

The enlarged abdomen causes a change in the woman's posture. This imposes a strain on the back muscles and brings on backache. To prevent this, the expectant mother should take enough rest and should avoid wearing high-heeled slippers.

Cramp in the legs

This again is due to the growing uterus pressing on the nerves and blood vessels of the legs. Anyone with this trouble should stand up and massage the painful part.

Sleeplessness

This is common during the last three months of pregnancy and is due to the movements of the foetus. Any exercise which is not too tiring, or an interesting activity will help to secure sound sleep.

Golden rules for expectant mothers

1. Engage doctor early.
2. Avoid constipation.
3. Pay strict attention to diet.
4. Take regular outdoor exercises.
5. Look out for danger signals like:
    a. Red discharge
    b. Swelling of face and legs or hands
    c. Scanty urine
    d. Dimness of sight
    e. Giddiness
    f. Severe vomiting
6. Carefully carry out the instructions of the doctor.

The object of prenatal care is to prevent trouble and to help the mother to go through pregnancy and labour with complete safety.

Systematic care of children

All the world over children are born in thousands almost every minute of the day and night. They need parental care for normal and healthy growth. Child care has developed into a highly systematized science over the past hundred years; but it is regrettable to note that in India, and some other parts of the world, parents still cling to antiquated, out-moded and superstition-riddled ways of bringing up children, which often have deleterious effects on them. For instance, if parents fail to give polio vaccine to their babies at stipulated intervals as per doctor's immunization schedule, there is every chance of their children becoming polio victims resulting in paralysis of the limbs or even death. Scientific child care is an absolute necessity to ensure healthy citizens for a resurgent India.

Classification of age groups

For the sake of convenience, the stages of the child, as it grows, are classified as follows:

Infant—Birth to one year.
Pre-school child—One to five years.
School child—Five to twelve years.

Basic needs of a child

The basic needs of a child for healthy growth and development are food, clothing, baths, fresh air, play and sleep.

Food

As the child is fed, so it grows. Well-fed children have a cheerful aspect, healthy skin and are plump and bonny, active and pleasant. Undernourished children are thin, weak and bony, with shrunken skin and a pathetic mien. They are restless and cry a lot. A Chinese proverb says, "A thousand mile walk starts with the first step". Likewise the first steps taken towards proper nourishment of children pave the way for their future health.

Understanding the small baby is very important. When he cries, he is telling the mother that he is not comfortable or happy but it may also be that he is simply exercising his vocal chords.

Food and infants

Babies are fed with mother's milk, cow's milk, buffalo's milk, goat's milk, donkey's milk, mare's milk or camel's milk and we have the fable of Romulus and Remus, the founders of the city of Rome having been fed by a she-wolf. Though there may be some sources of artificial milk, mother's milk is undoubtedly the ideal food for the baby. Sometimes when the mother is unable to feed the child, "wet-nurses" are employed, if available; otherwise cow's milk is the most common substitute. Fruit juices also form part of the baby's food.

Human milk

Mother's milk is the most natural and ideal food for the baby in the first year of its life. The composition of human milk best suits the human infant's digestion and rate of growth. It is the birthright of every infant to be breast-fed. The protein and fat in human milk are much more easily digested and absorbed than those of cow's milk.

Moreover, human milk is available at the proper temperature, there is no danger of bacterial contamination, and it is the healthiest. One need not have fear of errors in calculation and in the formulae for preparation as with tinned or fresh cow's milk. Further, human milk has antibodies which prevent children's diseases.

Psychologically, breast-feeding gives the baby a feeling of safety, security, protection and love, and the mother a sense of accomplishment. Breast-fed infants have a better chance of surviving the rather perilous years of early life than the less fortunate babies nurtured with artificial milk. The mortality rate is high in artificially-fed infants, especially in the lower economic classes.

Feeding the new born baby

Nature has so provided for the new born that breast milk is sufficient in quality and quantity. The first day or so, the mother's milk flows scantily. It is called colostrum. There is an unfounded belief that this is not good for the new born. In fact the opposite is true. It is a rich source of vitamins, especially Vitamin 'A' and feeding it to the new born should be encouraged.

In many rural areas, on the first day or so, the new born is usually fed with sweetened water, by dipping a cotton wick in it and allowing the child to suck on it. We should try to discourage this practice and emphasize on feeding of breast milk.

Feeding breast milk

When the mother begins feeding her child regularly, she must remember the following points:

1. Washing of the breast-nipple, before and after each feed.
2. Allowing the child to feed whenever hungry as the child at this stage feeds frequently and in small quantities.
3. Taking care to burp the child after each feed, so that

the air swallowed during sucking which might cause colic, is released.

Advantages of breast feeding

It is particularly important to breast-feed in India because of the difficulty in maintaining strictly germ free methods of preparing and giving artificial feeds in a hot climate. Breast milk is pure, clean and fresh. It is the surest way of giving the infant that feeling of love and security. It contains all the nutrition he needs for growth and development in the first months of his life. It is always exactly at the right temperature. It helps him to resist disease and there is no danger of infection. It saves a great deal of time and trouble. It costs nothing though the mother's diet must be good. It helps to form good teeth and well-developed jaws.

Feeding other milk

If the breast milk is insufficient or the mother is ill, cow, goat or buffalo milk can be given. These types of milk are called "top milk". There are two important points to remember.

a. The hygienic aspect.
b. The method of dilution.

The hygienic aspect includes the following points:

1. All top milk should be boiled.
2. Many diseases are caused through improperly boiled milk. Boiling kills the germs and makes the protein more digestible.
3. After boiling, the milk should be set aside in a cool place.
4. The milk should also be covered to prevent dust and flies from settling on it.
5. If a bottle has to be used, then both the bottle and teat must be boiled at least once a day and rinsed after every feed.
6. The left over milk should not be fed.
7. The baby must not be given too hot or too cold milk. It should be warm, a few drops can be tested on the hand.

To dilute the milk the following points must be remembered:

1. Cow's milk should be diluted in the proportion of one part of boiled milk to two parts of boiled water.
2. The dilution can be gradually decreased so that by the third month the proportion should be equal parts of water and milk, and by the end of the sixth month the child should drink whole milk or undiluted milk.

To every four ounces of diluted cow's milk, one level teaspoonful of sugar should be added to make the milk more sweet, as cow's milk has less sugar than the breast milk and dilution further reduces the percentage of sugar. Also sugar serves to supply energy to the baby. A few grains of sodium citrate or some cereal water may also be added to make the protein form a softer curd in the baby's stomach.

Fruit juice, fruit, etc.

Fruit juice should also be given to babies. A small quantity of orange juice, strained, sweetened and diluted is good for the baby as it is a source of vitamin C. Tomato juice may also be given.

In addition, Adexolin which is a capsule containing vitamins A and D, and which is easily soluble can also be added to the baby's feed. Cod liver oil, vitamin C pills dissolved in water, and a little iron in liquid form may also be given for additional nourishment.

Artificially-fed babies thrive well on bananas. The banana should be freed of fibres, mashed up in milk and then given to the baby. Banana feeds should be started only after the fourth month.

Intervals of feeding

A new-born baby's stomach can hold only about two tablespoonsful of food. Therefore feeding must be frequent. The infant requires 2½ ounces of breast milk per day per pound of its body weight. Three-hourly feeds will be suitable for smaller babies. For larger babies, needing six feeds a day, the schedule may be four-hourly feeds at 6 a.m., 10 a.m., 2 p.m., 6 p.m., 10 p.m. and 2 a.m. The 2 a.m. feed is not necessary after the second month. Water should be given between feeds from a bottle or spoon; but the intervals should be flexible. Rigid adherence to a time schedule or feeding the baby whenever it cries are extremes, one as bad as the other.

If the baby is satisfied at the end of the feed, it falls asleep promptly and sleeps quietly for several hours. This is an indication of its having sucked milk to its heart's content. If the baby gains weight satisfactorily from week to week it will be obvious that it is getting enough milk and nourishment. Normally, the weight at birth of a well-fed, healthy child, is doubled at the end of six months and trebled at the end of a year.

Weaning

Weaning is a gradual process whereby breast-feeding is substituted by artificial feeding. It is considered that the eruption of the first incisor tooth is an indication to start weaning the child. Normally weaning should be done when the baby is nine months old. In India, because of economic conditions, most mothers do not take the child completely off the breast even when it is a year old. Weaning is done by giving one or two bottle feedings at six months, and progressively increasing the number.

One has to bc cautious about weaning in hot weather or when the baby is uncomfortable because of a cold or teething.

Necessity for weaning

If the quantity of breast milk available daily is not enough or the mother is ill and is advised not to breast-feed the baby on medical grounds, the infant will have to be artificially-fed.

Most mothers can produce enough breast milk only for the first 3 to 4 months. On the other hand, breast milk alone is not able to provide sufficient amounts of all the nutrients needed to maintain growth after the first six months. At the same time, the milk output also diminishes, and if the baby is to maintain the expected rate of growth and remain healthy and well nourished, supplementary feeding has to be resorted to from the third month of life.

Method of weaning

Weaning must be gradual and should commence around the

third month of life when the first supplements are introduced. It may commence by omitting one nursing and in its place feeding a suitable quantity of the chosen supplementary food. Gradually the baby is given more frequently, small quantities of different supplementary foods and the frequency of breast feeding is reduced to the minimum. It is desirable to retain the early morning and late night nursings until the last. At the other times, the baby is allowed to take the breast for short periods only, to remove sufficient milk so that the mother's discomfort, if any, is relieved.

Supplementary food

Supplementary food is added gradually according to the infants age, development, growth and physical condition.

The foods to be introduced at different age levels and the recommended allowances are given below:

Age of the infant		*Foods to be introduced at different age levels*
3 - 4 months	:	Semi-solid foods like mashed banana. Porridge with atta, rice, ragi, etc. Any commercial baby cereal mix.
5 - 6 months	:	Mashed seasonal vegetables like greens, beans, peas, carrots, etc. Steamed potato. Boiled egg.
7 - 8 months	:	Solid foods like combination of rice and pulses with curds, egg and bread, etc.
9 - 10 months	:	Well-cooked, minced meat and fish.
1 - 1½ years	:	Soft foods without spices.

* Recommended allowances

Age	*Calories per kg body weight*	*Protein in gms/kg body weight*
0 - 3 months	120	2.22
3 - 6 months	115	1.88
6 - 9 months	110	1.63
9 - 12 months	105	1.44
1 - 2 years	114	1.25

* Gopalan, C., Ramasastri, B.V., Balasubramanian, S.C., 1978 : Nutritive value of Indian foods, National Institute of Nutrition, Hyderabad, India.

The mother should have some practical knowledge regarding the introduction of new foods to the baby. The first and foremost is that only one food should be given at a time to enable the infant to become familiar with that particular food. While starting boiled foods, the consistency of the food should be very thin and the amount, minimal. Both the consistency and amount can be increased gradually. The infant's likes and dislikes should be considered while introducing the supplementary food. Lightly-seasoned food is preferable.

At the beginning, smooth consistency foods can be given. When the baby is able to chew, chopped fruits and vegetables can be given. Mixed foods can be given according to baby's taste. Finally, one must remember to have variety while introducing supplementary foods to a baby.

Diet schedule for a 10-month-old baby

6 a.m.	1 glass of cow's milk.
7 a.m.	½ an idli and 2 teaspoonsful of yolk of egg.
10 a.m.	1 cup of cow's milk with 2 tablespoonsful of cereal such as Farex.
1 p.m.	Well-mashed cooked rice with greens, and water to drink.
3 p.m.	1 cup of orange juice.
4 p.m.	1 rusk and a little ripe banana mashed in milk.
7 p.m.	1 glass of cow's milk.

Choice and care of feeding bottles

Feeding bottles should be of heat-resisting material, and transparent. If bottles with one opening are used, the mouth, neck and bottom of the bottle should be large. The side should be smooth, rounded and without ridges. Round bottles are better. Nipples should not be of tough and rigid rubber, nor have large holes.

All articles connected with a baby's feeding should be kept clean to guard against illness. Bottles, nipples, etc., should be rinsed and cleaned thoroughly soon after use. Bottles should be brushed in soapy water to remove any oily matter and then washed in hot water. Nipples should be cleaned well. Brushes should be rinsed in clean water after use and dried. The feeding bottle should be boiled at least once a day. Rinsing the bottle immediately after use is a healthy practice. The feeding bottle and nipple should not be exposed to dust and dirt. The feeding bottle should be covered or immersed in water and the nipple kept covered

Fig. 69. Child's feeding equipments

in a container. If the nipples are kept in water, a teaspoonful of salt should be added to the water to prevent the nipples from getting soft.

Nursing mothers and nurses should be very careful about their own personal cleanliness, apart from keeping clean the articles used for baby's feeding. They should not handle feeding bottles without washing their hands clean. Since babies are very susceptible to diseases, and have not as much resistance as grown-ups, absolute cleanliness must be strictly observed by mothers.

Food for the pre-school child

By the time a child is one year old, all types of food in simple, easily digestible form, will have been incorporated in his diet. He will get sieved cereals, boiled vegetables and fruit, yolk of egg, etc., in addition to milk.

Foods that can be chewed should be given towards the end of the first year and gradually increased during the second year. As the child grows and develops, his diet should be enlarged. New foods should be introduced as soon as his digestive tract can handle them successfully. In between meals, children should not have snacks as these spoil the appetite.

Usually by the time a child is one year old, he is on a three-meal-a-day schedule. During the second year, increased quantities of the food to which the child is accustomed will suffice. By then his tastes will have widened. Having become used to more solids, he may refuse milk. But he should be made to drink at least half a litre of milk everyday. Cod-liver oil or any other rich source of Vitamin D should be given up to two years of age, especially if the baby is bottle-fed.

Mothers usually coax, cajole, threaten, scold or bribe children to make them eat. In their anxiety to make the child put on weight they attempt to stuff it with food by hook or by crook. Children should be taught to eat by themselves without any unnecessary fuss being made.

As the child passes the fast-growing period of infancy, he becomes more selective and more independent about food. The pre-school period is often difficult because the appetite lessens or wanes, growth is slow and irregular and weight often drops. It is during this period that the parents should adopt a psychological approach towards the food problems of the child. Parents should be careful not to foster bad eating habits. Appetite usually returns as quickly as it disappears and a spurt in growth and weight is bound to follow.

The same types of food as were used during the second year may be given in increased quantities. Milk, egg, pulses, cereals, millets, groundnuts, vegetables and fruit may be given. The diet should be made as appetising and varied as possible, to make the children develop a natural taste for food and eat independently and well.

Food for school-going children

School-going children of five to twelve years of age grow slowly and steadily. The meal schedule for them should be spaced in relation to the school routine. They must have sufficient time for all their meals, including breakfast. They must not be allowed to gobble food hurriedly in order to rush to school in the morning or at noon. Since they can eat and digest almost any food that is served on the family menu, the problem of their diet is not so hard as in the infant stage. Most of the items included in their diet should be energy-giving proteins, minerals or vitamins in order to meet their proportionately higher nutritional needs.

In India the diet differs markedly between the North and the South. Because of our long association with the British, in many upper-class Indian homes, European menus are followed. This gives great opportunity of variety in the menu, selecting from North Indian, South Indian and European items, and one should make the most of this possibility.

Dress

Some mothers make elaborate preparations for the baby, long before it arrives, stitching sets of clothes, napkins, etc. Others get dresses made soon after it is born. Since there is not much difference in the clothes for new-born babies, boys or girls, there is no harm in having clothes made beforehand. However, some people fight shy of doing so out of superstition.

A baby's clothes need not be full of frills or elaborate, since the baby's comfort should be the main criterion. His clothes are meant to protect him from colds and chills, while allowing enough freedom of movement for his limbs. Clothes should not be tight or they will hamper the circulation and breathing.

In the selection of a baby's clothes, his age and the climate should be taken into consideration. In warm weather the baby should be lightly clad and in cold weather, wrapped up well in warm clothes.

Baby-clothes should be so designed as to render them easy to put on and take off without discomfort to the little ones. They should be of thin, smooth, durable, soft and washable material and whenever possible white in colour. A dress should open right down the back or front to enable the mother to slip it on with ease. Draw-strings should not be used especially at the neck, as they may get pulled tight by baby's movements and strangle him. Cotton is the best material for any clothing that comes in contact with baby's skin. Outer garments such as a sweater, a warm woollen cap, etc., may be used in cold weather.

All clothes worn during the day should be changed before putting a child to sleep at night. A loose slip or night gown is excellent. Baby's clothes should be well-stitched, with strong seams and be attractive in colour and design.

Baby's bed

It used to be a common practice to have the baby in bed with his mother, but there have been instances where the mother has smothered the baby in her sleep, so this is not advisable. Cloth hammocks have also been used but these keep baby in a cramped position and it is better for him to have freedom of movement.

A rattan cradle is suitable. The mattress should not be too soft, but should be a firm one, covered with a piece of plastic or rubber sheeting where it is likely to be wet by the baby. Suitable light-weight washable blankets must be provided and used as necessary.

Diaper

Using a diaper or napkin for the baby is a sound practice. It prevents the soiling of bed clothes, or baby's or mother's clothes. Diapers are best made oblong, 36 inches long by 18 inches wide. They can then be doubled to form a square and again folded to form a triangle. This is wrapped about the hips and between the limbs in the form of drawers. The ends are either pinned together or tied up in a knot which is easily untied. The several thicknesses of the napkin are advantageous in keeping the body warm and preventing moisture from penetrating and spoiling the outer clothing. Diaper material should be of soft absorbent cotton and not of bulky or thick texture.

The napkin should be removed soon after the baby urinates or has a motion and a fresh one used. They should be kept clean, washed regularly, and dried in the hot sun on a line. Soiled napkins should not be thrown about on the floor. They should be put into a covered pail and later on taken out and washed. This will prevent flies from carrying germs from them to the feeding bottles or food of the baby. If the napkins smell strongly of ammonia, they should be properly boiled and dried before use. Napkins should not be tied too tight around the baby's waist or they may hurt his tender skin. Rough or dirty diapers will cause diaper-rash or reddening of the skin around the groin and buttocks. They may even cause sores and blisters. After removing a wet napkin, the wet parts of the body should be gently wiped with a soft cloth before a new one is tied or pinned on. It is a good thing to use bath powder during each change of napkin.

In very hot weather, a napkin is clothing enough for a baby, with a thin cloth spread over the chest.

Special care should be taken when changing napkins at night, since carelessness will affect the child's health. Wet napkins can cause a cold and lead on to more serious infections such as bronchitis and the like. When the child is trained in toilet habits, the diaper may be abandoned and drawers substituted. The drawers should be neither too tight nor too loose and cumbersome. They should be of soft material and not rough.

Disposable diapers are very much in vogue these days, especially in western countries and among the rich and upper middle class in our country. It is a boon to the mother as it saves a lot of labour for the diaper can just be thrown away instead of having to wash it. Also there is no danger of contamination of any food through contact with soiled diapers. Mostly all maternity hospitals in our country now only use disposable diapers.

Shoes

A baby's shoes serve no other purpose than to give protection to his feet and make him look attractive and well-dressed. During the crawling stage they protect his tender feet, especially if the floors are rough. The shoes used should be roomy and not so tight as to cramp his toes. They should be of soft leather, without heels, and be shaped exactly like the foot so as to fit comfortably. Socks, when used, should be of soft material. They should not crowd the baby's toes.

Baths

Almost all babies, unless they are sickly, enjoy having a bath. It is good for their general health, and they should be given at least one bath a day in warm water of a temperature of 37.8°C to 40.6°C. On very hot days they can be given more than one. Oil baths are also good for the baby, especially in hot weather, as they have a cooling effect. Bathing a baby should be done skilfully and carefully. It is good to be systematic about it, sticking to a particular time every day. A baby should not be given his bath within an hour after feeding. It is better to give it just before the feed. If he has a bath and is then fed and put to bed, he will sleep well.

Preparing for the bath

It is wise to have everything needed for the baby's bath close at hand. The mother or the nurse who bathes the baby should have within reach the basin or tub or the plank on which the baby is bathed; a pitcher of water, soap, towel, change of dress, powder, etc. The water should be lukewarm. Only a mild toilet soap should be used. The room in which the baby's bath is given should be reasonably large, comfortably warm, and sufficiently lighted. The doors and windows should be closed to prevent exposure to cold draughts. After the bath too, the baby should not be brought out of the room before it is properly dried and dressed; special care is necessary in cold and rainy weather. It is important to keep the baby warm at all times.

Bathing the baby

Babies are bathed in different ways in India; inside a basin or tub, as in western countries, or laid on the mother's or nurse's lap or outstretched legs, or on a plank.

The person who gives baby his bath should see that his neck and back are well supported since he cannot support them by himself. In soaping him, his body should be rubbed gently but vigorously to stimulate circulation. The soap must be carefully rinsed off afterwards. It must not be allowed to get into his eyes. While washing the hair and head, neither soap nor water should be allowed to run down the baby's face.

The baby should be dried with a soft towel. Mucus or dirt from the nose may be removed with the corner of the towel twisted like a wick, or with cotton twisted into a thread. When the skin is thoroughly dried, some talcum powder may be lightly sprinkled between the folds of the baby's skin, especially the axilla, elbow, neck, back of knees, groin, and buttocks.

Oil bath

Peculiar to India is the oil bath for children, usually with gingelly oil. This is cooling and refreshing. Soapnut powder is not to be used for a baby's oil bath. Usually green gram powder is used to remove the excess oil.

Sun-bath

A sun-bath is not an absolute necessity in hot countries, though plenty of sunshine is good for a baby. Weather permitting, a sun-bath may be given, but care should be taken not to keep the child exposed to the sun for too long, since it may have adverse effects. While sun-bathing a baby, great care should be taken to protect his eyes from too much glare.

Fresh air

The baby should have plenty of fresh air. Rooms where children live and sleep, should be well ventilated. There should be enough natural light and the room should have a sunny aspect with open windows and ventilators. Taking babies for a morning or evening stroll in a perambulator or carrying them in one's arms is a good habit, as the child will get plenty of fresh air. However, the baby should be properly covered and sheltered both from cold wind and hot sun.

Play—games and toys for different age groups

Children's play is not just meant to amuse the child, though that is an important part of its purpose. Playing stimulates learning in children and enables them to develop co-ordination of the various muscles. To a baby in the cradle, playing is just kicking the legs in the air and waving the arms. But as he advances in age, play becomes a serious affair, and proper selection of toys is necessary to enable the child to develop his muscles. Since the objects with which a baby plays are important, toys and other such articles should be carefully chosen to suit his age and ability.

Babies generally enjoy bright-coloured, fairly large objects which can produce some noise. Rubber balls, animals, composition beads, rattles, wooden spoons, spools, small pails, small and large bells, are appropriate. They can manipulate such things as they like. They will feel them, roll them and shake them; drop them, pick them up, and repeat the action over and over again in an exploratory manner, till they are tired of them.

Since the sucking instinct is strong in babies, the natural inclination for them is to put objects in their mouths. Therefore, care should be taken in the choice of playthings. The colours of the toys should not run, as the baby may suck them, which is dangerous. Similarly the paint should not be such as can be rubbed off by the baby's gums, since some paints cause lead poisoning. Toys should be smooth without too many ridges or sharp corners and without splinters. Pointed and sharp objects should be kept away or the baby may hurt himself by poking them into his mouth, nose, ears or eyes. Toys should be easily washable. Further, a baby's toys should not be too small for him to pick up or hold, since a very young child does not have control over his thumb or fingers to the extent of getting a proper grip on objects.

Toys that are interesting to the child should be kept near enough for him to see and reach with very little effort. They should be kept neither too far away, where it is difficult for him to get them, nor too near, where he can get them too easily. Babies should not be given too many toys to play with at a time. One or two playthings are sufficient to keep him amused or entertained. Any other than those with which he is playing should be kept out of sight in reserve. The moment he shows signs of boredom the toys should be changed.

The age of exploration

The first year of a child's life is a period of exploration. He explores all the possible ways in which a toy can be used. In his attempts to know more about the toys and the world around him, he pats the toys with his fingers and strikes or bangs them on the floor. He loves sound, and toys which can make a noise, such as rattles and bells will give him great joy. He will be able to roll a ball away from him in a sitting position but he will not be able to throw objects accurately. Since chewing is natural to a child, soft dolls and woolly toy animals which can be washed easily will please him very much.

When the baby is a year and a half old he will enjoy a three-wheeled push-cart and a two-wheeled drum-cart which produces a deafening noise when dragged along tied to a string.

The age of discovery

By the time a child is two, his muscles have grown and he wants to play the Columbus in life. This is the age of discovery in children. He likes to investigate his surroundings as he is able to walk about. He will look into every drawer and cupboard found open to satiate his curiosity. He enjoys climbing. He should be encouraged and given things like inclined boards to help him in this. He must be taught to climb up safely and get down properly. Climbing helps to make his back, legs and arms stronger. He will enjoy romping with a pet, but he must be properly supervised. Blocks will hold his attention. He will be able to throw a ball, though not accurately, in a standing position. He loves to play in the sand and with it. Linen picture-books with large coloured pictures of animals, flowers and familiar household objects may be provided for him to thumb through. He may be also given large sheets of coloured paper to play with. Dolls will represent babies for a child of two. Since outdoor games are desirable, babies of this age should be provided with a fenced-in play-area adjoining the house, to prevent their straying into the street. The child should be allowed freedom of play and liberty to choose his own activities, to encourage his developing a sense of independence and further his individual interests.

The age of imitation

The three-year-old child is an imitator. Sandcastles, mud cakes, construction of houses with building blocks, and the like are thrilling to him. The unreal becomes real in his childish imagination. Children of this age play at dressing, feeding and bathing dolls as though they were real babies, talk to them, lisping endearing nothings and prattling lullabies to put them to sleep. They recreate the home situation to which they are accustomed in their own lives, and play the role of a parent to their favourite dolls. The toy dog becomes a real one and a child may order it around and fondle it. Outdoors, swinging and climbing interest him.

Three-year old children should be tactfully taught to love and care for domestic pets. They should be allowed to feed the chicken or the dog, and thus be given lessons in kindness and gentleness. Simple jigsaw puzzles should be introduced to develop their powers of concentration. They may be given a paint box and paper to enable them to enjoy their own creative efforts as artists. Their playthings should be such as to kindle their creative interest, facilitate dramatic play and provide some exercise.

The age of make-believe

At four, children are ready for tricycles and cars that can be made to go fast. They have good co-ordination of muscles and can throw and catch balls better. They can use building blocks of different sizes and shapes. If modelling clay is given, they will be able to reproduce recognisable objects which interest them.

The age of achievement

On attaining the age of five, a child is no longer a baby. He is able to achieve things with his five years of experience in life. A definite change is apparent in a boy or girl at this age. Children now develop definite preferences of their own as to the toys they use, the games they play or the activities they indulge in. They can now get along with other children, having shed the selfishness of the earlier years. They enjoy handicraft sets such as carpentry or fretwork. They derive great pleasure from craft sets such as those for making paper-flowers or for needlework. Toys which enable them to accomplish something appeal to children of this age.

The age of group activity

At six, children are ripe for widening their circle of friendship, mixing with others freely and enjoying group games and activities. In proper surroundings they take pleasure in team games like football and cricket. Children of this age should have graduated from the tricycle to the bicycle stage. Some six-year-olds evince interest in gardening. They should be encouraged to select a plot of their own for planting, watering and growing plants.

Children of one, two, three, four, five and six years of age have been classified as balancing "the age of Exploration, Discovery, Imitation, Make-Believe, Achievement and Group-Activity", respectively. However, there are no hard and fast demarcations between two age levels or between children's behaviour patterns. It is a fallacy to say that a child of two should be a discoverer. Generally speaking he is expected to be, but if he does not, it does not prove in any way that he is underdeveloped or backward. The environment, the home, sisters and brothers, parents and playmates, emotional security, mental and physical well being, etc., play an important part in the life and development of children as in that of grown-ups.

Recreational activities for children

Rhymes and music

Children are often heard singing and chanting as they work,

rock and swing. They enjoy singing alone or in a group.

Music can contribute in many ways by offering opportunities for listening, creating, singing, rhythmical responses and playing instruments. Through these activities, the child experiences pleasure, joy and creative expression, develops listening skills and auditory discrimination. Young children are much less inhibited than others in the use of their bodies; they can be encouraged to move freely to music, permitting the music to evoke emotions and ideas as they respond towards it. It helps in promoting physical development and increases the range and flexibility of their voices. Music enables the child to be in a group which in turn develops discipline and harmony in him. Music helps to overcome boredom.

Rhymes lay the foundation for music. They give him a feeling of joy and make it easy for him to memorize. As he is memorizing rhymes, he picks up phrases thus moving towards mastery over the language.

Story-telling

Story-telling is an activity of great interest to children everywhere. This interest can be enriched through the use of pictures. The values of story-telling are:

1. It is a joyful activity and it is a source of enjoyment.
2. It promotes social development, i.e., observing group discipline while listening to the story. It also promotes emotional development because the child identifies himself with the character of the story as though it is happening to him. Further, it encourages intellectual development. Abstract concepts are made more concrete through story-telling. It enriches vocabulary and provides opportunity for thinking, reasoning and concentration.
3. It serves as a good foundation for future reading.
4. It is a gateway to imagination, creativity and self-expression.
5. It aids personality development.

Play

Play is a biological necessity through which growth and development take place. It prepares the child for harmonious living. It enables him to experiment and test his abilities without taking full responsibilities for his actions; through it he learns to distinguish between reality and fantasy.

Play is educational. The child learns a number of things through play— shape and size, colour, texture of objects and their significance. Play provides opportunity for exploring and collecting information.

Play is therapeutic. It provides an outlet for the surplus energy pent up in the child and it releases the tension that builds up through restrictions imposed on him by his environment. The child is able to formulate and carry out plans which help him to solve problems that are important to him.

Play provides training in social and moral aspects of life. The child learns to share, to give and to cooperate which enables him to learn social behaviour. Play enforces moral training in children. The child learns to be fair, honest, truthful and a good sport. He learns that he must be self-controlled if he is to be accepted in his play group.

Sleep

Sleep is as essential as food and play for the growth and development of children. Babies need abundant sleep. The very young baby sleeps most of the time, excepting when he is being fed or bathed. A new-born baby normally sleeps nine-tenths of the time, that is, more than 21 hours a day. When six months old he sleeps 16 hours a day, that is to say, two-thirds of time. As he grows older he gradually sleeps less and less, till at the age of one the average is about 15 hours or so. There is variation in the hours of sleep of an infant, a year old. Sleep periods are short but frequent at first; later they grow longer but less frequent.

Causes of sleeplessness

If the child shows signs of sleeplessness it means that he is not quite comfortable. This may be caused by lack of food, or by having been fed irregularly or too often. If the child is wet and cold, or oppressed with heat by excessive bed clothing, he may not sleep well. Thirst also may prevent sleep. Skin irritation, improper motions or constipation may be other causes for a baby not sleeping soundly. Loud noises and other such disturbances, mosquito bites or bed-bugs may also cause sleeplessness. Sound sleep is absolutely necessary for the sound health of the baby.

It is not advisable for mothers to sleep with their babies. Indian mothers often do go to sleep with the baby alongside on a mat or cot, whereas in European countries, babies are made to sleep separately in a cradle or baby-cot. It is inadvisable for the mother and baby to sleep in the same bed not only because it is quite unhygienic but also because it is very risky, since the mother may roll over the child during sleep and smother him to death unwittingly.

Mothers should see to it that the baby goes to bed in a happy frame of mind, because then he is much more likely to fall asleep easily and sleep soundly. A quiet room also helps him to sleep well. As babies grow older their hours of sleep decrease, and mothers should reduce the number of times they put them to sleep. The average child of 2 to 6 years of age requires about 12 hours sleep at night, while his daytime naps may get shorter as he grows older. In putting babies to bed, mothers should be guided both by their age and their apparent needs. Going to bed will be a pleasant experience for a baby if the mother does not rush him to bed or force him to go to bed, but leads up to it with an attitude of serenity and calm purposiveness. Story-telling and singing will help him fall asleep. If the child has had proper attention and companionship in the daytime, putting him to bed at night will not be a problem.

Tentative schedule: The following is a tentative schedule in a baby's life.

6 a.m.	...	First feed followed by sleep.
9.30 a.m.	...	Bath.
10 a.m.	...	Second feed.
10.30 a.m. to 2 p.m.	...	Sleep.
2 p.m.	...	Third feed.
2.30 p.m. to 4 p.m.	...	Sleep.
4.30 p.m.	...	Orange juice.
5 p.m. to 6 p.m.	...	Evening outdoors time.
6 p.m.	...	Fourth feed.
6.30 p.m. to 7.30 p.m.	...	Playing by himself in bed.

7.30 p.m. to 10 p.m. ... Sleep.
10 p.m. ... Fifth and last feed, and sleep till following morning.

Needs of children

The child needs spiritual, emotional, social and mental care, apart from the basic physiological needs such as food, clothing and shelter. If friendship between child and parents starts early, it is likely to continue and be a source of happiness which grows with the years.

Spiritual needs

Children have spiritual needs which must be satisfied. Good parents take the time to teach their children about their religion and to share their beliefs with them. The various religious festivals interest the child and he can be led to some understanding of the practical side of religion and how it should affect his actions, thoughts and indeed his whole life.

Emotional needs

A child shows emotions such as pleasure, joy, affection and love. Good mothering satisfies these emotions. There are other emotions such as dislike, annoyance, fury, shame, fear, worry, aggressiveness and jealousy and these may appear in the small child. The mother must try to channelize these negative emotions into positive ones by giving them some creative activities like clay modelling and painting. Jealousy is a very common emotion. He has to learn to share and to be made to understand gradually, that there is no need for him to be jealous.

Generally speaking, to help the child to handle his emotions, it is best to make a fuss over his good behaviour and not his bad behaviour.

Social needs

This simply means that a child needs companionship and friendship first from his family and gradually from other children and other people. He needs to learn to mix with others as he grows out of babyhood. With more confidence in himself, more strength and control in his body and more understanding, he should be given opportunities to learn what it means to be sociable.

Mental needs

The mental needs are met through nursery rhymes, stories, right toys and companionship. When his lively, enquiring mind makes him ask endless questions, he is indicating what his mental needs are. Patience is needed over his persistent "why" or "what" or "how". His simple questions early in life may be easily answered but later they may become difficult and he may have to be encouraged to turn to other sources of information such as a more knowledgeable person or an encyclopaedia. As young people grow up, they gradually take over more and more responsibility for themselves and to some extent it is up to them to see that they themselves satisfy their needs.

Habit formation

Habit formation results from the process of learning. Habits are formed by repetition, and thus they become mechanical and automatic. Once they are formed they do not require much effort and concentration.

There are Tamil proverbs which bring out excellently universal truths about habits and habit formation. They are: "What is not bent at five cannot be bent at fifty," and "Cradle habits persist to the grave". Good habits are a lifetime asset to children and the family, hence children should be trained in good, healthy habits very early in life. Though there are no hard and fast rules, the following facts may be borne in mind regarding habit formation in a child. The parents should take care that the child is physically and mentally ready before they start training him. They should see that he derives pleasure and satisfaction from doing the right thing at the proper time. A feeling of accomplishment and independence instilled by parents would go a long way towards helping a child to learn good habits. Psychologically, a word of praise and cheer and an occasional reward will also help a child in his efforts to acquire healthy habits.

Above all, parents and elders in the family should set an example for children to follow, since children learn mostly by imitating the elders with whom they live.

Bowel training

It is deplorable that proper bowel training is not given in most Indian homes. Answering nature's calls anywhere inside the house any time of the day or night, or in the streets, is a common habit with some children. The parents are responsible for this highly objectionable behaviour of children. This unhygienic behaviour, apart from being extremely filthy in itself, is also dangerous because it can lead to the spread of various diseases.

Apart from aesthetic considerations, hygienic methods of collection and disposal of excreta from babies should be learnt and practised since germs present in the stools can cause diarrhoea or typhoid in others. Children should not be allowed to pass stools in bed clothes or sarees. Napkins should be used by parents as a precaution. Soiled napkins should be kept covered up in an enamel pail with a lid or a similar utensil and cleansed at leisure. If it is not possible to put soiled napkins in covered vessels, they may be put into a basin containing phenol or Dettol solution or some other lotion which is a disinfectant.

The proper time to commence bowel training for a baby is when he is able to sit steadily on a commode, normally about the tenth month. The baby should be trained to sit on a pot for about 10 minutes at the time when he usually has his bowel movement. Early morning, soon after he has had his first feed for the day, is about the proper time. Indian mothers have their children squat on their legs and pass stools on paper, sand or a bit of cloth, which is placed underneath. This is a healthy practice. Once the baby develops the habit, he will find it comfortable to pass stools restfully sitting on the commode.

Toilet training

Bed-wetting and passing urine anywhere they please is a tendency that should be stopped early in children. It is an essential part of habit formation. At stated times, the mother should put the child on the pot and train him to use the receptacle. Urination will follow immediately. If the baby stays dry for two hours, it is a clear indication that he is able to control himself. This starts about the fifteenth month. By one and a half years of age, children are usually dry during the day time and when they are two or three years old, they are dry at nights too. By then the sphincter muscles of the bladder take control of the situation.

The parents should show children where to ease themselves. Before putting the child to bed, the mother should see that he evacuates the bladder. It is better not to allow the child to take too much liquid just before going to bed. Mothers may wake up and take the children from bed in the middle of the night and coax them to urinate in a pot to prevent them from wetting the bed. Systematic handling of the situation will help the child to gain control. Emotional stress, nervous debility and bad dreams may upset children and make them urinate in bed during sleep. It is desirable that children should not be subjected to any emotional stress at home or school, and should go to bed in a relaxed and happy frame of mind. When a young child stays dry for a longer period than usual, he should be praised.

Patience, perseverance and the utmost tact and caution should be employed by parents in training children. Children should not be rushed into doing things. They should not be given too many instructions, lest too many "do's" puzzle them. Parents should enlist the child's cooperation for achieving their purpose and assist him in all possible ways. Lapses on the part of the child should not be made much of; on the other hand, the parents should find out the real reason for the failure and help the child to rectify the mistake, without taking him to task for the lapse.

Neatness

Daily repetition of the same procedures in exercise, toilet, eating and sleeping will help the child develop suitable attitudes. Neatness and orderliness should be taught early, before a child develops untidiness and disorderliness. Work should be treated as a game to make children learn things fast. After playing, a child should be trained to put his toys away tidily instead of leaving them strewn all around the house. The parent should make a game of putting the play things away carefully and thus teach the child a lesson in neatness. Everything depends on the parent in making the child learn and develop good habits. Similarly, a lead could be given by parents in other directions for children to acquire and sustain other good habits.

Good discipline

Home is the first society known to any child. In the development of a child as a social being, home life plays an important role. Children of rich parents, especially only sons or daughters, are apt to be petted and pampered to such an extent that they may not acquire any discipline. Children should be disciplined properly, otherwise they will develop into wayward, disobedient, self-centred creatures. A sense of right and wrong should be instilled into a child early. While praise and recognition have their own place as an incentive to children to do things right, punishment properly administered will also have the same effect.

"Spare the rod and spoil the child" is a biblical truth. The goad (angus) for the elephant and the whip for the horse are effective instruments in disciplining. Similarly, a cane when used with caution can be an instrument in disciplining a child properly. However, before administering any sort of punishment, the punisher should weigh the pros and cons and be fully satisfied that he is justified in doing so. A child should not be ruthlessly or indiscriminately taken to task for an offence which may not be wanton but purely incidental or accidental. Punishment should not also be so severe as to have any detrimental psychological impact on the child, such as the creation of a fear complex, which may have adverse effects on the child's later life. Further, the punishment should be correlated to the offence committed to enable the child's mind to put two and two together, surmise the cause and effect, and thus refrain from repeating the offence. A disciplined child will know that by being good he is happy and makes others happy.

Stealing in children

Children may steal, unaware of any sense of wrong-doing. A gentle explanation may well cure this habit. If stealing still persists as the child grows up, it becomes a matter for alarm. When older children steal and persist in that habit, the parents should take steps to curb it. They should find out the root cause and remedy things. Normally, lack of parental love, poverty and penury, unhappiness in school, bullying by other children, want of friends, a feeling of loneliness and emotional upsets, are the reasons for a grown-up child stealing things. Bed-wetting, thumb-sucking, nail-biting, stammering, and handling or playing with the genitals are also symptoms of emotional upset in children. The parents should take more interest in the child, shower on it more care, affection and love and thus check the bad habit in its early stages. If children start stealing because of the company they keep and the environment and circumstances in which they are placed, it is better to overhaul the situation by separating the child from its unworthy friends and companions, or even change one's residence.

Minor ailments

Children suffer from a lot of minor ailments which, if neglected, may develop into serious, complicated, major diseases, causing great concern and alarm to the parents. The most common are colic, constipation, diarrhoea, common cold, convulsions, croup, scabies or itch, eczema and worms. Minor ailments can be minimized by ensuring that the child is fed and cared for properly.

Colic

Colic is a disease attended with severe pain and flatulent distension of the abdomen, without diarrhoea. It may be due to a variety of causes such as indigestion, constipation, or infection. The symptoms are the following: fits of irritable crying, hard and distended abdomen, gas in the stomach, clenched fists and cold feet tightly drawn up against the body and kicked out.

Warmth should be applied to the abdomen as a relief measure, with a slightly heated flannel cloth. Warm water with a little bicarbonate of soda dissolved in it may be given. Hotwater bags may be applied to the sides of the abdomen, or the child may be laid on his stomach over a hot water bag. Regular habits of emptying the bowels should be encouraged as a preventive against colic.

Constipation

Breast-fed babies seldom get constipated. Even if their bowel movements are infrequent or irregular, the faeces are never hard. Babies should not be given laxatives, which at best give only temporary relief. At times children get constipated when solid foods are introduced. Water given between feeds may relieve constipation. Prune juice is suggested by many doctors for constipation in infants. In bottle-fed babies adding more sugar especially brown sugar to the milk will help to relieve constipation.

Diarrhoea

Diarrhoea is a disease which causes too many loose motions. The stools are frequent and watery, often with mucus. Vomiting and fever may follow severe diarrhoea.

Diarrhoea is a common disease in India, and through neglect is often the cause of infant mortality. Especially between the ages of two months and one year, children should be guarded against its dire consequences. It rarely occurs in breast-fed babies. If it does, it may be due to some infection in the mother or to some medicine which the mother may be taking.

Normally, infantile diarrhoea is caused by germs gaining entrance to the baby's body, through the feeds. Feeds should be carefully protected from flies, and from contamination by unclean hands; and feeding utensils should be thoroughly sterilized.

Since a baby's intestines are very sensitive, too much sugar in the feeds, or any other food which does not agree with the baby and which the baby is unable to digest, may cause diarrhoea. As diarrhoea drains the tissues and depletes them of water, it will lead to serious complications if allowed to continue. One most important and immediate mde of treatment for diarrtroea is the Oral Rehydration Therapy

(ORT), using Oral Rehydration Solution (ORS). For common usage, the optimal formula for the ORS has been scientifically developed. The ORS package contains several ingredients of which the most essential are salt (soldium chloride), and an absorbable sugar (glucose). Other ingredients are important, but less critical for treating acute fluid loss in diarrhoea.

The optimal salt, sugar mix contains 4 gms salt; 20 gms glucose (or 40 gms sucrose) in a litre of clean water to make an optimal salt sugar solution. For practical purposes, for a person who may not have much education, the quick way of preparing ORS is to add a pinch of salt and one heaped teaspoonful of sugar in a glass of water and feed the child who has diarrhoea with this solution as often as possible. It will save the child from becoming dehydrated. Mothers should be told that ORS replaces essential fluids and electrolytes and diarrhoea may eventually end on its own. However, it is always good to consult a doctor also when the child has diarrhoea, even after starting Oral Rehydration Therapy or even if it is a mild attack.

Mild diarrhoea is improved by cutting down the sugar in the feeds and making them more dilute. The fat content in the milk feeds should also be reduced. As a short term measure, arrowroot *conjee* gruel may be given to babies suffering from diarrhoea. Semi-solids and solids should be avoided.

The after-care of babies who have suffered from acute diarrhoea is very important. They should be kept to a strict diet with no fat in it. Skimmed milk and half-cream milk should be given till such time as the child is absolutely normal. Though diarrhoea may be severe in babies, it is seldom acute or prolonged in children above two years of age.

Common cold

A cold is a common and oft recurring complaint in children. It is due to an infection by a virus. Since it is infectious, those suffering from it should not be allowed near the baby or his food and clothing. If the cold is accompanied by fever, a doctor should be consulted immediately. Infants catch it by exposure to a chill breeze, from wet napkins not being changed quickly, from staying in rooms which are too moist, or through wet clothes hung inside the room where they are cradled. Situations such as these should be avoided to prevent a child from catching cold. A running nose, sneezing and watering eyes are common symptoms of cold.

The child should be given heavy doses of vitamin C to combat colds. Plenty of lukewarm boiled water should be given and no cold water. If the child lacks appetite, he should not be forced to eat. If he has a cold and fever, he should be confined to bed. Laxatives and nose drops should not be given unless prescribed by a doctor. A neglected cold may lead to serious ear and throat infections and further develop into bronchitis or pneumonia.

Convulsions

Children sometimes get convulsions, especially when they have high fever. During convulsions or spasms, there is twitching of the muscles of the hands, feet and face, spreading to most parts of the body. Breathing becomes heavy, the body stiffens, the eyes become fixed or roll upward, there is occasionally froth in the mouth, and at times the child perspires profusely. A heavy cold combined with high fever and constipation, sore throat, infectious diseases, brain injury or brain infection may cause convulsions.

The most common cause of convulsions is fever, and steps should be taken to bring it down. An ice cap should be used if available. Otherwise a cloth soaked in cold water or with a little eau-de-cologne or spirit should be put on the child's forehead. A warm bath should be given to the baby's body. After the bath the baby should be dried, wrapped in a warm towel and put to bed. During convulsions the feet usually become cold. They should be kept warm by rubbing them vigorously. A doctor should be sent for at once.

Croup

When a child suffers from croup, he has inflammation of the vocal cords. Coughing, hoarseness and difficulty in breathing are the symptoms. Croup usually troubles the child at night.

Croup should be treated with hot fomentations to the throat. The room should be kept warm. The child should be kept out of cold draughts, but the room should have plenty of fresh air. Wet towels, the water wrung out, should be hung up to keep the room moist. A doctor should be consulted lest croup should develop into diphtheria or a "strep" infection.

Chafed or irritated skin

In the folds where moisture collects, the skin gets red and sore and later peels off. This is caused by dirty clothing and wet diapers. The skin should be kept clean and washed, and dried clothes should be used. Dirty and soiled napkins should be removed immediately. After removing the wet diaper, pat the skin dry and dust it lightly with powder.

Prickly heat or heat rash and heat boils

If the weather is hot and the child is heavily clothed and in consequence perspires profusely, heat rashes appear on the skin. He should be lightly clothed and kept in cool surroundings in hot weather. He should be sponged several times a day and powder should be liberally applied on his back and chest. Though heat rashes are not serious, they cause a lot of discomfort because of the itching sensation they excite. Application of a mild lotion may help to cure prickly heat.

Heat boils start as reddish pimples, accumulate pus and cause pain. These are common in India, especially in the summer months. Children are given frequent oil baths to keep their body cool, which spares them the suffering and pain caused by heat boils. If boils occur in profusion, a doctor should be consulted.

Scabies or itch

This is caused by a small insect called the itchmite. Children get it while playing in dirty soil. It spreads from person to person either through personal contact or by contact with the infected child's clothing. It causes a scratching sensation which increases in intensity at night. It is better to get the child cured of the itch by consulting a doctor in good time and thus also prevent others in the family from contracting it.

Eczema

Another common skin disease in babies is eczema. It occurs on the face and scalp and in the folds of the elbows and knees. It begins with redness and roughness. Then dampness develops and finally a crust develops. Scratching aggravates the condition.

Strong soaps should not be used. A doctor should be consulted, and his prescription followed carefully to fight the disease.

Worms

Children suffer from a variety of worm infections in India. The most common of these are the roundworm, the threadworm, the hookworm and the tapeworm.

The Roundworm

The roundworm, an intestinal parasite, is of most frequent occurrence in children. It resembles the earthworm and is round or cylindrical and pointed at both ends. The male is about 10.2 cms to 20.3 cms long and the female about 17.8 cms to 35.6 cms. The sources of infection are uncooked vegetables, contaminated food or drinking water. Infection is through the skin by the larvae, and also through the air by breathing embryonated eggs contained in dust. The roundworms, if present in large numbers, cause severe colic pain, irregular appetite and convulsions and other nervous symptoms in children.

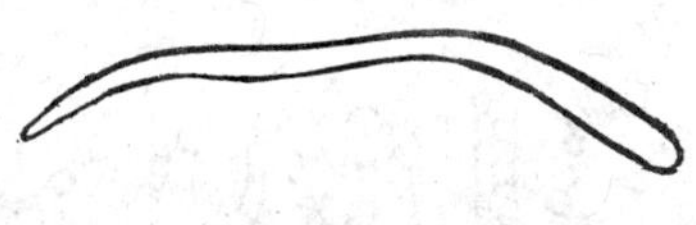

Fig. 70. The Roundworm

Threadworms

As the very name indicates they are threadlike. They measure about 6.35 mms to 12.7 mms and are found mainly in children, in enormous numbers. They inhabit the colon, especially the caecum. They usually cause irritation around

Fig. 71. Threadworm

the anus. Smearing the anus with dilute ammoniated mercury ointment at night, before going to bed, will not only allay the irritation but kill the worms and their eggs.

The hookworm

Fig. 72. Hookworm

The hookworm is also another common parasite of the intestines. It has a conical head and a threadlike body. Infection with hookworms is mainly a rural phenomenon. In older children going about the fields without any protection, the skin of the foot is the vulnerable spot. The symptoms vary. Indigestion, dyspepsia, lack of energy, apathy and anaemia are common symptoms in the early stages and are followed by dropsy, palpitation, shortness of breath and general debility in advanced stages of the infection.

The tapeworm

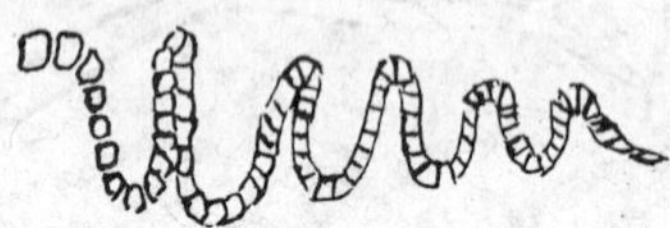

Fig. 73. Tapeworm

These worms are long, fat and tape-like and inhabit the intestinal canal. They are usually segmented, white or yellow in colour, and lead a parasitic life by attaching themselves to the intestinal walls. The tapeworm segments break and come out in the faeces. Animals such as the pig, which eat refuse, harbour them and act as the "intermediary host" till the eggs and larvae develop. They pass into the digestive system of human beings through such meat being eaten.

Combating worms

Only hygienic methods of living can help to combat worms. Children should not be allowed to play in the dust and dirt. Water should be boiled and filtered before being drunk. Food, especially vegetables, should be properly cooked before being eaten. Washing of hands before eating and careful cleaning of finger nails should be a regular and scrupulous habit. Proper sanitation should have top priority for the healthy living of children and adults. The practice in India of children and sometimes even adults passing stools around their houses, on open land or on the banks of rivers and tanks, deserves the severest condemnation. Effective steps should be taken to stop it. Walking barefoot in the streets and fields should be avoided. Adherence to careful hygienic principles and prevention of soil pollution through proper sanitation will ensure the enjoyment of buoyant health and a happy life by children.

Immunization

Immunization is the process of introducing a very small and harmless dose of the germs causing the disease into the body. Through immunization, the antigerms are multiplied, and therefore the body becomes sufficiently strong to fight the disease germs.

However, most immunizations have to be repeated over a period of time, when these antigerms become weak. These repeated immunizations are called 'boosters' i.e. they further strengthen the body against the particular disease for which the body has been immunized.

Immunization Schedule for Children

	Age	Vaccination
1.	After 24 hours of birth and before 15 days	Zero Polio (OPV)
2.	1½ months (45 days)	1st DPT and OPV
3.	2½ months	2nd DPT and OPV
4.	3½ months	3rd DPT and OPV
5.	After 270 days (9 months)	Measles Vaccine and OPV
6.	After 1½ years	Booster DPT and OPV
7.	5th year	DT (Diphtheria & Tetanus)
8.	6th year	TT 1st dose (Tetanus Toxoid)
9.	10th year	TT 2nd dose
10.	16th year (only for girls)	TT 3rd dose

Note: DPT is Diphtheria, Pertussis and Tetanus. OPV is Oral Polio Vaccine.

When the child has completed six months, give vitamin A 2 mls concentrate—first dose. Then every six months for three doses repeat the same amount of vitamin A. This is not immunization.

As per the WHO report, small pox has been eradicated and hence there will be no need for vaccination against small pox. Typhoid inoculations are recommended to be given in epidemic areas when threatened with local outbreaks.

Needs of adolescents

Adolescence is a period of transition when a person is neither a child nor an adult. It is a period during which marked changes occur in duties, responsibilities, privileges and relationships with others. According to Hurlock, the adolescence period is from 12 to 21 years of age.

Physiological needs of adolescents

Physical and psychological changes that occur with the gaining of sexual maturity provide the background for many of the problem situations encountered by adolescents who have not been prepared by intelligent and tactful adults for the onset of pubescence. The information or misinformation regarding sex that he acquires from other young people may result in the development of attitudes of fear or may stimulate the urge to experiment alone or with other children. The boy's first ejection and discharge of semen or the girl's first menstrual flow may become emotionally charged incidents in the young person's life.

Emotional needs

An adolescent is identified by high emotionality as reflected in the increase in emotional tension at adolescence. Matters relating to happiness, problems and worries, mental disease and suicide are only a few that need to be considered. An adolescent tends to be aggressive, self-conscious and withdrawn. Adolescents become increasingly moody. They shift easily from elation, hope or joy to the depth of gloomy despair. Instability is the common mark of adolescence.

Worry is a common characteristic of an adolescent's emotional behaviour centering around social activities and home relationships including friendship with members of both sexes. Adolescents are often very short-tempered. They are emotionally immature due to the growing feeling of independence.

Psychological needs

Every age has its problems. But for young adolescents, problems seem more numerous than at other ages. Even if they have parental love and affection, young adolescents think that their problems are their own and parents are too old to understand and help them. The feeling of insecurity makes them hide their feelings from their parents. So adolescents who feel that their parents do not understand them have greater problems than those adolescents who have more insight into their own problems. All the problems the adolescent faces are increased when the home situation is not satisfactory or when the home is broken up by death or divorce.

Measures to help adolescents

There are a number of things one can do to help adolescents to develop in a healthy way.

1. Elders must respect the adolescents individuality.
2. Parents should be consistent in disciplining the children.
3. Proper sex education must be given.
4. Recreational facilities should be provided.
5. They should have access to books.
6. The home environment should be so arranged as to provide for their increasing independence in order to solve the problems of inadequacy and insecurity.
7. He must be provided with a chance to express his feelings.
8. Too much of expectation from him and adult interference should be avoided.
9. Give him some chance to be responsible and do his own work.
10. Proper love and affection must be given.
11. Positive guidance should be provided.
12. Their activities must be encouraged.

Duties of parents

The family plays a predominant role in the socialization of the child, which starts from the day the child is born. It is the parents with whom the child comes into contact first. Parents are the conveyors of culture. The attitudes, values and prejudices which shape the human personality are mainly acquired by the child through his parents. In the words of Rousseau, "Man is good but if he is bad, it is the environment that has made him so."

Parenthood does not simply mean procreation and feeding of children but also includes the responsibility for developing the emotional, social and psychological aspects of a child's personality.

Here are seven clues to successful parenthood.

Spend time—not money alone

To demand parental love and affection is the birthright of every child. Parents have the responsibility of satisfying the emotional needs of children such as (a) the need for love and affection (b) the need for adventure (c) the need for security (d) the need for understanding and appreciation, and (e) the need for play. Many of the child's problems are attributed to the emotional disturbance in children caused by the lack of parental warmth and affection. Parents should therefore spend time with their children rather than only money. There should be proper communication and understanding of the child's mind in the family. The children would feel safe and secure and experience, what is called a "sense of belonging" if they find their parents loving and interested in their well-being.

Be a model

Children look upon their parents for everything and they are their parents' imitators. Let the parents, therefore, preach only those things, which they themselves can practise; any deviation will have a deleterious effect on the character of their children. If the parents want to inculcate a spirit of cooperation and accommodation in their children, this should be shown in their day-to-day life. Hence healthy husband-wife relations are the key to successful parenthood.

Successful parents are those who command love and affection from their children.

Don't condemn but correct

Right upbringing requires on the part of the parents great patience, tolerance, tenderness and self-restraint. Parents should never be hasty in condemning the actions of their children, especially of those who are in their infant stage as that is the stage when the children's mind can be very easily moulded. The parental role in the home should be supportive, helpful and nurturing rather than controlling, condemning and coercive.

Avoid unhealthy comparisons

The child should be allowed to learn things at his natural pace without any fear and any unhealthy competition arising out of parents making unnecessary comparisons. Parents should praise the child's sincere efforts at learning and guide him whenever necessary.

Never kill the child's curiosity

Grown-ups should try to recollect their childhood experiences and try to enter into the children's world while they are dealing with them. Children should be given a chance to express themselves and exhibit their innate potentialities. Parents should be particularly careful not to destroy the child's delight and enthusiasm or ridicule his budding aesthetic sense.

Keep pace with the changes in society

As the structure of society changes, the make up of the generations also alters correspondingly and if the parents refuse to keep pace with the changes by changing their attitudes and opinions accordingly, they would find their children uncontrollable and rebellious.

Don't dictate but educate

Education is not the job of only the school, but also that of the family. Parents have the duty to make the child develop an integrated personality endowed with healthy attitudes, desires and a sense of civic and moral responsibility.

Thus parenthood is a tough job. It involves being a dietician, a child psychologist, a patient listener and a social worker.

Family

Family is an institution existing in all human societies and continues to remain important despite the changes taking place in the world today.

Characteristics of a family

The following characteristics which define the human family differentiate it from other social groups.

1. The family is composed of persons united by marriage, blood or adoption—husband and wife by marriage and parents and children by blood or adoption.
2. The members of a family typically live together under one roof and constitute a single household.
3. The family is a unit of interacting and intercommunicating persons enacting their social roles.
4. The family maintains a common culture, derived mainly from the general culture.

Types of family

The family is a variable concept. In the narrow sense the conjugal family (nuclear type) consists of husband and wife and their children towards whom they assume the role of parents. In a broader perspective the family is a larger one (joint family), consisting of old relatives and their conjugal units.

In terms of authority, there are two types of families (1) patriarchal and (2) matriarchal. In the patriarchal system the father or male member has the authority in the family. In the matriarchal type of family, the mother or female member is the supreme authority.

The patriarchal type is also known as a patrilineal family and the matriarchal type is known as a matrilineal family. In a patrilineal family, children are recognized through male membership and in a matrilineal family it is through the female.

Inheritance of property rights is given to males in patriarchal families and to females, in matriarchal families, depending on where the married couple resides. On the basis of their residence the family can be either patrilocal and matrilocal. When the married couple live with the wife's parents, it is known as matrilocal and when they live with the husband's parents, it is called patrilocal family. As a result of supreme authority, the patrilocal type of family will be a patrilineal family and the patrilocal type of residence of the married couple will be present. Similarly, the matrilocal type of family will be a matrilineal family and matrilocal type of residence of the married couple will be present.

In the conjugal type of family also there are two types. (1) nuclear family (2) extended nuclear family.

Functions of family

Regardless of the type, each family has certain functions to carry out. These functions vary according to the standard of living, personality of members and other influencing factors. Some of these functions are:

1. Economic — The family has to support the members economically.
2. Protective — It must give protection to the members in the family, and also love and affection.
3. Recreational — It must provide facilities for recreation.
4. Religious — It must carry out the religious functions in the family.
5. Cultural — It must transmit culture to the family members.
6. Reproduction — To inherit the property of ancestors, it must give birth to children.
7. Education — It must give higher education to the children in order to make them ready to stand on their feet.
8. Social — It must teach them how to adjust with others in society.

Factors which promote harmony in family relationships

Marriage is the recognized union of husband and wife, which is the basis of the conjugal family. Adjustment is a continuous process leading to either greater or lesser understanding and solidarity between men and women.

Adjustment in marriage

There are a number of factors that go into making up a marriage, requiring adjustments from both husband and wife.

1. Personality characteristics: Emotional stability is very important to success in marriage. The emotional stability of the marriage partners has been shown to be related closely to their happiness. Happiness is positively related to the sharing of common interests among the couples.
2. Relationship with in-laws: In-law troubles were mentioned in second place by women and in third place by men as their most serious problem in achieving happiness in marriage.
3. Economic factors: Adequate income, savings, low indebtedness and steady employment of either the husband or wife or both are positively related to marital success. The person who considers financial security as the most important factor in marriage should not marry another who is careless and wasteful with money.
4. Sexual relationship: The sexual relationship between the partners should be good, if the marriage is to be a happy one. Consideration, gentleness and sensitivity are some factors that are important in regard to this aspect of marriage.
5. Influence of siblings: The only child more often is a problem child than a child with brothers and sisters. The only child makes poor adjustments in marriage as compared to families with two or more children.
6. Influence of parents: Happy parents usually give their child the kind of training that will ensure his ability to get along in marriage when he becomes an adult. Children who come from unhappy homes on the other hand are more likely to have marriage failures. Children of divorced or separated parents find adjustment in marriage more difficult than do children from united families.
7. Age at marriage: The happiness of couples depends upon the age at which they get married. Men and women who marry after they have achieved a reasonable amount of maturity may have good adjustment in their married life.

8. Education: Research shows that success in marriage is greater if the level of education of the partners is higher.

Other factors facilitating marital adjustment

The other factors which help marital adjustment are:
1. Similar family backgrounds of couples.
2. Attending the same church or temple or mosque.
3. Good health of husband and wife at the time of marriage.
4. Not having sex relations before marriage.

Part VI

Food and Cookery

12. General Functions of Food

"A sound mind in a sound body" is a well-known adage. A sound body is an impossibility without proper food and nourishment. The right kind of food has an important role to play in promoting good health. Healthy children have bright, clear eyes, smooth, glossy hair, a clean and shining skin, and firm, well developed muscles. They have excellent poise, bearing themselves erect on well formed, sturdy bones. Healthy children have good stamina and physique, are active mentally and physically, have endurance, vigour and vitality, have a cheerful mien and are good natured. Good food means good health. Good health is the source of good living, and good living is conducive to a full and long life.

All living organisms need food to keep the spark of life glowing. Food gives vitality by discharging the following functions:

It energizes.
It builds.
It renews body tissues.
It regulates body processes and internal conditions.

Nutrient groups or food classes

There are differences in the nutritive value of foodstuffs. The main nutrients of foodstuffs have been classified as:

Carbohydrates,
Fats,
Proteins,
Minerals,
Vitamins and
Water.

Functions of nutrient groups

Each nutrient serves one or more of the following general functions:

Functions

To supply heat, energy and power	To build and promote growth	To renew body tissues	To regulate body processes
Carbohydrates	...	...	...
Fats	...	...	...
Proteins	Proteins	Proteins	Proteins
	Minerals	Minerals	Minerals
	Vitamins	Vitamins	Vitamins
			Water

Protective foods

The foods which provide the different requirements of the human body in greatest measure are known as "protective

Fig. 74. Rich sources of energy-giving foods

foods." To this category belong milk, butter, meat, eggs, whole grain cereals, fruit, especially the citrus variety, and vegetables, notably the green or yellow varieties.

Energy values of nutrients

The main function of food is to supply energy. The energy value of nutrients is expressed in calories. A nutritional calorie or the physiological calorie is the amount of heat necessary to raise the temperature of 1 kilogram of water through 1°C. This is also referred to as Kilo Calories (K Cals.) This is 1000 times the physical calorie unit which is the heat required to raise the temperature of 1 gm of water through 1°C.

In recent years, a new unit of energy has been adapted which is referred to as Joule.

1 Kilo Calorie (Physiological Calorie) = 4.184 Kilo Joules (K.J.) For practical purposes, however, the factor 4.2 can be used for conversion of Kilo Calories to Kilo Joules.

When a pure carbohydrate food such as sugar or starch is burnt or oxidised, energy is released during oxidation which can be measured in terms of Calories. Scientific experiments have proved that:

1 gm of carbohydrate yields 4 calories or 4 × 4.2 = 16.8 Kilo Joules

1 gm of protein yields 4 calories or 4 × 4.2 = 16.8 Kilo Joules

1 gm of fat yields 9 calories or 9 × 4.2 = 37.8 Kilo Joules.

Energy requirements

If a person does not obtain the required amount of calories from the food he takes, he gets hungry quickly, and cannot do strenuous work. The caloric requirements of a child, a woman or a man depend on the age, sex, height, weight and the activity or profession pursued. Muscular work is the most important factor in determining the energy requirement. When a man is at rest he needs less energy than when he is actively engaged. He requires only basal energy for the functioning of the heart, lungs, liver, kidneys and other internal organs. Manual work, light or heavy, calls for an additional supply of energy above the basal rate. Normally women need less calories than men. The following is the scale of average calorie requirement per day in India as recommended dietary allowance for Indians taken from the book—*Nutritive Value of Indian Food,* 1993, National Institute of Nutrition, Indian Council of Medical Research, Hyderabad, India.

		Net Energy K. Calories per day
Man	Sedentary work	2425
	Moderate work	2875
	Heavy work	3800

Woman	Sedentary work	1875
	Moderate work	2225
	Heavy work	2925
	Pregnant woman	+300
Lactation	0-6 months	+550
	6-12 months	+400
Infants	0-6 months	108/Kg body weight
	6-12 months	98/Kg body weight
Children	1-3 years	1240
	4-6 years	1690
	7-9 years	1950
Boys	10-12 years	2190
Girls	10-12 years	1970
Boys	13-15 years	2450
Girls	13-15 years	2060
Boys	16-18 years	2640
Girls	16-18 years	2060

Carbohydrates

The body's most economical source of energy is carbohydrates. These derive their name from their component parts—carbon, hydrogen and oxygen. Hydrogen and oxygen are present in the same ratio as in water. Carbohydrates include every kind of starch and sugar, and such other substances as cellulose, pectins and gums.

Classification of carbohydrates

The carbohydrates in our food belong to three different groups known as:

The Monosaccharides or the Single Sugars;
The Disaccharides or the Double Sugars; and
The Polysaccharides or the Multiple Sugars.

Monosaccharides

These are single sugars and are the simplest and smallest of the carbohydrate molecules. They cannot be split up further into simpler forms. They are easily soluble in water. It is only in the form of monosaccharides that the carbohydrates are absorbed in the body. They are directly absorbed from the intestinal tract into the blood without undergoing any change whatsoever. All the end products of digested carbohydrates are single sugars.

The three important monosaccharides or single sugars are glucose, fructose and galactose.

Glucose is abundantly present in grapes. It is widely distributed in nature. It occurs in small quantities in the blood of all animals. It is present in human blood to the concentration of 0.1%. It is also known as dextrose. Because it occurs in grapes, blood and iron, it is called grape sugar, blood sugar and corn sugar. Sometimes it is also referred to as starch sugar. In grapes glucose forms 20% or at times 50% or more of the solid matter.

Fructose is also known as levulose or fruit sugar. It occurs in fruit and honey. In honey it forms about one half of the solid matter. Fructose is the sweetest of all sugars.

Galactose does not occur free in nature. It comes principally from the digestive breakdown of milk sugar. It is formed, along with an equal weight of glucose, when milk sugar is digested. Galactose occurs in plants combined with other sugars and starches. In brain and nerve tissues, it is found along with fats or proteins.

Disaccharides

These are double sugars formed when two monosaccharide units condense together with the elimination of one molecule of water. The three nutritionally important members of this group are **sucrose**, **maltose** and **lactose**.

Sucrose or ordinary table sugar is also known as saccharse, cane sugar and beet sugar. The sources of sucrose are the sugar and sorghum canes, the sugar beet, the sugar palm and almost all fruits and vegetables. Half of the solid matter in a ripe pineapple and the sweeter variety of carrots, is sucrose. Sucrose on hydrolysis yields glucose and fructose.

Maltose or malt sugar occurs in germinating cereals, malt and malt products. It is also formed in the digestive tract from the breakdown of starch. Since many foods contain starch, which is converted into maltose and then into glucose, this sugar is an extremely important source of heat and energy to the body. One molecule of maltose on hydrolysis yields two molecules of glucose.

Lactose or milk sugar occurs in the milk of all mammals and is synthesized in the mammary glands. Six to seven per cent of human milk and four to five per cent of cow's milk is lactose. It is less sweet than other sugars and is easily soluble in water. The sweeter form is known as beta-lactose. Physicians and bacteriologists consider lactose of great importance for maintaining a desirable state of the lower intestinal tract. Hydrolysis on lactose yields glucose and galactose.

Polysaccharides or multiple sugars

Starch, the dextrins, glycogen, cellulose and the hemicelluloses are the polysaccharides. As the name indicates, these are formed by the condensation of many monosaccharide units with the elimination of water.

Starch is the principal source of energy for human beings. It is found in all cereals, bread, potatoes, and many other roots and tubers. Three-fourths of the solid material in most cereal grains and in mature potatoes is starch.

Dextrin is formed from starch when grains sprout. When bread or similar starchy foods are toasted, dextrin is formed. Thus dextrin is an intermediary product in the digestion of starch. Any starch during digestion passes through the dextrin stage before it reaches the monosaccharide stage.

The liver is the principal storehouse of **glycogen**. Hence the liver is the richest food source. Glycogen plays much the same role in animals as starch in plants. It is sometimes known as animal starch. Excess sugar in the body is converted into glycogen and stored in the liver or muscles. Glycogen reserved in the body is used whenever it is required by the body. However, glycogen is converted into glucose before it can become a source of energy.

Cellulose is the framework of all plants. It is the chief constituent of wood, stalks and leaves, the peelings and fibrous parts of fruits and vegetable tissues, the outer covering of seeds and the bran or coating of grains.

The **hemicelluloses** belong to the walls of plant cells.

On hydrolysis they yield monosaccharides or mixtures of monosaccharides and disaccharides. A large portion of the hemicelluloses usually remains undigested and gives bulk to the intestinal residue. Although digested in considerable quantities, they are not utilised to any great extent.

Fats

Like carbohydrates, fats are composed of carbon, hydrogen and oxygen in different proportions. They consist of glycerol (glycerine) and complex fatty acids. They are the most concentrated form of energy and yield more than twice as much energy as carbohydrates. Fats differ in colour, taste and consistency and in vitamin value. Being unable to store a large amount of carbohydrates, the animal body converts carbohydrates not only into glycogen but also into fat and stores the fat in almost all parts of the body. The largest amount is stored directly under the skin. Although fats are mostly of animal origin, a few plants also have the power to store fats in considerable amounts in their nuts.

Nuts such as almonds and peanuts are very rich in fats. Vegetable fats are known as 'oils' because at ordinary temperature they are liquids. Ghee, butter, coconut oil, groundnut oil, cottonseed oil, olive oil, fish oils like cod liver oil and shark liver oil, are some of the familiar examples of foods consisting almost entirely of fat.

Fats which have a low melting point, like milk, cream and butter are easily digested. Those with a high melting point, like mutton fat, are hard to digest.

Uses of fat

The uses of fat are many. It gives energy value to the food. Storage of fat assists in the regulation of body temperature. It protects the body from mechanical injury and acts as a support to vital organs like the kidneys. It also acts as a carrier of essential fat-soluble vitamins and gives satiety value to a meal. Certain fatty acids found in foods such as butter and egg yolk are essential for normal health. Not less than 45 to 60 grams of fat should be consumed daily. At least 15 grams of fat should be derived from vegetable oils.

Lipoids

Fats are usually accompanied by lipoids which are fat-like substances soluble either in fat solvents or fat itself. Lipins and lipids are names sometimes used to cover both the true fats and the lipoids of all kinds.

Proteins

The word "protein" is derived from the Greek word *proteios* which means "the first place". Proteins hold the first place in the build-up of all living things. They are the fundamental constituents of tissue substances. Without proteins there can be no life. They are the very basis of life, because the cells of all forms of life, whether animal or vegetable, are built of protoplasm which consists of protein. Without proteins no plant can grow, no animal can thrive, no baby can be born or brought up.

Sources of protein

Proteins occur in nature together with fats and carbohydrates, and seldom alone. The purest forms of natural proteins are found in the white of eggs, the curd of milk, and fat-free meats. While plants synthesize or manufacture their own proteins, animals obtain theirs from food.

Uses of protein

The most important function of protein is body-building. Proteins help children to grow, and adults to renew their body tissues. Next to water, they constitute the largest proportion of the body. The hair, nails, skin and muscle tissues consist almost entirely of proteins. The body uses protein in many other ways which are of tremendous importance to health. Haemoglobin, the red corpuscles of the blood, are largely protein. The hormones produced by the glands in the body, are made of proteins. Enzymes are largely proteins. Proteins are responsible for the collection of urine and removal of wastes. They prevent blood from becoming either too acidic or too alkaline. They are of value in the clotting of blood. They form antibodies in the blood, which combat bacteria and injurious toxins produced by the bacteria. Thus proteins are so valuable that life cannot exist without them. They are of the very essence of life. Neither fats nor carbohydrates are of direct value for the purpose of body-building since they contain no nitrogen. Practically all the tissues of the body contain proteins which are nitrogenous. Proteins contain carbon, hydrogen, oxygen and nitrogen and in many cases sulphur and sometimes phosphorus also. Proteins, like carbohydrates and fats, can be used in the body as fuels.

There are many different kinds of proteins—animal, plant and human. However, all are alike in one respect, since they are all built up of similar substances known as "amino acids". They have to be hydrolysed into amino acids before they can be absorbed and utilised by the body. Animal proteins such as those of meat, milk and eggs are most completely digested. Those of legumes, peas, beans and grams are the lowest in digestibility. All proteins are not of equal value as food, because they do not all contain the amino acids we require. On the basis of their efficacy in promoting growth, amino acids can be differentiated into indispensable and dispensable acids.

Kinds of proteins

Taking into consideration the number and quantity of essential amino acids they contain, proteins can be classificed as complete, partially complete and incomplete or inadequate.

Complete of proteins

Proteins containing all the ten essential amino acids in generous amounts are called complete. When a complete protein is fed to young animals as the only source of protein, normal growth and development result. Complete proteins such as casein of milk maintain life and promote normal growth of the young.

Partially complete proteins

Partially complete proteins maintain life but do not support growth. Gliadin of wheat is a good example of a partially complete protein.

Incomplete or inadequate proteins

A protein which lacks the essential amino acids is called incomplete or inadequate. It is incapable of maintaining life or promoting growth.

The capacity to promote growth is called the Biological Value of proteins and is related to the amino acid content. Nut proteins have the lowest biological value. Pulse proteins and cereal proteins have a higher biological value. Meat, fish, milk and egg proteins are of the highest biological value. From the above it will be clear that animal proteins have a higher biological value than vegetable proteins. Growing children must be given some of the foods which furnish protein of excellent quality such as milk, eggs and meat.

Protein requirement

As already mentioned, proteins are required for maintenance (replacing the wear and tear in tissue) in adults, for growth in infants and children, for faetal development in pregnancy and milk output in lactation. The relative requirement of protein of the latter groups are higher than in adults. The actual amount of protein to be consumed daily to meet the above requirement will depend upon the quality of dietary protein. The higher the quality, lower the requirement and vice versa. The requirements are generally determined in terms of egg and for other proteins are computed after making adjustment for the lower quality of dietary protein relative to egg. Egg protein has the highest value as compared to other proteins and is therefore taken as a reference protein and the value of others are expressed as relative to egg (100). The adult requirement of egg protein is 0.7 gms per kg; while requirement in terms of mixed vegetable protein is 1.0 gm per kg. It is to be expected that children require more protein per unit body weight than adults, because of new tissues which are being laid down during growth are largely built from amino acids drawn from the dietary protein. Thus a young child of 1-2 years requires 1.2 gm egg protein/kg or 2.0 gms of mixed vegetable protein per kg. Likewise, protein needs of women are greater during pregnancy and lactation than during non-pregnant, nonlactating states. It must also be emphasized that figures for protein requirement are valid only when other nutrients particularly calories in diet are adequate. In other words, the diet must be. a well balanced one.

A mixed diet even solely based on plant proteins can meet the protein requirement of adults and older children, provided they consume enough of the diet to meet their energy needs. For this the protein content of the diet should be such as to contribute around 10% of the total calorie. For growing children and for women during pregnancy and lactation, the protein requirements are relatively greater and it is desirable that some animal foods which have protein of high nutritive value be included in the diet of these groups of population, particularly if the protein concentration in the diet is low (containing low protein cereals, roots, little of pulse, etc.) The best source of animal protein for growing children is milk. Milk also provides a good amount of calcium which is normally lacking in vegetarian diets. Eggs also can be used as source of good quality protein whenever possible. Besides providing good quality protein, it provides a good amount of a wide range of other nutrients, particularly B_{12} which is absent in vegetable foods. Skimmed milk is a rich source of protein as whole milk. Butter milk of good quality can also serve as a source of good quality protein. Fish also is a good source of protein whenever available and acceptable and should be included in the diet, particularly of older children and adults. In devising an inexpensive well balanced diet in India, economic considerations often preclude the inclusion of milk or often animals foods in adequate amounts. A judicious mixture of plant foods like cereals and pulses and vegetables can be relatively inexpensive and at the same time can provide a mixture of proteins with nearly as good an amino acid pattern as that of expensive animal foods.

Recommended dietary allowance for protein

In 1989, a subcommittee of the United States Food and Nutrition Board issued its updated Recommended Dietary Allowance for protein and amino acid, based largely on the conclusion of the 1985 report of the FAO/WHO/UNU

Committee. The 1989 Recommended Dietary Allowance (RDA) for protein was established by first estimating the average requirement for high quality, highly digestible protein, so called reference protein, according to sex, age and reproductive status.

For **adults**, the average daily requirement for reference protein was accepted to be 0.6 g/kg per day based on published data from long term and short term studies. This average was then increased by 25% to allow for individual variability, and the recommended allowance of reference protein for **young men** was at 0.75 g/kg per day. The limited available data for **women** suggests that their requirement levels, when adjusted for body weight, are similar to those of men. This value is rounded off resulting in an RDA of 0.8 g/kg per day for young men and women.

The RDA (Recommended Dietary Allowance) for protein for **elderly adults** is also assigned the value of 0.8 g/kg per day.

In **pregnancy**, the RDA for women is increased to provide additional protein for deposition in the maternal (i.e. blood, uterus, breasts) fetal, and placental tissues. To allow for a maintenance requirement of the added lean tissue and the uncertainty about the rate of tissue deposition, the new RDA for protein during pregnancy provides an additional 10 gms per day throughout gestation over and above the usual adult requirement.

The average protein requirement for **lactation** is estimated from milk composition and the mean volume of milk produced, resulting in a RDA increment of 15 g of extra protein daily over and above the usual adult requirement of 0.8 g/kg per day. After 6 months of lactation, the volume of milk produced decreases about 20% and in consequence, the RDA increment for protein is decreased to only 12 g of extra protein daily over the usual adult requirement.

The RDA for protein for **infants and children** is intended to provide adequate protein for a satisfactory rate of growth. During the first year, the infant increases in weight. Infants breast fed by healthy, well nourished mothers grow satisfactovily for about 3 to 4 months and are usually supplemented with additional foods thereafter. A study of breast fed infants in the United States demonstrated satisfactory growth at a mean protein intake of 1.6 g/kg per day during the first 3 months. The RDA Subcommittee has accepted this as the average human milk protein requirement from birth to 3 months of age. This estimate was then increased by about 25% resulting in the RDA of 2.2 g/kg per day for infants from 0 to 6 months of age. Thereafter the protein requirements again fall to 1.6 g/kg in the second 6 months of life i.e. 6 to 12 months, and then again to 1 g/kg for children upto 14 years of age. This in turn goes down to 0.8 g/kg for adults. The following is the table of Recommended Daily Allowance for proteins (FAO/WHO/UNU-1989).

Recommended Dietary Allwance for Protein (FAO/WHO/UNU-1989)

Adults Man or Woman	0.8 gms/kg per day
Pregnancy	Plus 10 gms per day
Lactation	Plus 15 gms per day
Lactation after 6 months	Plus 12 gms per day
Infants (0-6 months)	2.2 g/kg per day
Infants (6-12 months)	1.6 g/kg per day
Children upto 14 years	1 g/kg per day

Kwashiorkor is one of the most widespread protein deficiency diseases found in tropical and sub-tropical areas. The term Kwashiorkor means "red boy" and refers to the loss of pigmentation in the dark-skinned races. The disease is found among severely undernourished children and infants and is related to diets in which the protein is insufficient in quantity and poor in quality, i.e., proteins of low biological value.

The incidence of Kwashiorkor among children in India is due to prolonged breast feeding or early weaning or to diets consisting mainly of carbohydrates such as rice that are lacking in proteins.

The symptoms are alterations in skin and hair pigmentation, oedema, diarrhoea and fatty infiltration of the liver. If not treated early, it leads to high infant mortality.

Since foods of animal origin are not readily available to

the poorer classes, and to certain sections of the people owing to religious restrictions, foods rich in vegetable proteins such as legumes, peanuts, etc., could be introduced into their diet. Skimmed milk powder has been found to be very effective in the dietary treatment of Kwashiorkor.

Minerals

Apart from carbohydrates, fats and proteins, there are other substances in the body known as **mineral salts** which are of importance for the growth and well-being of the individual. These form the ash constituents of the body. They are present in simple form as inorganic salts or in complex organic combinations. Mineral elements are divided on the basis of their concentration in the body into major elements and minor or trace elements. Calcium phosphorus, potassium, sulphur, chlorine, sodium, magnesium and iron are considered major elements. Manganese, copper, iodine, cobalt, zinc and fluorine are present in smaller amounts and are considered trace elements. For the purposes of practical dietetics, particular attention is given to calcium, phosphorus, iron and iodine, because these are the elements which, as far as our present knowledge indicates, are most likely to be present in insufficient quantities in human diets.

Uses of minerals

The mineral salts found in the body form constituents of skeletal bodies. They occur as essential elements of the soft tissues of the body as in muscle cells, nerve cells, liver cells and brain cells. They are also found as soluble salts in the fluids of the body such as the blood, the lymph, the digestive juices and also in sweat and tears.

Calcium

Calcium is the mineral salt which occurs in the largest proportion in the human body. It occupies a prominent place among the mineral components of the animal body since it is one of the principal substances of which the bony skeleton and teeth are composed. The rigidity of the bone is due to the presence of calcium in it. Calcium deficiency during the period of growth results in defective development

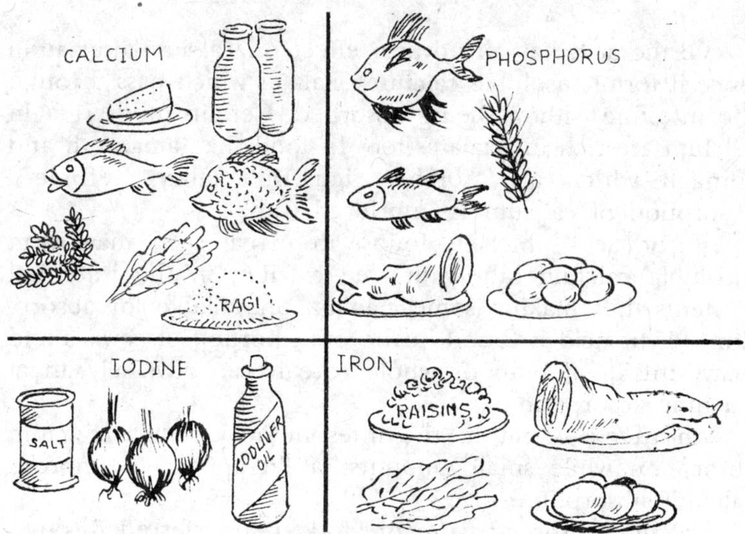

Fig. 75. Rich sources of minerals

of the bony skeleton, weakened bones, contracted thorax and pelvis, defective teeth and stunted growth.

The presence of calcium is necessary for the proper contraction of the heart muscle. Calcium promotes the clotting of blood, which is so necessary, since without coagulation of blood, fatal bleeding would follow even from a slight injury. It improves the conductibility of the nerves and increases the activity of the nerve cells. It aids in the curdling of milk in the stomach. It helps the body to assimilate iron. Calcium is a co-ordinator among mineral elements. It helps to maintain the proper balance of other minerals in the body.

Calcium absorption

Dietary calcium is absorbed in the small intestine. The amount absorbed is influenced by a number of factors. The greater the need, and the smaller the dietary supply, the more efficient is the absorption. Calcium absorption is facilitated in the presence of vitamin D and by a low intestinal pH which keeps the calcium in solution. Normal secretion of hydrochloric acid in the stomach is thus necessary to facilitate absorption. Lactose also stimulates absorption of calcium.

Oxalic acid has an adverse effect on calcium utilization since it forms insoluble calcium oxalates which pass through the intestine without being absorbed. Certain foods rich in calcium are rich in oxalates too. In foods like amaranth and spinach which are notably rich in oxalates, efficient absorption of calcium is interfered with.

Phytic acid which is found in cereal seed may form insoluble calcium salts with free calcium in the intestinal contents thus making some calcium unavailable for absorption. Phytic acid is found in the bran portion of cereals and heavy intake of bran or whole cereals can adversely affect calcium absorption.

An excess of fat in the intestine may reduce calcium absorption while small amounts of fat appear to improve calcium absorption.

Calcium absorbed from the food is transferred through the body by the circulation. It is withdrawn from the body by the bones and teeth during periods of growth and some calcium is incorporated into bones, at all ages. The calcium blood level is regulated by the parathyroid hormone. Calcium may be withdrawn from the bones to maintain normal blood levels during periods of dietary calcium deprivation.

Normally the kidney excretes any excess blood calcium. The parathyroid hormone regulates urinary calcium excretion.

Insufficient intake of calcium and phosphorus as well as marked imbalance in calcium and phosphorus intake may result in rickets although the principal cause of this disease in children is lack of vitamin D. In adults, calcium deficiency may cause osteomalacia—a generalized rarefaction and demineralization of bone. This condition is usually due to a deficiency of vitamin D and calcium. Osteoporosis is a metabolic disorder resulting in decalcification of bone with a high incidence of pathologic fractures following light trauma.

Sources

Milk and cheese are the richest sources of calcium. Fish, green leafy vegetables like spinach, amaranth and drumstick leaves are also rich sources. Ragi is rich in calcium, hence a rice diet should be supplemented with ragi. In India, chewing betel leaves with chunam is a common practice. The calcium provided by the chunam is well absorbed by the body.

Requirements

An adult requires approximately 0.5 grams of calcium per day and children require more. The calcium requirement in women is greatly increased during pregnancy and lactation. The requirement is 1 gram per day during pregnancy and lactation. Lack of calcium during pregnancy and lactation will not only affect the growth of the baby but also deplete the calcium in the mother's body. On the other hand the greater the intake of calcium by the mother during pregnancy and lactation, the stronger and sturdier the offspring will be.

Phosphorus

Phosphorus is very widely distributed in the body. Along with calcium it is an important constituent of the bones and teeth. It occurs in nerves, nerve cells and the brain. It plays an essential part in regulating the neutrality of the blood.

Phosphorus has more functions than any other mineral element in the body. A complex of calcium phosphate lends rigidity to bones and teeth. A greater per cent of the body's phosphorus, about 80 per cent is found in the skeletal tissues. The other 20 per cent is located in the body fluids and in every cell of the body and is vitally concerned with their metabolism and function. Phosphorus plays an important part in muscle-energy metabolism, carbohydrate, protein and fat metabolism, normal blood chemistry, skeletal growth and tooth development and the transport of fatty acids. Phosphate is a component of many enzyme systems and is involved in the storage and transfer of energy in phosphorylated compounds such as adenosine di-and triphosphate.

Sources

Milk and milk products have a large amount of phosphorus; so also eggs. Meat and fish have moderate amounts of this mineral salt. Cereals in their raw state are fairly rich in phosphorus. Considerable loss of this element occurs in milling, washing and cooking of rice.

Requirements

Calcium and phosphorus usually occur together. If a diet contains a sufficient quantity of calcium it means that it also contains a sufficient amount of phosphorus. Phosphorus deficiency seldom, if ever, develops in humans.

Iron

Though iron occurs in negligible proportions in the body, its functions are very vital. The body takes great care to preserve as much of its iron as possible. The chromatin substance of the nucleus of every cell and the haemoglobin of the blood contain iron. Lack of iron leads to lack of haemoglobin and results in anaemia. If the iron supply is insufficient owing to deficiency in the food, defective absorption or inefficient utilisation, anaemia will be the consequence.

Iron plays an essential role in oxygen transport and cellular respiration. The haemoglobin molecule is composed of 2 parts; globin (a protein) and heme (the iron containing pigment of the blood and responsible for its characteristic colour.) Haemoglobin combines with oxygen in the lung and normally releases it is the tissues. Haemoglobin also serves as a vehicle for some of the carbon dioxide produced in the active tissues, releasing it in the lungs. In the muscles some of the oxygen is taken up by another iron porphyrin protein, myoglobin, which serves as a temporary oxygen acceptor and reservoir. Iron is also found in the intracellular cytochrome enzyme system which functions in energy production.

Dietary iron is absorbed primarily by the mucosa of the duodenum. Ferrous iron is absorbed more efficiently than ferric iron. Absorption of iron is more efficient in the presence of ascorbic acid, sulphydryl compounds and similar reducing substances. An excess of phosphates, oxalates or phytates in the food may impair iron absorption because of the formation of insoluble iron compounds which pass through the intestinal tract without being absorbed. The main factor that affects iron absorption is the body's need for this substance. Thus absorption is increased during periods of rapid growth in youth, during pregnancy, as a result of blood loss, and in persons living at high altitudes.

Iron deficiency in man is known as hypochromic anaemia. In this condition the total quantity of circulating haemoglobin is low, the number of circulating red blood cells is either normal or reduced. Each erythrocyte has a reduced haemoglobin content and the red blood cells are pale. The blood thus has a decreased oxygen carrying capacity which reflects unfavourably on most body functions. Pallor of skin and tissues, weakness and fatigue, dysponea (laboured breathing) on exertion, headache, palpitation and a constant feeling of tiredness are some of the signs and symptoms of this condition.

Iron deficiency anaemia may develop as a result of inadequate diet or poor absorption. Even though absorption and the diet are adequate, chronic blood loss may lead to a severe exhaustion of the body's iron stores and to subsequent hypochromic anaemia.

Sources

Egg, liver, meat and dry fruits are good sources of iron. Green, leafy vegetables also contain iron. Useful amounts of iron may be absorbed from the water used for drinking. In egg yolk, along with iron, traces of copper are also found. Copper is essential for the proper absorption of iron. Therefore egg, which contains a combination of iron and copper, is an excellent donor of this mineral.

Requirements

Women need more iron than men. In general it is said that an adult's requirement varies from 20 to 30 mg per day. Pregnant women need more than others. Babies are born with a small reserve of iron. Since milk is a poor source of iron, care should be taken to supplement children's feeds with egg yolk, especially if they are bottle-fed.

Iodine

Iodine occurs in the body in the form of salts known as iodides. This is needed by the thyroid glands which are found on either side of the wind pipe at the base of the neck. These glands manufacture a substance called thyroxin which consists largely of iodine. Without thyroxin there can be no normal growth. It is an important regulator of energy metabolism. Deficiency of iodine leads to simple goitre. Lack of thyroxin disturbs the physical and mental well-being of an individual and causes the disease known as myxoedema in adults and cretinism in children. Cretins are under-developed and have a low intelligence level. Owing to an enlarged tongue they cannot shut the mouth. A cretin aged 15 may be of the stature of a three-year-old child.

Sources

Seafood in general are rich sources of iodine. Cod liver oil is of value because of its high iodine content and its richness in fat-soluble vitamins. Seafish and oysters are also good sources of iodine; so also watercress and onions grown in soil containing iodine. Natural unrefined salt contains iodine compounds, but these are lost during the process of refining.

Requirements

Balance studies indicate the daily requirement of adults as 0.05-0.075 mgs. Growing children and pregnant women may need more. Lactating women, specially need a liberal allowance because iodine is lost in the milk. It is usually adequate in non-goitrous regions. In iodine deficit areas, far from the sea, the iodine may be given in drinking water, in table salt, or even in chocolate.

Cobalt

This is a part of the vitamin B_{12} and has been found to help in the treatment of certain types of anaemia. Cobalt is found in many common foods. It is readily absorbed from the intestinal tract and most of the absorbed material is excreted in the urine. Very little of this element is retained. There is no known human cobalt requirement.

Copper

This is a component of the enzyme, tyrosinase, which is

necessary for melanin pigment formation in the body. It is also part of the molecule of uricase and of butyryl coenzyme, a dehydrogenase, and is probably associated with other oxidation-reduction enzymes in the body such as cytochrome C oxidase and ascorbate oxidase. Copper appears to play a role in the synthesis of iron into the haemoglobin and cytochrome molecules. Copper is also a constituent of the elastic connective tissue protein, elastin and is involved in the formation of myelin, the material which sheathes nerve fibres.

Zinc

This is a component of several enzymes which catalyze vital metabolic reactions. Zinc is an integral part of the molecule of carbonic anhydrase without which carbon dioxide exchange cannot take place. It is also a component of the digestive enzyme, carboxyl peptidase and of several dehydrogenases. Zinc also participates in nucleic acid and protein metabolism and is essential for normal maintenance of vitamin A blood levels by facilitating release of vitamin stores from the liver. The richest dietary sources of zinc are oysters and herring. Other high-zinc foods are meats, liver, milk, fish, eggs, nuts and legumes. Diets high in protein of animal origin supply large amounts of zinc. Diets containing mostly carbohydrates and containing only protein of plant origin provide considerably less zinc.

An excess of zinc may be harmful. Too much zinc may be dissolved from galvanized iron containers and cooking utensils by acid foods to produce untoward gastro-intestinal symptoms.

Manganese

This is part of the molecular structure of arginase, an enzyme necessary for the formation of urea. It also serves as an activator of several enzymes active in the "Kreb's" cycle reactions, particularly in the decarboxylation steps. Based on its role in enzymatic reactions, it is considered an essential micronutrient.

Manganese is widely distributed in foods of plant and animal origin. The human requirement is unknown.

Magnesium

Magnesium is a component of soft tissues as well as bone. Cardiac and skeletal muscle and nervous tissue depend on a proper balance between calcium and magnesium ions for normal functioning. It is an essential activator for all enzymes which transfer phosphate from adenosine triphosphate (ATP) to adenosine diphosphate (ADP). Physiologically, low magnesium body fluid levels enhance muscular irritability through increased nerve conduction, increased impulse transmission at the myoneural junction and increased muscular contractility. Magnesium occurs widely in foods.

Fluorine

Traces of fluorine are present in human tissues. Fluorine in traces help to protect the teeth against decay. However, excessive intake of fluorine leads to mottling of the teeth.

Fluorine is important as it is present in bones and teeth and a proper intake is essential to achieve maximum resistance to dental caries. Small amounts of fluorine helps in the prevention of dental caries in children and adults.

Fluorine is widely but unevenly distributed in nature. Water normally contains traces of fluorine. It is found in many foods, seafoods and tea being the most significant dietary source. Its intestinal absorption depends to a large extent on the solubility of the ingested fluorine compound.

The fluorine content of normal human blood is about 0.2 part per million (ppm) and that of saliva, 0.1 ppm. Almost all ingested fluorine is quantitatively excreted in the urine. Prolonged, higher intake may result in excessive storage of fluorine in the skeleton and teeth and in extreme cases, in abnormal hardening of bone and skeleton. Abnormalities usually begin with calcification between the radius and the ulna.

An excessive intake of fluorine leads to mottling of the enamel of the teeth. In extreme cases, the enamel may become pitted and the teeth appear stained and corroded. This condition of dental flourisis is endemic in areas where the natural water supply contains from 2 to 6 ppm of fluorine. On the other hand, when the fluorine content of drinking water is about 1 ppm, a marked decrease in dental caries is observed. There are strong indications that fluoride reduces mineral loss from not only the teeth, but also the skeleton in general, and renders bone more resistant to the degenerative de-mineralization of osteoporosis.

Molybdenum

It is an essential trace mineral as it is part of the molecular structure of two enzymes, xanthine oxidase and aldehyde oxidase.

Minerals	*Rich Sources*	*Functions in the body*	*Recommended daily allowance*
Calcium	Milk, cheese, egg, green vegetables	Bone and tooth formation, coagulation of blood; regulation of heart beat	Adult man 0.4 to 0.5 gram Adult woman 0.4 to 0.5 gram Pregnancy and Lactation 1 gram
Phosphorus	Liver, kidney, egg yolk, meat, fish, milk, cheese, cereals	Bone and tooth formation, constituent of cells, regulation of neutrality of the blood	—
Iron	Liver, meat, egg yolk, raisins, peas, fish, whole grains, green vegetables	Constituent of haemoglobin in the blood and tissue cells necessary for oxygen carrying power	Adult man 20 mg Adult woman 30 mg Pregnancy 40 mg Lactation 30 mg
Iodine	Seafood, iodised salts and iodised sweets	Necessary for normal functioning of the thyroid gland	Adults 0.05 to 0.75 mg
Fluorine	Seafood and tea water in traces	Constituent of bones and teeth, prevents dental caries, reduces mineral loss from the skeleton	In traces—1 ppm in water

Vitamins

The story of vitamins

The most important advance in the knowledge of foods made during this century so far is the discovery of vitamins. For many years scientists were of the opinion that carbohydrates, fats, proteins, minerals and water were all that the body required for health and growth. However, experiments on rats fed with pure carbohydrates, fats, proteins, minerals and water showed that the health of the animals deteriorated. Adding a little cow's milk to their diet produced improvement in health and growth. Scientists therefore became convinced that there was some other nutrient in milk besides the ones previously known.

The Cambridge scientist, Dr. Frederick Gowland Hopkins, published the results of his experiments on rats in 1912 and established beyond doubt that in natural foods there are other essential nutrients apart from carbohydrates, fats, proteins, minerals and water, which he termed "Accessory Food Factors". Therefore, Sir Frederick Hopkins is generally credited with the discovery of vitamins. Simultaneously the American scientists, Osborne and Mendel, McCollum and Davis discovered two factors in milk, one in the fat of the milk which they called "Fat Soluble A" and another in the water of the milk which they termed "Water Soluble B". Subsequent studies showed that each group contained a number of vitamins.

Dr. Casimir Funk, a Polish biochemist, suggested the name *vitamine* for these accessory food factors, *vit*—because it was so vital for life and *amine*—because he found evidence that it belonged to the group of chemical substances called amines. The final 'e' of 'vitamine' was dropped some years later when it became evident that the chemical nature of these substances was not what Funk had supposed it to be. Vitamins are now called by the letters of the English alphabet, as vitamin A, B, C, D and so on.

Every vitamin is a clearly defined chemical compound with distinct characteristics. Each one has a particular role to play and one cannot discharge the duty of another. For instance a cartload of oranges cannot cure vitamin A deficiency, while two oranges may prevent occurrence of vitamin C deficiency. Lack of any one of the vitamins leads to "deficiency diseases" and prolonged deficiency of any vitamin is fatal. Vitamins differ from proteins, fats and carbohydrates in that they do not supply energy. The actual amount of them that one needs daily is very small, but their importance is very great.

Classification of vitamins

Vitamins can be broadly classified as fat-soluble and water-soluble. These are further divisible as follows:

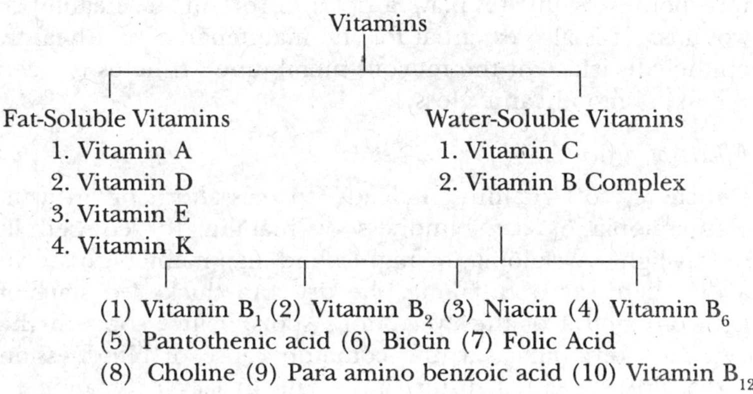

Fat soluble vitamins

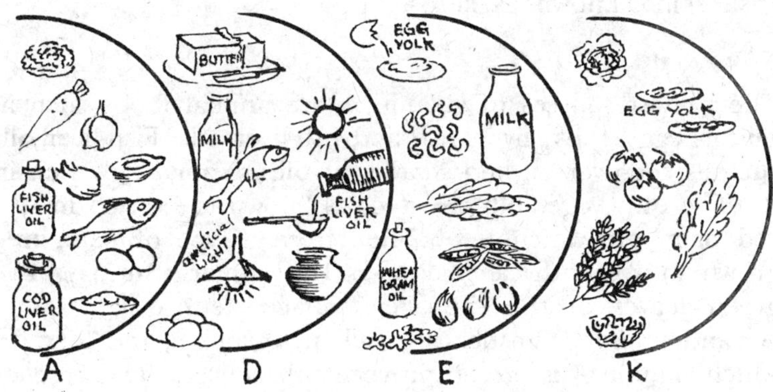

Fig. 76. Rich sources of fat-soluble vitamins

Vitamin A

Vitamin A is otherwise known as the 'Anti infective vitamin' since it plays a vital role in resistance against infection. It is scientifically known as axerophthol because vitamin A deficiency leads to an eye disease called xerophthalmia which, if neglected, will ultimately lead to blindness. It is a fat-soluble vitamin. It can be stored in the body to some extent. It is not lost or destroyed by cooking.

Uses of Vitamin A

Vitamin A is important for growth. It is absolutely necessary for good eye-sight. It plays a definite role in the healing of wounds. It is also essential for the maintenance of a healthy epithelial surface of the mucous membrane. It helps to keep the skin smooth and glossy.

Effects of deficiency

Deficiency of vitamin A leads to cessation of growth. Hemeralopia or day blindness or inability to see well in bright light, nyctalopia, or night blindness, inability to see in a dim light, xerophthalmia, the dry and thickened state of the conjunctiva of the eye, Bitot's spots, yellow spots in the eye, and keratomalacia, the common cause of blindness in India, are the visual disturbances due to lack of vitamin A. Deficiency of vitamin A may also affect the skin. The skin becomes dry, scaly and rough, resembling "goose flesh" or "fish skin", known as xerosis.

Sources

The richest sources of vitamin A are animal foods such as butter, eggs, milk, liver, fish and fish-liver oil. Fish-liver oils such as cod-liver oil and shark-liver oil are amazingly rich in it. The only vegetable oil which is known to be rich in it is red palm oil, which is obtained from a type of palm tree grown in West Africa, Malaya and Myanmar (Burma). The green leaves of the cabbage, spinach, lettuce, amaranth, coriander and drumstick are rich in carotene, the form in which vitamin A is present in vegetable sources. The greener and fresher the vegetable, the greater will be the carotene content. Carrots are also a rich source. Ripe fruits such as mangoes, papayas and tomatoes are rich in carotene. The carotene is converted into vitamin A in the body.

Requirements of vitamin A

Dietary allowance for vitamin A is expressed in terms of either retinol (vitamin A alcohol) or β carotene, depending upon the dietary source of vitamin.

1 μg of β carotene=0.25 μg of retinol. The average adult requirement of vitamin A (retinol) is 750 μ gm per day. During lactation a higher intake of 1150 μg retinol is recommended. Children also need from 250 to 600 μg retinol per day.

Vitamin D

The chemical name of vitamin D is calciferol. It is also known as calcifying vitamin, because it helps to strengthen the bones, sunshine vitamin, because a strong summer or mountain sunshine impels the body to manufacture it and antirachitic vitamin, because it prevents rickets in children. Vitamin D is soluble in fats.

Uses of vitamin D

Vitamin D is essential for the maintenance of normal bone structure and for the proper growth and development of the bones. It also gives increased resistance to infection.

Effects of deficiency

Deficiency of vitamin D causes rickets in children, a disease of childhood characterized by softened bones and chiefly found among ill-fed, undernourished children. Rickets may also be caused by deficiency of calcium or phosphorus in the diet, which may upset the calcium-phosphorus ratio. The bones of the legs become bent under the weight of the body resting upon them and cause "knock-knees" or "bow-legs". The trunk also undergoes various alterations. The chest may be contracted, forming "pigeon chest"; and nodules can be felt at the sternal ends of the ribs, forming "rachitic rosary". Swellings may be noted in the wrists and ankles. The liver is pushed outwards and the abdomen becomes protuberant causing "pot belly". The beginning visible symptoms in infants are profuse sweating and restlessness. If the deficiency appears during the 3rd and 4th month of life, when the skull is growing rapidly, the structure of head will be larger than normal. In the case of adults, especially women, a softened condition of the bone, similar to rickets in infants, may occur as a result of vitamin D deficiency. This is known as osteomalacia. The pelvis undergoes distortion to such a degree that serious difficulties may arise in the course of labour. Lack of vitamin D during pregnancy will affect both the mother and the child.

Sources

Sunlight, artificial light from mercury vapour lamps and food sources such as fish, eggs and milk can supply vitamin D to the body. The supply of vitamin D from food can be supplemented by the body itself in a remarkable way. When the body is exposed to bright sunlight, the fat-like substance called 7-dehydrocholesterol found under the skin is converted into vitamin D which the body is able to store and utilise. Vegetables also contain a vegetable sterol known as ergosterol which, when irradiated by the ultra violet rays of the sun, is converted into vitamin D.

Requirements of vitamin D

During the pregnancy period the need for vitamin D is great and 400 International Units (IU) are recommended for infants and children. Adults undoubtedly need some vitamin D when the vitamin benefits from sunshine are not available. For women the need for vitamin D is increased during pregnancy and lactation and 400 I.U. per day are recommended. In India where there is scope for meeting part of the vitamin D requirement by endogenous synthesis through sunlight an arbitrary level of 200 I.U. vitamin D per day has been suggested by the nutrition expert group of the Indian Council of Medical Research (1968).

Vitamin E

Vitamin E is known as antisterility vitamin. Its chemical name is tocopherol. It is a fat-soluble vitamin. Vitamin E is necessary for normal reproduction in many animal species. It is successfully used in cases of threatened or repeated abortions in women. Vitamin E is an anti-oxidant that preserves the vitamins which are easily oxidizable.

Sources

The richest natural sources of vitamin E are wheat-germ and wheat-germ oil. It is also present in considerable amounts in cottonseed oil, lettuce oil, rice-germ oil, other vegetable oils, legumes, nuts, leafy vegetables and egg yolk. Because of its wide distribution in natural foods, the chances of vitamin E deficiency in most human diets are small.

Requirements

The adult requirement is 10-30 mgm per day.

Vitamin K

Vitamin K, a fat-soluble vitamin, was discovered in 1935 by a Danish scientist of the name of Dam. He suggested the name Koagulation Vitamin or Vitamin K. It is sometimes called the antihaemorrhagic vitamin.

Uses

The specific function of vitamin K is to make possible the production of prothrombin in the blood. Prothrombin is necessary for the clotting of blood. Thus vitamin K is necessary for the coagulation of blood.

Effects of deficiency

Deficiency of vitamin K may lead to impaired coagulability of the blood which may in certain cases, such as surgical operations, lead to haemorrhage. The death rate from haemorrhage in newborn infants has been reduced by giving vitamin K to the mother before delivery or directly to the child immediately after its birth.

Sources

Vitamin K is fairly widely distributed in foods. It appears abundantly in green leaves, alfalfa, spinach, pork liver and vegetable oils. Tomatoes, cauliflower, egg yolk, liver and cabbage are also liberal suppliers of it.

This vitamin is synthesized by bacteria found in the

human intestines. Consequently, vitamin K deficiency is usually not a dietary problem in man.

Requirements

The dietary requirements for man are not specified. Newborn infants need special consideration in regard to vitamin K, as their blood is characteristically low in prothrombin content and clotting power. A single oral dose of 1-2 mg for the infant is considered adequate and is probably higher than the minimum requirement.

Water soluble vitamins

Vitamin C

Vitamin C is known as the antiscorbutic vitamin. Its chemical name is ascorbic acid. It is the most labile of the vitamins and is rapidly oxidized by heat and exposure to air. It is readily soluble in water and much vitamin C may be lost to the body if the water in which food has been cooked is not used. Bruising of fruit and chopping up of vegetables too fine destroys vitamin C.

Uses

Vitamin C is needed for buoyant health, vitality, and endurance. It ensures a clear skin, a fresh complexion, healthy gums and strong teeth. It is necessary for the healing of wounds. It plays a significant part in the formation and maintenance of an intercellular cement-like substance. A large intake of vitamin C is an effective preventive against the common cold.

Effects of deficiency

Vitamin C is essential for the prevention of a deficiency disease called scurvy. This is characterized by the occurrence of extravasations of blood in the tissues of the body. The gums become livid, spongy, ulcerated and they bleed. The teeth are loosened and drop out and the breath is foetid. Scurvy is also characterized by general weakness, pallor, poor appetite, sensitivity to touch, pains in the limbs and joints, and failure to grow. Anaemia may occur if there is significant blood loss.

Sources

Vitamin C is found in all fruit and vegetables, but specially rich sources are black currants and citrus fruits. Sprouted grams and sprouted pulses are rich in it. Cabbage, tomatoes and salad greens, eaten raw or lightly cooked, are rich yielders of vitamin C. Guavas are rich in vitamin C. *Nellikai* or *amla* have more vitamin C than oranges.

Requirements

The requirement of vitamin C for a normal adult is at least 50 mg daily. Young children need 30-50 mg per day.

Vitamin B_1

Vitamin B_1 is known as aneurine or antineuritic vitamin in England and as thiamine in America. It is familiarly called

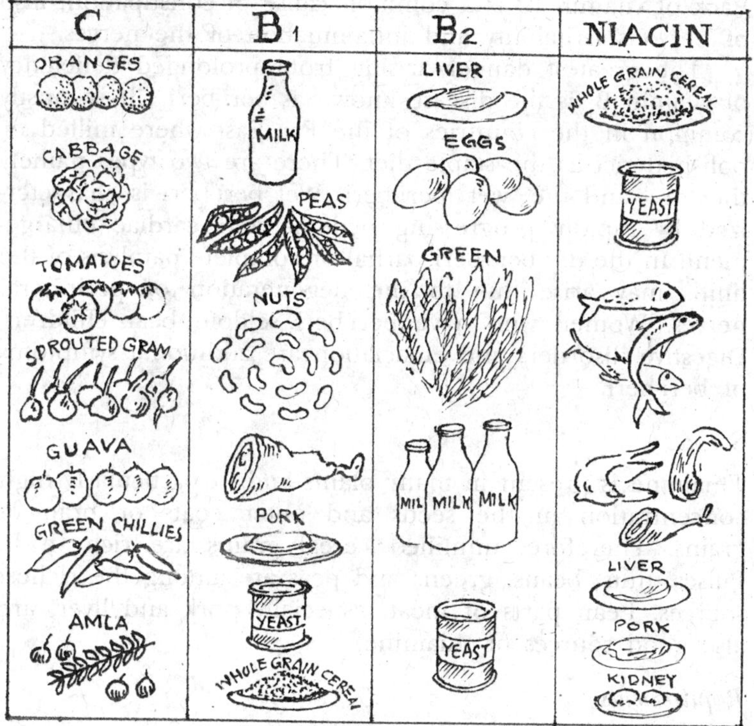

Fig. 77. Rich sources of water-soluble vitamins

the anti-beri-beri vitamin. It is water-soluble and nearly half of it gets into the water in which fruit and vegetables are cooked. It is destroyed by high temperatures and by alkali, for example, by the use of soda in cooking.

Uses of Vitamin B_1

Thiamine is necessary throughout life for tissue respiration. It is necessary for normal growth and development in the young. It creates appetite, prevents fatigue and constipation and gives a zest for life.

Effects and deficiency

Lack of thiamine leads to a decrease in the growth of children. Even a mild deficiency may cause anorexia or loss of appetite. Fatigue sets in, interest in one's daily tasks is lost and one becomes lethargic and develops a depressed look. Lack of vitamin B_1 is a common cause of constipation, also of nervous irritability and inflammation of the nerves.

The greatest danger arising from prolonged deficiency of vitamin B_1 is the disease known as beri-beri. It is mostly common in the countries of the Far East where milled or polished rice is the staple diet. There are two types namely the 'dry' and the 'wet' beri-beri. Wet beri-beri is characterized by rapidly progressing oedema and cardiac enlargement. In the dry beri-beri partial or complete paralysis of the limbs may arise due to the degeneration of peripheral nerves. Women who have beri-beri seldom bear children. Digestive disorders and emaciation are additional symptoms of beri-beri.

Sources

Thiamine is present in many plants and in particularly high concentration in the seeds and outer coats or bran of grains. Therefore, unmilled cereal grains are rich in it. Pulses, nuts, beans, greens and peas are among the richest sources. Lean parts of meat, especially pork and liver, are also good sources of thiamine.

Requirements

The daily allowance of vitamin B_1 falls between 1.2 to 2mg for men and 1 to 1.5 mg for women, varying with the energy requirement. More thiamine is required for heavy work and exercise. The fat content of the diet has a sparing effect on thiamine. The requirement is increased for women during pregnancy and lactation. Children need 0.6 to 1.0 mg, per day.

Vitamin B_2

The chemical name for the vitamin which was originally called B_2 in England and G in America is riboflavin. It is a water-soluble vitamin and therefore some of it is dissolved when foods are cooked in water. Riboflavin in aqueous solution is destroyed rapidly by light, even more than by cooking. It is a thermo-stable factor and withstands well the heat of ordinary types of cooking, particularly when the medium is acidic. However, losses do occur during frying and roasting. It is not stored in the body and, therefore, has to be supplied regularly.

Uses of vitamin B_2

Vitamin B_2 appears to be essential to normal digestion. It has an important contribution to make in relation to the eye. It is necessary for the metabolic processes. It is also important for the utilisation of food fats and amino acids. Riboflavin is essential for growth.

Effects of deficiency

Insufficient riboflavin leads to visual fatigue, blurred vision, photophobia, burning and itching of the eyes, soreness and swelling of the eyelids. The transparent front of the eye, the cornea, gets misted and hence the vision is impaired. The mouth gets inflamed. The skin is roughened, the pink parts of the lips become bright red, swollen and cracked, the tongue gets enlarged and lesions occur at the corners of the mouth which get sore, and a condition sets in known as angular stomatitis. The occurrence of riboflavin deficiency is called ariboflavinosis.

Sources

Rich sources of riboflavin are liver, yeast, kidney, eggs, milk, green leaves and the outer parts of cereals.

Requirements

The requirement of riboflavin for women vary from 1.0 to 1.7 mg per day and for men from 1.3 to 2.2 mg per day. Riboflavin requirement is increased during growth.

Nicotinic acid or niacin

Since the name nicotinic acid associates this compound with the poison nicotine in tobacco, another name was sought for it. The name niacin, coined by Dr. Cowgill of Yale University, was chosen. Niacin name is derived from *Ni* meaning nicotinic, *ac* denoting acid and *in* representing vitamin. It is also known as antipellagra vitamin or pellagra preventing factor. Niacin is soluble in water and is not stored in the body.

Uses of nicotinic acid

The function of niacin in the body, like that of the other B-vitamins, is to help in the release of energy from carbohydrate foods. It acts as a hydrogen transporter in tissue respiration. The main use of niacin is to prevent the disease known as pellagra.

Effects of deficiency

Pellagra is a disease caused by the deficiency of niacin. This is a disease called *Mal de la rosa,* a name, derived from the Italian *Pell agro,* meaning "rough skin". Pellagra occurs among people who live in extreme poverty. It is also called the disease of 3 D's because it causes dermatitis, diarrhoea and dementia.

Pellagra is characterized by dermatitis or skin lesions. The skin lesions become symmetric, occurring as bilateral dermatitis. If the back of one hand or cheek is affected, the corresponding part of the opposite side also gets involved. First they appear as severe sun burns, red in colour. Later, they become rough, thick and permanently dark. The skin eruptions are accompanied by soreness of the mouth, redness of the tongue, indigestion and diarrhoea. The entire alimentary tract, from mouth to rectum, becomes sore. In 60% of the cases the hydrochloric acid in the stomach is completely lost. Dermatitis is followed by very severe diarrhoea.

The neuralgic manifestations caused by pellagra may not be recognized early, but may develop later into definite mental derangement or dementia. Lethargy, characteristic of many of the victims, may be in itself an early symptom of niacin deficiency. Further the common symptoms are: loss of weight and strength, burning sensation all over the body, headache, nervousness, mental depression, irritability, apprehension and confusion, and last but not the least, insomnia. Dementia can be completely cured by suitable therapy, if the disturbance has not been present for too long a time. Mental symptoms vary from patient to patient and even in the same person from time to time.

Sources

Meat, poultry and fish are better sources of niacin than plant products. Liver, kidney and meat are the best animal sources. Yeast and the outer parts of grain are good natural sources and care should be taken to see that the bran is not completely removed while milling.

Requirements

The recommended daily allowance for adult men varies from 16-26 mg per day; and for women, from 13-20 mg per day.

Water

Water is of very great importance to diet. It is possible to live for several weeks without food, but it is not possible to survive only for a few days without water. Dehydration or loss of water will cause death quicker than starvation.

Water constitutes nearly three-fourths of the body weight. Every tissue or organ in the body contains water. Body water is classified as intracellular and extracellular. Intracellular water is inside the cells of the body. Extracellular water comprises water in the blood, lymph, spinal fluid and secretions and the water between and around the cells. Though the distribution of water in the body is not fixed and constant, the total quantity in the body remains relatively constant.

VITAMINS AT A GLANCE
Fat Soluble

Factor	*Uses*	*Sources*		*Requirement per day*
		Vegetable	*Animal*	
Vitamin A	Helps growth, prevents eye diseases, helps resistance to infection and keeps skin healthy.	Green and yellow fresh vegetables, mangoes, papayas.	Fish-liver oil, whole milk, butter, curd, cream and egg yolk.	Adult 750 μ gms retinol.
Vitamin D	Helps growth, builds bone and teeth, prevents rickets. *Note*: Action of sun's rays on skin produces vitamin D.	—	Fish-liver oil, egg yolk, butter.	200 I.U.
Vitamin E	Helps in reproduction.	Wheat-germ oil, lettuce, peas, vegetable oils.	Liver, egg yolk, milk.	10-30 mg.
Vitamin K	Helps in the coagulation of blood.	Green leaves, alfalfa, tomatoes, cauliflower, spinach and cabbage.	Egg yolk, liver.	—

Water Soluble

Factor	*Uses*	*Sources*		*Requirement per day*
		Vegetable	*Animal*	
Vitamin C	Prevents scurvy, prevents bleeding gums and painful joints, and in healing of wounds.	Citrus fruits, pineapple, cabbage, amla, sprouted legumes.	—	50 mg.
Vitamin B_1	Prevents beri-beri, prevents loss of appetite, keeps the nerves healthy, prevents constipation.	Yeast, whole grain cereals, cabbage, spinach, carrots, onions, tomatoes, lady's fingers.	Egg yolk, liver.	Adults 1.0 to 2. 0mg Children 0.6 to 1.0 mg.
Vitamin B_2	Prevents visual fatigue, essential for normal digestion, prevents angular stomatitis.	Yeast, wheat germ. carrot, cabbage, green leaves.	Meat, liver, eggs, whole milk, cheese.	Adults 1.0 to 2.2 mg.
Niacin	Prevents pellagra.	Yeast, outer parts of the grain.	Meat, liver, kidney, poultry and fish.	Adults 13-26 mg.

Uses of water

Water is absolutely necessary for the digestion and absorption of the foods taken in. It is the great solvent and neutraliser in the body. It is the substance in which bodily chemical reactions take place. Water is the carrier or transporting medium for all nutrients and body substances. Water regulates the body temperature. Water is the great purifying agent in the body and removes waste materials in tears, perspiration, urine and faeces. Water substances act as lubricants in the body, especially in the joints. It is a part of all body tissues and fluids.

Effects of deficiency

Acidosis, alkalosis and dehydration, oedema, fever, shock, uraemia and constipation are some of the clinical signs of inadequate salt and water in the body.

Sources

The body obtains water mainly from the fluids we drink, from the solids we eat and from the oxidation of energy foods. Fats and carbohydrates are oxidized in the body to carbon dioxide and water. It may be mentioned here that vegetables and fruits contain 60% to 98% water, milk 87% in its unadulterated state, meat 40% to 75% and even dried food such as raisins and figs 8% to 25%.

Requirements

Daily adult requirement of water is 2.5 litres. Much of this is found in the food we eat. Requirements depend on climatic conditions also. An average of 5-6 glasses of fluids should be consumed daily, either as water or as beverage.

RECOMMENDED DIETARY ALLOWANCES FOR INDIANS

Group	Particulars	Body wt	Net energy	Protein	Fat	Calcium	Iron	Vit. A retinol	mg/d β-carotene	Thiamin	Riboflavin	Nicotinic acid	Pyridoxin	Ascorbic acid	Folic acid	Vit B-12
		kg	Kcal/d	g/d	g/d	mg/d	mg/d			mg/d	mg/d	mg/d	mg/d	mg/d	μg/d	μg/d
Man	Sedentary work		2425							1.4	1.4	16				
	Moderate work	60	2875	60	20	400	28	600	2400	1.4	1.6	18	20	40	100	1
	Heavy work		3800							1.6	1.9	21				
Woman	Sedentary work		1875							0.9	1.1	12				
	Moderate work	50	2225	50	20	400	30	600	2400	1.1	1.3	14	2.5	40	100	1
	Heavy work		2925							1.2	1.5	16				
	Pregnant woman	50	+300	+15	30	1000	38	600	2400	+0.2	+0.2	+2	2.5	40	400	1
	Lactation															
	0-6 months	50	+550	+25	45	1000	30	950		+0.3	+0.3	+4				
	6-12 months		+400	+18					3000	+0.2	+0.2	+3	2.5	40	150	1.5
Infants	0-6 months	5.4	208/kg	205/kg					55μg/kg	65μg/kg	710μg/kg		0.1			
	0-12 months	8.6	98/kg	165/kg		500	350	1200	50μg/kg	60μg/kg	650μg/kg		0.4	25	25	0.2
Children	1-3 years	12.2	1240	22			12	400	160	0.60	0.7	8	0.9		30	
	4-6 years	19.0	1690	30	25	400	18	400		0.9	1.0	11		40	40	0.2-1.0
	7-9 years	26.9	1950	41			26	600	2400	1.0	1.2	13	1.6		60	
Boys	13-15 years	47.8	2450	70			41	600	2400	1.2	1.5	16	2.0	40	100	0.21.0
Girls	13-15 years	46.7	2060	65	22	600	28			1.0	1.2	14				
Boys	16-18 years	57.1	2640	78			50	600	2400	1.3	1.6	17	2.0	40	100	0.21.0
Girls	16-18 years	49.9	2060	63	22	500	30			1.0	1.2	14				

13. The Basic Seven

A committee of experts on Food and Nutrition set up by the National Research Council, U.S.A., made recommendations in 1941, on the daily dietary allowances for ten nutrients, namely carbohydrates, proteins, calcium, iron, vitamin A, thiamine, riboflavin, niacin, ascorbic acid and vitamin D. For practical purposes, the recommended daily dietary allowances have been classified into seven food groups which supply the ten nutrients listed above. These food groupings are called the "Basic Seven Food Groups." Apart from these ten nutrients, other nutrients which are necessary to the human body find no mention in the Basic Seven Food Groups, since the foods from which the essential ten nutrients are obtained usually supply the other nutrients.

The Basic Seven Food Groups contain the common food stuffs we use, grouped together on the basis of similarity in the type of nutrients which they contain. The foods in each of the Basic Seven Food Groups supply one or more of the nutrients not so well met by the foods listed in the other groups. There is a wide variety of choice within each group, so that it is possible to find several foods in each group which can be easily bought in the market, and which are also to one's own liking.

Group 1 includes green and yellow vegetables.

These can be eaten raw, cooked, frozen or canned. The vegetables or fruits in this group provide vitamin A. They are also rich in vitamin C, iron and riboflavin.

Everyday, at least one large serving from the foods in group 1 should be included in the diet for the supply of vitamin A.

Agathi, amaranth, coriander leaves, curry leaves, drumstick leaves, lettuce, mint, parsley, spinach, carrots, green peas, pumpkins, beans, sweet potatoes, mangoes and papaya belong to this group.

Group 2 includes high vitamin C foods. Vitamin C is more likely to be present in raw, uncooked, fresh foods. One or

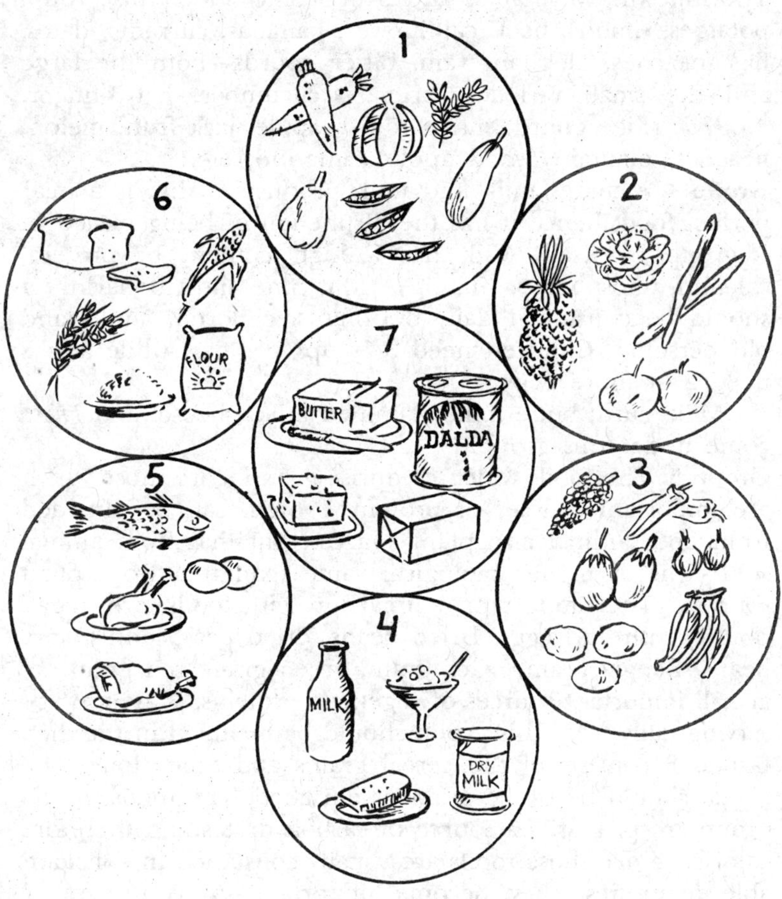

Fig. 78. The basic seven

more servings of the following should be taken daily: country guava, citrus fruits like limes, lemons, oranges; pineapples, *nellikkai* or *amla*; drumstick and raw cabbage. *Nellikkai*, the size of a large marble, ranks highest in vitamin C.

Group 3 consists of vegetables and fruits other than those mentioned in groups 1 and 2. They are of help in supplementing some of the other food groups and hence two or more servings of these should be consumed daily. The following vegetables and fruits come under this group: potatoes, onions, beet, cauliflower, bananas, currants, dates, figs, peaches, elephant yam, bitter gourds—both the large and the small varieties, brinjals, cucumber, lady's-finger, *noolkhol*, ridge gourd, snake gourd, apple, jack fruit, melon, peaches, plantain, wood apple, tamarind, etc.

Group 4 includes milk and milk products. Milk is a near perfect food; hence it has the distinction of being placed in a group by itself. Milk has a high content of protein, calcium, phosphorus, vitamin A, thiamine and riboflavin. It should be consumed daily by infants, children, adults and old persons. Children need 3-4 cups per day, while adults need 2 or more cups.

Milk, curd, buttermilk, skimmed milk, cheese, and *khoya* come under this group.

Group 5: The foods which comprise group 5 are those which are important sources of protein. Protein can be obtained from both animal and plant sources, but that from animal sources is of higher biological value than that from plant sources. The important animal protein foods are meat, poultry, fish and eggs. Dried beans, dried peas, lentils, soya beans, Bengal gram, black gram, green gram, red gram dal are all important sources of vegetable proteins. One average serving daily from this group should be included in the diet.

Group 6 consists of the cereal grains and their flour. The cereal should be whole grain or enriched. The foods in this group are primarily a source of carbohydrates and therefore calories. Since these foods are usually consumed in considerable quantities, they become important sources of many other nutrients, particularly the B vitamins and iron. This group is of special importance in low-cost diets, because the foods in this group form the cheapest source of carbohydrates. One or two servings per meal is necessary as they form the bulk of the diet. Cambu (which is a cheap cereal grain available in South India), cholam also known as maize and ragi (which is also a cereal grain available in South India and which is fairly cheap source of energy) home pounded parboiled rice, whole wheat, and whole wheat flour belong to this much used group.

Group 7: The foods in group 7 furnish fat. Butter, ghee and other oils are placed in this group. Butter or ghee must be included daily in our diet. For cooking purposes, other fats and oils such as *vanaspati*, gingelly oil or coconut oil may be used to reduce the cost.

A balanced diet is a diet that contains all the nutrients in the correct proportion, so that the minimum daily requirements of all these nutrients are obtained. Thus it will include protective foods, energy-yielding foods and body-building foods. The components of a balanced diet differ according to age, sex, and physiological state namely sickness, pregnancy and lactation.

Examples of a balanced diet consisting of the basic seven food groups

Breakfast	*Lunch*	*Dinner*
Puris and potato curry; egg omelette; coffee with plenty of milk and cream; orange.	Cooked par-boiled rice; dal curry served with ghee; amaranth pugath; salad with tomatoes and beet; curds; fruit salad with pineapple, mango and banana.	Wheat chappatis; fish-molee; mint chutney; guava; hot milk.
Bread with butter and jam, poached egg; coffee with milk, orange.	Dry chappatis with channa; curd rice, greens; beans pugath; carrot raita; any fruit in season.	Chappatis with minced meat curry or vegetable stew; cutlets and mint chutney; cabbage pugath, jelly with cream.

One serving each of the above must be eaten. This example of a balanced diet consists of the Basic Seven Food Groups as follows:

Group I: Amaranth pugath*, mint chutney, and mangoes used in fruit salad, greens, beans, carrots, cabbage.
Group II: Orange, tomato salad, pineapple used in fruit salad, guava.
Group III: Potato curry, beet, banana used in fruit salad.
Group IV: Milk in coffee, curds, hot milk.
Group V: Egg omelette, fish-molee, dal, curry, channa, minced meat.
Group VI: Puri made with whole wheat flour; par-boiled cooked rice, wheat chappatis, bread.
Group VII: Ghee used with rice; other oils used in the preparation of dishes, butter-cream.

Thus we see that the Basic Seven Food Groups are an easy food guide for good health and better living. They offer a simple method of choosing a balanced diet. They afford a scientific basis for selecting our breakfasts, lunches, and dinners day by day. We should be conversant with what food belongs to each group and eat the recommended amounts. In addition to the food from the Basic Seven Food Groups, we can eat any other foods we want.

The Basic Seven idea has undergone a change in the U.S.A. The present terminology is the "Daily Food Guide". The foods are grouped into four main classes with the emphasis on protective foods. The groups are as follows:
Group I: Milk, cheese and ice-cream. The main nutrients in this group are protein, riboflavin and calcium.
Group II: Meat, liver, fish, poultry, eggs and legumes. This group contributes protein, vitamins and minerals.
Group III: Vegetables, especially green, leafy and yellow vegetables and fruits. This group provides vitamins A and C and iron.
Group IV: Bread, cereals and potato. These foods serve as important sources of energy, protein, iron and B complex vitamins.

The number of servings of each group are so adjusted as to add up to a good diet. However, the grouping is just a framework to which other foods can be added as one

---

*Pugath is a vegetable preparation cooked by boiling in a minimum amount of water and then seasoning it for serving as a side dish with any main meal.

desires.

Another food guide for India is composed of five food groups. Appropriate quantities of foods from these five different groups will supply the nutrients needed by the body.

The basic five food groups

Group	*Foodstuff*	*Main nutrient contribution*
I	MILK and MILK PRODUCTS, Curds, panir (cheese), skimmed milk powder. PULSES Dried beans and peas, nuts MEAT Fish, poultry, eggs.	Protein Calcium Riboflavin.
II	FRUITS Orange, tomato, mango, papaya, amla, lemon juice, etc., GREEN LEAFY VEGETABLES Keerai, cabbage, carrot-tops, etc.	Carotene (Vitamin & value), vitamin C Mineral salts Iron (in leafy vegetables).
III	OTHER VEGETABLES Brinjal, gourds, fresh beans, pumpkin, ladies-finger, etc.	Vitamins and minerals (in small amounts).
IV	CEREALS Rice, wheat, maize, ragi, etc., STARCHY VEGETABLES Yams, colocasia, tapioca, potatoes.	Carbohydrate, B vitamins Protein (in cereals).
V	FATS AND OILS Vegetable Oil, butter, ghee SUGAR Jaggery, etc.	Fat (energy), essential fatty acids, vitamin A (in animal fats only), carbohydrate (in sugar only).

All these Food Groups, the Basic Seven, the Daily Food Guide and the Five Food Groups can be helpful in selecting one's foods. However, for our Indian economic conditions, the Basic Seven is more easy to follow, as an average Indian cannot afford many servings from an expensive group.

The following tables indicating the quantity of foods to be included per day in planning balanced diets have been taken from "Nutritive Value of Indian Foods", 1972, National Institute of Nutrition, Indian Council of Medical Research, Hyderabad, India.

BALANCED DIETS FOR CHILDREN

	PRE-SCHOOL CHILDREN				SCHOOL CHILDREN			
	1-3 Years		4-6 Years		7-9 Years		10-12 Years	
	Vegetarian (g)	Non-Vegetarian (g)	Vegetarian (g)	Non-Vegetarian (g)	Vegetarian (g)	Non-Vegetarian (g)	Vegetarian (g)	Non-Vegetarian (g)
Cereals	150	150	200	200	250	250	320	320
Pulses	50	40	60	50	70	60	70	60
Green leafy vegetables	50	50	75	75	75	75	100	100
Other vegetables Roots and tubers	30	30	50	5 0	50	50	75	75
Fruits	50	50	50	50	50	50	50	50
Milk	300	200	250	200	250	200	250	200
Fats and oils	20	20	25	25	30	30	35	35
Meat and fish, eggs	—	30	—	30	—	30	—	30
Sugar and jaggery	30	30	40	40	50	50	50	50

BALANCED DIETS FOR ADOLESCENTS

	BOYS				GIRLS	
	13-15 Years		16-18 Years		13-18 Years	
	Vegetarian (g)	Non-Vegetarian (g)	Vegetarian (g)	Non-Vegetarian (g)	Vegetarian (g)	Non-Vegetarian (g)
Cereals	430	430	450	450	350	350
Pulses	70	50	70	50	70	50
Green leafy vegetables	100	100	100	100	150	150
Other vegetables	75	75	75	75	75	75
Roots and tubers	75	75	100	100	75	75
Fruits	30	30	30	30	30	30
Milk	250	150	250	150	250	150
Fats and oils	35	40	45	50	35	40
Meat and fish	—	30	—	30	—	30
Eggs	—	30	—	30	—	30
Sugar and jaggery	30	30	40	40	30	30
Groundnuts	—	—	50*	50*	—	—

*An additional 30 g of fats and oils can be included in the diet in place of groundnuts.

BALANCED DIETS FOR ADULT WOMEN

	SEDENTARY WORK		MODERATE WORK		HEAVY WORK		ADDITIONAL ALLOWANCE DURING	
	Vegetarian (g)	Non-Vegetarian (g)	Vegetarian (g)	Non-Vegetarian (g)	Vegetarian (g)	Non-Vegetarian (g)	Pregnancy (g)	Lactation (g)
Cereals	300	300	350	350	475	475	50	100
Pulses	60	45	70	55	70	55	—	10
Green leafy vegetables	125	125	125	125	125	125	25	25
Other vegetables	75	75	75	75	100	100	—	—
Roots and tubers	50	50	75	75	100	100	—	—
Fruits	30	30	30	30	30	30	—	—
Milk	200	100	200	100	200	100	125	125
Fats and oils	30	35	35	40	40	45	—	15
Sugar and jaggery	30	30	30	30	40	40	10	20
Meat and fish	—	30	—	30	—	30	—	—
Eggs	—	30	—	30	—	30	—	—
Groundnuts	—	—	—	—	40*	40*	—	—

*An additional 25 g of fats and oils can be included in place of groundnuts.

BALANCED DIETS FOR ADULT MEN

	SEDENTARY WORK		MODERATE WORK		HEAVY WORK	
	Vegetarian (g)	Non-Vegetarian (g)	Vegetarian (g)	Non-Vegetarian (g)	Vegetarian (g)	Non-Vegetarian (g)
Cereals	400	400	475	475	650	650
Pulses	70	55	80	65	80	65
Green leafy vegetables	100	100	125	125	125	125
Other vegetables	75	75	75	75	100	100
Roots and tubers	75	75	100	100	100	100
Fruits	30	30	30	30	30	30
Milk	200	100	200	100	200	100
Fats and oils	35	40	40	40	50	50
Meat and fish	—	30	—	30	—	30
Eggs	—	30	—	30	—	30
Sugar and jaggery	30	30	40	40	55	55
Groundnuts	—	—	—	—	50	50*

*An additional 30 g of fats and oils can be included in the diet in place of groundnuts.

14. A Study of Common Foodstuffs

Cereals

Rice and wheat are the two most important cereals in the world. It has been estimated that approximately half the world's population live on rice as their staple food.

Structure

All cereal grains have several parts, but the following are common to them all. The outer layer acting as a protective coating is composed of several bran layers containing cellulose, minerals, proteins and small quantities of thiamine. Within these bran layers is the central portion or endosperm, the storehouse of the grain containing starch and protein. The germ or embryonic plant containing fat, minerals and vitamins is at one end of the grain.

Rice

Compared to other cereals, rice has a low protein content. It contains 6-7% of protein. Wheat contains considerably more.

Rice, like other cereals, is poor in fat. There is hardly any vitamin A in it. Therefore, the rice eater must rely on other foods for adequate supply of vitamin A.

Rice is also a poor source of calcium. Calcium deficiency is one of the chief faults of a rice diet. The amount of phosphorus present in rice of any kind is fairly high; hence rice eaters do not suffer from phosphorus deficiency. Rice is a poor source of iron, however. Unmilled rice is a good source of vitamin B. The nicotinic acid content of unmilled rice is high. Rice contains no vitamin C.

Par-boiling

Par-boiling is a process widely used in the preparation of rice for human consumption. By par-boiling we mean steaming of unhusked rice after soaking. Striking changes are brought about in the nutritive value of rice as a result of par-boiling. Some of the nutrients from the pericarp and germ or embryonic plant diffuse into the inner endosperm. Therefore, when par-boiled rice is milled, even though it loses the germ and the pericarp it will not lose all its nutrients. Par-boiled rice retains a considerable proportion of vitamin B, even when highly milled.

The milling of rice

When rice is milled it loses the outer layers, the germ and the pericarp. These contain more protein, mineral salts and vitamins than the starchy inner parts of the grain.

Rice is usually washed several times before cooking and may be boiled in a large quantity of water. The extent of the losses in food value depends on the number of washings and on whether the cooking water is discarded. In cooking rice, the minimum amount of water needed should be used, so that all the water used is completely absorbed and no straining is necessary.

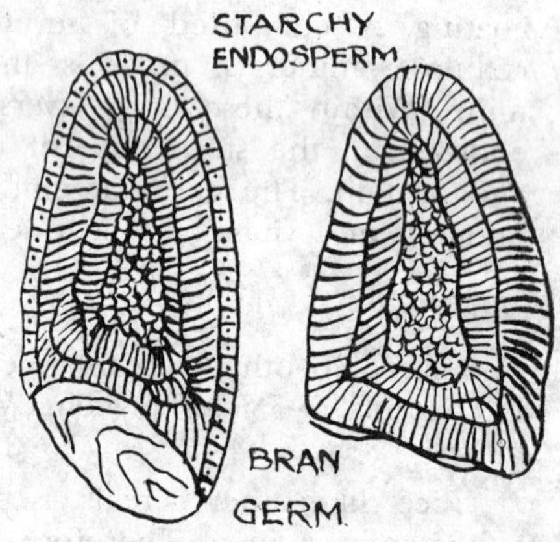

Fig. 79. The milling of rice (when rice is milled, the germ, and bran are lost)

Wheat

Wheat is the chief cereal food of north Indians. Like the rice grain, the wheat grain consists of three parts: germ, bran and endosperm. The outer layers can be removed by machine milling just as completely as the outer layers of rice. Very white refined wheat flour, like white highly milled rice, loses most of its vitamins. In India, wheat is nearly always eaten in the form of *chappatis, puris* or *parathas* which are made from flour (*atta*) containing the outer as well as the inner parts of the grain. *Atta* is in many ways a better food than milled rice, but it cannot by itself supply all the substances we need for growth, health and repair and renovation of body tissues.

Ragi

What has been said above of wheat is also true of ragi to a large extent. Ragi can be powdered to form flour and with it *rotis* or porridge can be made. Ragi contains more calcium and less protein than other millets. If germinated it becomes a rich source of vitamin C.

Germination of grains

The grain is first soaked in water for 24 hours and is then spread out on damp, thick material and covered with a moist cloth, which is kept moist by sprinkling water upon it from time to time. After two or three days it sprouts and is ready for use.

Pulses

Most people in India eat pulses such as dal, gram, etc., every day. Other familiar pulses are peas, beans and lentils. Pulses are richer in body-building materials than cereals and they also contain more of certain vitamins. Pulses form vitamin C in the gram when they are allowed to sprout or germinate.

Pulses are rich in protein, carbohydrates, calcium and vitamins A, B, and B_2. Most of them are also rich in iron. Though rich in proteins, they are not as good as the protein of milk, eggs, fish or meat, and are not a sufficient source of protein for growing children.

Fruits

Fruits are pulpy in character and often juicy. They have hardly any protein or fat, but contain cellulose which serves as roughage. In unripe fruits carbohydrate is found in the form of starch which gradually becomes sugar when the fruit ripens.

Fruits contain certain important vitamins. When fresh they are valuable sources of ascorbic acid or vitamin C. Since this is destroyed by cooking, it is better to eat fruit raw. The *amla* or *nellikkai,* ranks highest in vitamin C. The country guava comes next. Tight-skinned oranges are also high in vitamin C.

Yellow fruits such as mangoes and papayas are among the richest in vitamin A. Dates, jackfruits and oranges have a fair amount of it.

Dates, tamarind pulp, mangoes, peaches, apples, custard apples and guavas are good sources of iron. Wood apples contain as much calcium as milk. Other minerals such as phosphorus, potash, sodium salts and copper are plentiful in all common fruits.

Vegetables

As a group, vegetables are valuable for their cellulose content, vitamins and base-forming properties. Cellulose adds bulk to the diet and thus prevents constipation. The base-forming properties maintain acid base balance in the body. Vegetables have an aesthetic appeal because they are colourful, palatable, good in texture if raw or when properly cooked, and refreshing. They add variety and interest to the diet. Green leafy vegetables such as amaranth, etc., are useful because they contain minerals like calcium and iron and vitamins like A, C and B_2.

Flesh foods

Meat

Meat is chiefly the muscle tissue of animals which is used as food, such as beef, veal, pork, mutton, lamb and venison. The meat of cow is known as beef, that of calf, veal; of pig, pork or ham; of sheep, mutton; of lamb, lamb; and that of deer, venison.

Meat is an expensive food, but it furnishes excellent protein to the body. Meat also contributes minerals, notably phosphorus and iron, and vitamin B_1. Meat is prized for its flavour. The extractives of meat stimulate the appetite, and increase the flow of digestive juices.

Liver and kidney

Of all the edible internal organs, liver is the most useful food. Its richness in iron and copper is invaluable for building up healthy blood. It also contains manganese, a mineral which promotes growth. It contains almost all the B group vitamins in greater concentration than fleshy meat. The vitamin A content of liver is more than a hundred times that of milk. Liver and kidneys are rich in proteins.

Fish

This food resembles other flesh foods, being rich in protein. The amount of fat varies in different fishes. Vitamins B_1 and B_2 are present to an appreciable extent. The presence of certain minerals also adds to the nutritive value of fish. Sea fish is a rich source of iodine. Oils from the livers of various fish like the cod, the halibut and the shark are high in vitamins A and D content. Shell-fish are a source of protein. Oysters rank next to livers in iron and copper content.

Fish is easily digested, and therefore it is a valuable body builder for children and people of weak digestion.

Eggs

In composition the egg averages about 75% water, 13% protein and 12% fat.

Eggs are not to be depended upon for energy, since their fuel value is low; the average-sized egg yields only about 75 to 80 calories. They are valuable for their excellent and complete protein. The fat in egg is present in finely emulsified form and therefore can be easily digested and absorbed. The iron content of egg yolk is not only abundant but is also very easy for the human body to absorb because it

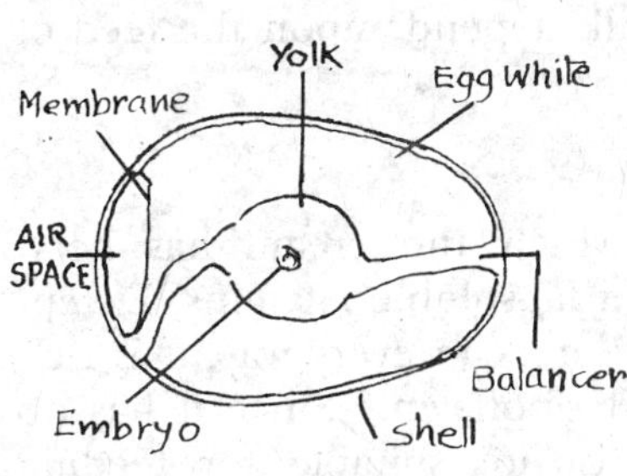

Fig. 80. Parts of an egg

contains a little bit of copper which is necessary for the proper absorption of iron. This is a definite asset because so many foods, although rich in iron, do not provide it in a suitable form. Another valuable contribution of eggs is phosphorus. Egg also contains a good amount of the fat-soluble vitamins A, D, E and water-soluble vitamins B_1 and B_2.

Milk

Milk is nature's nearest approach to a complete food. Fine physique, good health and vitality characterize the people of countries where milk has an important place in the diet. Milk is a valuable food for people of all ages.

It is particularly important in childhood, as it builds strong and healthy bones, teeth and muscles. It is an essential food for expectant and nursing mothers. Vegetarians need to include milk in their diet because the protein of milk is superior to the vegetable protein of nuts and pulses. Since vegetarians do not take meat, fish or eggs, milk is their only source of these superior proteins.

The fat of milk contains nutritionally essential fatty acids. The fat is present in an emulsified form; hence it is more easily digested by the body than fats of other common foods.

Milk is by far the most important of all foods as a source of calcium. Though rich in phosphorus also, it is poor in iron. It contains vitamin A, a fair concentration of thiamine and a high concentration of riboflavin. It is a poor source of niacin.

Milk freshly drawn from the cow contains some vitamin C, but most of it is destroyed before consumption by boiling. The content of vitamin D in milk depends upon the feed of the cow.

Skimmed milk

Skimmed milk is milk from which the cream has been separated. It is devoid of fat and fat-soluble vitamins. Except for this, it is equivalent to whole milk in every way; it is rich in proteins, sugar, minerals and riboflavin. Since it has no fats or vitamins A and D, it is not suitable for feeding infants. It can, however, be used as a supplement to the diet of children and adults, since it supplies protein in a concentrated form.

Nuts

Nuts are dry fruits consisting of an edible kernel enclosed in a woody shell. The most well-known nuts are almonds, cashew nuts, coconuts, groundnuts, walnuts and pistachio nuts.

Nuts are rich in protein but their protein is of low biological value and is not absorbed properly. Their calcium and iron are not all available to the body. They are rich in fats and hence have a high caloric value, but these vegetable fats lack vitamins A and D.

Spices and condiments

The general condiments and spices are mustard, pepper, salt, vinegar, caraway, cinnamon, cloves, ginger, mustard, mint, nutmeg, garlic, etc. They provide taste and flavour to our diet. Their aroma and taste are due mainly to the essential oils they contain. They also contain protein and carbohydrates. They do not contain fats in appreciable amounts. They contain minerals and some of them contain carotene and riboflavin also.

Beverages

A beverage is any material used as a drink to relieve thirst, introduce fluid into the body, nourish the body and stimulate or soothe the individual.

Beverages may be classified according to their functions as:

I Refreshing; to relieve thirst

1. Water, plain or carbonated.
2. Ginger ale and other bottled beverages.
3. Fruit juices.
4. Iced tea or coffee.

II Nourishing

1. Milk; pasteurized, skimmed, evaporated, dried, malted buttermilk, chocolate, cocoa.

2. Eggnog made with whisky, rum, brandy, fruit juices, coffee, chocolate.
3. Fruit juices with egg white or whole egg.
4. Glucose lemonade or orangeade.
5. Tube feedings—milk etc.

III Stimulating

1. Eggnogs made with whisky, rum, brandy or coffee.
2. Coffee and tea.

IV Soothing

1. Warm milk.
2. Hot tea.

Ingredients in beverages

Milk is the most important of all the liquid foods since it gives more nutritive value than any other food. Milk beverages add protein, calories, calcium and other nutrients to the diet. The mild flavour of milk permits it to be used in many ways—plain, malted or acidulated. It may also be reinforced with egg, skimmed milk powder, gelatin, yeast or various sugars. It may be flavoured with coffee, chocolate and flavouring extracts.

Eggs are especially useful for increasing the protein content of beverages. Eggnog made with strong coffee or brandy is mildly stimulating and lends variety to liquid diets. Fruit eggnogs contain egg, cream, milk, sugar and fruit juice.

Fruit and vegetable juice are refreshing, easily digested and especially useful in increasing the fluid intake. Citrus juices and tomato juice are excellent for their ascorbic acid content. Fruit juices may be served plain or sweetened with sugar, reinforced with egg white or whole egg.

Chocolate contains about 50 per cent fat and some protein and carbohydrate. A mild stimulant theobromine is present in chocolate. Sweet chocolate contains added sugar and milk chocolate contains chocolate, milk and sugar.

Cocoa should be boiled with water before adding milk in order to cook the starch and develop the flavour.

Sweetening and flavouring agents such as canesugar, glucose, honey and lactose may be used to sweeten beverages and to supply additional calories. Vanilla, various fruit flavourings, nutmeg and cinnamon lend variety.

Coffee, tea, cocoa, and milk are the beverages widely used all over the world.

Tea has been used as a beverage in China since as early as 2700 B.C. Different kinds of tea are available in India. The tea plant is a hardy evergreen which is kept down by severe pruning to a low shrub of convenient height for hand plucking. The leaves are plucked at intervals during the season. The size of the leaf varies according to age and position on the twig and determines the grade of tea. The smaller, younger leaves and buds at the top of the twigs are the finest grade; and the larger, older, tougher leaves lower down, the lowest grade. Unless taken with sugar and cream or milk, tea has no food value, being simply a stimulant. Theine found in tea is a mild nerve stimulant with no harmful after-effects. But if large amounts of the tannin contained in tea leaves are also extracted during the brewing of the tea, they have an unfavourable effect on the digestion.

Coffee grows on a plant that is an evergreen shrub. It is grown in the moist tropics. The beans or seeds are the part used for coffee as a beverage. They are roasted before use. This makes them brittle and easy to grind and gives them a pleasant aroma and flavour. The roasting should be done frequently, even daily, and it is best to grind the beans immediately after. The aroma and flavour are lost if the powder is not kept in an air-tight container. owing to the volatile character of the essential oils present in the seeds.

The stimulating effect of coffee is due to an alkaloid known as caffeine, present in it. Caffeine acts directly upon the central nervous system; it diminishes greatly the sense of fatigue, increases mental activity and quickens the power of concentration. A small cup of strong black coffee taken after a heavy meal is considered an aid to digestion, hence it is served as a final course at dinners.

Caffeine in excess causes insomnia, irritability and rapid heart action.

Cocoa and chocolate are made by grinding the seeds of pods of the cacao tree. The seeds are fermented to decrease their bitter taste after which they are roasted, shelled and cracked. Roasting develops their flavour.

The stimulant in cocoa is theobromine, which is similar to caffeine in coffee but milder in its action on the nervous system. In addition to theobromine, cocoa contains some tannin, fat, starch, protein, vitamin B and mineral salts. Therefore, cocoa has some food value.

TABLE OF FOOD COMPOSITION OF RICE, WHEAT AND RAGI

Name of foodstuff (edible portion)	Values are per 100 g of edible portion											
	Protein	Fat	Carbohydrate	Energy	Calcium	Phosphorus	Iron	Carotene	Thiamine	Riboflavin	Niacin	Vitamin C
	g	g	g	K.cal	mg	mg	mg	μg	mg	mg	mg	mg
Rice, raw, handpounded	7.5	1.0	76.7	346	10	190	3.2	2	0.21	0.16	3.9	0
Rice, parboiled, handpounded	8.5	0.6	77.4	349	10	280	2.8	9	0.27	0.12	4.0	0
Rice, raw, milled	6.8	0.5	78.2	345	10	160	3.1	0	0.06	0.06	1.9	0
Rice, parboiled, milled	6.4	0.4	79.0	346	9	143	4.0	—	0.21	0.05	3.8	0
Wheat, whole	11.8	1.5	71.2	346	41	306	4.9	64	0.45	0.17	5.5	0
Wheat flour (whole)	12.1	1.7	69.4	341	48	355	11.5	29	0.49	0.29	4.3	0
Wheat flour (refined)	11.0	0.9	73.9	348	23	121	2.5	25	0.12	0.07	2.4	0
Ragi	7.3	1.3	72.0	328	344	283	6.4	42	0.42	0.19	1.1	0

TABLE OF FOOD COMPOSITION OF A FEW PULSES

Name of foodstuff (edible portion)	Values are per 100 g of edible portion											
	Protein	Fat	Carbohydrate	Energy	Calcium	Phosphorus	Iron	Carotene	Thiamine	Riboflavin	Niacin	Vitamin C
	g	g	g	K.cal	mg	mg	mg	µg	mg	mg	mg	mg
Bengalgram dal	20.8	5.6	59.8	372	56	331	9.1	129	0.48	0.18	2.4	1
Blackgram dal	24.0	1.4	59.6	347	154	385	9.1	38	0.42	0.20	2.0	0
Greengram dal	24.5	1.2	59.9	348	75	405	8.5	49	0.72	0.21	2.4	0
Redgram dal	22.3	1.7	57.6	335	73	304	5.8	132	0.45	0.19	2.9	0
Soyabeans	43.2	19.5	20.9	432	240	690	11.5	426	0.73	0.39	3.2	–
Fieldbean, dry	24.9	0.8	60.1	347	60	433	2.7	0	0.52	0.16	1.8	0

TABLE OF FOOD COMPOSITION OF A FEW VEGETABLES

Name of foodstuff (edible portion)	Protein	Fat	Carbohydrate	Energy	Calcium	Phosphorus	Iron	Carotene	Thiamine	Riboflavin	Niacin	Vitamin C
	Values are per 100 g of edible portion											
	g	g	g	K.cal	mg	mg	mg	µg	mg	mg	mg	mg
Amaranth, tender	4.0	0.5	6.1	45	397	83	25.5	5520	0.03	0.3	1.2	99
Cabbage	1.8	0.1	4.6	27	39	44	0.8	1200	0.06	0.09	0.4	124
Curry leaves	6.1	1.0	18.7	108	830	57	7.0	7560	0.08	0.21	2.3	4
Lettuce	2.1	0.3	2.5	21	50	28	2.4	990	0.09	0.13	0.5	10
Mint	4.8	0.6	5.8	48	200	62	15.6	1620	0.05	0.26	1.0	27
Spinach	2.0	0.7	2.9	26	73	21	10.9	5580	0.03	0.26	0.5	28
Beetroot	1.7	0.1	8.8	43	18	55	1.0	0	0.04	0.09	0.4	10
Carrot	0.9	0.2	10.6	48	80	530	2.2	1890	0.04	0.02	0.6	3
Onion, small	1.8	0.1	12.6	59	40	60	1.2	15	0.08	0.02	0.5	2
Yam, ordinary	1.4	0.1	26	111	35	20	1.3	78	0.07	–	0.7	–
Bitter gourd, small	2.1	1.0	10.6	60	23	38	2.0	126	0.07	0.06	0.4	96
Brinjal	1.4	0.3	4.0	24	18	47	0.9	74	0.04	0.11	0.9	12
Cauliflower	2.6	0.4	4.0	30	33	57	1.5	30	0.04	0.10	1.0	56
Drumstick	2.5	0.1	3.7	26	30	110	5.3	110	0.05	0.07	0.2	120
French beans	1.7	0.1	4.5	26	50	28	1.7	132	0.08	0.06	0.3	24
Ladies-fingers	1.9	0.2	6.4	35	66	56	1.5	52	0.07	0.10	0.6	13
Pumpkin	1.4	0.1	4.6	25	10	30	0.7	50	0.06	0.04	0.5	2
Snake gourd	0.5	0.3	3.3	18	26	20	0.3	96	0.04	0.06	0.3	0

TABLE OF FOOD COMPOSITION OF CERTAIN NUTS

Values are per 100 g of edible portion

Name of foodstuff (edible portion)	Protein	Fat	Carbohydrate	Energy	Calcium	Phosphorus	Iron	Carotene	Thiamine	Riboflavin	Niacin	Vitamin C
	g	g	g	K.cal	mg	mg	mg	µg	mg	mg	mg	mg
Almond	20.8	58.9	10.5	655	230	490	4.5	0	0.24	0.57	4.4	0
Cashewnut	21.2	46.9	22.3	596	50	450	5.0	60	0.63	0.19	1.2	0
Coconut (fresh)	4.5	41.6	13.0	444	10	240	1.7	0	0.05	0.10	0.8	1
Groundnut (roasted)	26.2	39.8	26.7	570	77	370	3.1	0	0.39	0.13	22.1	0
Pistachio Nut	19.8	53.5	16.2	626	140	430	7.7	144	0.67	0.28	2.3	—
Walnut	15.6	64.5	11.0	687	100	380	4.8	6	0.45	0.4	1.0	0

TABLE OF FOOD COMPOSITION OF SOME CONDIMENTS AND SPICES

Values are per 100 g of edible portion

Name of foodstuff (edible portion)	Protein	Fat	Carbohydrate	Energy	Calcium	Phosphorus	Iron	Carotene	Thiamine	Riboflavin	Niacin	Vitamin C
	g	g	g	K.cal	mg	mg	mg	µg	mg	mg	mg	mg
Asafoetida	4.0	1.1	67.8	297	690	50	22.2	4	0	0.04	0.3	0
Cardamom	10.2	2.2	42.1	229	130	160	5	0	0.22	0.17	0.8	0
Chillies, dry	15.9	6.2	31.6	246	160	370	2.3	345	0.93	0.43	9.5	50
Cloves, dry	5.2	8.9	46	286	740	100	4.9	253	0.08	0.13	0	0
Coriander	14.1	16.1	21.6	288	630	393	17.9	942	0.22	0.35	1.1	0
Cuminseeds	18.7	15.0	36.6	356	1080	511	31.0	522	0.55	0.36	2.6	3
Garlic, dry	6.3	0.1	29.8	145	30	310	1.3	–	0.06	0.23	0.4	13
Ginger, fresh	2.3	0.9	12.3	67	20	60	2.6	40	0.06	0.03	0.6	6
Nutmeg	7.5	36.4	28.5	472	120	240	4.6	0	0.33	0.01	1.4	0
Pepper, dry	11.5	6.8	49.2	304	460	198	16.8	1080	0.09	0.14	1.4	–
Tamarind, pulp	3.1	0.1	67.4	283	170	110	10.9	60	–	0.07	0.7	3
Turmeric	6.3	5.1	69.4	349	150	282	14.8	30	0.03	0	2.3	0

TABLE OF FOOD COMPOSITION OF A FEW FRUITS

Values are per 100 g of edible portion

Name of foodstuff (edible portion)	Protein g	Fat g	Carbohydrate g	Energy K.cal	Calcium mg	Phosphorus mg	Iron mg	Carotene µg	Thiamine mg	Riboflavin mg	Niacin mg	Vitamin C mg
Amla	0.5	0.1	13.7	58	50	20	1.2	9	0.03	0.01	0.2	600
Apple	0.2	0.5	13.4	59	10	14	1.0	0	–	–	0	1
Banana, ripe	1.2	0.3	27.2	116	17	36	0.9	78	0.05	0.08	0.5	7
Grapes, blue variety	0.6	0.4	13.1	58	20	23	0.5	3	0.04	0.03	0.2	1
Guava	0.9	0.3	11.2	51	10	28	1.4	0	0.03	0.03	0.4	212
Lime	1.5	1.0	10.9	59	90	20	0.3	15	0.02	0.03	0.1	63
Lime, lime, sweet (Musambi)	0.8	0.3	9.3	43	40	30	0.7	0	–	–	0	50
Mango, ripe	0.6	0.4	16.9	74	14	16	1.3	2743	0.08	0.09	0.09	16
Orange	0.7	0.2	10.9	48	26	20	0.3	1104	–	–	–	30
Papaya, ripe	0.6	0.1	7.2	32	17	13	0.5	666	0.04	0.25	0.2	57

TABLE OF FOOD COMPOSITION OF FLESH FOODS

Name of foodstuff (edible portion)	Values are per 100 g of edible portion											
	Protein g	Fat g	Carbohydrate g	Energy K.cal	Calcium mg	Phosphorus mg	Iron mg	Carotene μg	Thiamine mg	Riboflavin mg	Niacin mg	Vitamin C mg
Fish, (Sea)	22.1	1.1	—	98	40	300	1.6	5	0.10	—	2.5	—
Prawn	19.1	1.0	0.8	89	323	278	5.3	0	0.01	0.01	4.8	—
Egg (duck)	13.5	13.7	0.8	181	70	260	3.0	540*	0.12	0.26	0.2	—
Egg (hen)	13.3	13.3	—	173	60	220	2.1	600*	0.10	0.4	0.1	0
Fowl	25.9	0.6	—	109	25	245	—	—	—	0.14	—	—
Liver (sheep)	19.3	7.5	1.3	150	10	380	6.3	0**	0.36	1.7	17.6	20
Mutton (muscle)	18.5	13.3	—	194	150	150	2.5	0***	0.18	0.14	6.8	—

* Contains also 1200 i.u. of vitamin A.

** Contains also 22,300 i.u. of vitamin A.

*** Contains also 31 i.u. of vitamin A.

TABLE OF FOOD COMPOSITION OF MILK AND MILK PRODUCTS

Values are per 100 g of edible portion

Name of foodstuff (edible portion)	Protein g	Fat g	Carbohydrate g	Energy K.cal	Calcium mg	Phosphorus mg	Iron mg	Carotene µg	Thiamine mg	Riboflavin mg	Niacin mg	Vitamin C mg
Milk, buffalo's	4.3	8.8	5	117	210	130	0.2	160	0.04	0.1	0.1	1
Milk, cow's	3.2	4.1	4.4	67	120	90	0.2	174*	0.05	0.19	0.1	2
Milk, goat's	3.3	4.5	4.6	72	170	120	0.3	182	0.05	0.01	0.3	1
Milk, human	1.1	3.4	7.4	65	28	11	–	137	0.02	0.02	–	3
Curds	3.1	4.0	3.0	60	149	93	0.2	102	0.05	0.16	0.1	1
Buttermilk	0.8	1.1	0.5	15	30	30	0.8	0	–	–	–	–
Cheese	24.1	25.1	6.3	348	790	520	2.1	273	–	–	–	–
Skimmed milk powder (cow's milk)	38.0	0.1	51	357	1370	1000	1.4	0	0.45	1.64	1.0	5

* Cow's milk contains in addition 6.0 µ.g. carotene.

TABLE OF FOOD COMPOSITION OF FATS AND OILS

Name of foodstuff (edible portion)	Values are per 100 g of edible portion											
	Protein g	Fat g	Carbohydrate g	Energy K.cal	Calcium mg	Phosphorus mg	Iron mg	Vitamin A i.u	Thiamine mg	Riboflavin mg	Niacin mg	Vitamin C mg
Butter	—	81	—	729	—	—	—	3200	—	—	—	—
Ghee (cow)	—	100	—	900	—	—	—	2000	—	—	—	—
Ghee (buffalo)	—	100	—	900	—	—	—	900	—	—	—	—
Hydrogenated oil (fortified)	—	100	—	900	—	—	—	2500	—	—	—	—
Cooking oil												
(Groundnut, gingelly, coconut, mustard)	—	100	—	900	—	—	—	0	—	—	—	—

TABLE OF FOOD COMPOSITION OF MISCELLANEOUS FOODSTUFFS

Name of foodstuff (edible portion)	Values are per 100 g of edible portion											
	Protein	Fat	Carbohydrate	Energy	Calcium	Phosphorus	Iron	Carotene	Thiamine	Riboflavin	Niacin	Vitamin C
	g	g	g	K.cal	mg	mg	mg	μg	mg	mg	mg	mg
Betel leaves	3.1	0.8	6.1	44	230	40	7.0	5760	0.07	0.03	0.7	5
Biscuits, salted	6.6	32.4	54.6	534	–	–	–	–	–	–	–	–
Biscuits, sweet	6.4	15.2	71.9	450	–	–	–	–	–	–	–	–
Bread, brown	8.8	1.4	49	244	18	–	2.2	–	0.21	–	2.5	–
Bread, white	7.8	0.7	51.9	245	11	–	1.1	–	0.07	–	0.7	–
Coconut water	1.4	0.1	4.4	24	24	10	0.1	0	0.01	0	0.1	2
Fish liver oil	–	100	–	900	–	–	–	–	–	–	–	–
Jaggery (cane)	0.4	0.1	95	383	80	40	11.4	168	0.02	0.04	0.5	0
Papad	18.8	0.3	52.4	288	80	300	17.2	0	–	–	–	–

15. The Cooking of Food

Most of us who have read Charles Lamb's essay, "Dissertation on a Roast Pig" will remember the hilariously funny story of how a father and son accidentally learnt the art of roasting pigs by a fire in their hut and made it a regular feature, and how the neighbours followed suit by setting aflame their abodes. Primitive men ate roots and fruits, fish and the raw meat of the animals they hunted. Greek mythology tells the story of how Prometheus stole fire from heaven and brought it to man, while science says that man made fire by using flint or rubbing wood. With the discovery of fire man learnt to cook his food. Though civilized man has the choice either to eat food raw or cooked, he normally prefers the latter.

Advantages of cooking food

The advantages of cooking food are many. Cooking aids digestion, particularly carbohydrates. The appetising, natural flavour of what we eat depends entirely on cooking. Further, the addition of flavouring agents like condiments, spices, etc., enhances the flavour and taste of the food. Cooking enables us to prepare a great variety of dishes. Cooking partly sterilizes food and makes it easier to preserve and store for long periods. It renders food, especially of animal origin, more pleasing to the sight. Foods properly cooked and attractively served are inviting and are a stimulus to the secretion of the digestive juices. Cooked food is more palatable than raw food.

Disadvantages of cooking food

The most deplorable factor of cooking food is that in the case of certain foods, the vitamins and minerals are lost. It is better for a part of one's daily diet to consist of raw foods. If food is not cooked carefully, it will either get charred or messy and sticky. Since fried foods are difficult to digest they should not be given to invalids.

Methods of cooking

The types of food available, the climate and the fuel, have been largely responsible for the ways in which methods of cooking have evolved in various countries through the ages. However, whatever be the method of cooking, the principles involved everywhere are just two. They are: either to keep the flavour "in" or to bring the flavour "out". For instance in the preparation of mutton broth or vegetable soup, when meat is chopped up and vegetable cut up and put into cold water and slowly cooked, the flavour is drawn "out". On the other hand, when meat or potatoes are fried or roasted the flavour is kept "in".

The different kinds of cooking are boiling, steaming, stewing, frying, baking, cooking under pressure, roasting and broiling or grilling. According to its value in making food tasty and nutritious preserving its quality and saving cooking time, each method has its own distinctive advantage. Different methods may be used at different times to suit the circumstances.

Boiling

In this method food is cooked in boiling water. The notion that boiling violently will cook the food faster is erroneous. Violent boiling is unwise, since it wastes fuel, breaks up the food and spoils its appearance. Further, the quick evaporation of the water may result in the food getting burnt.

Fig. 81. Boiling

Boiling is not a tasty way of cooking food. The food is usually completely immersed in water, so that the flavour and the water-soluble vitamins get extracted into the water. If this water is kept, it makes nourishing gravy or sauce or soup. Since boiled foods are easy to digest and do not surfeit the appetite, they are a pleasant change from heavy and rich foods. Most vegetables are better simmered in a small amount of water than boiled in much water.

Steaming

Fig. 82. Steaming

Steaming is also a method of cooking food with water, but in this case the food does not come into direct contact with the water. It is done in two ways: direct and indirect.

In the direct method of steaming, the food is placed on a perforated plate above boiling water and the vessel tightly covered with a lid, as in making *idlis.*

In the indirect method, the food is packed into a vessel with a lid. The vessel is then immersed in another vessel of boiling water. The heat for cooking the food is supplied by the boiling water all round the immersed inner vesssel, as in the case of making puddings. This method is good since there is very little loss of nutrients, and the food is easily digested. This indirect method of cooking can be used to advantage for heating up food.

Steaming is better than boiling since the flavour is not lost in the water. The food does not shrink due to evaporation of water. But it is a slower process than boiling. Nevertheless it will be economical if several compartments are used at the same time. Further, foods, such as new rice, which become pasty when boiled, can be cooked well without the grains sticking to one another by steaming.

Stewing

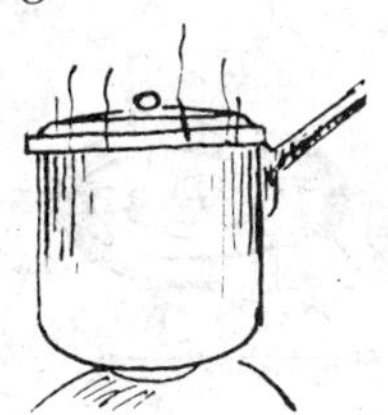

Fig. 83. Stewing

Stewing is another method of cooking food in water, like boiling. However, while a large quantity of water is heated quickly in boiling, only a small amount of water is used in stewing and the cooking is done for a prolonged period of time over a low fire. Long, slow simmering is the secret of preparing a good stew. For cooking tough cuts of meat and dried vegetables, stewing is the best method. Since foodstuffs are cooked in covered pans and the juices are retained as gravy, stewed foods are nourishing. However, there is some loss of vitamins in stewing.

Frying

While water is used in boiling, steaming and stewing, fats and oils are the mediums used in the method of cooking food known as 'frying'. There are two kinds of frying. Deep fat frying and shallow fat frying.

Deep fat frying

The food to be cooked is completely immersed in hot melted fat or oil. For frying, the oil should be hot and perfectly still with a pale blue smoke emanating from it, so that the outer surface of the food put in will harden immediately and prevent the oil soaking in and making the food soggy. If a fresh quantity of oil is added, it must be allowed to get hot before a further quantity of food is put in it to fry.

Deep fat frying
Fig. 84.

Fried food should be thoroughly drained of oil before being served. It should be served as quickly as possible so that its crispness is not lost.

Although a large amount of fat or oil is used for deep frying, it is not a wasteful method of cooking. The oil or fat left over can be used again and again if strained and carefully stored.

Shallow fat frying

This method is handy in cases where it is not possible to practise deep fat frying. However, there should be a sufficient amount of oil or fat in the pan and the food should be turned to cook both sides equally, as in the case of pancakes.

Shallow fat frying
Fig. 85.

Baking

Normally baking denotes oven baking. Good results can be obtained in sigree baking if an even temperature is maintained

Fig. 86. Baking

on the top and bottom of the tin in which food is baked. Usually, the dry heat inside an oven is used for baking. To obtain good results it is necessary to place food properly in the oven. The instructions of the baker or recipe should be strictly followed, as stoves vary a great deal. Baking with a little fat is known as "roasting."

Cooking under pressure

Food is placed in a sealed container with very little water and cooked by the pressure of steam in this method. The pressure cooker has gadgets for regulating the pressure by allowing the escape of steam. These cookers save fuel because a whole meal can be cooked at the same time. The number of compartments inside the pressure cooker facilitate the preparation of different dishes, simultaneouly. Food can be cooked very rapidly. Pressure cookers are widely used for bottling jams.

Cooking under pressure
Fig. 87.

Broiling or grilling

Broiling or grilling
Fig. 88.

Cooking food by exposing it directly to fierce red heat either of coal, gas or electricity is known as broiling or grilling. It is necessary to have strong heat to begin with. Broiling food is the most ancient and primitive method of cooking. It is the simplest method of preparing food. In this method of cooking there is very little loss of vitamins and the food cooked has a good flavour. In broiling or grilling, the fire should be free from smoke or ash; otherwise the food will become sooty. A little salt sprinkled on the fire will keep it clean.

Pan-broiling

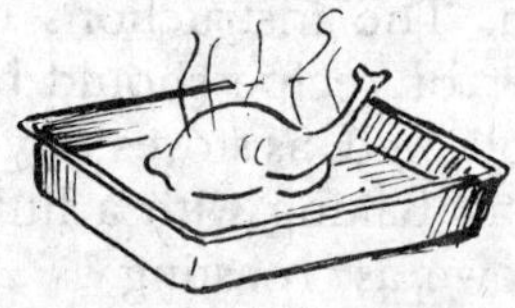
Fig. 89. Pan broiling

Instead of cooking food by exposing it directly to fire as in broiling, it is placed on a pan and cooked by pan-broiling. The dry heat is applied to the flat or deep frying pan in which the food is broiled. Coffee seeds, groundnuts, etc., are pan-broiled. Chapatis are first pan-broiled and then broiled.

16. Essential Equipment and Utensils

It is as important where food is cooked as how it is prepared. Cleanliness, tidiness and economy in utilization of space, time and material are essential factors in the kitchen set-up. The kitchen should be designed and planned for maximum efficiency and convenience. The finished product of an artisan depends on his equipment or tools as well as his own skill. A cake cannot be baked at home without a proper oven, nor a *dosai* fried without a flat frying pan. A kitchen has to be well equipped to enable a person to combine pleasure with work for the benefit of all the members of the family.

The choice of essential equipment and utensils for the kitchen and dining room depends on the tastes of the cook and her purse.

Different types of equipment are needed and used in the kitchen. They can be classified as "major kitchen equipment" and "minor kitchen equipment".

Major kitchen equipment

The major equipment consists of a stove, a refrigerator, if one can afford it, a sink, a table, a cooker, a meat safe, cupboards and racks.

Stove, oven or fire place

This is the first requisite in any kitchen. Cooking stoves may be heated by solid fuel, oil, gas or electricity. A good variety of them are available. Their choice depends on the cost and personal preference of the cook.

A refrigerator

A refrigerator is a costly piece of equipment found only in wealthy homes in India. It is a luxury article not within the reach of every person in economically backward countries.

Refrigerators are used for preserving foodstuffs for some days.

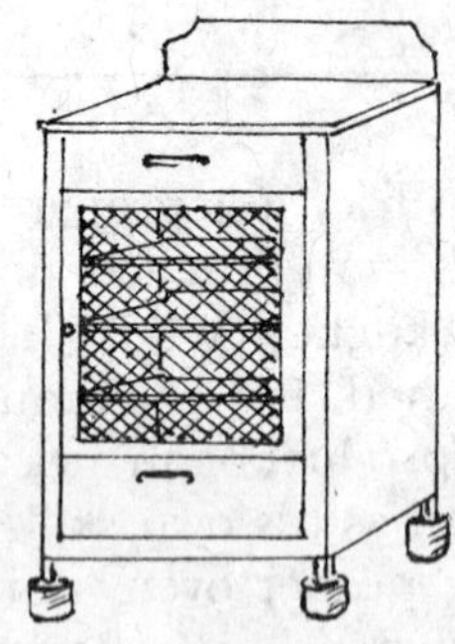

Fig. 90. Meat safe

Fig. 91. Refrigerator

The temperature within a refrigerator can be regulated.

Sink

As every vessel and article used for cooking has to be cleaned from time to time, a sink is an absolute necessity in the kitchen. The cook also has to wash her hands and keep them clean while cooking; hence a sink is needed in the kitchen.

Fig. 92. Sink

Table

The table used in a kitchen may be marble-topped or plain, inexpensive, wooden-topped. In some houses people use tables with stone tops. Since the preparations for cooking are mixed or cut on the table, its height is important. It should be of the right height for the cook to work standing upright or low enough to work, sitting.

Cooker

Various types of pressure cookers are available and their

cooking range differs very much. The larger and advanced types have many mechanical gadgets like clock, pressure and temperature gauge, safety valve and pressure regulator or "whistle" fitted to them. They make cooking quick and easy. The detailed instructions supplied with them should be strictly followed for proper results.

Haybox cooker

The Haybox cooker is a good illustration of cooking by heat insulation. It is a means by which partly cooked foods can be cooked to completion without any fuel and kept warm for a few hours. It consists of a hollow wooden box of suitable size, usually rectangular, with a lid. The hay is packed in sacking cloth and stitched and attached to all sides, including the top and bottom, to a depth of 3". The vessel with the partly cooked food in it, usually rice, is covered and kept in the haybox cooker in the centre (covered with the packed hay all round). The rice gets cooked in about 2 hours and it can be kept warm for a longer period if necessary.

The principle employed in this method is that hay acts as a poor conductor of heat. The heat is prevented from being conducted away by insulation. Thus the partly cooked food is cooked to completion in its own heat and the food also remains hot. It must be remembered that the amount of water used for cooking should be the correct amount so that all the water is completely absorbed and the rice is fully cooked.

Precautions to be taken

The hay should be clean, dry, free from dust and insects and should surround the vessel to a depth of at least 3" all round. The vessel should have a rim with a tight-fitting lid.

Cupboards and racks

Cupboards are required in a kitchen for keeping materials like seasonings, spices, condiments, etc. They should be insect-proof. Racks are useful for keeping cups, saucers, plates, tumblers, spoons and ladles, tidily arranged.

Minor kitchen equipment

A large number and a good variety of minor or smaller

utensils and articles of equipment are absolutely indispensable for the kitchen, for increased efficiency. Which of them are used and when depend on the needs and individual taste of the cook.

Pots

Pots are necessary for cooking rice and for making many other food preparations.

Pans

Pans are of various types such as saucepans, frying pans, baking pans and roasting pans.

Pots and pans are usually made of stainless steel, aluminium, enamelware or iron.

Trays

Cake tray, vegetable tray, etc.

Bowls

For mixing foodstuffs.

Tins

For storage.

Other equipment

Set of jugs, set of basins.

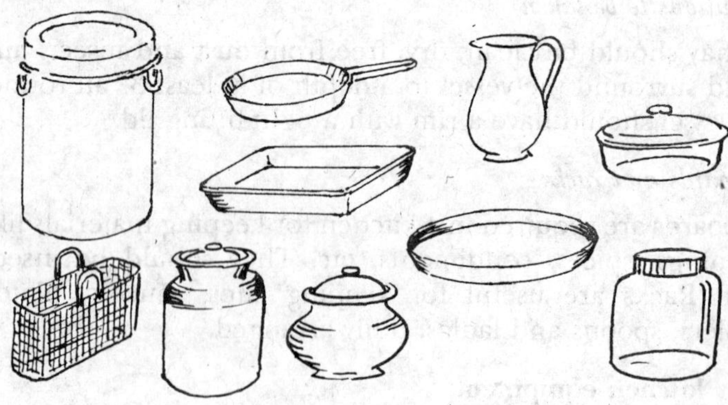

Fig. 93. Minor kitchen utensils

Measuring equipment

Measuring cups, tablespoons and teaspoons. As every cooking material needs measuring, we must have a pair of scales or some form of weighing machine. Whether we have one or not, it is useful also to set aside special cups and spoons for handy measuring.

Boards

Chopping boards for chopping up vegetables, a larger board for kneading dough, rolling pastry, etc., moulding and pastry boards.

Rolling pins.
Sieves—flour sifters.
Strainers.
Juice extractor.
Lemon squeezer.
Jelly moulds.
Set of graters.
Grinding stones (or *mixer/blender*).
Grease-proof paper and dish paper.

Knives

Vegetable knife, one set of vegetable-cutters, egg-slicer, dough-nut cutter, pastry cutter, biscuit cutter.

Palette knives are invaluable for many purposes such as mixing pastry, cleaning round basins and removing cakes and buns from baking pans and, in frying, to loosen the cooked food from the pan.

Spoons and ladles

Tablespoons and dessertspoons for measuring, one large ladle, a set of wooden spoons and perforated spoons.

Wooden spoons are useful for mixing and for creaming fats and sugar together. They are also useful for stirring sauces, custards, porridge and cereals.

Tin opener and **bottle opener** for opening tins and bottles.

A cork-screw for removing corks.

Cloths

Dish cloths, kitchen cloths, oven cloths and roller towels, dusters and floor cloth.

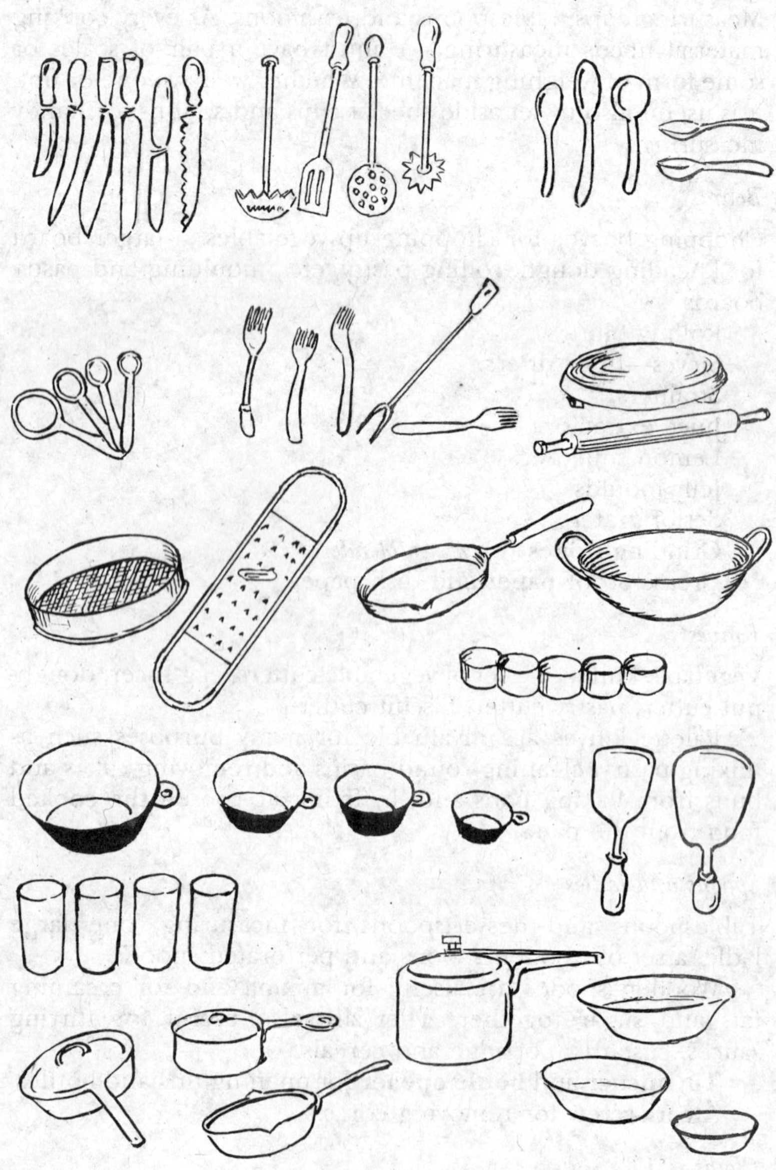

Fig. 94. Minor kitchen utensils

Refuse-bin

Finally one needs a **refuse-bin** for disposing garbage. It should have a tight-fitting lid. It should be cleaned, washed, dried and disinfected from time to time.

A study of kitchen equipment includes the question of its arrangement also. We must plan the kitchen so as to get the utmost use out of the equipments we have in it.

Dining room requirements

If the kitchen is scientifically planned, even a verandah will serve as a dining room. The dining room should be located as near the kitchen as possible.

Equipment

A **dining table**: if the room is long, an oblong table should be chosen; if square, a square or round or oval table will be suitable. If plate-glass is fixed on the top, a table-cloth may be dispensed with. Glass is a very clean material and saves considerable labour and if a paper with colourful floral design is spread under it, it will create a cheerful atmosphere.

Sideboard or side-table with drawers specially for cutlery and glass-ware.

Built-in cupboards.

A **wash-basin** in a corner.

The other requirements are chairs, table-mats, trays, tumblers, fruit bowls, flower-vases, salt and pepper shakers, lemonade set, serviettes, plates, cups, saucers, tea-pot, crockery stand, coffee pot, cutlery, spoons, tray-cloths, etc.

These are the chief articles of equipment required. Others such as a coffee percolator, mixer, etc., may be bought if one can afford them.

Cost of kitchen equipment

The cost of equipment varies very much depending on its size and quality. Further, if the equipment is worked by electricity it is costly. If it is operated by kerosene or any other fuel, its price is lower.

Stove

Ordinarily, the cost of the stove varies from Rs. 65 to Rs. 200.

The cost of a gas stove will range from Rs 950 to Rs 2000,

(gas cylinder with regulator Rs 500).

An electric cooking range will easily cost over Rs 5,000.

Refrigerator

From about Rs 6000 upwards to Rs 20,000.

Sink

The cost of sinks vary according to the size. One steel sink of average size costs about Rs 2000 and a cement one about Rs 500.

Table

An ordinary wooden table costs anywhere between Rs 1,000 and Rs 2,000, depending on the size. If it is ordinary wood, it is cheaper.

Cookers

Pressure cooker costs vary from Rs 450 to Rs 1200, depending on the size.

Meat-safe

Rs 500.

Kitchen cupboards (Storage)

Prices vary according to size and material used and the finish. The cost will be anywhere from Rs 2000 and upwards.

Minor equipment

Pots

The cost varies according to the material. Aluminium costs less, brass a little more and stainless steel still more.

Aluminium pots	— from Rs 50 to Rs 200.
Brass pots	— within Rs 120 to Rs 550.
Stainless Steel	— within Rs 70 to Rs 250.

This again varies according to size.

Pans

Aluminium and iron pans are commonly used.

Aluminium pans	— from Rs 40 to Rs 80
Iron pans	— from Rs 65 to Rs 140.

Kettles

These are made of various materials.

Enamel-coated iron, aluminium and stainless steel.

Enamel — Rs 150 to Rs 400, according to size.
Aluminium — Rs 55 to 200, according to size.
Stainless steel — Rs 50 to Rs 200, according to size.

Bowls

Usually of aluminium and stainless steel.

Aluminium — within Rs 30 to Rs 150.
Stainless steel — Rs 50 to Rs 250.

Measuring equipment

Set of measures

one litre
half litre
quarter litre
An aluminium set will cost about Rs 50.
Pint measure (Pyrex Measuring Cup)—Rs 25.
Plastic Measuring Spoon—Rs 10.
A set of kilogram weights (iron)—Rs 65.

Boards

These depend on quality, size and material.

Chopping boards—About Rs 20 to Rs 120.
Pastry boards—Rs 15.
Sieves—Rs 15.
Strainers:
Stainless steel—Rs 50.
Aluminium—Rs 20 to Rs 30.
Lemon squeezer (glass)—Rs 15.
Grinding stones—Rs 120.
Mixie (electric)—Rs 2000 to Rs 4000.
Large kitchen knife—Rs 20.

Cutlery

Table spoons and teaspoons—Rs 5 to Rs 10 per piece.

A complete set of dinner
Crockery (a dozen)—Rs 500 to Rs 1000.

17. Cleaning of Utensils and Equipment

Kitchen and dining utensils and equipment can be kept and used for a long time with proper care and careful handling. Cleaning things properly after use is not only hygienic but also gives them long life. Used equipment get dirty or stained easily and should therefore be washed soon after use. This will facilitate easy and quick removal of grease, stains, soot, etc.

It saves time and energy to have a regular plan of cleaning utensils.

The following order is to be recommended in washing: glassware first, silver next, china third, pots and pans afterwards. All articles should be cleaned immediately after use. Things to be washed should be stacked tidily near the sink. A tray is useful for carrying a number of articles at the same time.

Particles and remnants of food should be scraped off the dishes. All garbage should be collected and deposited in the refuse or garbage bin. Greasy dishes should be wiped with newspaper to make washing easier. The utensils should be washed in hot soapy water, rinsed, and finally dried with a clean absorbent towel or they can be air-dried if rinsed with hot boiling water.

Equipment of various types is used in Indian homes, made of various materials such as silver, aluminium, stainless steel, brass, iron, glass, china-clay and so on.

Cleaning materials and aids for cleaning

The cleaning materials that are commonly used are soap, a scouring powder like Vim, soapnut powder, tamarind, lime, ash or brick powder, washing soda, whiting power, etc. Coconut fibre, steel wool, straw, newspaper, net cloth and dusters are some of the aids for cleaning.

Glass

If milk-stained, cold water should be used to rinse off the grease and prevent it from sticking to the glass. Then it should be washed with warm water and soap, rinsed in cold water and dried. Once a week, vinegar should be added to the washing water to brighten the glass.

Silverware and cutlery

Grease should be removed by wiping the knives, spoons, forks, etc., with newspaper. In the case of knives the blade should be washed in hot soapy water with a piece of cloth. The knife may then be washed in clean water and dried. If the handle happens to be of wood or bone, it should not be allowed to get wet, or it will get loose and become yellow.

China

Chinaware should be first rinsed in cold water and then washed in hot soapy water. Finally, it may be washed in hot water and dried. When there are spouts, grooved spots or embossed designs with curves, a brush should be used for scrubbing corners and crevices.

Brass, bronze or copperware

Tamarind should be applied with a little water and rubbed well. Fine brick powder may also be used with coconut fibre. The article may then be rinsed thoroughly in clean water and dried.

Brasso or any other metal polish can be used for cleaning and polishing the ornamental articles. Stains, if any, can be removed by applying a piece of lime smeared with salt.

Aluminium

If greasy, aluminium vessels should be steeped in hot water, otherwise in cold water. They may be washed with hot soapy water, using steel wool or coconut fibre; or cleaned with tamarind or lime. Stains and smoky deposits may be removed with steel wool or coconut fibre, using a scouring powder . If the inside of the vessel is stained badly, water to which a little vinegar is added, should be boiled in it for about half an hour. This will loosen the stains. After removal of stains, they should be rinsed with cold water and dried with a cloth.

Stainless steel

Stainless steelware can be cleaned in the same manner as aluminium. After steeping it in cold water, it should be washed with soapy water. It may also be cleaned with soapnut powder and finally rinsed with clean water and dried with a cloth.

Steel wool and coconut fibre should not be used as they leave scratches on the vessels.

Iron

First the grease should be removed with waste paper and the vessel scrubbed well with steel wool and wood ash in hot soap water. Then it should be rinsed in clean cold water and allowed to dry. A small amount of grease applied to the surface of the vessel will prevent it from rusting.

Utensils used mainly for cooking purposes and placed directly on the fire collect a lot of soot at the bottom. Care should be taken to remove this. In some Indian homes a mild coat of wood ash or cow-dung ash mixed with a little water is applied to the bottom of the vessel. This facilitates the easy removal of soot.

Cleaning of equipment

Stoves or ovens

Stoves or ovens should be kept spotlessly clean. In the case of oil stoves, the reservoir containing oil should be only 3/4 full and should not be allowed to get too low. The stoves and ovens should be carefully wiped with a soapy cloth and any grease or food particles removed, after which they should be wiped again with a clean cloth.

Refrigerator

The refrigerator should always be wiped clean both inside and outside. At regular intervals, it should be defrosted, that is, the excess ice should be removed from the freezer.

Sink

The sink should be thoroughly cleaned with fine scouring

powder. If it is greasy, a little soda may be put in the plug hole and boiled water poured on it to clean the pipe. The sink should then be well flushed with hot and then with cold water.

Table

The kitchen table should be kept spotlessly clean. The top of the table (stone-slab top or marble top) may be cleaned with a soapy cloth and then wiped with a clean wet cloth.

Meat safe and cupboards

Meat safes and cupboards should be emptied and cleaned periodically. They should be dusted first and wiped with a clean wet cloth. When dry, the shelves should be lined with a clean set of papers. Before replacing the jars and bottles that have been removed from the meat safe or cupboards, each article should be wiped clean. The ant-wells under the four legs of the meat safe should always be kept full of water to prevent ants from getting in.

18. Purchasing and Storing Food in a Home

Purchasing food

What one buys depends on the funds at one's disposal. To cut one's coat according to one's cloth is a well-known maxim which comes in handy where purchasing is concerned. A buyer normally wants to bargain well and shrewdly buys the things he wants, eliminating waste. Those who have sufficient storage space go in for bulk purchases, for convenience and economy. Economy should be the keynote of all purchases. However, this does not mean stinting money and running short of food, but buying wisely and using every scrap of food bought in the best manner possible. For purchasing food systematically, an orderly shopping list is the prerequisite. It will save time for the buyer as well as the seller.

Every housekeeper must know how to choose food and recognize its worth. Only fresh meat, fish, eggs, vegetables or fruit should be bought. One should not buy more than is necessary for consumption. In buying dry condiments, spices, rice, ghee and other cooking medium, one should select good brands in reliable shops.

It is better not to buy prepared or cooked foods since they are distinctly uneconomical. In these days of rampant adulteration, in order to enable people to buy the best unadulterated food, the Government of India has taken steps to put the seal "AGMARK" on certain foodstuffs. The word "Agmark" means "Ag" Agriculture, and "Mark" for marketing. It is a symbol of purity and a guarantee that the product which bears it possesses the declared attributes of quality. Agmark products mean for the consumer a high level of quality, purity and freshness and better value for money, since the "Agmark" graded articles are supervised by the Government, and backed by legislation. An association called the Madras State Consumers' Association exists in Madras and it is very desirable for housekeepers to join such associations so as to gather in full strength as consumers.

Marketing should be done by the housekeeper if possible. Buying directly from the market is better than having foodstuffs delivered at the house, since in the delivery system the food supplied may not always be good, and the weights may not be correct. One should be conversant with the grades and brand of food and know what grades can be used for which dish. It is better to buy foods which are in season and in abundance in the market since they will cost less.

It is not worth buying wilted vegetables just because they are cheap, since they will have lost their vitamins. When buying tinned foods, one should make sure that the tin is not bloated.

Storage of food

Great care should be taken in storing foodstuffs. If properly stored they can last for several days, weeks or months. Careful storage will help to retain their appearance, flavour, general quality and food value.

If foodstuffs are carelessly stored they will deteriorate and there will be wastage through withering, discolouration, mould and decay. Further, foods will lose their natural flavour, attractive appearance and vitamin content. Sometimes they may prove a complete loss.

Rice

Rice should be bought from reliable shops. It is advisable to buy bags with 'Agmark' stamped on them.

The common mode of storing rice is by keeping it in the form of paddy in properly constructed granaries. It will last for a year without deterioration if stored thus.

Highly-milled rice, free from weevils, if stored in suitable receptacles, will remain in good condition for more than a year.

Hand-pounded rice and under-milled rice deteriorate more rapidly than highly milled rice. However, under-milled, par-boiled rice can last for a longer period than under-milled, raw rice, if carefully stored.

Rice is best stored in air-tight tins. Storing rice in earthen vessels or keeping it in open vessels is not advisable since it is liable to be spoilt by dampness or moisture.

Pulses

The general rules for the purchase and storage of cereals like rice hold good for pulses also.

Flour

Flour from fresh stock should be bought from the shops, as old stock may contain worms and weevils. Flour should not be kept exposed to damp air since it will absorb moisture. It will become lumpy and mouldy even if subsequently stored in air-tight tins. Flour containing germs will not last long, since the fat in the germs is likely to become rancid.

Fruit

Only fresh, firm fruit, free from blemishes should be bought. It is not advisable to buy badly bruised or decayed fruit however cheap it may be. Fruit may be judged for ripeness by its firmness. If it is very hard, it is unripe. On the contrary, if it is too soft it may have decayed.

Fruit should be stored in a cold place. Bananas are an exception to this general rule, since they should be kept in an airy place and not in a refrigerator, as the skins go black.

Vegetables

Only fresh vegetables should be bought. Limp or wilted ones should be rejected. Fresh vegetables are firm and crisp and they should be preferred to wilted, shrunken and shrivelled ones. Vegetables should be heavy in proportion to their size. Medium-sized vegetables are better than large ones since the latter are often fibrous. It is best to use vegetables soon after they are bought. Most vegetables do not store well and lose their vitamin content, especially vitamin C.

Onions and potatoes should be put in a wire basket and hung up in a dry place. If kept in a moist atmosphere they will get mouldy. They should not be put in a refrigerator. Cauliflower should be stored with its green leaves. However, soiled or wilted leaves should be removed before storing, or they may cause decay in the other leaves also. Peas should be stored in their pods, since these protect them and keep them fresh. Brinjals shrink if kept inside the refrigerator.

Green leafy vegetables should be washed of dirt and sand.

The excess water should be shaken off. Only then should they be stored in a refrigerator. One of the cheapest ways of keeping vegetables fresh at home is to put them in an earthen pot covered with a piece of wet sacking. This keeps them fresh even for three or four days. However, it is always better to buy the vegetables fresh and use them straightaway.

Meat

Only fresh meat which is firm, elastic to the touch, moist and of bright colour should be bought. Such meat will be mottled with pale yellow fat.

It is best to store meat as large cuts. It should be kept in the coldest part of the refrigerator under the freezing or ice compartment. Before storing in the refrigerator, it should be wiped with a damp cloth but never washed in water. A little drying of the surface is desirable as it checks bacterial growth.

Poultry

One should always choose young, tender birds since old birds are tough. Birds which are plump in appearance with smooth soft legs, bright eyes and red combs are a good buy. Abundance of pin feathers will indicate that the birds are young. Male birds which are free of spurs and young are preferable to those with long spurs and full crop.

Fish

Fresh fish usually sinks in water and has no disagreeable odour. Fish with bright red, clear gills are fresh; the flesh is firm; the tails do not droop; and the scales do not come off easily. Still another test of fresh fish is that pressure on the body does not leave a depression on the flesh. Fish can be iced and stored for a few days.

Eggs

It is better to buy eggs with an Agmark stamp on them. A new laid egg has a rough surface. As the egg ages, the shell becomes shiny. Since the contents of the egg shrink with keeping, it is possible to gauge the staleness of eggs by gently shaking them. Rotten eggs when shaken produce dull thuds. The easiest way of selecting fresh eggs is by immersing them fully in water. Fresh ones lie flat, whereas stale ones tend to float or stand up on their narrow ends. Another way of determining the quality and freshness of eggs is to hold them up in front of a candle or any bright light or in sunlight. If the egg is fresh the light passes through clearly. This is also done in selecting eggs for hatching.

Eggs can be stored by keeping them chilled. They can also be kept by pickling them in solutions of water-glass, lime or borax. Another way of preserving them is to seal the pores on the shell by coating them with melted paraffin wax. This prevents micro-organisms from entering the egg and spoiling it. If eggs are to be stored in a refrigerator, they should not be washed, as the protective dull coat known as "bloom" is lost by washing and odours and flavours enter the egg through the porous shell.

Milk

Great care should be taken in buying milk. Government sponsored or other co-operative milk supply units exist in many cities which supply milk in a hygienic manner. Milk should be bought only from sources which are sanitary, since adulterated, impure milk may contain germs that cause typhoid, tuberculosis and other contagious diseases. Only the milk of a healthy cow, milked under conditions of perfect cleanliness, should be bought.

To keep milk, it should be boiled or pasteurized. Pasteurization is done by heating milk to 63°C for about 30 minutes and then cooling it quickly. Milk should be kept in a cool place, away from flies and dust. As far as possible, it should be stored in the vessel in which it was boiled and kept in the coldest part of the refrigerator. Since few homes in India have refrigerators, the following method may be adopted for storing milk in hot weather. The vessel containing milk should be kept in a basin of cold water and covered with a piece of wet muslin cloth with the edges dipping in the water. This will help to keep the milk cool.

Milk should never be kept near foods with a strong smell such as onions, as it easily absorbs odour. New milk should never be mixed with the old, since the bacteria in the old milk will infect the new.

Butter and ghee

Only good brands of butter or ghee should be purchased, and that too from reliable shops.

Like milk, these milk products also absorb odours easily. Therefore, they should not be kept near foods with a strong smell. They should be stored in a cool place, as otherwise they tend to become rancid.

Spices and condiments

It is not advisable to buy spices and condiments in large quantities as they tend to lose their smell and flavour with time. They should always be kept in a cool, dark, dry place, in tightly covered containers.

19. Practical Cookery

Weights and measures

It is customary for the cook in Indian homes to take handfuls or so of various ingredients and use them for cooking. Out of long experience she is able to take out the precise amount with accurate judgement. Questioned, she will retort, "The eye's precision guides the hand's measure". But her experience in cookery cannot be of much value to others since she cannot impart her culinary art to them. There is no scientific basis in such measuring, hence there will be difficulty in interpretation.

People in different parts of the world are not only interested in the clothes and habits of those of other countries but are also eager to know about their delicious dishes and the methods of preparing them. Even in the same country, people are interested to know each other's ways of preparing various dishes. Standardization of recipes with clear indications of the weights and measures of articles to be used will help in the diffusion of know-how in such matters.

In the market, articles of food like cereals and pulses are sometimes sold in heaped measures. From the point of view of weight, this method is not satisfactory, because the weight of the heaped measures of the articles may vary at different times. Since heaped measures differ in weight, level measures only should be used for a record. Even the weight of levelled measures may not be constant. In measuring flour for instance, there is bound to be some difference of weight according to whether the measure is loosely filled or pressed down even though it may be levelled off. It is important to measure the ingredients accurately, especially for making cakes and pastries. The following suggestions may be borne in mind in measuring.

Dry ingredients may be measured in a measuring cup. The cup should be filled with the foodstuff and the edge of a knife or the handle of a spoon passed over the top of the cup to level off. In case a teaspoon or a tablespoon is used for measuring dry ingredients, after heaping the spoon first, the edge of a knife should be passed across the top to level off.

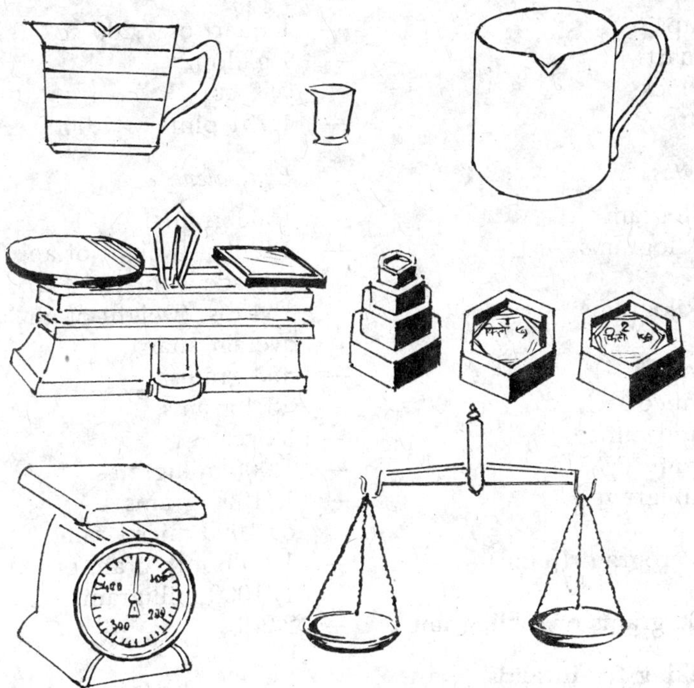

Fig. 95. Weights, measures and scales

Flour should be measured after being sifted. The measuring cup should be loosely filled and not tapped every time flour is added, as this will cause great variation in the quantity taken.

Solid fats should be packed into the spoon and levelled.

Till recent times, different types of weights and measures were used in different parts of India. After the introduction of the decimal coinage in the country, the government brought in a bill to unify weights and measures by introducing which the metric system comprises grams and litres.

The following conversion table will be of help:

Measures		*Equivalents*
1 teaspoon	—	60 drops.
1 tablespoon	—	3 teaspoons.
1 cup	—	16 tablespoons or ½ pint or 10 fluid ozs.
2 cups	—	1 pint.
4 cups	—	1 quart or 1,200 cc.
4 quarts	—	1 gallon.
1 ollock	—	7/8 cup.
1 litre	—	1.761 pints or 1,000 cc.

Weights		*Equivalents*
1 kilogram	—	1000 grams.
60 kilograms	—	132 lbs. (weight of an average woman).
70 kilograms	—	154 lbs. (weight of an average man).
1 pound	—	454 grams.
1 ounce	—	28.4 grams.
1 fluid ounce	—	30 cc.
1 gram	—	1,000 milligrams.
1 milligram	—	1/1000 grams. or 1000 microgram.
1 microgram (μ gm)	—	1 millionth gram or 1/1000 milligram.
1,000 grams or 1 kilogram	—	2.2 lbs.

Cooking for invalids

Food prepared for and consumed by normal, healthy people cannot be digested by invalids. The sick have little or no appetite for food. The food prepared for them should be so cooked as to be easily digested and should be served in such a fashion as to tempt them to eat. Normally, liquid or soft diets are given to them. Invalid diets include conjees (gruel) made of broken rice, arrowroot, sago, barley, whey; vegetable and mutton soups; fruit juices and custards.

Rice conjee

Broken par-boiled rice	—	1 tablespoon.
Water	—	½ cup.
Milk	—	½ cup
Sugar	—	to taste.

Cook the rice in water till it is very soft. Then add milk and sugar and serve.

If unbroken rice is used instead of broken rice, it should be boiled for a longer period to make it soft and easily digestible.

Arrowroot conjee

Arrowroot — 1 tablespoon.
Milk — ½ cup.
Water — ½ cup.
Sugar — to taste.

Put half a cup of water on the stove to boil. Make a paste of arrowroot powder using 2-3 tablespoonful of cold water. Add this paste slowly to the boiling water, stirring all the time and let it simmer for 5 minutes. When the mixture appears to be of uniform consistency and the arrowroot is cooked, remove it from the stove, add milk and sugar and serve.

Arrowroot conjee is often given to infants suffering from diarrhoea. Since it has no protein value it will not help invalids to recuperate, if given as the sole food for long periods.

Sago conjee

Sago — 1 tablespoon.
Milk — ½ cup.
Water — ½ cup.
Sugar — to taste.

Boil the sago in water till it becomes transparent. Add milk and sugar and serve.

Barley water

Pearl barley — 1 tablespoon.
Water — 1 cup.

Boil the barley in water till it gets soft. Decant the fluid and use.

Barley water has little nutritive value. Since it helps to make milk curd softer and finer, it is added at times to the milk feed of infants and invalids.

Whey

Milk — 1 cup.
Lime juice — 2 tablespoon.
Sugar — to taste.

Boil the milk. While it is still very hot, add the lime juice and leave it to stand for 5 minutes. The curd will separate. Now filter through a thin cloth and serve the whey water only, with a little sugar, if desired.

Soup (Vegetable)

Tomato (big)	— 1
Carrot	— 1
Onion	— 1
Water	— 1 cup.
Seasoning	— salt and pepper.

Chop the onion, cut the tomato and carrot into small pieces and simmer the vegetables in a covered pan for 10 minutes. Press through a sieve and season with pepper and salt. Other vegetables may also be used.

Cream of tomato soup

White sauce

Butter	— 1 tablespoon.
Flour	— 1 tablespoon.
Salt	— ½ teaspoon.
Pepper	— ½ teaspoon.
Milk	— 1 cup.

Tomato stock

Tomatoes	— 2
Onion	— 1
Coriander leaves	— a few.

Melt the butter and then stir in the flour until smooth. Gradually add milk and stir constantly until the mixture boils and thickens. Then cook for about 3 minutes more, stirring occasionally. Place over hot water to keep hot and cover tightly to prevent a skin forming on top. Chop up the vegetables and simmer them in a covered pan for 10 minutes. Press through a sieve and add to the white sauce; heat thoroughly and season with salt and pepper to taste.

Mutton broth or soup

Meat	— 180 g.
Water	— 3 cups.
Onion	— 1
Pepper and salt	— to taste.

Wash the meat and cut it into small bits and crack the bone to loosen the marrow. Chop up the onions and add the pieces of mutton and crushed bones along with pepper and salt to the 2 cups of water in the saucepan. Heat slowly and allow to simmer for nearly 2 hours. Strain and serve hot.

Steamed custard

Egg — 1
Milk — 1 cup.
Vanilla essence — 2 drops.
Sugar — 2-3 tablespoon.

Beat the egg and sugar. Warm the milk. Add the warmed milk to the beaten egg and sugar mixture. Add the essence. Pour into custard cups and steam. The custard is cooked and ready when the handle of a spoon or the blade of a knife inserted into it comes clean.

Preparation of beverages

Boiled coffee

Coffee powder — 2 teaspoons.
Boiling water — 1 cup.
Milk — to taste.
Sugar — to taste.

Put the coffee powder in freshly boiling water and stir well.

Allow to infuse for 5-7 minutes.

Strain and serve hot.

Milk when used with coffee should be hot but not boiling.

Care should be taken to use clean coffee pots for preparing good coffee. A pot which retains the stale smell of coffee will spoil the flavour and taste of the beverage.

Freshly ground coffee powder has a good flavour. The aroma and flavour quickly disappear after grinding, particularly if the coffee powder is not kept covered in an air-tight tin.

Tea

Tea — 1 teaspoon.
Boiling water — 1 cup.
Milk — to taste.
Sugar — to taste.

Pour hot water into the teapot. When the pot is hot, pour

the water out. Put in the tea leaves, allowing one level teaspoon for every cup and one for the pot.

Pour boiling water over the tea leaves.

Allow the tea to infuse for 3 or 4 minutes only. Stir well before pouring out. Serve at once.

In serving tea, the milk should be poured into the cup before the tea. This helps to precipitate any tannin present in the tea. Tannin gives a bitter taste to the tea.

It is better to use a china pot rather than a metal one.

Fruit juice

Lime juice

Lime — 1
Water — 1 cup.
Sugar — to taste.

Extract the lime juice. Remove the pips with a spoon; add sugar and water and mix well. Chill and serve.

Orange juice

Oranges — 2
Water — 1 cup.
Sugar — to taste.

Extract the orange juice and strain. Add sugar and water. Mix well. Chill and serve. (If the oranges are sweet do not add sugar, since, for many people, the added carbohydrates are unnecessary).

Preparation of snacks

Uppuma and chutney

Uppuma
Clean, fine *rava* (semoline) — 120 g.
Water — 240 ml.
Mustard — ½ teaspoon.
Black gram dal — 1 teaspoon.
Bengal gram dal — 1 tablespoon.
Salt — 2 teaspoons.
Fried cashewnuts — 4 or 5
Green chillies — 2
Red chillies — 2

Curry leaves — a few.
Ghee (or Oil) — 2 tablespoon.
Onion — 1

Heat the ghee. Fry mustard, black gram dal, Bengal gram dal, chopped onions, chillies and curry leaves. Add water and salt and stir well. When the water boils, add the *rava* slowly, stirring briskly all the time to prevent lumps forming. Cook till the *rava* gets soft. Add the fried cashewnuts, stir and remove from the fire. Serve hot with *chutney*.

Chutney

Coconut scrapings — 60 g.
Broiled Bengal gram dal — 1 tablespoon.
Salt — 1 teaspoon.
Green chillies — 2
Tamarind — 1 pea-size ball.
Mustard — 1 teaspoon.
Gingelly oil — 2 teaspoons.

Grind the coconut scrapings along with the dal, salt, chillies, and tamarind into a rough paste. Fry the mustard in the oil and add to the ground paste; mix well. Serve with *uppuma*.

Puri and potato curry

Wheat flour — 120 g.
Water — enough to make a dough.
Salt — 1 teaspoon.
Ghee — 3 teaspoons.
Dalda — 1 cup.

Mix the flour, water and salt and prepare the dough. Knead the dough well, adding ghee. Allow the dough to stand covered for at least 10 minutes and then divide it into 8 equal balls. Roll them one at a time on a floured board into circles 2" in diameter. By folding and refolding during rolling, the dough is aerated. Heat the Dalda and when it is very hot, deep-fry the puris one by one till they puff up well.

Potato curry

Potatoes — 4
Oil — 1 tablespoon.
Green chillies — 3
Salt — 2 teaspoons.
Onions — 2

Black gram dal — 1 teaspoon.
Ginger — 1 small piece.
Mustard — ½ teaspoon.
Curry and coriander leaves — a few.

Boil the potatoes in water. When they are cooked, remove from the stove, peel and mash them.

Chop up the onions, green chillies, coriander leaves and ginger. Heat the oil in a frying pan. When hot, put the mustard in. When the mustard seeds burst, add the black gram, and when this turns light brown, add the chopped ingredients. When it is browned add the mashed potatoes, stir well for a few minutes and remove from the stove.

Toffees

Coconut toffee

(Scraped) coconut — 120 g.
Sugar — 120 g.
Cardamom — 6
Cochineal (colouring) — 2 drops.
Water — ½ cup.

Add the water to the sugar and boil the sugar in a frying pan, and when the soft ball stage is reached, add the coconut scrapings and keep on stirring till the sugar begins to caramelize. Add the colouring and powdered cardamom and immediately remove from the fire and transfer to a greased plate. When nearly set, cut into desired shapes.

Groundnut toffee

Shelled roasted groundnuts — 120 g.
Jaggery — 120 g.
Water — ½ cup.

Remove the outer skin of the shelled groundnuts. Boil the jaggery with water in a frying pan. When it boils, add the groundnuts, stirring all the while. Remove from the fire when the syrup thickens and pour on to a greased plate. Cut into slabs of the desired shapes and sizes.

Mysore pak

Bengal gram flour — 120 g.
Sugar — 240 g.
Ghee — 240 g.
Water — 60 ml.

Boil the sugar with the water in a frying pan till the syrup stage is reached. Add the Bengal gram flour to the syrup, little by little, stirring all the while to prevent the formation of lumps. When the contents do not stick to the sides of the pan, remove from the stove. Transfer to a greased plate and cut into desired shapes while still hot.

Cooking a simple balanced meal

The majority of people in India suffer from malnutrition. Due to economic conditions, they are unable to afford milk, fish, etc. Most Indian diets consist mainly of cereals which contain only small quantities of proteins and protective elements. Malnutrition is caused by want of proteins, calcium and certain vitamins in the food. With a view to meet the requirements of the economically backward people, the Central Food Technological Research Institute, Mysore, has produced a low cost food of high nutritive value. This has been prepared from specially processed low-fat groundnut flour and Bengal gram flour, strengthened with minerals and vitamins. One gram for children and 2 gram for adults, of the Indian Multi-purpose Food (I.M.P.F.) will supply the consumer with approximately 1/3 of his minimum daily requirements of proteins, minerals and vitamins.

The Indian Multi-purpose Food can be incorporated to the extent of 20% in any of the common food preparations. It does not require any change in food habits. The I.M.P.F. is available in a **seasoned variety** for use in the preparation of savouries; an **unseasoned variety** for sweets; and an **unseasoned variety with 20% skimmed milk powder** for children and convalescents.

Therefore any simple balanced meal must include IMPF.

Menu of a simple balanced meal

Such a meal would consist of:

Rice.
Sambar.
Tomato Rasam.
Mint chutney.
Beans Pugath.
Pappads.

Curds.
Ripe plantains.

Rice

Rice	— 180 g.
Water	— 1½ cup.

Clean the rice and cook by the absorption method till all the water is absorbed and the rice is well cooked. Remove from the stove and transfer to a flat plate so that the cooked rice is well exposed to air. Otherwise rice cooked by this method is likely to be sticky.

Sambar

Red gram dal	— 90 g.
I.M.P.F. (Seasoned)	— 90 g.
Brinjal or any other vegetable	— 4 (medium).
Coriander seeds	— 1 teaspoon.
Mustard	— 1 teaspoon.
Red chillies	— 6
Salt	— 3 teaspoons.
Fenugreek	— ½ teaspoon.
Asafoetida	— a little.
Tamarind	— 15 gm.
Curry leaves	— for flavour.
Oil	— 2 tablespoons.
Turmeric powder	— ½ teaspoon.
Water	— 2 cups.

Fry the coriander seeds, turmeric powder, red chillies, fenugreek and asafoetida together to a reddish brown colour. Fry the coconut scrapings next. Grind all the fried ingredients. Soak the tamarind in a little water and extract the juice. To this add salt and the ground spices.

Boil the red gram dal in 2 cups of water. When the dal is nearly cooked, add the I.M.P.F. and cook it for 10 minutes more. Mash the dal well and mix in the tamarind juice containing salt and the ground spices.

Fry mustard and curry leaves in oil in a vessel and pour the sambar in it. Add the cut brinjals and leave the sambar on the stove till they are cooked.

Tomato rasam

Tomatoes	—	2 (medium).
I.M.P.F. (Seasoned)	—	30 g.
Salt	—	2 teaspoons.
Turmeric	—	a little.
Asafoetida	—	a little.
Mustard	—	½ teaspoon.
Red chillies	—	3
Curry leaves	—	a few.
Coriander leaves	—	a few.
Oil	—	1 teaspoon.
Water	—	2 cups.

Cook I.M.P.F. for 10 minutes in 2 cups of water containing asafoetida and turmeric powder.

Wash the tomatoes and cut each of them into 4-6 pieces. Heat the oil, add mustard, chopped red chillies, tomatoes, then curry leaves and coriander leaves and fry for a few minutes. Add cooked I.M.P.F and salt and boil for about 10 minutes.

Mint chutney

Mint leaves	—	90 g.
I.M.P.F. (Seasoned)	—	90 g.
Salt	—	1 teaspoon.
Red chillies	—	3
Garlic	—	1 pod.
Black gram dal	—	1 teaspoon.
Tamarind	—	15 g.
Mustard	—	1 teaspoon.
Curry leaves	—	for flavour.
Oil	—	2 teaspoons.
Water	—	a little.

Soak the tamarind in a little water and prepare a thick extract. Wash the mint leaves and fry them in a frying pan for 2 or 3 minutes. Then grind all the ingredients given above to a coarse paste. Add the tamarind extract. Season with mustard and curry leaves fried in oil.

Beans pugath

Beans	—	180 g.
I.M.P.F. (Seasoned)	—	90 g.
Oil	—	2 teaspoons.
Mustard	—	½ teaspoon.
Black gram dal	—	1 teaspoon.
Chillies	—	3
Salt	—	1½ teaspoons.

Wash the beans and cut them into small pieces. Cook with the I.M.P.F. in just enough boiling water with salt till they are fairly cooked. Place a *degchi* with oil on the stove. Add the mustard, then the black gram dal and split chillies, and fry till the dal becomes golden brown. Add the cooked vegetables and fry for 5 minutes till the water left, if any, is evaporated. Finally add the coconut scrapings, mix well, and remove from the stove.

Pappads

Heat the oil in a deep pan. When hot, fry the pappads one by one.

Curds

3 tablespoons skimmed milk powder.
1 cup warm water.
1 teaspoon buttermilk.

Dissolve the milk powder well in one cup of warm water without forming any lumps. Add one teaspoon of buttermilk, stir well and set it aside in a covered dish for 6 hours, by which time the milk will have become curds.

Dessert

Bananas, guavas, *amlas,* papayas or any other fruit in season, available at a low cost, can be served for dessert.

Suggestions for a Days's Menu

6 A.M.	Bed Coffee/Tea/Milk/Ragi malt.		
8 A.M. Breakfast	Idlis, chutney, egg omelette, fruit juice, coffee or tea or milk.	or	Puri & potatoes or alu paratha with sweets and fruit juice, milk or coffee or tea.

Lunch 12 Noon	Chapatis with dal, potato fry, vegetable salad, rice, rasam, curds, pickle, any fruit.	or	Ghee rice or egg rice, vegetable kuruma, curd rice, cucumber raita, cutlets, any fruits.
Tea 4 P.M.	Groundnut masala, carrot halwa, tea.	or	vadais groundnut, toffee tea.
Dinner 8 P.M.	Rice or Idiappam with vegetable kuruma, greens pugath, cultets custard or ice cream fruit.	or	Chappatis with thick dal, cabbage and peas pugath fruit salad with ice cream.
Bed Time 10 A.M.	Hot milk	or	Hot chocolate.

Effect of supplementary foods on poor rice diet

It is a well-known fact that a rice diet is deficient in calcium, vitamins and protein. Hence experiments on animals using cheap, commonly available foods as supplements to a rice diet were conducted as early as 1937 by Dr. Aykroyd and his associates. Their work is reported in the Indian Journal of Medical Research, vols. 24 and 25 (1937).

Experiments on white rats have proved that ragi and amaranth are good cheap supplements to a rice diet. Small dried fish used as supplements have also been found to be very effective, since fish is a rich source of protein as well as calcium. Dal also has been found to be a valuable source of protein; but dal supplements have been effective when calcium supplements are also added.

An Indian home scientist investigated the growth of white rats on supplemented rice diets in 1959. She supplemented the polished rice diet with groundnut. Groundnuts have a high protein content, and are grown abundantly in India and are well liked by the people. Her results proved that the rats fed with the groundnut supplemented diets grew better than those fed on the unsupplemented rice diet.

India joined the race of soya producing countyries during the seventies only. Soya flour is used for fortifying wheat flour. Soya flour has all the desirable attributes like aeration, porosity, whippability, blendability and excellent emulsifiability. During hospitalisation, pregnant, lactating women, convalescents, anaemic and diabetic patients can be given soya products. To combat protein-energy malnutrition, soya flour will prove to be a very timely and rich source. Soya milk can be used as beverage. Soya meal is used as one of the most important animal feed ingredient also. Refined soya oil has more than 85% polyunsaturated fatty acids. It is totally free of cholesterol and has a very significant effect of reducing the existing high level of cholesteric patients. Soya oil does not give any taint or off flavour in the fried products and the true naturai flavour of the ingredient mix of the products are exhibited better, giving better taste and crispness. One of the by-products of soya is lecithin which has a excellent cholesterol reduction effect. Hence it is presently capsulated and marketed as an anticholesterol drug.

20. Preparing the Dining Room —Western and Indian Styles

Western style

The dining room may be prepared for serving meals in different ways to suit the occasion. Normally, in a house, the various times when the dining-room is set for meals are breakfast, lunch, tea, and supper or dinner. Table-laying should be such as to enhance one's enjoyment of food and simplify eating. The two most important things to be observed during table-laying are convenience and practicality.

Requisites for table-laying

Apart from the dining table, which may be oblong, square, oval, or round, to suit the shape and size of the dining-room, and other furniture, such as armless, straight-backed chairs, etc., linen, crockery and cutlery play a vital role in table-laying. Since the enjoyment of a meal depends upon table appointments, their choice is important.

Table linen

The tablecloth should fit the table with the edges hanging over uniformly on all sides, say, 8" to 12". The linen should only supply a background for the crockery and cutlery used. Table linen should not be highly decorative or brightly coloured, but simple, providing a clean framework for the food served. It is advisable to use a clean, white damask, tablecloth.

Dishes and silverware

Plain, white porcelain crockery with no decorations beyond a few simple bands is best suited for daily use. Cream or light yellow is the next best choice. Such dishes show up the food to the best advantage.

For daily use, plain cutlery with no ornamental workmanship on the handles is the best, as it is the easiest to clean.

Glassware

Clear, smooth, colourless glass, free from scratches, cracks or bubbles, is most satisfactory for ordinary table use. The more cutwork it has, the more difficult it is to clean. Water is most attractive in clear sparkling glass without colour. Coloured glass does not show up the colours of beverages to advantage. Glassware adds greatly to the attractiveness of the table. One should take care to see that the glassware harmonizes with the other dishes in colour, shape, size and quality.

Table decorations

In addition to table linen, crockery and cutlery, vases, bowls and candlesticks of various types are used on the dining-table for decorative purposes.

Setting the table

Till the invention of spoons and forks, food was eaten with the hands, a custom which exists in Africa, India and several other countries even today. Many of the rules concerning table-setting and service are a few centuries old. They were derived from the castles of medieval times and adapted to suit the interests, needs and customs of the individual families and groups.

The most important thing to be borne in mind in serving food is cleanliness and tidiness, so linen should be clean and well ironed; glass and china should be well washed and clear and sparkling; the table should be neatly set with simple but attractive decoration; and well-prepared food should be carefully served on the plates and dishes. Food should not be allowed to spill on the floor or on the table, nor should it drip over the edges of the vessels from which it is served. Custom, convenience and commonsense should guide one's choice of linen, crockery and cutlery, and one's plan of service.

The dining table and chairs should be dusted and cleaned. A silence cloth of heavy material should go under the tablecloth, unless the tablecloth is of lace. The heavy, silence cloth is used to muffle the clatter of dishes, protect the table, and to keep the table linen smooth. If place mats and table runners are used, no silence cloth is needed. The tablecloth should be laid with the middle lengthwise crease up and

PLACE SETTING FOR INFORMAL MEAL

Fig. 96. 1. Table knife and Fork. 2. Small Bread Knife. 3. Dessert Spoon and Fork. 4. Table Napkin on the side plate. 5. Tumbler.

PLACE SETTING FOR FORMAL MEAL

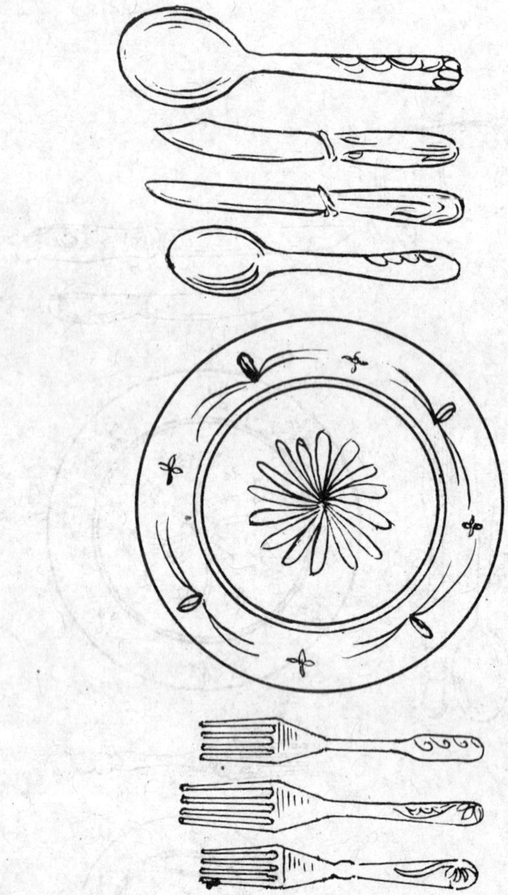

Fig. 97. 1. Soup Spoon. 2. Fish Knife and Fork. 3. Table Knife and Fork. 4. Dessert Spoon and Fork. 5. Table Napkin on side plate. 6. Tumbler.

extending exactly along the centre of the table. Decorations, if any, should be in the centre of the table. A flower vase or fruit centre-piece should be low.

The place set for each person at the table is known as 'the cover'. The term includes the crockery, cutlery and napery arranged for the individual's use. The space allowed for each person should be 20" to 24" in length and 15" to 16" in breadth so as not to crowd the guests. If an even number of people are to be catered for, the covers should be directly opposite one another.

Plates should be arranged at the centre of the cover, one inch from the edge of the table. One inch from the edge and perpendicular to the plate, is where the flat silver should be placed. The fork should be on the left side of the plate, tines up, and the knife on the right, sharp or cutting edges towards the plate. The spoon should be to the right of the knife. Additional forks should be placed to the right of the first fork and additional knives and spoons to the left of the first spoon.

On a side plate to the left of the fork the table napkin or serviette should be placed with the open corner toward the edge of the table. The water glass should be at the tip of the knife, slightly to the right of it.

All pieces of silver should be so arranged as to enable the guest or diner to work toward the plate starting at the outside piece on either side. The silver required for the dessert and after-dinner coffee is usually brought in with the dessert bowl or coffee cup.

Seating arrangement

Places at the table have always been assigned according to rank, the seats of honour being those nearest the host. The host occupies the head of the table and the hostess the foot. The guest of honour is seated at the host's right, if a woman, and if a man, at the right of the hostess. One should stand beside the chair and wait till the hostess sits down. When the hostess rises from her seat, it indicates that the last course has been served and the dinner is over. One sits and rises from the left side of the chair.

General rules for serving food

Water glasses should be filled three-fourths. Ice may be put in, if desired. Bread, when served, should be cut into small slices and placed on a plate on the table along with butter and other cold foods before the meal is served. Food should be arranged in a uniform manner on the plates. The meat should be on the lower left side of the plate with potatoes on the upper left and other vegetables on the right side of the plate. As a general rule food is passed to the right. Food, if served, is held in the left hand of the maid and offered from the guest's left. Only beverages like coffee or water are served from the right. Plates are removed one at a time from the left.

Sometimes fruit juices are served before dinner.

After eating, the knife and fork should be placed on the dinner plate close together in such a way that they do not topple down when the plates are being removed. The butter knife should be placed in the centre of the bread plate after use.

Strictly speaking, there are no rigid rules of etiquette except at formal dinner parties. Most of the details of service, etc., should be dictated by convenience and courtesy. The two important watchwords for the guest are: to watch the hostess and take the cue from her actions; and, while eating, to start with the food from the outside and proceed inwards.

The general rules for the hostess are: she should keep everything in readiness before dinner is announced. She should not be over-anxious and jumpy, but cool and collected. If no servants are available, she should enlist the help of a friend for serving, and not unnecessarily fret herself.

The following is a typical western menu for dinner:

Cream of tomato soup.
Fried fish and chips.
Roast chicken with stuffing.
Gravy.
Vegetable salad.
Hot Rolls.
Jelly.
Coffee.

Buffet service

There are no strict rules or regulations for buffet service. Informality is the general rule. Guests have the privilege of moving around. They are at liberty to take the foods that appeal to them. They may sit or stand and eat their food and choose their own companions. In buffet service there is freedom of movement and an air of ease. The arrangement of foods for buffet is planned for the convenience of the guests. The plates should be stacked at one end of the table from which the guests approach. Food for the main courses come next. Then the salads, breads and beverages. Hot food comes last. Each food should be kept in a large vessel with the proper cutlery for serving the dish beside it. The silver which the individual takes for use is placed in an attractive pattern and serviettes are kept last.

Buffet may be self-service or the hostess or a maid may serve from the dishes on to the plates of the guests as they move along. Coffee should be served last.

The meal is announced informally by the hostess. The guest of honour is ushered to the table and serves himself first; the others follow suit.

Small tables such as card tables that can seat four are arranged in groups. If one can balance the food on one's knees, the tables may be used to hold the beverage cup or glass containing water. The food may also be placed on the table and eaten.

In buffet service, one should start from the table end where the plates are stacked and proceed to the main and other dishes. Lastly one should pick up the napkin, hold it under the plate, and take up one's seat around any one of the tables provided.

Indian style

The Indian style of serving food differs widely among Hindus, Muslims and Christians. The food may be served on tables on plates or leaves; and even in serving the dishes there may be differences. Various customs and manners in serving and eating food are observed in orthodox Hindu homes. Further, there are wide differences between the North and South Indian styles of serving food.

In the Indian style, a person always uses his right hand and eats with his fingers. Plantain leaves are often used in South India instead of plates. They are washed and placed on the floor with the tip to the left of the guest. Among North Indians a *thali*—a stainless steel plate with small bowls—is used. A plank or mat is placed for the person to sit on. A silver, brass, stainless steel or glass tumbler of water is placed at the top left side of the leaf. On festive occasions, sweets find a place on the menu. In the South Indian way of serving food, they are served at the right hand corner of the leaf at the side nearest the person. In some homes sweets are served first; in others, last. Next *pachadis (chutneys)*, dry curries, *koottu* (wet curry) and *appalam* are served on the top half of the leaf. Then pickle is served at the left side, near the tip of the leaf. Rice is served in the centre of the leaf. Ghee and *sambar* are served next. This is the first course.

The second course consists of rice with *rasam*, followed by another round of *pachadis* etc.

The third course comprises rice and curd or buttermilk and a pinch of salt, along with some pickles.

Payasam (sweet dish) is served before curds usually, but sometimes it may be served first.

After eating, the guests wash their hands. Pan (betel leaf) is then distributed.

In the Indian style, the guest is offered water to wash his hands before he enters the dining room. Usually one removes one's shoes before sitting down to eat. The hostess takes pride in serving food to the guests and gives them her personal attention. She seldom sits and eats with the guests.

Further Reading

1. Needham, M.A. and Strong, M.A., *Better Homes,* Oxford University Press, London.
2. Deshpande, R.S. *Modern Ideal Homes for India,* The United Book Corporation, Poona.
3. Raju, S.P. *Smokeless Kitchen for the Millions,* The Christian Literature Society, Madras.
4. Harris, Tate and Anders *Everyday Living,* Houghton Mifflin Co., Boston.
5. McDermott, Irene, E. and Nicholas, Florena W. *Home Making for Teenagers,* Vol. I, Chas, A. Bennett Co. Inc., Publishers, Illnois.
6. Goldstein, Harriet and Goldstein, Vetta *Art in Everyday Life,* Macmillan & Co., New York.
7. Graves, Maitland *The Art of Colour and Designs,* McGraw-Hill Book Company, New York.
8. Ishimoto, Tatsuo, *The Art of Flower Arrangement,* The Crown Publishers Inc., New York.
9. Pal, Rampa *Arranging Flowers:* Extension Pamphlet No. 3, Directorate of Extension and Training, Ministry of Agriculture, New Delhi.
10. St. John Ambulance Association, *First Aid to the Injured.*
11. St. John Ambulance Association, *Home Nursing.*
12. Ghosh, B.N. *Hygiene and Public Health,* The Scientific Publishing Co., Calcutta.
13. McCullough, Wava *The Illustrated Handbook of Child Care from Birth to Six Years,* McGraw-Hill Book Company, New York.
14. Parbhu, M.B. *Mothercraft and Child Care,* Orient Longman Ltd., Madras.
15. Achar, S.T. *Child Care in India and Neighbouring Countries,* Macmillan & Co. Ltd., Madras.

16. Gopalan, C. Ramasastri, B.V. and Balasubramanian, S.C. *The Nutritive Value of Indian Foods,* National Institute of Nutrition, Indian Council of Medical Research, Hyderabad.

17. Hildreth, E.M. *Elementary Science of Food,* Allman & Son Ltd., London.

18. Chaney, Margaret *Nutrition,* Houghton, Mifflin Co., Boston.

19. Kilander *Nutrition for Health,* McGraw-Hill Book Company, New York.

20. Swaminathan, M. and Bhagavan, R.K. *Our Food,* Ganesh & Co., Madras.

21. Krause, *Food, Nutrition and Diet Therapy,* W.B. Saumders Co., Philadelphia.

22. Gopalan, C. and Narasinga Rao, B.S. *Dietary Allowances for Indians,* Special Report Series No. 60, Indian Council of Medical Research, 1968.

23. Bogert, Briggs and Callow *Nutrition and Physical Fitness,* W.B. Saunders Co., 1966.

24. Bennion, M. and Hughes, O. *Introductory Foods,* 6th edn, Macmillan Publishing Co. Inc., New York, 1975.

25. Swaminathan, M. *Handbook of Food and Nutrition,* Ganesh & Co., Madras, 1977.

26. Edwards, F.A. and Durham, A.W. *Medical Dictionary and Health Guide,* The New English Library, Great Britain, 1964.

27. Florence, E. and Inman, Lydia L. *Equipment in the Home,* 3rd edn, Harper and Row Publishers, New York, 1973.

28. Bronson, Joan, C. and Lennox, Margaret, *Hotel and Hospital Housekeeping,* 3rd edn, Arnold Heineman Publishers, New York.

29. Mager, N.H. and Mager, *S.K. The Household Encyclopadia.*

30. *Hints 'N' Helps Household Dirctionary,* 1988 edn, PSI & Associates Inc., Miami.

31. Shils, M.E., Olson, J.A. and Moshe, Shike *Modern Nutrition in Health and Disease,* Vol. I 8th edn., Lea and Febiger.

32. Gopalan, *C. et.al, Nutritive Value of Indian Foods,* National Institute of Nutrition, Indian Council of Medical Research, Hyderabad.

Model Questions

Part I. Home-making

Chater I

1. Give details of plan and equipment for a good storeroom in the house. Why is it important to plan for storage place ? What are the types of food materials you can store and how should you store them ?

2. Plan a kitchen for a middle class family in South India. What arrangements will you make for the equipment needed and for the washing of such equipment in the kitchen ?

3. If you were to plan a house for a middle class family in South India, how would you assign the rooms for essential purposes ? How would you make the best use of a one-room apartment ?

4. What are the various activities carried on in a home ? How would you allocate space for these activities in a middle class home ?

5. How and where would you allocate the space in a house for the dining room ? How would you furnish it ? What is the equipment necessary for dining in Indian style and in the Western style ?

6. What are the essential points that you would consider in choosing a site for a house ?

7. Discuss the essential features of a good house.

8. While planning your new home, how will you allot space for cooking, dining, sleeping, study, toilet, store room and reception of guests. Draw a rough plan to illustrate your answer.

9. How would you plan a house while building it ? Describe the rooms and mention the sizes of the rooms.

10. Discuss the different types of fuels commonly used in South Indian homes. What fuel would you suggest for an average middle class family ? Give reasons for your choice.

11. Explain the working of the different types of stoves and ovens. Which of them do you like best and why ?

12. Write notes on a lavatory and its sanitation.

13. List the factors to be considered while planning for building a house.

14. How would you furnish a living room ?

15. Draw a floor plan of an efficient kitchen indicating work areas.

Chapters II and III

1. In what ways will you make your home beautiful ? How does your interest in colour shemes help to enhance the beauty of your home ?

2. In the furnishing of a house, what are the chief considerations that should influence your selection ? Describe how you would furnish and decorate a drawing room.

3. How would you furnish and decorate a sitting room 12'x12', making use of some colour combinations that you like ?

4. Explain how you would choose and hang suitable pictures on the walls of the different rooms in a house.

5. Give practical suggestions as to how you would furnish, arrange and decorate a dining room.

6. Write short notes on :–
   (a) Arrangement of flowers in a home
   (b) Triad
   (c) Analogous
   (d) Split complementary

7. How would you use flowers in a house for interior decoration ?

8. (a) Why is it important to have good taste in the planning of interior decorations of a room ?
   (b) What part does colour play in the arrangement of a room ?

9. State how you will furnish your bedroom. What principles will you bear in mind in the choice of curtains and pictures for that room ?

10. Define the principles or elements of design.

11. Mention the different types of complementary colour harmonies, with one example each.

12. Describe the styles of flower arrangement.

Chapter IV

1. State briefly the plan of work which a housewife should follow in her daily and weekly cleaning campaigns.

2. Discuss the importance of cleanliness and its value with regard to the home and its surroundings.

3. Explain clearly how you would clean the following :–
   (a) A brass vase
   (b) An aluminium teapot
   (c) A mirror
   (d) Bronze vessels
   (e) Cutlery and crockery
   (f) Furniture

4. Write short notes on :–
   (a) Making furniture polish at home.
   (b) Cleaning and polishing window panes.

5. Describe any two methods of preparing furniture polish at home.

Chapter V

1. Write short notes on :–
   (a) How to launder a dirty silk blouse.
   (b) How to launder and iron a cotton choli.
   (c) How to launder a woollen sweater.

2. What are textile fibres ? How are they classified ?

3. What care should be taken regarding the laundering and storage of the household linen in the home ?

4. List the natural fibres and give the characteristics of any one natural fibre.

5. List the different types of household linen with examples.

Chapter VI

1. Name the common household pests. What are the dangers

of having a house infested with pests ? State some simple measures to free the house of them.

2. How would you protect the kitchen against flies ?

3. How would you control and eradicate the following pests in your home ?
   - (a) Bugs
   - (b) Cockroaches
   - (c) Flies

4. (a) What are the pests that destroy household linen ? How are these pests destroyed ?
   (b) How will you protect your kitchen from flies, rats and cockroaches ?

Part II Income and expenditure

1. Give an account of the different methods of saving that could be adopted by a household.

2. (a) Explain the working of a Nidhi.
   (b) Why is it important to save money ?
   (c) Name the different institutions for saving.

3. Define household budget. What are the chief budget items ? Draw up a budget for a family of three members–father, mother, and son aged 16–with a monthly income of Rs. 2000/-.

4. Define Engel's Law. List the different institutions of saving.

5. Plan a budget for a family living at Madras, the members being father, mother, and two children aged 3 and 10–monthly income Rs. 5000/-.

6. Enumerate the chief methods of saving possible for a middle class family.

7. Write short notes on :–
   - (a) Chit Funds
   - (b) Insurance
   - (c) Saving banks
   - (d) Co-operative societies

8. Describe the importance of the household budget. Mention the details to be included in it.

9. Mention five important reasons for saving.

10. List the factors that are to be kept in view while investing one's savings.

11. Mention types of chit funds ? Describe their advantages and limitations ?

Part III. Personal hygiene

1. Discuss the importance of personal cleanliness.

2. What is personal hygiene ? Discuss its importance in daily life.

3. What advice would you give a young girl on the following ?
   - (a) Care of teeth
   - (b) Care of skin
   - (c) Care of hair
   - (d) Care of nails

4. (a) What points should be observed in the cleanliness of one's person ?
   (b) Describe the items in personal cleanliness that are likely to be overlooked in the care of young children.

5. How will you teach a 5 year old child to care for his teeth of skin ?

Part IV. First aid and home nursing

1. (a) How would you render first aid for the following ?
   1. A simple cut on the finger
   2. Bleeding from the nose
   3. Sprain of the ankle
   4. Burn of the arm

   (b) What are the sign and symptoms of sunstroke ? Mention the treatment for sunstroke.

2. How would you prepare a room in the house to receive a typhoid patient ? Draw up a diet schedule for the patient.

3. (a) What is a fracture ? How would you render first aid in the case of a simple fracture, snake bite and bleeding from the ear ?

(b) What is the use of a clinical thermometer ?

4. Define first aid. Mention qualities needed in a first aider.

5. Describe the three main types of fractures.

6. Mention the different types of wounds and suggest treatment for the same.

7. List the different types of shock. Hou would you render first aid for electric shock ?

8. State the factors to be considered while selecting a sick room.

9. What are the different items required for making a bed in the sick room ?

10. (a) How would you prepare a room in the house for a patient and how would you disinfect a room in the house ?

(b) What are the different kinds of poison ?

11. What are disinfectants ? How would you proceed to disinfect a room occupied by a cholera patient ?

12. When should artificial respiration be rendered ? Describe how it is administered.

Part V. Child care

1. (a) What are the minor ailments of childhood years ?

(b) Discuss the importance of habit formation in a child during the "toddler stages."

2. What are the basic needs of a child ? Explain how you would care for a child who is three years of age.

3. Describe the daily routine of a ten month old baby.

4. Mention the causes and treatment of any four children's diseases.

5. What toys would you recommend for a child five years of age ?

6. Mention some of the ailments of early childhood. Describe the preventive measures you would adopt against them.

7. Describe any four suitable toys for a four year old child or state four reasons for organising play activities for children.

Part VI. Food and cookery

1. (a) What are the uses of carbohydrates, fats and proteins ?
   (b) What are the sources of calcium, iron and Vitamin A ?

2. Explain the different methods of cooking employed in a house, giving examples.

3. What is a balanced diet ? What are the uses of proteins ? What are the sources of Vitamin C and Vitamin B ?

4. (a) What are your nutritive requirements of calories, proteins, calcium and Vitamin A ?
   (b) What are the good sources of Vitamin D, iron and phosphorus ?

5. What are the advantages and disadvantages of cooking ? Explain the best method of cooking vegetables.

6. What is a nutritional calorie ? An adult man doing light work gets 30 g proteins, 45 g fats, and 80 g carbohydrate per day. Calculate the calorific value in his diet and compare it with his daily requirement.

7. Describe the functions of minerals in the body. Give examples of foods rich in minerals.

8. Explain briefly how you would prepare the following :–
   (a) A cup of tea
   (b) Puri and potatoes
   (c) Groundnut toffee
   (d) Uppuma and chutney

9. Discuss the importance of Vitamin B_1 and B_2 in our food. What are their sources ?

10. Explain clearly how you would prepare the dining table for a lunch in Western style and how you would serve the lunch.

11. What is the Basic Seven ? Plan a balanced meal for a day for an adult using the Basic Seven.

12. Give two examples of foodstuffs which are prepared by the following methods of cooking :– frying, steaming and boiling. Explain the advantage and disadvantages of such methods of cooking.

13. Write short notes on :–
    (a) Pellagra

(b) Scurvy
(c) Ragi
(d) The value of milk in diet
(e) Par-boiled rice

14. From the point of view of suitability, cost, and durability, consider the relative merits of the different kinds of materials used for making cooking vessels.

15. Write short notes on :–
(a) Cleaning of cutlery and crockery
(b) Weights and measures
(c) Purchasing foods
(d) Rickets
(e) Preparation of a fruit drink

16. Describe basic food groups. Give two examples for each group.

17. State the functions of Vitamin C, and mention four good source of the same.

18. List the functions of proteins.

19. What are the points to be considered while planning meals for a family ?

20. Give a daily diet plan for a pregnant or nusing woman.

21. State the cleaning method you would use for cleaning a brass flower vase or a cooking vessel made of stainless steel.

22. What are the Basic Five food groups ? State the main nutrient content of each group. Plan a balanced meal for a day using the Basic Five food groups.

Index